GALE FORCE

GALE FORCE

Owen Laukkanen

G. P. PUTNAM'S SONS
New York

G. P. Putnam's Sons
Publishers Since 1838
An imprint of Penguin Random House LLC
375 Hudson Street
New York, New York 10014

Library of Congress Cataloging-in-Publication Data

Names: Laukkanen, Owen, author.
Title: Gale force / Owen Laukkanen.
Description: New York : G. P. Putnam's Sons, 2018.
Identifiers: LCCN 2017020483| ISBN 9780735212633 (hardcover) |
ISBN 9780735212657 (ebook)
Subjects: LCSH: Deep-sea sounding—Fiction. | Salvage—Fiction. |
Suspense fiction.
Classification: LCC PR9199.4.L384 G35 2018 | DDC 813/.6—dc23
LC record available at https://lccn.loc.gov/2017020483
p.   cm.

Printed in the United States of America
1   3   5   7   9   10   8   6   4   2

BOOK DESIGN BY LUCIA BERNARD

FOR MY DAD, WHO BROUGHT ME TO THE BREAKWATER;
AND FOR JOEY AND SUZI, WHO TOOK ME TO SEA

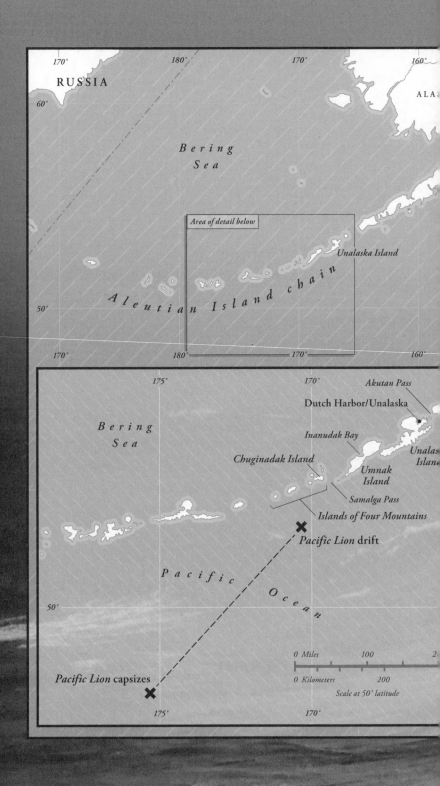

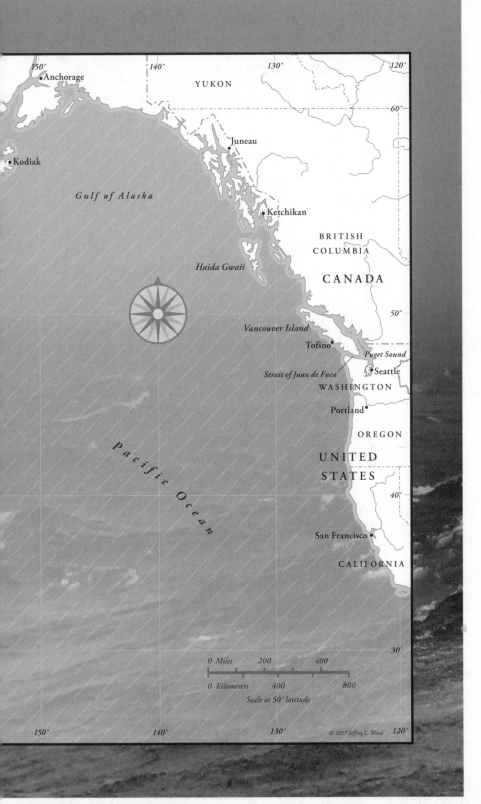

© 2017 Jeffrey L. Ward

PROLOGUE

The freighter loomed in the distance, six hundred feet of black steel and burning light, lurching, punch-drunk, in the face of the storm. The ship was the *Argyle Shore*, a bulk carrier with fifteen thousand net tons of Columbia Basin grain, dead in the water and broadside to the swell, waiting on the knockout punch that would send her to the bottom.

In the wheelhouse of the salvage tug *Gale Force*, fifty yards away, McKenna Rhodes watched the lights of the freighter and aimed for the bow. She was used to nights like this; she'd grown up on her dad's boats, spent most of her thirty years on the water. She'd worked summers on barge jobs, all over the Pacific Coast, up the Columbia River, and to the farthest reaches of Alaska. But the salvage business wasn't much like towing barges. The money came sporadically, when it came at all, and you took risks to earn it—risks like tonight, the *Argyle Shore* in one hell of a nasty storm.

"Keep her face to the sea, McKenna."

Randall Rhodes's voice came into the wheelhouse through the loud-hailer from the afterdeck, barely audible over the roar of the wind. McKenna stood at the tug's controls, wrestling the bow into the roiling sea, the oncoming waves spilling white water everywhere.

She still wasn't sure she was comfortable up here, warm and dry at the wheel, her dad down on deck with the crew, preparing to launch a messenger line to the bow of the freighter. Her father, though, had insisted.

"You're going to run this boat one day," he'd told his daughter, often enough that she could hear him in her sleep. "You've been on the water long enough; you're plenty qualified. Might as well get used to that captain's chair."

The Coast Guard had taken care of most of the *Argyle Shore*'s crew. They'd sent a Jayhawk from Astoria almost as soon as the ship's captain had put out the distress call, and the crew of the helicopter had plucked all but the ship's master and a couple of seamen from the deck below, the wind blowing a hurricane around them, seventy-knot winds whipping white froth off the wave tops.

That left only the freighter. Enter the *Gale Force*, one hundred and forty-four feet of stout steel, a couple brawny engines and a crew hungry to enter the fray. Under maritime law, the *Argyle Shore* was up for grabs as soon as her crew abandoned ship, fair game for any salvage team who thought they could save her. Success meant a share of the wrecked freighter's value, ten percent minimum, but paid only on completion. There'd be no points for effort. No sympathy offered.

No matter. Within an hour of the distress call, Randall Rhodes had assembled his crew and pointed the *Gale Force* into the teeth of the storm. And now, after sailing through the night into waves as tall as apartment buildings, the *Gale Force* had arrived. With rival tugs just hours behind, it was time to get to work.

Through the closed-circuit TV mounted beside her chair, Mc-Kenna could see her dad and the crew on the afterdeck, preparing the messenger line and gesturing her onward. Through the front windshield, she could see the master of the *Argyle Shore* standing on the bow of the freighter with his few remaining crew, waiting to draw the line in, along with the towing bridle behind it—the heavy three-inch wire that would fasten the two vessels together.

Might as well get used to the captain's chair.

"Crossing the *t*," her dad called it—rigging a tow in rough seas. It meant running the *Gale Force* into the waves and across the freighter's bow, then, from the tug's starboard side, shooting the messenger line, some six hundred feet of rope fired off with a rocket.

The waves came in sets, mountains of water fifty, sixty feet high, launching the *Gale Force* skyward, then plunging it down to the trough. To McKenna's right, the *Argyle Shore* rolled; the men on her bow fought to keep upright. McKenna watched on the monitor as her dad struggled forward with the messenger line as another wave broke, sending a surge of water over the wheelhouse windows. She felt her breath catch as her dad disappeared from view, then relaxed again, but just slightly, when the water receded and he was still there, coughing and spitting water and soaked to the bone—and, damn him, was he *smiling*?

Never ask the crew to do a job you're not willing to take on yourself, McKenna. The skipper leads from the front.

Randall Rhodes hauled the messenger line up the starboard side of the tug, then reappeared at the bow, below McKenna's window, holding the launcher, a bright yellow device about the size of a tool-box. McKenna kept her hand on the throttle, modulating the tug's power as the next wave rose, the *Argyle Shore* almost in line with the bow of the tug now. It was almost time to fire.

Her dad twisted around, found her eyes through the window. He *was* smiling, the maniac, and McKenna couldn't help but smile back. *The old man's built for this stuff,* she thought, reaching for the radio.

"*Argyle Shore*, this is *Gale Force*. We're going to launch the messenger line."

A moment later, the radio crackled. "*Affirmative.*" An accent, heavy static. "We're ready."

McKenna leaned forward and gave her dad a thumbs-up. Watched as he aimed the launcher and pulled the trigger.

Pop.

The shot was a beauty. The line arced high over the water and landed across the bow of the freighter with plenty of rope to spare. McKenna's radio came to life again.

"Hello, *Gale Force*, we are hauling in the line."

Bingo. One step closer to a seven-figure payday.

Randall disappeared again, headed aft. McKenna checked the monitor, saw Matt Jonas and Al Parent back there making a last-minute double check on the winch. She waited for her dad to show up on-screen again, knew she'd breathe easier when he'd made it back around, when everyone was inside and dry, when all that mattered was to ride out the storm and keep the towline intact.

She felt the wave coming before she saw it. Felt the *Gale Force* drop into the trough, that same sickening, roller-coaster feeling, but this time it was worse; this time, the drop seemed to last a fraction of a second too long, the crash at the bottom like a swan dive into concrete, and McKenna knew without looking up that the wave was a bad one.

She grabbed for the radio. "*Rogue! Rogue wave!*"

She'd barely said the words when the wave hit, and hit hard, came plunging over the bow and driving the tug under, green water at the windows now, the crest somewhere above, knocking McKenna nearly off her feet, the tug shuddering, rolling, water roaring past, and for a moment McKenna caught herself thinking, *This is it, we're done, this is how it all ends.*

But the *Gale Force* was a tough boat. It plowed through the wave and surfaced again, shook itself off and kept going, no harm done. McKenna picked herself up and reached for the radio handset where it dangled, meaning to check on the crew, but the crew beat her to it; the loud-hailer was live.

"Man overboard!" someone called, and suddenly the *Argyle Shore* and that seven-figure payday were about the last things on McKenna's mind.

The voice on the loud-hailer was too garbled to place, but on the monitor McKenna could see bodies in bright orange rain gear rushing to the starboard rail. She hurried to the window and looked out to the passageway, where her dad should have been. There was nothing, no sign of him, just water and spindrift and random, scattered jetsam. McKenna felt it like a punch to the stomach.

She picked up the radio. *"Someone get eyes on him! You find him, and don't let him get away!"*

They'd trained for this. Randall Rhodes was a maverick, but he wasn't reckless. His crew ran emergency drills as a matter of course— ship evacuation, fire suppression, first aid. Everyone on the boat had to prove they were able to climb into their bright red survival suit in less than one minute flat or they didn't go out on a job. They'd trained for disaster. But training didn't count for very much with waves the size of apartment buildings and your old man in the water.

McKenna switched on every spotlight the *Gale Force* could

muster. Picked up the radio and called the master of the *Argyle Shore*, telling him to forget the messenger line and to hold tight. She tried to keep the panic out of her voice as she broadcast *Man overboard* over the distress channel, knowing it was pointless; there was no one close enough to respond in time.

On the afterdeck, Matt Jonas was throwing a life preserver in the water. That wouldn't matter a bit, though, if McKenna couldn't turn the tug around.

The waves kept coming, ship-swallowing monsters. McKenna knew if she timed the turn wrong, those waves would bowl the *Gale Force* over, rolling her and dooming them all. On the other hand, if she waited too long, the crew would lose sight of the old man, or hypothermia would set in, numbing his faculties and pulling him under.

Shit, shit, shit.

It was her failure to make the turn, McKenna decided later, that had killed her father.

She stood frozen at the wheel, searching for a break in the waves—but, of course, the sea wasn't going to give it to her that easy. The waves weren't letting up; there was no safe way to do it. There was no way to turn back without risking the boat.

She'd frozen. Afterward, Matt and Stacey Jonas would try to console her, telling her it had been only a minute, two at the most. But that minute mattered. By the time she'd regained control, swung the boat around—a harrowing, life-before-your-eyes turn—the life preserver Matt had thrown was drifting four or five boat lengths away, disappearing in the trough and only reappearing intermittently. There was no sign of Randall Rhodes anywhere.

"*I lost him,*" Nelson was shouting, over the hailer. "*That last wave, I had him, but I just bloody lost him.*"

McKenna urged the boat back, the sea following now, the tug surfing down monster waves and closing in on the life preserver, spotlights chasing the dark away. She still couldn't see the old man anywhere. The minutes ticked onward, and the storm kept coming, and McKenna stood in the wheelhouse and looked out at the black water, knowing in her heart that her dad was gone.

1

The cargo ship *Pacific Lion* stretched 650 feet along the pier, her hull rising a hundred feet out of black water. At her stern, on a massive loading ramp, a long line of brand-new Nissan cars waited to be loaded, while amidships, a man smoked near a gangway leading from the pier to a small hatchway in the hull, the cherry end of his cigarette a beacon in the darkness.

Tomio Ishimaru stuck to the shadows as he hurried toward the man. He'd bribed a customs officer to let him access the docks, but at that moment, customs officers were the least of his problems. In his briefcase, he carried bearer bonds worth more than forty-five million euros—nearly fifty million American dollars—property of the Inagawa-kai syndicate of the yakuza, Japanese organized crime.

The bonds were a simple game. The syndicate funneled money from its numerous criminal enterprises into stock certificates for an anonymous corporation based nominally in Switzerland. Basic money-laundering—except, instead of delivering the bonds as he'd been contracted, Tomio Ishimaru had made a play. Now the bonds were his, and that made him—for the moment—a very rich man.

Assuming he could get out of Yokohama alive.

The man with the cigarette stepped out of the shadows as Ishimaru approached. His name was Okura, and, once upon a time, he'd been a teenage friend of Ishimaru. Now he wore the dress uniform of an officer in the Japanese Overseas Lines, and his face had aged considerably since those early years.

Okura took another drag of his cigarette. Regarded Ishimaru with a wry smile. "Ishimaru-san," he said. "I thought you were going to miss the boat."

Ishimaru didn't bother to return the smile. Okura hadn't any idea how much effort he'd expended to be there. There were bodies in his wake. There were members of the Inagawa-kai close behind. There was no time for idle banter.

"The bonds took more effort to obtain than expected," he replied. "When can we board the ship?"

Okura looked up and down the dock. The row of Nissans, five thousand of them, was nearly at its end. Soon, the ship would sail.

"Patience," he told his old classmate. "When I go back inside, I won't set foot on dry land again for two weeks."

Ishimaru shifted his weight. Followed Okura's gaze. "You're sure you can hide me. Nobody is aware?"

"You'll be fine," Okura replied. "This ship is filled with hiding spaces. If you stay silent and keep out of sight, we'll be okay."

Ishimaru nodded. Scanned the dock again with nervous, darting eyes. Wondered when Okura had become such a shark, wondered just how much debt his old friend had accrued in the parlors. Wondered how he, Ishimaru, had found himself here.

Finally, Okura flicked his cigarette away. *"Iiyo,"* he said, stepping back to the gangway. "Welcome aboard."

. . .

IN POINT OF FACT, Tomio Ishimaru's path to the *Pacific Lion* had begun months ago, in one of Yokohama's many dimly lit and smoky *jansou*—underground mah-jongg parlors operated by the Inagawa-kai. At first, he'd imagined that this path had been accidental. Lately, he wasn't so sure.

By nature, Ishimaru wasn't much of a gambler. He was an accountant, a numbers man, and anyone with even a weak grasp of numbers could see that it was near impossible to win money consistently in the parlors. In the first place, the rakes charged by the operators were obscene. It took skill to beat the house, much less one's opponents. Ishimaru hadn't the skill, nor the gambler's desire. He wasn't sure why he'd come to the *jansou* at all.

He was a bachelor, was the reason, little more than a hardworking salaryman. He had few friends, but his coworkers, fellow accountants with the Inagawa-kai, and associates of the syndicate drank for free at many of the parlors in the city. Ishimaru went to be social, to get drunk. He went to stare at the pretty hostesses who flitted about the crowded rooms, draping themselves on the arms of the high rollers.

It was in one of these parlors, late at night, that he'd reconnected with Hiroki Okura. And it was there, in the bar, as the hours grew long and the conversation turned from old classmates and memories to the present day, that Ishimaru had carelessly let slip his position with the syndicate—and it was in a similar bar, in a similar parlor some nights later, that Okura had first broached his idea.

"It's suicide," Ishimaru had replied as his former classmate explained the plan. "We'd never make it out of Yokohama, much less the whole country."

Okura had laughed, poured more sake. "You haven't been paying attention, Ishimaru-san," Okura had said, clapping him on the shoulder. "*I* can get us out of the country, no problem. *You* just get us those bonds."

Okura had persisted. Needled, angled, flattered, cajoled. And Ishimaru? He'd realized, as Okura spoke, that he was sick of his boring, unglamorous life. He was sick of working to death on behalf of the syndicate, trading his youth and seeing no real reward; sick of returning to his tiny apartment alone every night.

Okura had kept speaking. Ishimaru had listened. And, eventually, he'd agreed to join with the sailor, to steal the yakuza bonds and stow away to America.

THE LION *SAILED AT MIDNIGHT.* From a storage locker at the rear of the ship's accommodations deck, Ishimaru sipped tea and peered out through a porthole as the crew cast off lines and a fleet of tugs moved the ship from the pier. He could feel the *Lion*'s massive engines rumble beneath him. Watched the lights of the harbor swing past.

Before he left Ishimaru to his new, cramped confines, Okura had assured him that he was safe. "No one should disturb you here, but just in case, keep the door locked," the ship's officer had said. "I'll bring you food when I'm able."

"Bring me a book, too," Ishimaru replied. "Two weeks in this cave and I'll surely go crazy."

"For ten percent of your cut, I'll see what I can do," Okura replied, and Ishimaru couldn't be sure he was joking. Then an alarm sounded, and Okura left him, making his retreat to the bow to supervise the big ship's departure.

Alone now, Ishimaru was in his hiding place, stowed away in secret, watching the lights of the harbor slowly recede in the distance, and feeling the tension in his muscles dissipate.

Though his body relaxed, his mind wasn't able to. The adrenaline rush—the urgent, electric thrill of his flight to the docks—had subsided. All that remained was a mounting fatigue, and the inescapable truth of what he had done. The memory of the warm pistol in his hands, the shocked looks of his colleagues—his friends—as he'd turned on them, betrayed them, murdered them in cold blood.

He'd made it on board the *Lion*. He was now a rich man. But as Ishimaru stretched out in his locker and tried to relax, he thought of the money, and of the three friends he'd killed for it, and he couldn't quite chase the feeling that he'd just sold his soul.

SEVEN DAYS LATER

Second officer Hiroki Okura checked the *Pacific Lion*'s coordinates on the ship's GPS instruments. Then he crossed the bridge to the intraship telephone and placed a call to the captain's quarters.

It was nearly midnight, and the ship was approaching the American territorial limit, two hundred miles from the Alaskan Aleutian Islands. It had been an uneventful voyage so far, with reasonable weather; they were making good time. Lately, however, the North Pacific had developed some bite. The *Lion* was plowing through a steady fifteen-foot swell, twenty-knot winds. Hardly dangerous stuff for a ship of this size, but lumpy enough to be noticeable.

Nobody had yet discovered Tomio Ishimaru. The yakuza accountant remained safe, secreted away in his unused storage locker, the stolen bonds secure in his briefcase.

Fifty million dollars. Okura had been able to think of little else since the *Lion* began her voyage.

The telephone rang twice, and the captain answered. "Yes?"

"Second Officer Okura, sir," Okura said. "We are approaching the American two-hundred-mile limit. I request your clearance to dump the ballast water."

The captain grunted. "Seems a little rough, doesn't it?" he replied. "Might be safer to jog into these seas for a while, wait for the swell to die down."

"As you wish," Okura replied. "Though we risk missing our window at the Port of Seattle if we wait too long."

The captain was silent a moment, and Okura could almost read his thoughts. Unlike most cargo ships, whose payloads rested close to the waterline, the *Pacific Lion* was a car carrier, a large, bricklike vessel with a high center of gravity. Consequently, the *Lion* carried seawater as ballast to retain stability, but American law required the ship to change out the ballast water before entering U.S. territorial waters, to prevent the spread of invasive marine species.

It was a delicate procedure, involving the release of the ship's old ballast simultaneous with the intake of new seawater, and Okura knew the captain would prefer to wait for the calmest seas possible. But Okura also knew that the captain had a schedule to maintain, and that the shipping company gave close scrutiny to any unforeseen delays. Captain Ise risked his yearly bonus if he dawdled too long; no ship's master wanted a reputation as a laggard.

Okura had a schedule, too. He had a buyer in Seattle lined up for the bonds, but time was of the essence. Sooner or later, the syndicate in Yokohama would trace Tomio Ishimaru to the docks, to the *Lion*. And the syndicate's reach extended across the Pacific Ocean; the yakuza had friends on the American shore. Okura wished to liquidate the bonds quickly, before the syndicate could catch up. From there, he'd have enough money at his disposal to disappear completely.

Finally, the captain came back on the line. "At your discretion, Mr. Okura. Proceed with the ballast changeover as you see fit."

"Very good."

Okura ended the connection and made another call, this time to the engine room. "This is the bridge," he told the engineer who answered. "Please stand by for ballast changeover."

A pause. "Are you certain? It feels rough out there."

"Captain's orders," Okura said. "Would you like me to tell him the engine room wishes to delay?"

"That won't be necessary" came the reply. "Five minutes and we'll be ready."

As he waited, Okura's mind drifted to Ishimaru. The accountant still believed this was all a coincidence; that Okura had found him in that parlor by chance. In fact, Okura's debts to the parlors had been precarious even then. He'd seen Ishimaru, known his old classmate had taken a job with the syndicate. Gradually, he'd worked out a plan.

All that remained was to off-load the bonds. And to take care of

Ishimaru, of course. The accountant had played his role, and could now be discarded. Sometime soon, in the days ahead, he would suffer a tragic accident by falling overboard far from land. He would disappear into the ocean, and never be heard from again.

And the entirety of the syndicate's fifty million dollars would belong to Hiroki Okura.

The phone rang. The engine room calling back. "Ready to begin," the engineer reported.

Okura shook Ishimaru from his mind. Surveyed the bridge, verified with the helmsman that the ship was in position. "Very good. Clear to open the starboard ballast tanks."

"Opening starboard tanks," the engineer replied. Okura put down the phone and crossed to the front of the bridge. Stared out over the bow at the black ocean beyond as slowly, almost imperceptibly, the ship began to list to the portside.

This was normal. The water rushing out of the starboard tanks would create an imbalance that the engineers would rectify by refilling the tanks with new, American seawater. Okura had personally overseen the procedure more than fifteen times since he'd come aboard the *Pacific Lion*.

Still, he couldn't remember ever feeling the *Lion* heel over this quickly.

Twenty degrees, twenty-five, thirty. The ship continued to list, slow and sickeningly steady, as the bow launched up and lurched down in the teeter-totter swell. Okura hurried back to the bridge telephone, nearly losing his balance on the slanted deck. "What is going on down there?" he asked the engineer. "This is far too much list."

The engineer's reply was panicked. "The tanks aren't refilling.

All the old water's pumped out, but I can't get any new water in to replace it. We're high and dry down here!"

No. Okura stared out the window at a world gone cockeyed. In this awkward position, the ship was increasingly vulnerable.

"Maintain current heading," Okura told the helmsman. "Keep our bow to the waves, whatever you do."

This was bad. As the engineer pumped water from the *Lion's* starboard ballast tanks, the ship had not only heeled over to port—as Okura could currently attest—it had been rendered lighter, displacing less water, sitting higher on the ocean's surface.

The center of gravity, already above that of a normal ship, was now dangerously high. Any force exerted from the starboard side of the ship could send the *Lion* into a full capsize.

"*Steady,*" Okura told the helmsman. "Keep us *steady.*"

No sooner had he said this, though, did the ship lurch beneath him, and the bottom fell out of his stomach. A rogue wave from the starboard side, large and unpredictable, had pummeled the *Lion's* exposed hull and keel with precisely enough force to ruin the big ship's precarious equilibrium.

On the phone, the engineer swore. "*I can't fix this,*" he said. "*It's no use! We're going over!*"

The *Lion* continued to tip, faster now. At the wheel, the helmsman stumbled, fell to the deck, slid down toward the port wall. The wheel stood unattended, the ship at the sea's mercy, the swell helping her over now, books falling to the floor, paper charts and coffee cups, too.

Okura dropped the phone. Gripped a railing. "Brace yourself," he told the helmsman as the whole world went sideways. "*Sound the alarm.*"

. . .

THE WAVE AWOKE ISHIMARU from dreams of a beach, sunshine, a pretty companion. He awoke in midair, then slammed into hard steel a split second later, landing in a heap, dazed, and unable to remember where he was.

He wasn't on the beach, anyway. It was dark here, and cold, and the walls were all cockeyed. Somewhere in the darkness, an alarm began to blare.

Nante koto? What the hell?

Then he remembered. His little locker. The *Pacific Lion*. Hiroki Okura's plan, and the promise of America. Only now something had gone terribly wrong.

Ishimaru tried to sit up, failed, the whole ship funhouse slanted. He fumbled in the dark for a handhold, found a shelving unit and pulled himself upright, the deck still listing, faster now.

This ship is capsizing.

The alarm continued to blare. Voices from outside the door. *"All hands. Abandon ship!"*

Ishimaru reached around for a sweater, a blanket—anything warm—but there was no time. It was too dark in the locker to see anything, and he knew if he didn't move now, he might very well die.

He felt his way to the door. Wrenched it open and looked out into the hallway. The hall ran the beam of the ship. It was slanted like a children's slide. The exit to the portside deck—and the door to Ishimaru's locker—lay at the very bottom.

Get to higher ground.

Ishimaru gripped the railing on either side of the hall. Stepped through the bulkhead and began to climb toward the starboard weather deck. Made it halfway there when he remembered the brief-case. The bearer bonds.

Fifty million U.S. dollars.

He could picture the briefcase where he stored it, under the shelv-ing unit. It wouldn't take but five minutes to go back and retrieve it. And Okura would kill him if he left it behind.

The ship rocked as another wave hit. Somewhere in the cargo decks below, heavy objects creaked, shattered, fell. The ship groaned with the stress; a wounded animal in its death throes.

Fifty million dollars.

Slowly, his hands tight on the railings, Ishimaru turned himself around. Climbed back down the hallway to the locker door, released his grip on the railings and tumbled into the little room. Crawled across the floor to where he pictured the shelves.

He found the shelves, fumbled underneath them. Found the briefcase and pulled, but couldn't coax it out. The ship groaned again.

"Chikusho," Ishimaru swore, gritting his teeth. "Come *on.*"

Another heavy swell lifted the ship, rocking him across the little room. He clawed his way back. Gripped the briefcase, pulled, strug-gling for purchase. Dragged it out from underneath the shelves and held it tight as he staggered back to the door, kicked it open, and peered out into the hall.

The list had increased. The hallway was a mountain. At the bot-tom, just below Ishimaru's locker door, was the doorway to the port-side weather deck, and through the window, he could see green water and white roiling foam.

This ship is dying. Save yourself.

Every step took forever. Ishimaru hugged the briefcase to his body and pulled himself up the railings, inch by inch, gripping the briefcase with his left hand and reaching with his right, hanging on for his life. He made it to the middle of the ship, where a long hallway ran longitudinally. There was a gap here. Ishimaru leaped across, grabbed the railing with his right hand, and hung there, dangling in the air, holding on for dear life. He pulled himself across the gap and kept moving. Slowly, he climbed nearer to the starboard door.

Then another swell hit. It shuddered through the ship like the coup de grâce, shaking Ishimaru from the railing like fruit from a tree, and he fell, scrabbling at the walls for some kind of purchase and not finding it, gripping the briefcase to his chest as he hurtled down the slanted hallway and collided heavily with hard, unforgiving steel.

2

SEATTLE, WASHINGTON

One thirty in the morning and McKenna Rhodes was still wide-awake as, two thousand miles to the northwest, the *Pacific Lion* foundered.

As Tomio Ishimaru fought to reach higher ground, McKenna stood in the engine room of the salvage tug *Gale Force*, staring at the boat's twin Electro-Motive V20-710 diesel engines, and wondering where in hell she'd get the money for a new starboard turbocharger.

If she was smart, McKenna figured she'd have walked away from the boat, the whole outfit, just as soon as her boots hit the dock on the morning after her dad washed away. Anyone with a lick of sense, she knew, would have jumped in her truck and headed east. Back to Spokane and her mom's place, and real life, leave the tug and the rest of her dad's legacy—debt, mostly—for the banks to fight over.

For a spell, she'd done just about that. She'd left the *Gale Force* tied to the dock in Seattle, laid off the crew, and drifted, beat-up by guilt and unsure what to do with herself. The idea of going back on the water only reminded her of her father—specifically, how she'd killed him when she'd failed to make that turn the night they'd tried to save the *Argyle Shore*.

But dry-land therapy hadn't really worked out. McKenna had known since she was a girl that she'd inherited her dad's sailor's blood, and even if he was gone, she couldn't just turn her back on what made her a Rhodes. There was no job onshore that appealed to her, no life she liked better than being out at sea.

Finally, she'd compromised. She wasn't cut out for the gold rush, the kind of salvage job that had been the end of her father. But she couldn't just let the old man's name die out, not without putting up a fight. A good boat like the *Gale Force* could do more than just salvage.

She didn't have enough work to call back the salvage divers, Matt and Stacey, and the less said about Court Harrington, her dad's wunderkind naval architect, the better. McKenna mostly kept to contract work—barge tows and the like—from Alaska to Mexico and anywhere in between. It was hardly the glamorous life the old man had in mind, but the tug was still earning, and that had to count for something.

So, together with Nelson Ridley, her dad's indefatigable engineer, and a skeleton crew, McKenna had spent the three years since her father's death working her butt off, bidding on towing contracts, trying to convince herself she was doing the old man proud.

But the tug business was what you'd politely call a boys' club, and contracts weren't easy to come by. More than a few potential clients had bailed once they'd heard her voice on the phone. She'd debated getting Ridley, with his thick Irish brogue, to make the calls for her.

She was going to have to do something, anyway. Three years of slim margins and deferred maintenance took tolls, and Gale Force Marine was maxed out, overextended, leveraged to the hilt. And now McKenna found herself down in the engine room, well after midnight, trying to figure out how to scrape up enough cash to get the tug back to sea.

THE TROUBLE HAD STARTED midway through the last job, a log tow gone haywire off Cape Disappointment at the mouth of the Columbia River, winds gusting to fifty, seas thirty feet. There'd been no way to cross the Columbia Bar to shelter, not in that weather, so they'd jogged offshore in the brunt of it, waiting for the weather to break and hoping they weren't losing too many logs off that barge in the meantime.

Of course, even in fine weather, the Columbia Bar was no joke, and when you were dragging a three-hundred-foot barge and bucking six knots of river current, it could get downright hairy. Especially if your starboard turbocharger decided to crap out at the same time you were staring down an outbound oil tanker.

Not that it was the tug's fault. Randall Rhodes had known what he was getting into when he'd purchased the *Gale Force*, which was to say a twenty-year-old boat with a lot of big seas under her keel, a couple of decent engines with too many hours on them, good bones beneath her, and a reputation up and down the coast as one heck of a deep-sea tug.

She'd had to be, for what the old man had in mind for her. Spent every last dollar—and a million of the bank's—on the tug, traded the barge pulls for the treasure hunt, bringing ships back from the dead for seven-figure scores, minimum.

It had worked pretty well, until one night it didn't. And now the old man was gone, and McKenna kept slogging, trying to do the guy proud.

HER PHONE WAS RINGING, somewhere. McKenna wiped the grease off her hands and checked the caller ID. Her engineer—her dad's engineer—Nelson Ridley, a stubborn son of a bitch who loved the *Gale Force* so much it blinded him to the writing on the wall. Ridley could have bailed out about the same time McKenna should have, found a gig with one of the big outfits on the coast, Commodore Towing or Westerly Marine, something good paying, steady hours, reliable boats. But he stuck around, poured as much sweat equity— and almost as much cash—as McKenna into the operation, and McKenna had about given up trying to talk him out of sticking around.

She answered the phone. "Ridley."

"I've got something here, boss." The engineer's voice sounded too excited for the middle of the night. "Something pretty darn interesting."

"You should be sleeping," McKenna replied. "Or you should be down here helping me fix this turbo."

"Couldn't sleep," Ridley said. "I watched a movie with the wife, another ridiculous romance, and then she fell asleep and I didn't. And, boy, are you going to be glad, lass."

"Yeah? Why's that?"

"It's better if I tell you in person," Ridley said. "I'm coming your way."

3

Hiroki Okura had had just enough time to send out a Mayday before the captain ordered the crew to abandon ship.

The captain was still wearing his dressing gown. He clung precipitously to the chart table at the rear of the bridge, looking more like a bewildered old man than the master of a fifty-thousand-ton cargo vessel. But his voice was strong, and the meaning clear: Time to go.

The *Pacific Lion* lay at a sixty-degree angle, the portside all but completely submerged. The ship's bridge ran the width of the ship, and from the portside entrance, Okura could look out the window and see green water just a few feet below. The ship shuddered with every swell, threatening to topple. The crew would have to launch a lifeboat in the frigid Alaskan waters—and the starboard boats were too far from the water. They would have to take their chances and hope the portside of the ship didn't collapse on top of them.

The rest of the ship's twenty-six-man crew was already assembled at the forward portside lifeboat. One seaman wore nothing but a towel; none of the others had had time for survival suits. If they couldn't make it to a lifeboat, they would die in the water within minutes.

Okura muttered a quick prayer. Then he crawled his way aft to assist with the launching of the boat.

The lifeboat was fully enclosed and watertight, equipped with food and water and a GPS beacon. There were four of these boats on the *Pacific Lion*, and each had enough room and supplies for the entire crew. One by one, the crew climbed aboard as the sea continued to rock the freighter, threatening to push the ship over and kill them all.

But the *Lion* didn't capsize. Within minutes, the lifeboat was loaded and ready to be lowered into the ocean, just a few feet below the deck railing. Okura counted the crew and found every man present—all but one.

Tomio Ishimaru. The accountant, and the briefcase. *Damn it.*

Okura stepped back from the rail and signaled the third officer, who waited at the hatch. "Go. Call the Coast Guard. I'll make my own way off the ship."

The third officer stared. Called after Okura as he turned away from the lifeboat, clambering back toward the bridge and the interior of the ship. Whatever the man was saying, Okura couldn't make it out. The wind was too strong, and the ship's stance too precarious.

4

"She's called the *Pacific Lion*," Ridley told McKenna. "Six-hundred-and-fifty-foot roll-on/roll-off car carrier out of Yokohama. She screwed something up swapping ballast and nearly capsized at the territorial limit, a couple hundred miles southwest of Dutch Harbor, Alaska."

McKenna and Ridley were sitting at a table in a bar near the docks. Last call had come and gone, but Ridley seemed to know the bartender and he'd sweet-talked a couple of beers and the private use of the lounge.

"You aren't really the going-home type, are you?" McKenna asked him. "I send you back to Carly for some family time, and you're still dragging me to bars in the middle of the night."

Ridley looked around the empty bar. Leaned across the table, conspiratorial. "This ship is carrying a full load of brand-new Nissans."

"Happy with my ten-year-old Ford," McKenna replied. "You're going to have to do better."

"Five thousand brand-new Nissans," Ridley repeated, his eyes alight. "All of them fully insured. That ship must be worth a hundred million clams, easy. And as of an hour ago, skipper, she's officially up for grabs."

"An hour ago." McKenna studied her engineer. "I don't know why you keep tabs on this stuff, Nelson. We've been out of that game for years."

"Guess I can't take a hint." Ridley grinned. "Anyway, I can't sleep at home without my radio scanner hooked up. Some people have whale noises, thunderstorms? I have distress calls, everywhere from Panama to Siberia. Makes me feel like I'm still on the job, I guess."

"My god. How does Carly stand it?"

"Earplugs, skipper. Industrial strength. And thirty years of true love."

McKenna said nothing. The bar was empty, save the bartender polishing glasses and stifling yawns. McKenna yawned, too, didn't bother to hide it. She suddenly felt pretty damn tired.

"We're out of commission," she reminded the engineer. "The turbo, remember? Anyway, the *Gale Force* doesn't run salvage anymore."

"I'll fix the turbo," Ridley said. "If I start working tonight, I can have it straight by dawn. We can sail by noon, probably, if we bust our humps." He arched an eyebrow. "Whoever puts a line on this ship, they're taking home ten million dollars, minimum."

McKenna figured her engineer was right. By the rules of salvage, the *Pacific Lion* had become fair game to any outfit willing to risk the rescue. Of course, the rules of salvage also dictated that the crew wouldn't be paid one salty dime if they couldn't save the ship. Mc-Kenna had borne witness firsthand to that kind of heartbreak—and worse.

"You're asking me to sail to Alaska," she said. "Our first salvage gig since the *Argyle Shore*. The first job I've ever done on my own. A hundred-million-dollar ship. Are you nuts, Nelson?"

"Not in the slightest, lass. You're cut out for this work. Your dad knew it. I know it. Only thing to do is jump in, get your feet wet."

"This is a hell of a leap," she said. "And even if I was interested,

Christer Magnusson at Commodore will get the contract. Or Westerly Towing. One of the big boys."

"The *Commodore Titan* is laid up in Los Angeles," Ridley said. "Westerly's best boat is towing an oil rig to the Persian Gulf. We've got a couple days, easy, on anything else they can send."

Geez, Ridley. The engineer couldn't hide his enthusiasm, and McKenna felt a pang of something—guilt, maybe, or regret—as she watched him from across the table. McKenna knew, for all of Ridley's good humor and carefree demeanor, that he missed the days of tearing across the high seas in search of fortune and adventure with her father.

Her dad had found Ridley on some dock in Fiji, the *Gale Force* in dire straits after Ridley's predecessor fell in love with an island girl and bailed on the crew. He'd offered Ridley the job, and Ridley had taken it, no questions asked, never looked back. For a while, he'd even brought Carly along on the voyages.

Now Ridley got his adrenaline fix by carving up the Pacific Northwest back roads on his restored '71 BSA Rocket 3 motorcycle. The rest of the time, he helped McKenna keep the *Gale Force* running, at the docks or on jobs up the coast. He took a nominal salary, and he paid back more than he earned in parts, tools, and free labor. He'd never asked McKenna for a return on his investment, and McKenna knew he never would.

This pitch, she decided, was probably as close as he would ever come.

So she found herself mulling the question over. Commodore and Westerly were the two biggest operations in the Pacific Northwest. If their big boats were out of the hunt, the *Lion* was anyone's for the taking. And assuming that Ridley could rig up a fix for that starboard turbo, the *Gale Force* should have just enough oomph to handle the job. If everything broke right, it would mean a massive payday. But that was a big *if.*

"We'd have to call the crew back," she told Ridley. "Matt and Stacey, at the very least. I don't know if they'd even be interested. I haven't talked to them since . . ." She trailed off. But Ridley was unfazed.

"I'll fix the turbo. You call the crew. Tell them the *Gale Force* is back."

JUST LIKE THAT, HUH? Despite herself, McKenna could feel the adrenaline. This was the drug, she knew. This was why the old man turned his back on job security and a steady paycheck. This was what kept Nelson Ridley around, what convinced the best crew in the business to set sail on the tug.

Heck, this was why McKenna wasn't waiting tables in Spokane.

"I guess I kind of owe you this," she told Ridley, but he waved her off.

"You don't owe me anything, lass," Ridley said. "But we can't keep scraping for tow contracts much longer. Not at the rate we're going."

That was true, too. Gale Force Marine was just about out of money. In a year, maybe less, she'd be selling the tug, looking for new work. Her time and effort, Ridley's time and effort—all of her *dad's* energy—sold out from under them, nothing left behind.

"We'd have to leave quickly," McKenna said. "By morning, every salvage outfit on the coast will have the same information we do. They'll realize that Commodore and Westerly are out, and they'll set their own courses for that ship."

"Aye," Ridley said. "So we'd better not waste any time."

Are we doing this? Is this really what's happening?

"Get that turbo fixed," she said. "Then we'll talk."

"There is one other thing," Ridley said slyly. "The Coast Guard says the ship's leaning to port at about sixty degrees. If we want to do this, we're going to have to turn the thing upright."

"So we'll bring pumps," McKenna said. "Got it."

"Not just pumps, skipper. We're going to need Court for this job."

5

"I'm all in."

Court Harrington pushed six towers of poker chips into the middle of the table and stared down at the felt through his mirrored sunglasses. Around him, the noise of the casino faded into a dull murmur, replaced, more or less, by the pounding of his heart.

Hope the guy in seat eight can't see it, Harrington thought, stealing a glance across the table at his opponent, an older man in a LAS VE-GAS baseball cap—a tight player who hadn't shown down a bluff all day. Now, with three clubs on the board, Harrington was really hoping the guy would make him for the flush.

Time slowed as seat eight thought things through. It was day four of the World Series of Poker Main Event, a ten-thousand-dollar buy-in spectacular that, this year, had attracted more than six thousand hopefuls gunning for their shot at fame and fortune. Seven hundred players remained, and all but sixty of them would make a profit for their efforts. Based on seat eight's tacky ball cap and his careful play, Harrington made him for a tourist and assumed he would prefer to fold his way to the money, avoiding any big risks.

But the guy was sure taking his time, studying Harrington across the table, really staring him down—chatting to him, too, nonchalant, friendly. "You got clubs, do you?" the man said with a good ol' boy drawl. "Guess I should have raised you on the turn."

Harrington didn't reply. No sense giving the guy any tells. He shuffled his chips instead, looked out at the cards on the board, tried to will the guy into making a move.

Finally, seat eight sighed. Leaned back, checked his cards, and threw them into the muck. "Nice hand," he told Harrington. "Next time, I won't let you stick around to chase that flush."

We'll see about that, Harrington said, checking his own hand, a pair of red sevens, and throwing it into the pile before stacking his chips. *I just have to remember to stay out of your way when you actually get a hand.*

BREAK TIME, TWENTY MINUTES; the last break of the day. Harrington followed the other hopefuls out into the casino hallway. Seven hundred gamblers descending on the restrooms, heading outside for a smoke, whatever. Harrington wandered out to the food tent and checked his phone idly as he waited in line. Saw he'd missed one call, from an out-of-state number. Harrington didn't recognize the number, not at first.

Then he did, and it stopped him where he stood.

Harrington hit redial as he made the front of the food line. He ordered a cheeseburger and dug out his wallet to pay as the phone rang in his ear. Then the call went through, and there was McKenna Rhodes, exactly the same as she ever was.

"Court. Hey."

"Hey, you," Harrington answered, taking his cheeseburger and waving off his change. "Long time, no talk. How long's it been, anyway?"

McKenna paused. "It's been a few years, I guess." There was something strange in her voice. "Listen, this is going to sound weird, but do you have a minute to talk?"

Harrington carried his burger to a table. Sat down, unwrapped it. "I have about five minutes," he said. "But that's literally it. I can call you in a couple hours, though, call you tomorrow?"

"No time," McKenna answered. "Listen, do you want a job?"

A job.

At thirty-six years old, Court Harrington was still one of the youngest naval architects in the United States—and one of the most accomplished in the world. A graduate of the prestigious Webb Institute on Long Island—and, later, of MIT—he'd fallen into the salvage trade on the advice of an old professor, who'd referred him to Randall Rhodes for a one-off job down in Colombia, a container ship run aground on some undersea rock. The ship's hull had been breached, and the ocean nearby was considered very environmentally sensitive. Rhodes had hired him to plot a strategy to get the ship off the reef without spilling any fuel oil—though he'd cautioned, when he met Harrington at the airport in Cali, that the local authorities already considered the project a lost cause.

"Nothing's a lost cause," Harrington had replied, shaking the captain's hand and brandishing his laptop. "The models I make on here, we could refloat Atlantis."

Admittedly, that was something of a stretch, but not by much. Harrington's proprietary hydrostatics program had earned him his doctorate; with it, he could create accurate, highly detailed models of any vessel, afloat or sunk, in the world, and determine how any environmental change, man-made or natural, would affect the ship's equilibrium. This was particularly useful when it came to raising wrecked ships for big paydays.

He'd helped Randall Rhodes save the ship in Colombia, and the master of the *Gale Force* had been so impressed that he'd offered to keep Court on full-time retainer. Harrington—once he'd established that he could still spend the off-time on his sailboat in Myrtle Beach, relaxing and playing video games and flirting with coeds on spring break—had hired on instantly.

It had been the beginning of a fruitful and lucrative partnership that lasted four years and had earned Court a fairly decent sum of money, and plenty of notoriety besides.

In the process, though, he'd screwed things up royally with the boss's daughter. Who was now calling to offer him a job.

"IT'S A CAR CARRIER," McKenna was saying. "Up in Alaska. The crew screwed up the ballast transfer coming into American waters, and she tipped over onto her side at about a sixty-degree angle."

"Oh." Harrington felt his stomach rumble. Figured he should scarf down the cheeseburger and stop by the restroom before poker started again. "Well, shoot, McKenna, I don't know how much help I can be without knowing the specifics. Maybe if you want to, I dunno, fax the pertinent information to my hotel here in Vegas?"

McKenna hesitated. Then she laughed a little bit. "I guess I'm not really asking for your opinion so much as I'm hoping you'll consider heading out with us."

"Out . . . where? To the ship?"

"You're the best in the business," McKenna said. "Regardless of what happened between you and me . . ." She trailed off. Then came back, stronger. "Look, I could really use you, Court. The crew could really use you."

Two minutes left of the break. No time for the restroom. Court realized he would have to eat at the table, kind of a faux pas. He hurried out of the food tent and back through the casino to the poker room, the last of the stragglers ahead of him.

"Gah," he said. "Listen, McKenna, I'd really like to help you, but I'm in the middle of something here, something big, and I can't leave just yet."

"How big?" Rhodes replied. "This is a ten-million-dollar payday."

"I get it," Harrington said, "but this is the World Series of Poker. Eight thousand people, and I'm second in chips. First place is eight point six million."

The line went silent. Harrington ducked through the swinging doors into the poker room. Started through the sea of tables toward his seat.

"How long do you need?" McKenna asked finally.

"To win this thing? Another week or so, maybe. Then another couple days to celebrate."

"Too long. This ship could be at the bottom of the ocean in a week."

Harrington reached his table. "It's only half sunk?" he said finally. "I've never done that before. Hell, I don't think *anyone's* ever done it."

"I know," McKenna said. "It's a pretty big deal, Court. For all of us."

She let it hang there, and, despite himself, Harrington started mulling it over. Figured the notoriety for saving this wreck would just about make up for not winning the tournament. Figured the money would be nearly as good, too.

Nearly as good, but not quite.

The dealer was dealing the first hand. Seat eight was watching him, eyeing his stack. Harrington sighed. "I just can't do it," he said. "I can't walk away now, not while I'm second in chips. I'm sorry."

He ended the call. Sat down at the table just as the dealer was finishing the deal. Tucked his phone away, set his burger in his lap, and checked his cards: pocket queens.

Well, never mind that shipwreck, he said, reaching for a stack of chips. *Let's play some cards.*

6

Ishimaru was gone.

Passage from the bridge to the storage locker near the stern of the ship had taken Hiroki Okura the better part of an hour. The *Lion* hadn't capsized yet, but it hadn't recovered, either; the interior of the ship remained skewed at a maddening sixty-degree list, the portside walls now effectively a floor. Okura had to leap across doorways, intersecting halls, and push open watertight bulkhead doors as he made his way down the ship's longitudinal passages. Twice, the *Lion* had lurched against a particularly violent swell; both times, the sailor had imagined he was finished.

Fifty million dollars.

His career was over. Even if his arrangement with Ishimaru remained a secret, he'd been on duty when the *Pacific Lion* wrecked. He'd overseen the disastrous ballast transfer in rougher seas than were usual for the procedure. He would have to answer for the calamity that resulted.

He had planned for this eventuality. In his stateroom, he'd stashed twenty-five thousand American dollars in cash, the last of a large line of credit extended to him by a yakuza gambling parlor— at usurious rates of repayment. But twenty-five thousand dollars wouldn't buy him much of a future. He would need to find the briefcase if he wanted to move the plan forward.

. . .

BUT ISHIMARU WASN'T IN his hiding space.

The storage locker where Okura had left him was empty, its door hanging open, Ishimaru's bedding a tangle, and detritus strewn everywhere.

"Tomio!" Okura called. He heard nothing but the accountant's name reverberating through the ship's empty halls. The locker was dark. From the portside door below came the sound of water crashing against the hull. The ship might flood. The cargo doors might fail. The *Lion* might sink, taking Okura with it.

Okura searched the locker for the briefcase. Couldn't imagine Ishimaru leaving without it, but he looked anyway. Tried to imagine how the accountant had reacted when the alarm sounded, what he'd done, where he'd gone.

He would have been terrified. Survival would have been his first instinct. He would have grabbed the briefcase and made for the weather deck outside. He would have been panicked, but he'd know to go up.

The *Lion*'s crew had launched a lifeboat from the portside, nearest the water. Could Ishimaru be waiting on the starboard deck, wondering where everybody had gone?

Only one way to find out.

Okura abandoned the locker. Gripped the railings in the hall and began pulling himself skyward. He would check the starboard deck for his old classmate. That was the likeliest place he could be.

. . .

HIGH ABOVE THE DARK OCEAN and the *Pacific Lion*'s tiny lifeboat, United States Coast Guard pilot Sean McCloud glanced across the cockpit of his Sikorsky MH-60T Jayhawk rescue helicopter. "Another man," he repeated. "So where is he?"

In the copilot's seat, Jim Bute shrugged. "Captain has no idea. According to his third officer, the guy watched his buddies all pile into the lifeboat, then turned tail on them. They thought the ship was sinking, so they cut loose and left him there."

It was 0345 hours. Ninety minutes prior, the Jayhawk and its Kodiak-based flight crew had scrambled into the air from its forward deployment station in Dutch Harbor. McCloud and Bute had easily located the *Pacific Lion*'s lifeboat, dropped flares in the water, and conferred with the freighter's captain over the radio, telling him that they didn't have room in the chopper for all twenty-five men, but the cutter *Munro* was en route and would be on the scene in approximately four hours. Fine, the captain had replied. No injuries on board, plenty of food and water. And then he'd dropped the bomb.

One man missing. Somewhere on the ship.

Now McCloud looked out through his windshield at the night beyond. "Dang."

"That lifeboat has GPS and a distress beacon," Bute said. "We're not going to lose them."

"And meanwhile, this crazy SOB is somewhere else entirely." McCloud squared his shoulders. "Guess we've gotta go look for him."

He radioed back to the two crew members in the flight bay.

"Drop a couple more flares by that lifeboat. Apparently, these guys forgot someone."

In the back of the Jayhawk, flight technician David Denman slid open the helicopter's side door while aviation survival tech Tyson Jones readied a couple more flares. The chance that the chopper would lose the life raft on GPS was minimal, but McCloud didn't want to take any chances. There was no sense trading twenty-six lives just to take a shot at saving one more.

When Jones and Denman had dropped the flares, McCloud pulled up on the Jayhawk's collective, lifting the helicopter up and away from the sea.

"Find me that ship's last reported position," he told Bute. "Let's see if there's anything left."

RESCUE SWIMMER TYSON JONES clipped his harness to the winch above the Jayhawk's rear door. Flashed David Denman a thumbs-up, and stepped out of the cabin and into thin air.

The wind was moderate outside the helicopter as Jones descended to the *Pacific Lion*'s starboard weather deck, looking for a decent place to land. The ship hadn't sunk, not yet. It sat low in the water, listing heavily to port and rocking in the swell, but it was still floating, and its three remaining lifeboats remained on board and intact—the survivor hadn't launched his own boat.

Doesn't look so bad down there, Jones thought. *Hundred bucks says we find this maniac in the galley, eating all the cake.*

Denman and McCloud put him down aft of the bridge, high above the water. The ship was listing so much that Jones landed on the side of the accommodations superstructure, the wall more like a deck now. He braced himself as he touched down, keeping hold of the safety wire, as if his sudden added weight could be the final push that sent the ship over.

The ship swayed beneath his feet—a sluggish roll, heavy. The ship was partially filled with water, Jones realized, and there was probably more water flooding in. He unclipped his safety wire and muttered a prayer. *Come out, come out, wherever you are.* Then, carefully, he inched his way down the wall of the house to the bridge.

Through a doorway, Jones studied the bridge. Long and dark, no movement anywhere. No sign of the missing sailor.

"Entering the ship," he radioed up to the Jayhawk. "I'll let you know when I find this guy."

"Copy," McCloud replied. "No hero business, Tyson."

"Who, me?" Jones stepped through the doorway, found a railing on the wall, gripped it tight, and began to edge his way deeper into the ship. "Hello?" he called. "*Konnichiwa*, man. I'm here to take you home."

He unclipped a flashlight from his shoulder strap and surveyed the bridge. The whole place was a mess—paper everywhere, spilled coffee, ruined electronics. No maniac sailor. No one at all.

"No dice," he told McCloud over the radio. "Guess this guy's somewhere else."

He reclipped his flashlight. Looked around the bridge again, saw a bulkhead at the rear—a door to the rest of the ship.

"Going to check out the crew quarters," he radioed.

"If he's not on the bridge, he's probably overboard," McCloud replied. "We're getting low on fuel and that ship is unstable in those seas. Come on back."

"Two minutes." Jones dropped himself down the slanting deck, using chart tables and the wall for support. He made the bulkhead and pulled open the door. Flipping his light on again, he found himself staring down a long hallway, the spine of the ship. Nobody there. Nothing moving. No sounds.

"Jones." McCloud on the radio. "Topside. *Now.*"

"Dang it." Jones closed the bulkhead door. Climbed his way up to the starboard side of the bridge, and stepped back out onto the wall of the accommodations superstructure. Looked up into the night sky, the lights of the Jayhawk, motioned to Denman to send the safety wire down. Steadied himself on the deck, ready to receive the wire, and that's when he saw the guy, climbing out of a starboard doorway a hundred feet down, this Japanese sailor half-drenched with sweat, staring back at Jones with a look on his face like the kid who got caught breaking curfew.

Got him. Jones waved to the guy. "Hey, man," he said. "Come on over here a minute."

The sailor stared at him. Looked up at the helicopter. Looked ready to run.

"Don't you do it," Jones said, wishing he spoke Japanese. "The game's over. It's time to go home."

The sailor still didn't move. He looked down through the doorway. Then he sighed, and Jones took it as a good sign, a gesture of surrender. The sailor straightened up. He didn't move for a beat.

Then, as Jones watched, he dropped back down through the doorway, and disappeared out of sight.

OKURA COULDN'T LEAVE THE SHIP. Not now. Not without the briefcase.

He dropped down the transverse passage, sliding on his ass,

grabbing at the railings on either side of the hall to slow him down. He was sliding too fast; he would be injured when he landed. He reached out as he fell and clutched on to an open bulkhead, wrenching his arms and holding tight, fighting gravity and his momentum as it pulled his body down.

He clawed his way through the bulkhead and out of the hallway. Found himself in the crew lounge, a couple of sofas bolted to the floor, a library of paperback novels spilled over onto the carpet. There was a movie playing on the TV, something American, a cowboy kissing a pretty woman against a spectacular sunset backdrop.

The light from the TV flickered on the walls. The soundtrack swelled, a tinny, disorienting accompaniment. Okura pulled himself to his feet and knew he couldn't stay here. He would have to keep going, deeper into the ship; hide out and hope the Coast Guard abandoned the search.

This was bad.

He staggered to the open doorway, preparing himself mentally for another long drop. Made the hallway and peered out. Just as he did, the American Coast Guard airman dropped down in front of him, hooked into a safety wire and smiling a wide, toothy smile.

"Hey, man," the American said, breathing heavily. "That was fun. How about I take you on a chopper ride next?"

There was no way past this man. There was nowhere to go. Behind Okura, the movie music died away. The ship rocked in the swell.

The Coast Guard man put his hand out. Okura hesitated, but it was no use. He was finished.

"*Kutabare,*" he swore, but he took the man's hand.

7

Ridley had the turbocharger torn apart when McKenna poked her head into the engine room. The engineer was covered in grease, and he might have been bleeding. But he was grinning at McKenna, and he sure didn't look tired.

"Figured it out," he told the skipper. "Just have to pick up a couple parts when the stores open and we're good to go."

McKenna surveyed the engine room. Like any self-respecting towboater, Ridley kept the place spotless. It was a good-looking engine room—the twin twenty-cylinder diesels, the shiny diamond-plate flooring, every pipe and wire color-coded and labeled. Ridley was proud of these engines, and McKenna's dad had been, too. She couldn't come down here without seeing the old man.

Her mom had split after her dad bought the *Gale Force*, the purchase the final blow to the Rhodes's long-suffering marriage. She'd moved inland, Spokane, and dragged McKenna with her. There was a lot of bitterness, resentment, a lot of awkward, stilted phone calls, and months-late birthday cards, postmarked places like Hawaii, Panama, Vladivostok, Hong Kong. And McKenna marooned and landlocked, waiting tables and growing old fast, missing the water something terrible.

That was years ago. She'd ditched Spokane as soon as her mom remarried. Split for the coast and caught up with the *Gale Force* on a turnaround, the crew licking its wounds from a busted run to California, an oil tanker, eight figures easy, another soul-crushing loss to Christer Magnusson's *Titan*. Found her dad here, in this engine room, grease stains and coveralls. She'd picked up a wrench and tied her hair back and been crew on the tug ever since.

She'd upgraded the auxiliary with the last of her dad's insurance payout. Swapped in a brand-new 450-horse Caterpillar to keep the lights on, and the cranes, winch, and firefighting equipment working whenever she wasn't using the main engines. There wasn't quite enough money to cover the cost of new mains, though, and for all of Ridley's late nights and sweat equity, they'd put in their time.

Ridley caught her eyeing the mains and read her expression. "Don't stress the motors, skipper. They'll get us there."

"Yeah," McKenna replied. "But will they get us home?"

"They'll get us to eight figures, and that's all that matters. We get up to Alaska, put a line on that *Lion*, tow her to the first port that'll fit her. After that, who cares? We'll overhaul this old girl the minute the check clears."

McKenna rubbed her chin. "Just keep her running, Nelson."

"She'll run, skipper. Right as rain." Ridley turned back to the disassembled turbocharger. "Give me to lunchtime, we'll be ready to go. You get a hold of the whiz kid?"

McKenna didn't answer. Waited until Ridley turned back around to study her face. He nodded. "I guess that means you did," he said. "And I guess that means he's not coming."

"Poker," she replied. "He said he's playing poker."

Ridley wiped his brow with the back of his hand, said nothing, and McKenna wondered if he was thinking about the last time they'd all seen one another at her dad's memorial in Ridley's living room, McKenna drunk on wine and shots of somebody's whiskey, trying for a eulogy and missing the mark something awful.

She'd wound up telling Harrington, in front of the whole room, that she guessed he had no reason to be there anymore, now that the old man was dead and she wasn't worth settling down for. Told him maybe it was good that things had ended this way. The whole spiel had culminated with McKenna in tears and Ridley spiriting her away from the party. The next thing she remembered, she was in the engineer's upstairs bathroom, puking up the whiskey and trying not to ruin the one good dress she owned. By the time she'd regained control and come back downstairs, Court Harrington was gone, and none of the rest of the crew wanted to look her in the eye.

Christer Magnusson had sent a floral arrangement, damn him, on Commodore's behalf.

"You know," Ridley was saying now. "I know you two had your differences, lass, but we could really use the boy. Court's the best shot we have at raising that—"

She cut him off. "I know, Nelson. I tried. He just didn't want to give up on that poker game. That's it."

She held his gaze. "Must have been some game," he said at last. "I guess we'll make do without him."

"He's not the only architect," she said.

"No," Ridley agreed. "But he's damn well the best."

8

Christer Magnusson awoke at first light. He rolled out of bed, stood and stretched, and stared out through a wall of windows at the expanse of blue beyond. Then, as he'd done every morning for the past month, he walked into his kitchen and fired up his laptop computer and cursed the shipyard workers who'd tied up his boat for so long.

The master of the *Commodore Titan* wasn't used to spending this much time on land, and it was making him crazy. But with the pride of the Commodore fleet—and, hell, the Pacific Coast—tied up all month for a refit, he'd been forced to adapt. Grocery stores. Starbucks. Netflix. Traffic jams.

Magnusson could adapt, but he'd never learn to like it. He belonged on the ocean, and he itched to get back.

Three more weeks.

It felt like an eternity.

Magnusson's computer loaded, and he logged on to the Commodore database. Commodore kept an in-house ship-tracking server with real-time GPS monitoring of every registered cargo ship and passenger liner on salt water, the easier to anticipate lucrative salvage assignments. On a normal day, with his tug in the water, crewed and fueled and ready, the salvage master would have kept the server live around the clock, would bring his laptop to bed, even, so as to know instantly when a ship ran into trouble.

Lately, though, he'd had to shut down the computer, leave it in the kitchen if he wanted to sleep. It was torture otherwise, watching the ships pass, each one a potential million-dollar award, and none of them remotely accessible, not for twenty more days at the earliest.

This was the danger with the salvage profession. Heck, it was the danger with any life lived at sea. Sooner or later, you'd find yourself stuck on dry land for a spell of time, and if you hadn't planned for it—well, it was a prison sentence.

Magnusson was forty-six years old, descended from a long line of blue-water sailors and merchant mariners. He'd crossed the ocean on cargo ships and ocean liners more times than he could count, had been working the sea since before he could drive a car; he'd simply never had time to build out the normal, onshore, storybook life.

And so he found himself in this vast, empty condo, no wife for company, no children or even a dog, just a laptop computer, a list of transient vessels, and a gnawing impatience he feared might just drive him mad.

ON MOST DAYS, the Commodore database looked like a slow-speed video game, an air-traffic control screen on the water. But today, up near the Aleutian Islands, Magnusson saw a hazard alert flashing.

Cargo vessel Pacific Lion *involved in deep-water incident,* the alert read when Magnusson clicked to open it. *Crew evacuated to Dutch Harbor. One survivor still missing.*

Magnusson muttered an oath. Stared at the map on the screen, the little dot where the *Lion* was last reported, the vast expanse of blue around it. Dutch Harbor, Alaska, sat in the middle of the Aleutian Islands, closer to Russia than to any meaningful part of America, literally in the middle of nowhere.

And the *Pacific Lion*, a 650-foot cargo vessel, was in trouble up there.

WITHIN TEN MINUTES, Magnusson had Commodore headquarters on the phone.

"Nobody's really sure how it's going to play out," he was hearing from a man in the home office named Mueller, a vice president of something, a bottom-line, corner-office, dry-land kind of guy. "Crew abandoned her, expecting the ship would sink, but she hasn't yet. Just lying there on her side, drifting into American waters."

Magnusson walked back through his unlived-in condo to the windows. Stared out at the water.

"The vessel," he said to Mueller. "Is there any sign that sinking is imminent?"

Mueller didn't answer right away. Magnusson could hear him typing something. "No," the vice president said finally. "According to the Coast Guard, it looks pretty stable."

"And the weather?"

"The weather." Another pause. "Decent for the foreseeable future. It was rocky last night, but it calmed down some this morning. Looks like there's a window, anyway, before the wind starts to blow again."

"And the Waverly boat is unavailable."

"Right."

"So who is going to salvage the ship?"

Mueller let out a long breath. "No idea," he said. "Damn it, Christer, if the *Titan* wasn't still laid up, we could save that old hulk and make the company a pile."

This, obviously, was the worst-case scenario. A freighter in trouble, a potentially lucrative payday, and, someone else would win the award.

This, Magnusson figured, must be what it felt like to be stuck in prison, watching some other man marry your bride.

But Magnusson hadn't built a career on the water by doing what he was told. And he hadn't turned his *Titan* into the envy of the Pacific Coast salvage fleet by backing down from an obstacle, be it wind, weather, wave, or lack of proper equipment.

"We can still save the ship," Magnusson said, and he knew immediately that he was finished with dry-land living.

"What? The way that ship's drifting, it either sinks or makes landfall long before the *Titan's* even back in the water. It's impossible."

"So I don't use the *Titan*," Magnusson said. "Get me a couple good crew and a flight to Dutch Harbor immediately."

The master could sense the vice president's confusion on the other end of the line. "Christer, I don't—"

Magnusson ignored him. He'd been doing this for too long to let a chance like the *Lion* slip away. "And a boat," he told Mueller. "Find me the best boat in Alaska, right away."

9

McKenna spent the morning running errands around town. Came back to the docks with the bed of her old Ford full of food and assorted provisions. Nearly ten in the morning, and the first of the crew had arrived—Matt and Stacey Jonas, the divers.

They were an interesting couple. Matt was tall and lean, his skin tanned and leathery. Stacey was just as tanned, but nowhere near as weathered; she was three years Matt's junior, but it could just as well have been a decade. The Jonases had been happily married for as long as McKenna had known them, so she tended to think of them as a unit, but despite their mutual love of all things adventuresome— hang gliding, cave diving, BASE jumping, and the like—the two shared markedly different pasts.

Matt was an Ohioan by birth, a rust belt refugee who'd always wanted to see the ocean, and who'd thus found himself migrating to San Diego after dropping out of college. There, he'd met Stacey, a California girl through and through, a surfer girl and all-around thrill seeker.

According to *Gale Force* lore, the Jonases' first date had been a skydive—at Stacey's suggestion.

"She got me up into that plane and opened the door," Matt liked to say, "and then she winked at me and told me if I wanted a second date, I'd better jump fast. And then she was gone."

He'd jumped, of course, and when he'd touched down, he found himself not only with a new girlfriend, but with a taste for adventure, to boot.

"And the rest," Stacey would add, raising her glass for a toast, "is history."

The Jonases had been running dive charters in Baja since the *Gale Force* quit the big salvage stuff after Randall Rhodes's death, but they'd jumped at the *Lion* job, no questions asked, as soon as McKenna had called them.

"Love it," Stacey told her when she'd explained the score. "We're in."

McKenna laughed a little. "You want to check with Matt before you sign on? This is a big change from sand and snorkels."

"Matt's down for whatever," Stacey replied. "He's as sick of baby-sitting rich guys as I am. This sounds like an adventure." She went away, came back. "Matt's already got the plane gassed. We're wheels-up in a couple hours. See you on the dock!"

Now they'd arrived, and watching them cross the tug's after-deck to greet her, McKenna was struck by a sudden sense of sadness, an acute reminder of loss. Her dad had hooked up with Matt and Stacey early on. Found them in a dockside bar in Monterey, hired them, and leaned on them for years. They were competent and fearless, willing to dive anywhere, and when diving wasn't on the menu, they'd do just about anything else Randall asked of them—from welding, to climbing, to heavy-equipment operation. Matt had even earned his pilot's license, and the two traveled private, flying to gigs and new adventures in their personal Cirrus SR22 propeller plane.

Matt and Stacey had made plenty of money with Randall, but beyond that, they'd all bonded with one another, grown close as family—heck, they were family to McKenna, and she'd missed them nearly as much as she missed her own father.

Avoiding Matt and Stacey's eyes, McKenna hugged them both, tried to push her dad from her mind. She caught Matt and Stacey swapping a glance behind her as she helped them stow their kit bags in their stateroom in the tug's fo'c'sle, but ignored it. *Sooner we're at sea and working, the better.*

By the time they'd returned to the deck, more of the crew had arrived.

AL PARENT, the first mate and relief skipper, was a big, barrel-chested man with two shocks of red hair on his temples and none in between. He was a longtime sailor and an experienced towboater, and he would run the *Gale Force* while McKenna oversaw the salvage operation.

Al had stuck around, too, after Randall Rhodes's death. He was quieter than Nelson Ridley, and more laid-back than McKenna, but McKenna knew he was as fiercely loyal as she and her engineer were when it came to the *Gale Force* and maintaining her father's good name. As he came down the dock, she could tell he was excited by the way he barely glanced back at his grandson, who was following in his daughter-in-law's arms.

Al's son, Jason, trailed his father, walking down the wharf with his young wife, Angel, and their infant son, Ben. Your typical wharf rat, Jason was twenty-five or so, slimmer than his father, with a little more hair. He'd been raised on the water, grew up around boats, and there'd never been any question he would wind up at sea, though he'd barely started with the *Gale Force* when Randall Rhodes died.

Jason hadn't seen much of the salvage business, not yet, but he would soon enough, McKenna figured. He'd be the de facto deckhand on the tug; aside from tending to the lines and helping with the grunt work, he'd cook meals for the crew in the tugboat's small galley.

McKenna shook hands with both men, waved hello to Angel and to Ben, who gave her a big smile and looked around at the boats, as if he were already planning his own trip to sea.

The kid was adorable, McKenna thought, with rosy cherub cheeks and a patch of blond hair, that big beaming smile.

"I don't know how you're going to say good-bye to him," she told Jason. "He's such a handsome devil."

Jason looked back at his son and wife. He blushed a little bit, scuffed his boot on the wharf.

"Hoping we'll hit a big score on this, skipper," he said. "Set aside a little something for the kid's education, his future, you know?"

"Looks like he's pretty happy around boats," she said, grinning. "We might have to save a job on this tug."

She smiled at little Ben again, then looked past him just in time to see a black flash hurdle the bulwarks and career across the deck. "Cat came back, huh?" she said, grimacing.

Al grinned. "Ship's cat, skipper. Don't leave port without him; you know that."

The ship's cat, Spike, was as grouchy as ever, and McKenna figured she wouldn't mind so much if the *Gale Force* did leave him behind. Three years into her command of the tug and the cat still hadn't warmed to the new regime; he barely paused to give McKenna a petulant once-over before darting over the bulkhead and into the tug—headed, no doubt, to stake a claim on the wheelhouse.

"I'll know I've made it when that cat deigns to let me sit in my own captain's chair," McKenna told the crew. "That's when I'll know I'm a real tugboat skipper."

Matt and Stacey laughed, and Jason smiled, too. But Al wasn't paying attention. He was looking around the afterdeck and the dock, frowning. "I guess Ridley's in the engine room," he said. "But where's the whiz kid?"

Court.

McKenna felt every one of her crew's eyes turn toward her. Knew they were flashing back, too, to her dad's sloppy memorial.

"The whiz kid's not coming." She sighed. "We're going to have to make do without him."

She watched Al Parent's expression as she relayed the story of Court and the World Series of Poker, watched Matt and Stacey share another look and felt herself going red.

"Job needs an architect, doesn't it?" Al asked.

"Definitely," Stacey said. "I saw the pictures of that ship. We need to get her upright somehow."

"Are you sure you can't convince Court to come along?" Matt said. "Heck, I'll chip in a part of my share, if it helps."

McKenna closed her eyes. Tried to chase the feeling that she wasn't cut out for this game, just an amateur, playing pretend.

"We're going to have to do this without Court," she told them. "I'll get us another architect, don't worry."

10

There was no more time to worry about Court Harrington, not with a voyage to prepare for. Matt Jonas and the Parents helped McKenna stow the groceries in the tug's hold as Stacey stocked the lockers inside the house. By the time the crew had McKenna's truck unloaded, the pumps and generators had arrived, and Jason Parent worked the crane to offload them from the dock to the afterdeck: heavy, boxy things, a hundred pounds apiece. Jason stowed them behind the wheelhouse, affording them as much protection as possible from the elements. They'd be indispensible for moving water out of the *Lion*, and McKenna knew she'd need every one of those pumps in working order when she arrived on the scene.

McKenna was checking over her deckhand's work when Ridley emerged from the engine room, wiping his brow. "Turbo's a go," he told the captain. "Let me do an oil change on the auxiliary and we're all set."

"Perfect," McKenna replied. "We should be all squared away here by the time you're finished."

"Fine." Ridley glanced at Jason Parent, then leaned closer to McKenna. "Can I talk to you in private for a minute?"

McKenna followed his eyes, frowned. "Sure." She walked with Ridley to the stern of the tug, where a pair of chocks stuck up from the bulwarks to guide the towline over the rail.

"I went to the shop this morning," Ridley said. "Had to pick up the parts for the turbo, like I said."

"Yeah," McKenna said. "I remember. So?"

"So, they wouldn't give me credit." Ridley scratched his head. "Skip, they say we're used up. I had to put the parts on my wife's credit card."

McKenna closed her eyes. "Damn it. I'm sorry, Nelson."

"It's no big deal. I'll pay off the card before Carly even sees it, but, I mean—" He studied McKenna's face. "Are we really in it that bad, lass?"

McKenna looked back at the wheelhouse. Jason was hosing off the deck, the rest of the crew inside the tug somewhere. She said nothing.

"I knew we were right on the edge, but—" Ridley shook his head. "How are we going to put diesel in this boat? Are we that dry?"

McKenna hesitated, just a beat. "We're going to be fine. I called the bank this morning, soon as they opened. Took out another equity loan on my dad's old house, a hundred grand. It'll give us enough operating capital to get up to the *Lion* and see what we can do."

Ridley looked dubious. "Yeah," he said. "All right, skipper."

Just don't ask me how we're going to get home, Nelson, McKenna thought. *Or what I'm going to do if I can't find us an architect.*

BY NOON, the *Gale Force* was ready to go.

McKenna fired up the mains, feeling the big tug rumble and shudder to life beneath her. The engine room was insulated with about a mile of soundproofing, but still, the big 20-710s sounded like a freight train when they came to life.

Spike jumped up onto the dashboard, picking his way along the instrument panel, shying just out of McKenna's reach. He stopped and sat and studied the skipper while he cleaned one black paw with his tongue, his yellow eyes wide and inscrutable.

The cat leaped away when McKenna tried to pet him, jumping down off the dash and padding out of the wheelhouse. McKenna watched him go, trying to ignore the sting of rejection, feeling stupid for even feeling it.

Someday, she thought. *Someday, cat, you'll respect me.*

It was a ridiculous thought, but it buoyed her, nonetheless. She turned back to the wheel, ducked her head out the portside window, and surveyed the dock, where Jason and Al Parent stood ready to loosen the mooring lines.

The main engines were warmed. The crew was aboard. The *Gale Force* was as ready as she was going to get. McKenna nodded to the men. "Cut her loose, fellas," she told the Parents. "Let's go catch us a *Lion.*"

11

The American Coast Guard brought Hiroki Okura and the rest of the *Pacific Lion*'s crew to Dutch Harbor—eventually.

First, the airmen flew Okura to the cutter *Munro*, where he rejoined the *Lion*'s crew in a helicopter hangar at the stern of the ship. The Coast Guard seamen brought the crew blankets, hot coffee, and soup, and the sailors from the *Lion* eyed Okura warily. They'd heard how he'd fought to remain on the ship.

The first Coast Guard airmen had flown back to Dutch Harbor. Now, in daylight, the *Munro* sent its own helicopter, a bright orange Eurocopter HH-65 Dolphin, to survey the ship. The *Munro's* crew had opened the hangar doors, and the *Lion's* survivors wandered out to watch.

Morning had broken, sunny and brisk, a beautiful day, the sea as close to flat-calm as Okura had ever seen in this part of the North Pacific. In the distance, three hundred yards off the starboard quarter, the *Pacific Lion* languished.

If only I'd had more time.

The crew of the Dolphin helicopter boarded the *Lion* and stayed there for about an hour. Okura smoked cigarettes on the *Munro's* afterdeck and watched, until the Dolphin's crew was winched back up to their helicopter and flying to the cutter. He did not see any sign that the crew had found Tomio Ishimaru.

Within five minutes, the Dolphin had touched down on the deck of the *Munro*. The pilot and his crew climbed down and hurried across the landing pad, conversing briefly with the *Lion's* captain, before disappearing inside the ship.

The captain gathered his officers. "The ship is still very unstable," he told the men. "The Coast Guard expects it will sink. There is no chance of retrieving our belongings."

"So what are we supposed to do?" Okura wondered.

"They are sending us home to Japan," the captain replied. He looked at Okura, and his eyes narrowed. "I expect the company will want to know why the ballast transfer failed, Okura—and why you behaved so erratically after the disaster."

. . .

A DAY LATER, Okura surveyed the small town of Dutch Harbor as he descended the *Munro's* gangplank to the government dock. The town was pretty, that was for certain, a ramshackle crescent of houses and small buildings hugging the harbor bay, surrounded by lush mountains. The air was crisp and bracing and, here and there, the sun shined through the clouds. It was a beautiful day.

On the dock, a school bus was waiting to take the *Lion's* crew to the town's community center, where they would stay until a plane could take them home.

"Welcome to Alaska," a customs official told the crew as they found their seats on the bus. "Your plane should arrive sometime this afternoon. Until then, we'll make you as comfortable as we can."

The chief engineer, a chubby man in overalls, raised his hand. He'd been on his way up from the engine room when the *Lion* had capsized. "We have no clothes," he said.

The customs official nodded. "We're going to try to scrounge up clothing for you. Everything we can provide, we will."

"Food?"

"Yes, definitely. We have volunteers cooking you a meal as we speak."

"Will we be allowed to go for a walk?" someone else wanted to know. One of the deckhands, a reputed alcoholic. Okura suspected he knew where the man wanted to go.

"No walks," the official said. "As of right now, you're not officially admitted into the United States. We're just giving you a place to stay until you can go home."

"What if we have our passports?"

The bus was moving now, rumbling across the dock toward a stretch of gravel road. The customs officer lost his balance and hit his head on the ceiling. Winced.

"We'll deal with that on a case-by-case basis," he said. "If you have any more questions, come and see me when we get there."

The officer sat down, rubbing his head. Some other crew members shouted questions in halting English. Okura turned to stare out the window. *If I had my passport, I wouldn't need to go back to Japan.*

But he didn't have his passport. It was locked in the safe in his stateroom on the *Pacific Lion*, two hundred and fifty nautical miles to the southwest. And anyway, where would he go? What would he do?

If I had my passport, and fifty million dollars. Then I would be set.

But he had neither, and he sat and brooded in silence as the bus lurched and jostled its way into town.

12

SEATTLE

McKenna guided the *Gale Force* out of its berth and into Lake Union, past rows of fishing boats, pleasure craft, and tugs to the George Washington Memorial Bridge, where the water narrowed northwest into the Fremont Cut, splitting north Seattle in two. The ship canal was narrow and crowded with traffic, and McKenna piloted the tug carefully as she approached the system of locks at Salmon Bay that would drop the *Gale Force* twenty feet to the Puget Sound.

It was never the most relaxing way to start a journey, but McKenna felt calm anyway as the tug waited its turn and descended through the locks, ducked under the train bridge, and turned north into Shilshole Bay, leaving Seattle behind for the open water of the sound. She was happy, at least, to have escaped the city. The water was where she belonged.

There were problems to consider, of course, and all of them pressing. There was the problem of money; namely, that the *Gale Force* didn't have much. There was the issue of the *Pacific Lion*'s pronounced list—the Coast Guard was reporting sixty degrees—and how McKenna would reverse it without the whiz kid in the picture.

She'd called around, tried every naval architect she could think of, some of them salvage experts with whom her dad had worked before Court Harrington, others she knew only by reputation. The response had been singularly depressing.

"No offense, but I just don't know you, Ms. Rhodes," a professor at the Webb Institute told McKenna. "I'm sure you're just as good as your father at this stuff, but if you're asking me to fly across the country to work with an unknown entity, I'm going to need at least a hundred thousand dollars up front."

"I can't offer you that much," McKenna replied, "but I can assure you a share of the profits. We stand to make—"

"I know what you *could* make," the professor interrupted. "I also know you could very well walk away with nothing. And I just can't take that risk. Not with an unproven captain."

The story didn't change much, no matter who McKenna called. Nobody knew her, except as Riptide Rhodes's little girl. No one trusted her ability to bring the *Lion* to safety.

BEYOND THE ARCHITECT CONUNDRUM, there was always the possibility, too, that the ship would sink before the *Gale Force* arrived, or that some other salvage outfit would put a line on her first. By rights, McKenna knew she should be pulling out her hair right now, or turning the tug back toward the dock and looking for a nice job in an office or something, but instead, she felt calm. Serene. She felt her dad here, somehow.

It would have been impossible *not* to feel Randall Rhodes's presence in the wheelhouse. The man had molded the command center in his image, from the carpet on the wheelhouse floor to the leather on the captain's chair. The wheel, salvaged from an old steam tug in Prince William Sound. The pewter picture frame beside the depth sounder, a Christmas gift from McKenna from aeons ago. It had held a picture of McKenna for as long as Randall Rhodes ran the boat, the same picture, Little League, age eight. Braces and a ponytail and a wide, awkward smile. She'd always been embarrassed when she caught a glimpse of that photo. Wondered how her dad could expect the crew to take her seriously.

But they had taken her seriously, or they hadn't lasted long. Randall Rhodes had seen to that—not that he'd cut her any slack, either, not while they worked. The girl in the picture might as well have been someone else's daughter when they were out on a job; the old man worked every member of his crew just as hard as he worked himself, no quarter given, no excuses. She'd found it unfair at first.

Hated her father. Thought about quitting, packed her bags plenty, stalked off in a huff every time the *Gale Force* made land.

Somehow, though, she was always aboard when they cast off again. And now that old pewter frame held a picture of her father, faded flannel shirt, beard going to gray, a stained Baitmasters hat. And a smile for the camera that still caught McKenna off guard when she'd see it, even now.

NELSON RIDLEY CAME UP into the wheelhouse as the *Gale Force* approached Dungeness Spit, the top end of Puget Sound, some five hours after setting out from the Seattle docks. He handed McKenna a cup of coffee and stood beside her at the wheel. "How's she looking, lass?"

"So far, so good," McKenna replied. "Forecast is just fine, and we're making steady time. Should clear Cape Flattery right on schedule."

Ridley looked out through the forward windows. Up ahead, the Strait of Juan de Fuca stretched ninety-five miles to the open Pacific, the snowcapped mountains of the Olympic Peninsula to port, Vancouver Island and Canada to starboard, as far as the eye could see.

"How are the mains doing?" McKenna asked her engineer.

"That turbo's humming like a champ," Ridley replied. "All good so far."

So far, McKenna thought, then admonished herself. No sense jinxing the operation any more than normal. Seafarers were a superstitious lot; you didn't leave port on a Friday (it was Tuesday, thankfully), you didn't dry your coffee mugs upside down (invited capsizing), and on some boats, you didn't bring bananas on board—or women. McKenna was no fan of bananas, but she'd be damned if she was staying on shore, so maybe she wasn't superstitious. Still, she wouldn't be trimming her nails or running any laundry until the job was over, lest she anger the sea gods, or whatever.

Ridley let her stand in silence for a minute or two. "You getting anywhere with the architect situation, skipper? Any news from Court?"

"Not yet," McKenna said, avoiding his eyes. "I've been calling around, other contacts, don't have any leads yet. But I will."

"Not many people can do what the whiz can."

"Yeah, well, the whiz isn't coming." It came out rougher than she'd planned. "He's busy, Nelson, and that's all there is to it. We'll make do."

Ridley didn't say anything for a moment, and McKenna could practically read his doubt.

"Yeah," he said finally. "Yeah, we'll make do. We always do, right?"

"We have a long run up to Dutch, anyway," McKenna said. "I'll have a replacement by the time we make the wreck. I promise."

13

The Commodore headquarters had found Christer Magnusson the only working salvage boat in Dutch Harbor. It wasn't much to look at.

Magnusson had flown up from Los Angeles with a couple of crew, Foss and Ogilvy—young men, strong, more or less interchangeable. They'd caught a connection in Anchorage, a little Pen-Air turboprop, spent two and a half hours shuddering and bouncing through ragged clouds and harsh turbulence before the plane made its final, merciful descent.

They'd filed off the plane with about a dozen other passengers, walked through the tiny airport, and found a dirty minivan waiting, a decal on the side reading UNALASKA TAXI.

Magnusson dug in his coat for the name Mueller had given him. He leaned in through the cab's open window.

"Bering Marine," he'd told the driver. "Do you know it?"

Now Magnusson stood on the Bering Marine dock, surveying a tug called *Salvation*. She was about a hundred and twenty feet long—a modest white wheelhouse above raised blue bulwarks at the bow, a heavy-duty A-frame crane directly behind it, and then a long expanse of deck. The hull was blue in some places and grimy black in others; not the prettiest boat in the world by a mile, but the owner swore to Magnusson that she ran like a champion.

"Built for the war," the man said. His name was Carew. "The Second World War, that is. Navy ship. She's been repowered a couple times, but her bones are the same. There's nowhere in the Pacific this ship can't take you."

Magnusson looked the ship over. The boat's Caterpillar engines growled somewhere beneath its filthy hull; a greasy plume of exhaust smoke belched from the stake. Beside him, Foss and Ogilvy exchanged glances. Foss raised an eyebrow, an expression that meant *I'm not sure about this hulk.*

Neither was Magnusson. The *Salvation* was ancient, underpowered, and ill-equipped for a deep-sea salvage job. But Bering Marine was the only outfit in town, and Magnusson wasn't ready to give up an eight-figure charter so soon.

"When can you be ready?" he asked Carew.

The captain shrugged. "Take me a day or two, get the gear your boss requested. We weren't exactly prepared for this kind of operation, you know?"

"One day," Magnusson said. "We don't have time to screw around."

Carew rubbed his chin. Mulled it over.

"One day, fine," he said finally. Then he grinned. "Listen, when we save that ship, you make sure they know it was the *Salvation* that done it, all right?"

14

There was nothing to do but wait.

Okura had eaten until he was sure he would never feel hungry again. He'd smiled and attempted to make conversation with the well-meaning Americans who'd brought food to the little town's community center. Now all but a few of the Americans were gone, and Okura stood alone in the corner of the center's gymnasium, waiting for the customs official to return and tell them their plane had arrived.

Outside, it was no longer sunny. A thick layer of fog was settling on the mountains above the town. Okura watched it drift down. It did nothing to help his mood.

He'd given his life to the shipping company. No woman would marry a man who was away at sea for nine months of the year. He'd missed the death of his mother and the marriage of his younger sister. There was nothing else in his life but the work. Work, and the gambling parlors.

When he climbed aboard that plane, he would no longer have a job. That was a certainty. He might even face criminal charges for his role in the *Lion*'s disaster—especially if Tomio Ishimaru ever surfaced. And even, if by some miracle, Okura managed to escape with his professional life intact, he would still owe debts he was incapable of paying, huge debts, to men who regularly called on the yakuza to help them collect.

Put plain, he was finished. There was simply no hope.

TWO WOMEN WORKED at the front of the gymnasium, clearing empty dishes from the table. They talked, and their voices carried in the silent space.

"That was Robbie who just called," the first woman said. "Some bigwigs just came down to the dock, want to charter Bill's boat and head out to the wreck."

Her friend cocked her head. "What, the *big* wreck? What for?"

"See if they can save it, I guess," the first woman said. "I didn't really get the whole story. Anyway, they're leaving first thing tomorrow morning. Probably gone for a week, ten days, Robbie said. So you know what that means."

The second woman smiled. "Girls' night."

"Girls' *week*. If the guy's going to leave, I'm having a party."

The women walked out of the gym, laughing. Okura watched them go. So someone was going out to the *Lion*. Probably, they would find Tomio Ishimaru, and his briefcase. Maybe they would even take a cut of his profits.

Good luck to them. May they live long and happy lives. I will think of them often, from prison.

He dwelled on this unhappy thought for a while. Then the customs officer came into the room, and everyone straightened and shifted and looked at him. The man wasn't smiling.

"There's a delay," he told the crew. "It's too foggy to land your jet. They're going to fly on to Kodiak and try again tomorrow."

15

The *Gale Force* chugged north up the west coast of Canada, skirting the wild western edge of Vancouver Island, dodging freighters and log tows, fishing boats with their trolling lines, and pleasure craft under sail and power.

In the Queen Charlotte Sound, between the north end of the island and the southern end of the Haida Gwaii archipelago, a pod of Dall's porpoises appeared alongside the tug. It was morning, and McKenna was brushing her teeth on the afterdeck when the porpoises appeared, speed demons, racing alongside the tug and frolicking in the waves.

Some of the creatures were so close that McKenna imagined she could reach over the gunnels and touch them. They were so fast and carefree that she couldn't help but smile as she watched.

"Beautiful, aren't they?" Stacey Jonas said. She'd come out of the wheelhouse with her own toothbrush and a mug of water. "So fast and sleek."

"They sure look like they're having fun out there," McKenna said, making room at the rail so Stacey could join her.

"Sure do." Stacey grinned. "I love watching them. Any sea creatures, really. Sometimes I think I like animals more than I like human beings—present company excluded, of course."

"Of course. And Matt, too, I hope."

"Matt, too," Stacey said. "And he's the same way. I never love him more than when we're both underwater, guiding a bunch of folks around some coral reef. We can't talk to each other, but I still feel him there with me, and that's more than enough for both of us. I don't know what I would do if he didn't feel the same way."

You'd get divorced, McKenna thought. *Like my parents did.* Randall Rhodes had tried to get his wife aboard the *Gale Force,* when he first bought the tug. Come along for an adventure, he'd told her. You won't even have to cook. But Justine Rhodes loved the city, loved her home, the proximity of the grocery store and the coffee shop and the park. Try as her father might, McKenna's mom had never budged. And there was surely no way Randall Rhodes was coming in from the sea, so the marriage had wilted, fallen apart, leaving bitterness, hurt feelings, and a lonely, landlocked daughter, passing time in Spokane and dreaming about the ocean. Some romantic idea of what being a salvage master looked like.

It looks like this, McKenna thought. *A beautiful sunny morning, a fresh wind off the water, a pod of porpoises leaping and splashing off the starboard rail. And a thousand gnawing worries. A lonely life lived in suspense, waiting for the moment the whole operation falls apart.*

Stacey picked up on the look on her face. Wrapped an arm around her shoulder. "Smile, kiddo," she said. "You're living the dream. People pay big money for this view."

McKenna laughed. "I'm paying big money, too," she said. "Didn't Ridley tell you the tricks I had to pull at the bank just to get us out of Seattle? I don't know what I'm going to do if we don't—"

"We will," Stacey said. "*You* will. You think hubby and I would fly all the way up here if we didn't think you had the chops? It isn't cheap buying fuel for Matt's little plane, you know."

McKenna said nothing. Stared out over the water, the blue sky. The low, purple mountains on the horizon. Wished she shared Stacey's confidence.

The diver punched her on the shoulder. "Your dad raised a tug captain, girl. We're going to kick this thing's ass."

"Hell," McKenna said, turning back to the wheelhouse as the porpoises fell astern. "Just find me a decent architect and I'll feel a lot better."

At that moment, the rear wheelhouse door swung open above them, and Jason Parent poked his head out on deck. "Phone call for you, skipper," he called down. "Sounds like Court."

Stacey raised an eyebrow. "Good things to those who ask?"

"Apparently," McKenna replied, starting up toward the wheelhouse. "Whatever you did just there? Keep that around. We're going to need more when we get to the wreck."

. . .

"**SOME OLD BOY CRACKED MY ACES**," Harrington told McKenna. "I'm out."

McKenna frowned at the handset. The satellite phone's connection was a little spotty; she wasn't sure she'd heard correctly.

"Out," she said. "Like, for good?"

"Didn't even make my buy-in back." Harrington sighed. "I swear, two days ago I was doing great. I just ran like crap yesterday, is all. And then today, with the aces."

"Bad beat, huh?" McKenna hoped he couldn't hear her grin. Wondered if grinning made her a bad person.

"Anyway," Harrington continued, "my loss is your gain, if you still have that job open. I can catch a cab to the airport in a couple of days, meet you by the time you get up to the wreck."

"How about you catch that cab now?" McKenna replied. "Meet us in Ketchikan tomorrow morning."

"What, and ride the boat all the way up there? I was thinking I'd just take some time here in Vegas, you know, regroup and relax."

Typical Court, McKenna thought. "You want the job, I need you up here," she told him. "You wait around in Vegas, you might find another game. And where does that leave me and my crew?"

"*Our* crew," Harrington said. "I know the score, McKenna. You don't have to treat me like—"

"Ketchikan," she said. "Tomorrow morning."

Harrington went quiet. "Geez," he said finally. "Okay, McKenna. I'm in."

McKenna hung up the phone and crossed back to the wheel.

Couldn't hide the fresh bounce in her step. With Harrington on board, the *Gale Force* had a weapon that no other salvage outfit could top, not even the big guys. The whiz kid and his computer models could raise ships from the depths of the ocean. McKenna was certain he could figure out a way to save the *Pacific Lion*.

The radio squawked to life; the Coast Guard coming through with the latest long-range forecast. McKenna listened, but she was only half interested. The forecast was clear across the gulf to Dutch Harbor, and it was too early to think beyond that. Anyway, Harrington was en route, and McKenna was in no mood to worry right now.

As long as the Pacific Lion *stays afloat, we just might have a chance.*

16

DUTCH HARBOR

The community center was dark. The rest of the crew slept on cots and blankets provided by the people of the community. But Hiroki Okura lay awake. He couldn't sleep.

The fog that had descended over Unalaska Island had granted him a reprieve, however brief. The jet the company had chartered had flown on to Kodiak, and would try again to land tomorrow. Sooner or later, it would succeed, and the crew would be taken home to Japan.

Okura knew he should be preparing to face his fate with honor. An honorable man would return to Japan and face the consequences of his actions. But however appealing honor may have seemed in the abstract, in practical terms, Okura found the concept lacking.

He sat up from his cot and surveyed the gymnasium. The American customs officers had posted a guard at the front of the community center, more symbolic than anything. There was a police officer, also, patrolling the grounds. Okura could see the intermittent flash of his light through the windows of the gymnasium. Outside, the night was foggy. A plan slowly formed in his mind.

Quiet as he could, Okura stood and dressed. He rolled up his bedclothes on his cot, fashioned them into the form of a sleeping man. Then he crept down the row of cots to the rear of the gymnasium, where there was a fire door.

Someone whispered his name. *"Okura-sama."* It was the alcoholic deckhand. *"Where are you going?"*

Okura hesitated. "Cigarette," he said.

It was the wrong answer. The deckhand propped himself up on his elbow. "Lend me one?"

"Last one," Okura told him. "Sorry. Go to sleep."

"Damn it." The deckhand sighed. Looked around the gymnasium and finally lay his head down again. Okura waited in the shadows until the man was breathing heavily, and the police officer's flashlight had passed outside the window. Then he pushed open the fire door and slipped out into the night.

17

Christer Magnusson stood on a Bering Marine barge and watched his men load gear aboard the *Salvation* in the first light of day. It wasn't especially early—dawn came to Dutch Harbor around six thirty this time of year—but the men had worked all night to prepare, and Magnusson was eager to set sail. The *Lion* was drifting toward land, and the weather wouldn't hold forever. And who knew if Waverly was planning an attempt of their own?

One of Bill Carew's men coiled lines on the stern while Carew himself watched from the wheelhouse, hand on the throttle. He gave Magnusson a nod. *Ready to go?* Magnusson nodded back and bent down to release the spring line, preparing to step aboard.

There was a noise behind him, and Magnusson turned to see a small Japanese man step onto the barge. He wore the uniform of an officer aboard a Japanese Overseas ship.

"Good morning," he said in accented English. "I've heard you are going to salvage the *Lion*."

Magnusson said nothing. He would let the man reveal his angle before he made any response.

"My name is Okura," the man continued. "I need to get back to that ship."

Magnusson glanced back at Carew in the wheelhouse. "What's your business with the *Pacific Lion*?" he asked.

"I was second officer," Okura replied. "There's something on board that I would like to retrieve. If you could take me with you, I would gladly pay."

"We intend to bring this ship to harbor," Magnusson said. "Why not wait?"

"If I stay on this island, the authorities will send me home. I cannot allow that to happen."

"This thing you lost is valuable?"

"It is to me."

Magnusson studied the man. After a moment, he spit. This was unusual, to say the least. The man, Okura, was clearly into something unsavory, something that would no doubt bring trouble on land. Were he approached in the supermarket with a request like this, Magnusson knew he would turn Okura down without a second thought.

But the high seas weren't bound by the same laws as land. If you sailed far enough, you could outrun any law—and anyone who wished to enforce it. Magnusson had built his career in that wild, anarchic space. He wasn't the type to shy away from opportunity.

And there was opportunity here; that was plain.

"Ten thousand dollars," he said. "Plus expenses. And you stay out of our way."

Okura nodded. "Fine."

"*Each*," Carew called from the wheelhouse.

"I have twenty-five thousand dollars in American cash in my stateroom," Okura told them. "If you bring me to the *Lion*, you can have it."

He held Magnusson's gaze. Waited.

"You stay out of our way," Magnusson said again, turning back to the *Salvation*. "Hurry up and climb aboard."

18

KETCHIKAN, ALASKA

By morning, the *Gale Force* was tied to the dock in Ketchikan. McKenna topped up the tug's fuel tanks with diesel while Jason Parent and the Jonases headed into town for groceries. In the engine room, Nelson Ridley gave the twin EMDs a look over.

"Everything seems solid," he told McKenna, wiping sweat from his brow with a greasy hand as he stepped out onto the afterdeck. "That turbo's holding up nicely."

"Haven't really tested it yet," McKenna replied. "The real question is, can she hold up when we have that freighter in tow?"

"She'll hold up, skipper. You just worry about getting us to the job site."

"I'm working on it." McKenna watched the fuel gauge. Handed over the company credit card when the tanks were filled. The bank had come through with the hundred-thousand-dollar loan, and she'd paid down Gale Force Marine's overdrawn credit card, clearing enough breathing room to get up to the *Pacific Lion*. It was a slim margin, though.

Ten million dollars, easy. Just get up to that ship and put a line on her.

They'd arrived a little early. Court Harrington's plane hadn't arrived by the time the tug was refueled, and McKenna paced the dock, impatient. Time was a-wasting.

She was still worried about Harrington. They hadn't exactly ended things on the most amicable of terms, Randall Rhodes's

untimely demise pretty well killing any spark that had existed between them. Not that they'd been headed for any great romance.
Though the whiz kid was older than her, barely, he was still a boy at
heart, and she'd been the fool who'd tried to make him grow up.

They'd been drunk the first time it happened, at some fisherman's bar in Busan, high on salvage success and an exotic locale.
She'd kissed him, spontaneously, shocking the hell out of them both,
but he'd taken that first kiss and run with it. They'd spent the rest
of that voyage sneaking between each other's staterooms, hooking
up between wheel watches, and trying to keep the old man from
catching on.

Randall *hadn't* caught on, and they'd kept hooking up, though
there'd been warning signs from the very beginning. Court wasn't
much for hanging out between jobs, preferring to fly home to Carolina and his sailboat, to spring break and poker, no matter how many
times she'd tried to pitch him on, say, sticking around Seattle for an
actual *date*. He'd give her that big cocky grin and flash those green
eyes, change the subject or move in and kiss her. And, damn it, she'd
let him off easy, deluded herself, figured it was only a matter of time.

To his credit, Court had acted surprised when she'd spilled her
heart to him. And maybe he was. The guy was a drifter—he didn't
want a real job, so why had she ever thought he'd want a real relationship?

They'd been in his stateroom when she'd done it. A rocky trip up
the California coast, Randall on wheel watch. She'd freaking told
Court she loved him, watched him turn seasick-green, and after a
boatload of tears and some stilted conversation, all that remained
was one last walk of shame to her own stateroom, and some long,
lonely nights.

Then her dad died and she'd pushed Court away, and away he had drifted and never looked back. He'd done fine for himself, she was sure of it. She, on the other hand, was nearly broke, and hadn't had a real relationship since high school. Neither figured to change without a fair bit of luck.

HARRINGTON HAD TALENT, ANYWAY. The first job she'd worked with him, the architect had refloated a grounded bulk freighter that everyone aboard the tug figured was unsavable. He'd constructed a model of the ship on his laptop—every hold and compartment, measured the water level in each—and told the skipper and his crew where to install every pump, and how much water to pump out and when, and then stood back and watched as the freighter lifted like magic from the rocks.

It was a tour de force, a masterful performance—and for Harrington, it was just another day's work. By rights, the architect should have earned himself a long and glorious career with Commodore or Westerly. But Harrington was a slacker genius; he didn't want a real job, and, anyway, he'd grown fond of McKenna's dad. Commodore wanted to pay him a salary, keep him in an office most of the time. Harrington told them he'd done most of the work saving the ship, so he should get a percentage of the spoils, like the *Gale Force* operated—and moreover, he wanted to work on the boats. It hadn't gone over well with the suits.

AROUND THE MIDDLE of the morning, a white minivan pulled up at the foot of the docks. The rear door opened, and Court Harrington climbed out. He cut a striking figure—tall and lean, artfully mussed hair, and that cocky, mischievous smile, his eyes a startling gold-flecked green. He hoisted a duffel bag over his shoulder, paid the driver, and walked down the gangway to the dock.

"Whiz." Ridley wrapped him in a bear hug. Took his bag as he climbed over the bulwarks. "Glad you decided to join us."

"Had to keep you in suspense, didn't I?" Harrington replied. "Hello, McKenna."

"Court."

McKenna held out her hand. Harrington moved in for a hug. They settled on something in between, and it was awkward as hell. McKenna could feel her cheeks burning, and fought the embarrassment and insecurity she could tell were quite obvious.

You're the boss here. Act like it.

She stepped back, fixed Harrington with her most confident smile. "Welcome aboard," she told him. "Let's get to work."

GULF OF ALASKA

"So, okay," McKenna said. "Here's what we know about the *Lion* so far."

She and Court Harrington were in the *Gale Force*'s wheelhouse, seated at a table behind the captain's chair, where Al Parent monitored the autopilot and the radio. Outside, the weather was calm and sunny, the ocean kicking up about a three-foot swell, the wind behaving itself. It was a beautiful day for a boat ride, and the *Gale Force* was making good time.

Harrington had his laptop open, entering the *Pacific Lion's* dimensions into the complicated drafting program he'd designed himself. It was about a million light-years beyond McKenna's capabilities; just looking at the screen gave her a headache. If she didn't look at the screen, though, she would have to look at Harrington. And she still wasn't sure she could handle much of that yet.

"Six hundred and fifty-two feet, eleven inches," Harrington read. "One hundred and five feet, ten inches abeam."

McKenna checked her notes. "That's right."

The *Lion* was almost as wide as the *Gale Force* was long. Not that it should matter. As long as the weather cooperated, and the engines didn't crap out, the tug would be able to tow the freighter to wherever McKenna needed to take her. The only question was how long the tow would take. And whether Court Harrington could figure out how to get her upright first.

"So," Harrington said, studying his screen, "it should be pretty easy. I'll build a model of the ship as it lies, and then we'll go on board and figure out how much water's inside the hull, and how much fuel she's carrying, and whether any of the cargo has shifted and by how much, and that will give us a good idea of the *Lion's* weight distribution. From there, we can map out a strategy for pumping out the water that's causing the list, and pumping in ballast the way the crew should have in the first place."

McKenna blinked. "That's all?"

"We're going to need to be precise, though," Harrington continued. "If we screw up and pump water out of the wrong tanks at the wrong time, we could overcorrect and tip the ship over the wrong way. Or worse, we could sink her."

"Yeah," McKenna said. "Let's not do that."

Losing the ship would be disastrous, and not just for the millions of dollars they would forfeit. In order to obtain the measurements Court Harrington was talking about, the team would have to venture deep inside the *Pacific Lion*, in cold, dark labyrinthine holds and passageways. If the ship sunk while they were aboard, there wouldn't be any hope for survival—just miserable, lonely death as the freighter plunged to the ocean bottom. It was a grim thought.

Harrington caught McKenna's expression. "I'm not going to let us sink her, don't worry," he said. Then he smiled wryly. "Hey, if this stuff was easy, you wouldn't have been so desperate to get me back, right?"

"Sure," McKenna said, and she forced a smile in return.

"How've you been, anyway?" Harrington asked, leaning back in his seat. "I have to admit, my heart kind of skipped a beat when I saw your number on my call display. Kind of a blast from the past, right?"

Ah, shit, she thought. *Here it comes.*

"You're the best architect I know," she said. "I figured an eight-figure score was motivation enough for you and me both to put the past behind us."

"Definitely," Harrington said. He turned those green eyes on her. "Some things aren't that easy to forget, though."

She could feel herself blushing. Hated herself for it. Harrington picked up on it, laughed, and raised his hands. "Sorry, I just— It's good to see you, McKenna."

"Yeah," she said. "You, too."

"So you took over the boat, huh? Making a run at this captain thing, just like the old man. That's really cool."

"And you're, what—playing poker?"

"Weighing my options," he said. "Commodore offered me a job again, after I got my second doctorate. I don't really like their style, though. And, hey, if the *Gale Force* is back in the game . . ."

His smile wasn't going anywhere. He was still cocky as hell, sprawled out in that settee like the prodigal son, like this boat was *his* birthright.

He has the chops, though, McKenna thought, and that made it even worse. *He can handle this work. Everybody on this boat has the chops for this job. But do you? Who's the imposter here? Harrington? Or daddy's little girl?*

"We're not back in the game yet," she said lamely. "I'd wait until we get a line on that wreck before I made any big career decisions."

20

ABOARD THE *SALVATION*, TWO DAYS OUT OF DUTCH HARBOR

Okura woke up groggy. He'd spent the first day's run cooped up in the old tug's galley, watching Schwarzenegger movies on the tiny TV. Tinny little explosions and staticky one-liners, machine-gun fire everywhere. He'd escape to the back deck for fresh air every now and then, when the swell got too lumpy. Okura was a career sailor, but the *Salvation* was a lot smaller than the cargo ships he was used to, and it took the waves a little rougher.

He slept poorly. Saw the *Lion* in his dreams—endless hallways, dark nightmare cargo holds, Ishimaru always in his peripheral vision, gone when he turned to confront him. Ishimaru and that briefcase, fifty million dollars. Okura woke up sweaty, tangled in his bedsheets, didn't know where he was.

Imagined, for a split second, he was in a Yokohama prison already.

I need that briefcase.

He dressed and splashed cold water on his face, checked the galley and found Magnusson's men nursing cups of coffee. There were voices upstairs in the wheelhouse and he followed them, climbing the stairs to find Magnusson and Carew deep in conversation.

Magnusson turned to Okura as he entered. "This is where your distress call came in."

Okura looked out through the boat's windows. Saw nothing but open ocean, a growing swell, patches of sun through the clouds. There was no sign of the *Lion*.

"She has drifted," he said.

"Current's taking her up toward the Aleutians. We're going to have to chase her."

"How much longer?"

"A couple of hours, maybe. Enough time to get a good breakfast, get your gear ready. I'll give you some notice when we're closing in."

Okura looked out the window again, the empty sea. Then he descended the stairs to the galley, poured himself a mug of coffee. Picked out another action movie and tried to get comfortable.

. . .

SCHWARZENEGGER HAD JUST ABOUT killed the bad guy when the *Salvation*'s horn blew, long and loud. Okura paused the movie, and he and the Commodore men climbed back up to the wheelhouse.

Magnusson and Carew stood by the wheel, Carew's deckhand, Robbie, beside them. They gazed out through the forward windows. Okura followed their eyes. Gaped.

"*Iya,*" he said. "What a catastrophe."

They'd found the *Pacific Lion*. The ship lay on its side, dead ahead, and Okura could see the white of the ship's superstructure, the blue of its hull, and the red of its naked keel, laid out almost horizontal to the sea. Along the keel, way back at the stern, Okura could see a couple blades of the ship's propeller. The angle of the list was unsettling. The *Lion* looked ready to sink beneath the waves at any moment.

Okura shivered. Realized he hadn't been prepared to see his ship again. To see the damage he'd done.

The radio crackled.

"Vessel approaching the freighter *Pacific Lion*, this is the United States Coast Guard Marine Patrol aircraft above you. Please state your business in these waters."

There was momentary silence in the wheelhouse, and Okura could hear the drone of an aircraft engine above the boat. Carew craned his neck out of the starboard window, searched the sky.

"It's a Hercules," he said. "HC-130, probably out of Kodiak."

Christer Magnusson already had hold of the radio. "Coast Guard patrol aircraft, this is Captain Magnusson on the salvage vessel *Salvation*. We're here on behalf of Commodore Towing. We intend to salvage this wreck."

A pause. "Stand by, *Salvation*."

Okura caught Magnusson's eye. "Do you think they'll let us operate?"

"They have to," Carew said. "The Coast Guard isn't equipped to run an operation this big, not in the middle of nowhere like this. Right now, they're racking their brains trying to figure out how to keep that ship from wrecking on a rock and spilling oil over every duck, whale, and cuddly sea otter in the North Pacific. They need the *Salvation*. You wait."

Okura waited. So did the others. The Hercules droned on overhead, circling the wreck.

Then the radio hummed to life again. "*Salvation*, Coast Guard patrol. Captain, we appreciate your initiative. This ship is drifting deeper into American waters, and it's starting to scare a few people around here. Are you in touch with the ship's owners?"

"My office is in the process of negotiating a salvage agreement as we speak," Magnusson replied.

"Copy. Please advise when you're ready to commence operations. We'll continue to monitor the situation from up here, and we'll have the cutter *Munro* back on-site shortly to assist as necessary."

The radio operator wished them luck, and signed off. Overhead, the big Hercules waggled its wings. Magnusson hung up the headset. "There," he said. "The ship is ours."

21

The *Lion* was a mountain up close. Carew guided the *Salvation* around the *Lion*'s keel. There was a swell building, and the underside of the wreck was awash with breaking waves. Okura stood on the *Salvation*'s bridge wing and stared up and watched. Apart from the sound of the surf, the ship was eerily quiet.

Carew circled the *Salvation* around the stern of the freighter, where its massive propeller hung half submerged in the icy water, the flat slab of rudder sitting useless, hard-over to port.

There was an access walkway on the stern of the ship, and an opening just above where the name PACIFIC LION was painted in big white letters against the blue hull. At its lowest point, the walkway was maybe ten feet from the surface of the water, but it angled up so sharply that it might as well have been a wall.

Good thing we have rope, Okura thought. *This is going to require some agility.*

Carew idled the *Salvation* around to the portside of the ship, the weather deck at the top of the superstructure now just a few feet from the water. Okura could see the whole of the accommodations house, the plain, low boxes above the white hull that served as home and working space for the crew. The aft lifeboat remained in place, hanging from its stanchions near the giant exhaust funnel at the stern.

So Ishimaru hadn't stolen away. Not in a boat, anyway.

The bridge appeared empty as well. No sign of life anywhere. If the stowaway was still aboard, he'd had a lonely time at sea.

When the *Salvation* had completed its circumnavigation of the wreck, Okura turned and walked off of the bridge wing and into the wheelhouse, where Magnusson was on the satellite phone. He hung up as Okura entered.

"The shipowners have faxed an agreement to the Commodore headquarters," he told the men. "No cure, no pay. If we don't salvage this ship, we don't earn a dime."

He stared out at the *Lion*, silent. The rest of the men followed his gaze. Finally, Magnusson squared his shoulders. "First things first," he said, fixing his eyes on Okura. "We'd better get you on board to retrieve your lost item—and our fee."

MAGNUSSON AND CAREW DECIDED that the best way aboard the *Lion* was from the portside weather deck, the same way that Okura and his shipmates had evacuated the vessel days earlier.

"*Best* best way on board is with a helicopter," Magnusson told Okura. "We wait until the *Munro* shows up and they'll put you down nice and easy at the top of the starboard rail. You can drop in and search how you please."

"No Coast Guard," Okura told the salvage master. "They can't know that I'm out here."

Magnusson smirked, like he'd anticipated that response. "No helicopter, then." He nodded to Carew, who sidled the *Salvation* alongside the *Lion*'s empty lifeboat station on the portside, forward deck. The freighter was just a few feet away from the salvage boat now. It loomed high above the *Salvation*, skewed at its impossible angle. It looked seconds away from crashing down on them all.

Carew ducked his head out the wheelhouse window, called back instructions to Robbie, who stood at the starboard rail with a pike pole.

"Grab a tie-up line," Magnusson told Okura. "Make it fast to something when the deckhand grabs the rail."

The *Salvation* inched closer to the *Lion*, its bow thruster grumbling and churning up water, the propeller doing the same at the stern. Robbie stretched with the pike pole, hooked it around the freighter's side railing, and used it to guide the *Salvation* closer, until the railing nearly touched the smaller ship's bulwarks. Okura looped his rope around the railing, tied it off.

Robbie hoisted himself up and onto the freighter, two more coils of rope on his shoulder, a duffel bag in his free hand. He steadied himself, reached for Okura's hand, and pulled him aboard.

"You have three hours," Magnusson called up to them. "If the weather gets dire or the situation changes, we'll sound the horn. When you hear the horn, you return to this vessel immediately, understand?"

The tug motored away from the wreck, headed toward the stern. Okura listened as the sound of the engines died away. Then he turned to where Robbie waited.

Fifty million dollars.

"Right," Robbie said from beside him. "How about we go find your twenty-five thousand, before we do anything else?"

THE DECK WAS SLICK AND BARE, and the *Lion* groaned and wallowed as the sea battered against it. Okura followed Robbie along the railing to the bridge, conscious of the roiling sea beneath the grate of the rail.

Robbie reached the bridge, pushed a door open. It fell in and hung there, suspended by gravity. Okura followed the deckhand inside.

The bridge was dark. Its width spanned the ship, save for a couple of abbreviated wings on either side. Okura looked around, took in the shadowy instruments, the chart tables, the cupboards with books and coffee cups and creamers scattered on the floor. Everything looked familiar, but at the same time so alien. The last time he'd been here, he'd caused a disaster.

It was cold inside the bridge. Robbie reached into his duffel bag and switched on a headlamp. Passed it to Okura and produced another for himself. Then he reached up to a chart table and pulled himself skyward, toward the aft bulkhead door in the middle of the bridge.

Okura followed, sweating a little from the exertion, and they reached the bulkhead door and carefully negotiated the long, angled corridor. The thin light from the bridge windows disappeared quickly. The howl of the wind quieted, as did the drone of the Coast Guard rescue plane overhead. The only sound Okura could hear was the occasional groan of the five thousand Nissans still lashed down in the cargo hold.

"What are you looking for, anyway?" Robbie asked as they made their way aft toward Okura's stateroom.

Okura glanced back at him. Said nothing.

"Just so I know what I'm looking for," the deckhand explained. "Like, is it big, is it small, what is it?"

"It's a briefcase," Okura told him. "Silver."

"A briefcase." Robbie went silent for a moment, waiting, no doubt, for Okura to elaborate. He didn't. "Okay," the deckhand said finally. "A briefcase it is."

A briefcase. And the man who owned it.

But Okura kept his mouth shut about Ishimaru.

THEY REACHED A BULKHEAD door about thirty feet down from the bridge. Okura stopped. "The officers' staterooms are beyond."

He hesitated there as Robbie watched him. He didn't want to return to his stateroom, he realized. He would have liked to forget he ever lived here, ever worked here. He would have liked to forget, period.

He opened the bulkhead to another hallway, a line of doors on either side. Climbed into the hallway and across to his stateroom door, pushed it open. It smelled musty inside, like a forgotten room in an old house. the porthole was dim; it looked up at the gray, featureless sky, the sun obscured by thick clouds. Okura's belongings were pretty much as he'd left them, though anything loose had fallen onto the floor—the paperback novel he'd been trying to read, the photographs he'd arranged on his desk.

Okura picked up one of these, a framed picture of his sister and her husband, their young daughter. The girl was three now, and he could count the number of times he'd seen her on one hand, so long had he been out at sea. She was a beautiful little girl, intelligent and inquisitive, and her parents were kind and loving. Okura studied the picture and wondered what his sister would think, if she knew what he'd done.

Robbie coughed from the doorway. "I don't see any briefcase," he said. "How about that twenty-five grand?"

Okura looked up from the picture. "Just give me one minute," he said. "I didn't expect I'd be back here."

"It's your money," Robbie said. "You want to spend it on memory lane, be my guest. But my boss is going to want to get paid."

Okura glanced down at the picture again. His sister was smiling, as happy as Okura could ever remember seeing her. Her husband was a hardworking man, a lawyer. His life must have been stressful, but he was smiling, too, his arm around Okura's sister, his hand mussing his daughter's hair. They were a happy family.

Robbie sighed, his impatience obvious. Okura set the picture aside. Climbed over to his desk and withdrew his passport and the twenty-five thousand dollars he'd hidden away.

THEY MADE THEIR WAY to Ishimaru's hiding space, the storage locker aft of the ship. The stowaway wasn't there, hadn't returned, and the briefcase was still absent, too.

Damn it, Okura thought. *Why couldn't this be easy?*

Ishimaru could have been anywhere on board the ship by now, if he was even still there. Okura hoped the stowaway had at least had the sense to remain on the accommodations deck; the prospect of venturing farther below, to the cargo holds, was a nightmarish proposition.

So Okura and the deckhand searched every stateroom for the stowaway, inch by painstaking inch. There were two guest staterooms, the captain's suite, the first officer's suite, and Okura's. Beyond that, more staterooms, and the general crew quarters.

Okura searched the third officer's quarters and the cadet's modest suite and found nothing. Continued aft and found two more doors: to starboard, the deckhand's berths. To port, the galley and the crew mess.

"Which do we check first?" Robbie asked.

Okura considered. "The galley." *Perhaps Ishimaru got hungry.*

But the galley showed no sign of the stowaway. It was a long, low kitchen, stainless-steel islands and cooking areas, a walk-in refrigerator and a similar freezer. The meat had gone bad; the stench inside the freezer was horrific. Robbie gave it a sweep with his headlamp and slammed the door shut again.

"Dang it," he said, gagging. "I don't even know why I did that."

The galley floor was covered in foodstuffs: sauces and stale breads and broken eggs. The galley was a 24-7 operation, and even in the middle of the night, someone would have been working, setting out food for the midnight watch. The food was spilled everywhere, but there were no telltale footprints in the flour, nothing obviously stolen from the dry-goods locker. If Ishimaru was still aboard the ship, he hadn't made it to the galley.

The crew mess was adjacent to the galley. It was a small cafeteria, the tables bolted to the floor, the benches loose and scattered. There was spilled food here, too, but no Ishimaru.

Suppose we'll have to check the crew berths, Okura thought, but before he could tell Robbie, the *Salvation* sounded a blast on her horn from somewhere outside.

The deckhand emerged from another locker. "You hear that?"

"I heard it," Okura said. "I need more time."

"No more time. They blow the horn, we come running, remember? Get back down to the boat and try again tomorrow."

Shit.

Okura looked at the deckhand, who shrugged. *It is what it is.*

"Tomorrow," Okura said finally. "We come back early."

22

The *Gale Force* made Dutch Harbor the next morning. Sailed up through Akutan Pass into the Bering Sea, around the top of Unalaska Island, into Unalaska Bay, and down toward the village.

Court Harrington joined McKenna in the wheelhouse as the *Gale Force* motored across the bay. "So this is Dutch Harbor," he said.

"The one and only," McKenna replied. "You never made it up here with my dad?"

"Not this far out. Most I know about this place, I learned from that fishing show, the crab guys. Kind of doesn't seem real."

It was a beautiful little town, and the mariner in McKenna was fascinated by the mix of traffic in the harbor, from deep-sea container ships to Coast Guard cutters to fish packers and freezer boats to trawlers and crabbers. Harrington pointed out the window at one of the boats. "Right there," he said. "I definitely saw those guys on TV."

"You want to motor on over there, see if they'll give you a spot?"

The architect laughed. "I don't think I'm cut out for it. It's tough work on those crab boats. Hardest job in the world, they say."

"Psh. They never worked on a salvage tug."

"Settled, then. As soon as we save that *Lion*, I'm coming back to Dutch and ditching you for a crab boat. You can look for my ass on TV."

McKenna throttled down, pointed the *Gale Force* at the fuel barge. "I'd better get your autograph now, then," she told him. "Just in case."

. . .

McKENNA BROUGHT THE TUG into the fuel barge, nodded hello to the owner as Jason Parent and his dad secured the mooring lines.

"*Gale Force,*" the owner said, admiring the tug as he passed McKenna the fuel hose. "I remember this boat. Hell of a tug. Riptide Rhodes's, wasn't it?"

"Yes, sir," McKenna replied. "My old man."

"Your old man." The owner squinted up at her, appraisingly. "Well, what brings you to Dutch, anyhow?"

McKenna shrugged. The law of the gold-rush mariner, whether fisherman or salvage speculator, was to keep one's mouth shut, especially on the docks, where gossip was often the primary industry.

"Just come up to have a look around," she told the owner. "The crew always wanted to meet those crab guys, and I figured maybe we'd run into somebody who could use our services."

"Always a lot of guys needing help around here." The owner gestured across the water. "Especially with Bill Carew and his gang out with those Commodore boys."

McKenna felt her insides go a couple degrees colder. She followed the man's eyes to some ramshackle barges tied up in the elbow of a long spit of land. "Commodore guys are in town?"

"You bet. You heard about that big car carrier that nearly flipped over the other day? No sooner had the Coast Guard rescued the crew than a couple of those Commodore guys were climbing off a plane, scrounging for somebody's boat to take them out there." He spit on the dock. "Dunno how they plan to actually *save* that wreck, but they're the experts, I suppose."

"They put a line on her?" McKenna asked.

"That's what I heard from the Coast Guard." The guy grinned up at her. "Pity your old man isn't still around, huh? Tug like this, he could rack up a hell of a payday out there."

"Yeah," McKenna agreed, and she felt it like a punch in the gut. "A real pity, all right."

23

Christer Magnusson could tell this job wouldn't be easy.

Rescuing a ship was never a simple task, but in Magnusson's experience, some salvage jobs came easier than others. A bulk freighter dead in the water and adrift in the open ocean with calm weather? Fairly straightforward. An oil tanker aground on a shoal in a storm, one hundred thousand tons of crude in the balance? A little more complicated. And this job, the *Pacific Lion*, definitely ranged closer to the latter.

She wasn't filled up with oil, thank god; just Nissans. But the freighter would still make a mess if it landed on the rocks, a hundred nautical miles now to the north. Its bunker fuel alone would have a devastating impact on the Aleutians' marine environment, would kill fish, birds, and mammals alike, coat the shore with black tar. Magnusson wanted to avoid that, and the bad publicity that would accompany such a spill. Anyway, if the *Lion* wrecked, he wouldn't get paid.

Saving her, though, would be a challenge. He would need to get aboard, make sure she wasn't taking on more water. Then he would have to figure out a way to reverse that list. And it was here that Christer Magnusson knew he was at a disadvantage.

There was one man—one person—in the northern hemisphere who Magnusson knew could save the *Pacific Lion*, and he wasn't answering his phone. Magnusson had a fair idea as to why: Court Harrington had hired on with another operation somewhere. He was trying to save the ship for himself.

But which operation? Waverly's best tug was out of commission. There were no other outfits on the coast that could handle the *Lion*. Hell, even this tug, the *Salvation*, would barely be up to the task. There was only one other name, Magnusson figured, that even remotely made sense.

Rhodes.

Gale Force.

Court Harrington had been close with Randall Rhodes. He'd spurned Magnusson's entreaties to come work for Commodore time and again, even at the promise of better pay, steady work. If Harrington was allied with any tug, it was Riptide's *Gale Force*.

But Riptide Rhodes was dead. And his daughter was towing barges. Could she really be making a run at the *Lion*?

Magnusson supposed he would find out soon enough. Knew he had the edge on experience over McKenna Rhodes, even if she had Court Harrington. But he would need to work quickly, secure the *Lion* for Commodore. Arrest the wreck's drift north toward landfall, secure it offshore, and set to work on that list, Harrington be damned. With any luck, the weather would hold long enough for Commodore HQ to find him another architect. And maybe a bigger boat.

Either way, it was time to get working.

Magnusson descended from the *Salvation*'s wheelhouse, found the Japanese sailor, Okura, making coffee in the galley. Magnusson gathered the man's search yesterday had not gone to plan, but that was hardly his problem.

"This tug will not be your taxi today," he told Okura. "We came here for the *Lion*, and today we put a line on her."

He turned on his heel before the sailor could answer. Climbed back up to the wheelhouse, a full day's work looming ahead.

24

McKenna gathered the crew in the *Gale Force*'s galley. Matt and Stacey, Nelson Ridley, Court Harrington, and the Parents. The only crew missing was Spike, and McKenna figured the ship's cat wouldn't exactly have any sympathy to contribute, anyway.

"Commodore's at the *Lion*," McKenna told them. "According to the local gossip, they had a line on the wreck as of yesterday."

From his corner of the galley, Al Parent muttered a curse. Matt and Stacey swapped pained looks. Jason Parent stared at the floor.

"Commodore?" Ridley scratched his head. "I thought the *Titan* was laid up in California."

"It is," McKenna replied. "That's the funny thing. I thought we knew all the salvage outfits on the coast, but Commodore chartered a boat from in town. I guess the locals have a tug that can do the job."

"Be kind of crazy to go all the way out there if they didn't," Ridley agreed.

"What does this mean for us?" Court Harrington asked. "They can't really expect to right that list, can they?"

"What this means—" McKenna sighed. "What this means is that Commodore has a claim on the *Lion*. It means we're too late."

"So what are we going to do?"

McKenna looked around at her crew. The guy at the fuel dock had disappeared into his office about halfway through the *Gale Force*'s refueling. Came back with a story about a processing ship needing a tow, Kodiak to Seattle, ten thousand dollars a day.

"Probably a ten-day trip," the guy had said. "Hundred grand in your pocket, right there."

A hundred grand. It would keep the lights on, anyway. Get the *Gale Force* back down to the lower forty-eight on a paying run. Maybe they could pick up another job, quick and easy, in Seattle.

Maybe.

"There's a tow job available, Kodiak to Seattle," McKenna told her crew. "I'll need Al and Jason and Ridley aboard. Matt and Stacey and Court, I'll pay you for your time, fly you anywhere you want to go." She shrugged. "I wish I could do better, guys."

"Kodiak to Seattle." Ridley rubbed his chin. "How much are they paying?"

"Ten grand. Day rate."

"Cripes. That barely covers our expenses. And what about the engine overhauls? We were counting on this score to fix up the tug."

"I know, Nelson," McKenna told him. "I wish I had better news. We're just too late. That's all there is to it."

Ridley stared at her, his brow furrowed, his eyes dark, the rest of the crew's expressions a match. McKenna figured she could read what they were thinking, every one of them.

This never would have happened if your dad was still around.

25

Okura followed Robbie off the flimsy skiff and back onto the wreck of the *Lion*. They climbed up through the bridge again, all the way to the top this time, and inched across the starboard deck as the wind roared in their ears and the wounded ship rolled in the swell.

It had not been a pleasant ride from the *Salvation* to the freighter, not in the tug's tiny lifeboat. The weather was picking up; overnight, the swell had increased to approximately six feet, and the wind gusted strong enough to send an eerie howl through the stay wires on the *Lion*'s foremast. According to Carew, the weather wouldn't get really nasty for another few days, but Okura knew forecasts could be wrong. And in his experience, the North Pacific rarely stayed peaceful for long.

Carew and the Commodore men had motored the *Salvation* to the rear of the freighter, where they would attach a towing line to the stern and attempt to keep the wreck under control as the weather built up. Tethered to the *Lion*, they wouldn't be able to retrieve Okura and Robbie, who would have to navigate two football fields' worth of water to return to the safety of the tug. It wasn't a comforting notion.

They reached a door in the accommodations house, a couple

hundred feet from the bridge. "The crew quarters are down here," Okura told Robbie. "We'll search them next."

Robbie tied off a length of rope to a railing inside the doorway. Beyond was a long, gloomy hallway. It looked like a garbage chute, or some sadist's slide.

Okura took the rope in his hands and began the descent, walking his feet down the steep hallway floor as he held himself upright. The thin light from the doorway above was all but gone by the time he reached the central passage with the galley to one side, the crew berths on the other. Okura turned on his headlamp and peered into the first of the crew's rooms, could see two rumpled beds and a flimsy table. He couldn't see Ishimaru. Couldn't see the briefcase.

"Tomio?" Okura whispered.

There was no response.

26

McKenna sat in the skipper's chair, staring out through the wheelhouse windows at the mountains surrounding Dutch Harbor. They were a luscious, verdant green, almost shockingly so, plain of trees or any significant foliage. To McKenna's eyes, they looked as smooth as a painting, grassy carpet rising up from the water, interrupted here and there by jagged rock.

Weather was coming. The forecast predicted fog, and then increasing wind. Eventually, in a few days, a gale. McKenna had been on the phone through the morning, trying to scrounge a couple extra grand out of the day rate. The rate stayed firm, though. Ten thousand. Ten days. One hundred grand.

Then she'd called the airport. "Next flight's at four thirty," the PenAir guy told her. "Plenty of room for your crew. If you want off the island, I'd take it. Hard to say when we'll get the next plane out, the weather forecast how it is."

Four thirty. A few hours. It was time to make a decision, kiss the *Lion* good-bye. Anyway, a hundred thousand dollars wasn't nothing. It was a job, a couple weeks on the water. Who could really complain?

McKenna called the airport back, booked tickets to Anchorage for Matt, Stacey, and Court. Matt and Stacey would fly back to Seattle, she imagined, to pick up Matt's plane, and from there it was anyone's guess. They might fly that bird down to Patagonia, or maybe leave the plane and fly commercial to Nepal. Whatever they did, it was bound to be more fun than this.

And Harrington? He'd fly back to Las Vegas, or maybe home to Carolina, ghost from her life yet again. This time, she wouldn't be calling him back with any blockbuster jobs.

McKenna was about to call the guy in Kodiak, tell him she'd pick up that tow. She stopped when she saw Nelson Ridley steamrolling down the wharf toward the *Gale Force*, coming in hot.

McKenna watched her engineer climb aboard the tug. Heard him take the stairs so the wheelhouse double-time, burst in so fast he scared Spike off the dash.

"So, I've been asking around," Ridley said, nearly breathless. "I figured it was kind of shady how we'd never heard of this Carew fella, thought I'd find out what he's all about."

Ridley had the ghost of a grin as he caught his breath.

"Yeah?" McKenna said. "And?"

"And, first of all, I hear it's Christer Magnusson himself up here on that boat," Ridley said. "But forget about that for a second, lass. Carew and his gang spend most of their time helping out the crab fleet, repairs and overhauls, that kind of thing. Sometimes they help out with the merchant ships, but not often."

"Just our bad luck they decided to get frisky this time around, huh?"

"Maybe, or maybe not." Ridley smiled now, full-on, wide. "See, the word is they went out on their biggest boat, the *Salvation*, a few days back. But skipper, that boat, it's not the right equipment for the job."

McKenna didn't reply. The engineer's smile was infectious, and so was his enthusiasm, but McKenna was still smarting from the big reveal at the fuel dock that morning. Whatever Ridley had to tell her, the skipper wasn't about to fire up the mains and go roaring back out to sea just yet.

"The *Salvation*," Ridley continued, "is an old navy ship—seventy years old, in fact. A hundred and twenty feet long, twin Cat 3508s for power." He looked at McKenna. "That's barely fifteen hundred horses."

Now McKenna paid attention. The *Gale Force*'s twin EMDs put out 4,300 horsepower *apiece*, and though horsepower wasn't the be-all and end-all in the towing business, it did tend to be pretty damn important if you were trying to haul a twenty-five-thousand-deadweight-ton cargo ship across the North Pacific. By McKenna's calculations, anything above seven thousand horses should have handled the job easily, assuming the weather didn't go hurricane. The *Salvation* and her engines would hardly be able to *move* the

Pacific Lion, much less bring her to safe harbor, in anything less than dead calm and flat seas. And nowhere on the North Pacific was anything dead calm and flat for any length of time.

"Cripes," McKenna said. "You sure they don't have another tug on the way?"

"Not as far as I can figure," Ridley replied. "Best I can tell, they're going to hold the *Lion* for Commodore until they can get the *Titan* up here, the whole team, the works." He exhaled. "I mean, heck, it's almost criminal what they're trying to pull off."

Criminal might have been an overstatement. But if Magnusson and his crew were telling the Coast Guard that they could keep the *Lion* off the rocks, maybe not. The ship was drifting north, and the weather was rising. The whole thing was a disaster in waiting.

"Fire up the mains," McKenna told her engineer. "Get the crew aboard, and tell Al and Jason to be ready to cut us loose as soon as possible. Sooner or later, Christer Magnusson is going to realize he's bitten off more than that old tug can handle." She gave Ridley half a smile. "And I'd kind of like to be there for the moment of epiphany."

Ridley was already halfway out of the wheelhouse. "Aye-aye, captain," he called over his shoulder.

McKenna watched him go, felt her adrenaline pump as her eyes fell on her dad's picture in that old pewter frame.

We're still in the game, Dad.

27

There was a Coast Guard cutter off the *Salvation*'s starboard quarter when Okura woke up the next morning. It was the same ship that had brought the *Lion*'s crew to Dutch Harbor, long and sleek and white, a single-deck gun mounted ominously on the bow.

"The *Munro*," Christer Magnusson said. "They showed up last night. Hailed us while you were sleeping, asked if we'd seen any sign of a Japanese sailor. Seems one went missing back in Dutch Harbor."

Okura sipped his coffee, tried to calm his nerves, though the Coast Guard cutter outside loomed large. "What did you tell them?"

Magnusson spat into an empty microwave noodles cup. "I told them no," he said. "I told them I had a couple of salvage specialists going over to the ship, trying to work out the optimal towing strategy."

"Did they believe that?"

"They seemed to." Magnusson put down the noodle cup, looked him in the eye. "But my fee just went up, Mr. Okura."

Okura said nothing.

"I don't know what you're looking for, but I know it must be valuable," Magnusson continued. "And I *won't* lie to the Coast Guard forever, not for ten thousand dollars. So whatever you're looking for, if you intend to use this ship as a base of operations, you'll be handing twenty-five percent over to me."

Twenty-five percent. More than twelve million dollars. The idea made Okura feel faintly sick. But what choice did he have?

He nodded.

"Good."

The *Salvation* rolled into a swell with a sickening lurch. Magnusson checked the barometer at the back of the wheelhouse. "Weather's going to kick up," he said. "By tomorrow, the day after, you won't want to go far in that skiff. Better get back to searching while you still have the chance."

The salvage master throttled up the *Salvation*, glanced back through the aft windows at the *Lion* behind them. Overnight, the team had hooked up a towline to the stern of the freighter, managed to turn her into the wind. But the little tug's engines were working hard, and as best as Okura could tell, the tug wasn't doing much more than keeping the freighter in place.

Where are you, Tomio? he thought, studying the ship, contemplating the vast expanse of cargo area left to be searched, the rapidly building waves outside. *Where have you taken that briefcase?*

28

The seas were building.

McKenna lay awake in her bunk as the *Gale Force* plowed through the swell, the engines running full-out toward the *Pacific Lion*.

The good weather wasn't going to last. McKenna had checked the long-range forecast before passing the watch over to Al Parent, and the forecast was grim: winds fifteen to twenty knots by the time they arrived at the *Lion*, growing to twenty-five to thirty within a couple of days. There was a gale coming, the growing seas the first indication of bad weather, the distant wind building the waves bigger and bigger, pushing them ahead of the storm.

As the weather got closer, the swell would keep rising, and the *Lion* would wallow and lose stability. It might take on more water and sink, or it might drift faster toward the rocky coast of the Aleutian chain. However you looked at it, the gale was bad news.

McKenna didn't sleep much. She tossed and turned in her bunk, listening to the waves break over the bow, the pitch of the engines. The night passed slowly, the tug grinding along, and when the first light of dawn began to show through the portholes, the skipper forced herself to her feet, dressed and splashed water on her face, brewed a strong pot of coffee in the galley, and returned to the wheelhouse, where Al Parent sat in the skipper's chair with the satellite phone to his ear, talking to home while he monitored the tug's progress, the cat curled up asleep in his lap. It sounded like he was singing a lullaby.

Spike woke up as McKenna walked in. Stretched, yawned. Jumped down from Al's lap and padded out of the wheelhouse, nary a look in the skipper's direction.

Al watched the cat go, saw McKenna standing there. He stopped singing, and gave her a sheepish smile, quickly signed off the call.

"Little Ben isn't sleeping too well," he told her. "I thought if his mom put me on speaker . . ."

He trailed off, made a show of looking embarrassed, though

McKenna suspected her first mate would be doting over his grandson until the day the kid drove off to college—and probably longer. She smiled and handed him a cup of coffee.

"Heck, we should put you on the hailer," she told Al. "With that rock-a-bye baby, you'll have us all zonked right out."

Al laughed. "A little early, aren't you?" he asked McKenna. "Still have a couple hours left on my watch."

"Couldn't sleep," she said.

Al glanced at the autopilot, punched in a slight course correction. "Weather's building."

"That's what kept me from my beauty rest. Couple days, it'll be howling out there."

"Tough to tow a boat in that kind of wind. That *Lion*'s big hull will turn into a sail, send her sliding all over on the end of our towline."

"Assuming we can even right the thing. I don't want to be clambering around inside that wreck, trying to get the pumps working in twenty-foot seas."

Al nodded.

"*Assuming* we can even get a line on the thing," McKenna added. "Convince Christer Magnusson his tug isn't cut out for this work."

Al snorted. "Bunch of pretenders. One look at us, skip, and Magnusson will scurry off with his tail between his legs."

"Let's hope so," McKenna said.

The two sat in silence. Watched the light grow over the slate-gray sea, the never-ending procession of heavy, scudding waves, the rise and the crash of the hull though the peaks and troughs, the grind of the engines.

The night faded away. Morning passed. Al had the radio on the satellite channels, a country music station, all lonely husbands and runaway dogs, broken-down trucks and whiskey-bottle blues. It did nothing to help McKenna's mood.

She crossed the wheelhouse, ready to flip the station to something a little more uplifting, some classic rock, maybe, when Al called over from the radar. "I got a hit"

McKenna forgot about the radio. Crossed back and peered over Al's shoulder. The radar had picked up something dead ahead, thirty nautical miles or so, something large and uneven. As the *Gale Force* sailed closer, the radar slowly separated from one large hit into three smaller, distinct dots.

"That big one's the *Lion*," McKenna said. "The smaller one's gotta be the *Salvation*."

"And the third one?" Al asked.

McKenna scratched her head. "Coast Guard. Or another Commodore tug."

"Gotta be the Coast Guard," Al said. "We'd have heard if Magnusson had another tug here already." He glanced at the autopilot, set the tug on course. "Twenty miles away now," he told McKenna. "An hour or two, tops, we find out."

AT FIRST, the stricken ship was just a smudge on the horizon, a formless mirage, visible only from the tops of the swells. As the *Gale Force* plowed closer, the smudge separated, and McKenna could see the Coast Guard cutter, stately and proud, and the *Pacific Lion* herself, a half-sunk bathtub toy on an enormous scale, ungainly and wallowing in an uneasy sea.

"Holy hell," Al muttered. "What a wreck."

The ship had been ugly to begin with. It boasted none of the classic lines of a traditional cargo vessel. Looked more like a brick than a ship, blocky and angular and top-heavy, an affront to any sailor's sense of style and tradition.

Now, though, lying wounded in the water, it looked like disaster. The list was pronounced. The ship lay almost fully on its portside, the bulbous red chin of its bow almost parallel to the waves.

It's incredible nobody died when that ship flipped, McKenna thought. *Let's hope we can save her and still say the same.*

The *Lion* wallowed, waves breaking over her keel, but she looked more or less stable. Certainly, she didn't appear to have taken on much water, at least not drastically. There was still time to save her—assuming the *Salvation* relinquished its claim.

McKenna could see the little boat, low and blue and grungy, in a tow position at the stern of the freighter. The towline stretched taut between the two vessels, and exhaust billowed from the smaller boat's stack, but neither vessel was moving.

"What do they think they're doing out here?" Al asked. "If they're moving at all, it's backwards."

"Probably the best they can do," McKenna replied. "Slow down the drift and hope to ride out the gale."

A quarter mile or so off the *Lion*'s port quarter, the Coast Guard cutter silently stood guard. McKenna assumed the Coast Guard was aware of the situation, but if they had any concerns, they weren't showing it.

Soon enough. McKenna marked her position on the GPS screen. Less than seventy nautical miles south of the Aleutian Islands, and the weather building, but the *Gale Force* was finally on scene.

It was time to flex some Rhodes muscle.

29

Christer Magnusson was in the *Salvation*'s galley, pouring a fresh cup of coffee, when the radio crackled in the wheelhouse.

"*Salvation, Salvation*, this is the *Gale Force*. Are you on here, Christer?"

A woman's voice. McKenna Rhodes. *Shit.*

Magnusson crossed to the galley porthole, peered out, and saw nothing but ocean. He hurried through the house to the bulkhead door and the afterdeck, walked out under the mammoth A-frame crane, and peered back across the stern, beyond the hulk of the *Lion*.

For a moment, he saw nothing but gray swells and whitecaps, the turbulence of the building sea. Then the *Salvation* rose on a wave, and Magnusson spied the tug a half mile or so off of the starboard quarter.

"*Helvete.*"

It was the *Gale Force*, all right—big and brawny as always, and as pretty as the days Randall Rhodes had run her, a fresh coat of paint on her red-and-white superstructure, her hull black as coal. Magnusson had spent many trips racing that tug to a wounded freighter, and more than a handful shaking his fist at her stern from the *Titan*. She still looked good, Magnusson had to admit. She looked like a tug that could save the *Lion*.

But could the Rhodes girl?

McKenna Rhodes was an enigma to Magnusson. He'd spoken to her rarely, on those brief occasions when the *Gale Force* and the

Titan found themselves in the same harbor and he'd dropped by Riptide's galley for a cup of coffee with his rival.

She'd been quiet during those meetings, as far as Magnusson could remember. But she'd sure kept her eyes on him, studied him while he talked, as if she were committing every word to memory. He'd liked her, as much as he liked anyone on Riptide's boat: she carried herself like crew, not like Riptide's daughter, and by any account, she worked hard. Certainly, she had guts, sailing the old man's tug all the way here on a gamble.

Magnusson hurried back inside the *Salvation*, up into the wheelhouse, where Riptide's daughter was still trying to raise him on the radio.

"*Salvation, Salvation*, I know you're out there," McKenna was saying. "This is McKenna Rhodes on the *Gale Force*. How do you read?"

Magnusson glanced back at the tug again, through the rear windows. Then he picked up the radio. "*Gale Force*, this is *Salvation*." He forced a smile, kept his voice nonchalant. "Fancy meeting you all the way out here, McKenna. How are you?"

But McKenna Rhodes wasn't having any small talk. "What are you up to, Christer? You know damn well you can't save that ship with that old boat you're running."

Magnusson spit into his ramen cup. "We have a line on her, and we're holding our own. If you came out here thinking you'd push me off this wreck, I'm sorry, but you wasted a trip."

"Unless you're hiding about five thousand horsepower, the wind will give you all the pushing you can handle," McKenna answered. "Weather's building, and I have a team here who can get that ship upright. I suggest you stand down and let us do our jobs."

Magnusson pursed his lips. McKenna had her dad's audacity, that was for certain. And she probably had Court Harrington on board, too. But she was still in second place, and Magnusson wasn't about to back down.

"Sorry, McKenna," he replied. "We signed an Open Form with the owners, and we're salvaging this ship. We'll keep you in mind if we require assistance. Over and out."

He hung up the radio. Then he picked up the sat phone. Dialed in to Commodore home base, waited on the connection.

Pick up, damn it, he thought, studying the *Salvation*'s lack of progress on the GPS screen. *I need another boat, and an architect,* now.

30

Okura led Robbie down the *Lion*'s central hallway again. The waves outside were bigger now, the wind stronger. Okura winced every time the ship swayed, with every groan from the hull and the shifting cargo below.

They had covered every inch of the accommodations deck. Every stateroom, every hallway, every locker. No sign of Tomio Ishimaru. No sign of his briefcase. If the stowaway was still on board, he was in the engine room somewhere, or in the cargo holds.

Or he'd washed overboard.

But Okura wasn't ready to consider *that* possibility. He couldn't afford to lose faith, not yet. He led Robbie down the hall to a stairway amidships. Pushed the bulkhead door and it swung open, revealing the dark, cockeyed stairway beyond. The stairs descended into the gloom of the cargo holds. At this angle, there was no way to follow them but with ropes.

"These stairs go all the way to the last cargo hold, deck four," Okura told Robbie. "There are nine cargo decks in all. Five thousand cars."

Nine decks. Each deck six hundred feet long and a hundred feet wide. Miles upon miles of ground to cover, all of it dark and deadly. Okura watched Robbie rig up a climbing line. Tested the strength of the knot and hesitated at the edge of the bulkhead, his headlamp beam reflecting against the carnival funhouse angles of the listing stairway beyond.

Fifty million dollars. Okura took the rope in his hands and stepped off into the darkness, began to lower himself deeper into the *Lion*.

OKURA WAS HALFWAY TO the first cargo deck—deck twelve—when Robbie called down from the hallway above.

"Just heard the horn," the deckhand reported. "My radio's crapping out in here. I gotta get back to the surface."

"We can't turn around yet," Okura replied. "We haven't even started our search."

"Skipper sounds the horn, I gotta jump to it," Robbie said. "I'll be right back."

Okura listened to the deckhand picking his way down the passage, leaving him alone in the stairwell. He steadied his breathing. Gripped the rope tighter and pushed off from the wall. The darkness seemed almost alive beneath him, all drips and moans and swirling shadows rising up to meet him as he made his descent.

Robbie returned just after Okura had reached the bulkhead at deck twelve. "Bad news," the deckhand called down, his headlamp piercing the gloom from above. "Urgent. There's a salvage tug just showed up outside, the *Gale Force*, from Seattle. They're trying to bump us off the tow, and Bill says they have the boat that could do it."

Okura looked around the landing. The hatch to the cargo hold hung open on the wall opposite, now nearly vertical with the slant of the ship. This struck Okura as unusual; the door was supposed to be locked and secured while the ship was at sea. This was an aberration.

"I might have found something," Okura called up the stairway. "I want to continue the search."

"Not today," Robbie said. "Look, we'll keep poking around this damn ship as soon as we can, but right now I need to get topside and see what my boss wants us to do."

Okura pushed open the hatch wider and peered inside. The light from his headlamp was dim and abbreviated, but what it illuminated was astonishing: row upon row of cars, all hanging at the same awkward impossible angle, suspended in space by a system of high-strength straps, ropes, and chains. They swayed almost as one with the motion of the swell, the whole fragile mess a chorus of straining material and groaning steel every time a wave hit. The cars hung in place, and they stretched to the end of Okura's light and beyond, an obstacle course, a death trap, hanging by the proverbial thread.

"There is a storm coming," Okura called. "We need to keep looking while the weather still allows it."

"Look, if the other tug bumps us off the tow, they'll kick you off this ship with the rest of us." Robbie paused. "I'm heading back. You can stay, or you can go."

Okura steadied himself at the bulkhead and searched in his bag for another length of rope. He had plenty of fresh water in the bag, a supply of energy bars. "Very well," he said. "I'm staying."

He gritted his teeth and swung across the bulkhead, listening to the echoes from above as Robbie made his retreat to the surface. He tied his line to a beam above the doorway, and let it fall down the deck between a long row of cars. Reached out, prepared to lower himself into the hold, to continue his search. Then he glanced to his left, inside the bulkhead door, and stopped and stared.

There was a structural pillar beside the door, climbing from the bottom of the ship to the top. The way the ship listed, the pillar made a sort of cradle, just as the wall and the floor of the passageways above did the same.

In this particular cradle, though, was a pile of darkness that Okura assumed were just rags. Then the darkness moved, mumbled something, and Okura looked closer, saw the bruised and battered face, the parched lips, the limbs hanging at awkward angles.

This was a human being, wounded and starved. This was Tomio Ishimaru.

31

Tomio Ishimaru blinked in the bright light, and wondered if he was dead at last. He'd been in this black purgatory for almost as long as he could remember, blind and shivering, his whole world the inhuman groans from the depths around him. The memory of what he'd done devouring his conscience.

Naoko. Saburo. Akio. His colleagues. His *friends*. They'd believed it was a joke when he'd first pulled the gun, the pistol Hiroki Okura had obtained for him from god knew where. He'd *wished* he'd been joking. He'd been shaking so hard, so nervous.

He remembered the look on Saburo's face when he'd first pulled the trigger. Couldn't escape the memory, no matter how long he languished here. Akio had shouted in anger. Naoko had begged for his life.

Ishimaru hadn't been able to look at him, not at the end.

He'd stolen the briefcase. *Fifty million dollars*, just as he'd told Okura. And Okura had delivered him from Yokohama, just as he'd promised. But there was no escaping what he'd done, not here on this ship, and not anywhere else.

This was Tomio Ishimaru's personal hell, and he knew he deserved to be here.

He'd tried to make his escape when the ship began to capsize. Remembered the briefcase and returned to his hiding place to retrieve it. Tried again to climb the passage to safety but lost his balance, his grip. He slipped and slid and crashed against steel, feeling his leg crack and break underneath him as he landed, dazed and disoriented, in a long transverse passage without any windows.

He had no idea where he was. He knew he'd fallen, but the impact of his collision had knocked the sense out of him, probably left him concussed, and he lay half on the floor and half against the wall, the briefcase beside him, the ship steadily and inexorably tipping over.

He'd heard Okura call to him, somewhere, the second officer's voice resonating against the steel, echoing from all angles. It was impossible to tell where it was coming from.

Ishimaru had tried to pull himself to his feet. Tried to respond. The pain was agonizing, so bad it had nearly knocked him unconscious. He crawled, instead, in the direction he'd landed. Couldn't map the ship in his head because he'd never left his little locker until now. How could he know where to go?

He'd dragged the briefcase behind him as he crawled. Reached a doorway just as the generators failed, taking the lights with them. The passage was suddenly very quiet. No throb of the engines, no voices. Even the ocean was barely audible. It was pitch-black, and Ishimaru was in pain. He had no idea where he was.

It was impossible that the ship would survive. Sooner or later, the water would rush in, dragging the ship down and Ishimaru with it, drowning him in the darkness. He reached for the door, fumbled with it and pulled it open, hoping that it led to the outside world.

It didn't. It led to more darkness, a gaping, yawning maw. Blinded and crippled, he gripped the briefcase and crawled across the threshold, realizing too late that he'd found a staircase skewed crazily by the list of the ship, the walls and the floors not where they should have been.

He fell. Tumbled through darkness, too surprised even to call out, his body battered against unforgiving steel walls and railings, against the stairs themselves. He came to land again, a heap of broken bones and sprains, lay there for a while, vomiting and passing out and waking to vomit again.

He gradually came to realize he'd landed near another door. A hatch. It could lead to daylight. It could lead to a flooded compartment and certain death. It could lead to nothing at all, to more darkness. But there was nothing else that Ishimaru could do.

He struggled to open the hatch. Propped himself up and wrenched at the lever and, finally, pushed the hatch open. It swung down into nothingness. Ishimaru took the briefcase and crawled through, more carefully this time. Searched with his hands for a suitable landing spot.

There was a wall to his left. It met the listing deck so as to form a triangle. Ishimaru crawled into its cradle, intending to follow the wall to wherever it led. He was thirsty and hungry and in constant pain. He must have spent a day on the wreck by now, maybe more, and he realized with a surprising aloofness that he would probably die in the darkness. But he took the briefcase anyway, dragged it behind him through the hatchway until it came to its end, a few feet beyond.

There was nothing after it. There was a hole. It might have been six feet deep, or sixty feet; there was no way to tell. Ishimaru was exhausted, and his whole body was sore. He'd lain against the wall and the deck of the ship and listened to the monstrous, primeval noises around him. He closed his eyes and waited to die. Waited to be released from the memory of what he'd done.

Naoko. Saburo. Akio.

He'd killed them all.

EXCEPT NOW, HERE WAS LIGHT, and a man's voice calling his name. "The briefcase, Tomio," the man was saying in Japanese. "Where is your briefcase?"

Ishimaru struggled to straighten himself. Failed to move his head more than a few inches. He blinked in the sudden brightness, surveying the platform in the light of the man's headlamp. It was narrow, an ugly yellow, hard steel. Beyond it were the ghostly forms of cars hanging in rows to oblivion. And where *was* the briefcase?

The briefcase was not on the platform. Ishimaru remembered dragging it through the hatchway, remembered setting it down as he lay his head against the wall. He remembered now the sudden shudder of a large wave, jolting him awake from his delirious state. He remembered feeling the briefcase at his feet, kicking at it reflexively, then not feeling the briefcase anymore. He realized what he must have done.

"The briefcase, Tomio. Where is it?"

The man's light was blinding. Still, Ishimaru recognized the voice. *"Hiroki?"*

"Yes," Okura said. "It's me, Tomio. All is safe now. But where is your briefcase?"

Ishimaru rolled his eyes to look over the edge of the platform. Okura followed his gaze with the light. There was no sign of the briefcase amid the cars and the darkness, but Ishimaru knew it must be down there somewhere. Okura grabbed him, rough. Shook him. *"Talk to me, Tomio."* His voice desperate, urgent, unhinged.

Ishimaru lifted his chin and gestured over the edge. *"Down."*

Okura peered over the edge of the platform. He swore. He looked at Ishimaru and swore again.

32

Okura stared down at Ishimaru. The stowaway was filthy and bruised and broken, a pitiful creature. The sight of him filled Okura with hot, sudden anger.

All you had to do was hold on to the briefcase, he thought. *You could have made us rich. Well, me, anyway.*

Ishimaru clawed at him, weak as a baby bird. *"Water,"* he rasped out. *"Please."*

Okura ignored him. Shined his headlamp into the gloom again. Searched for any sign of the case, couldn't see it. He kicked Ishimaru's hand aside. Inched across the bulkhead to stand over him on the platform. Stared down at him for a long time—the stowaway feeble, blinking, near blinded by the light—and felt his anger only worsen.

Before Okura realized what he was doing, he'd put his foot down on his old classmate's throat, stepped down hard.

It would be impossible to bring Ishimaru to the surface. The stowaway's presence would bring more complications. It would raise questions that would stand in the way of Okura's freedom.

This is the only way.

Ishimaru was too weak to fight. He clawed ineffectually at Okura's boot. Gasping, his eyes bulging. Okura maintained the pressure, watched the desperation in Ishimaru's eyes turn to surrender. And then those eyes went vacant and his old classmate was finally dead.

33

McKenna watched through her binoculars as the man emerged from the bridge of the *Lion*, climbed into a skiff tied to the freighter's railing, and navigated it, slowly and perilously, back to the *Salvation*. Beside her, Court Harrington shifted his weight.

"What's that about?" he asked. "Who's that guy?"

McKenna shrugged. "One of Christer's guys, I guess. Could be his architect. You recognize him?"

She handed Harrington the glasses, and the whiz kid studied the man in the skiff. "Nobody I know," he said. "Whoever he is, he's got guts to be running that dinghy through those waves."

"Or he's just crazy." McKenna took the glasses back. The man had reached the *Salvation*, which rode the waves at the stern of the *Lion*, tethered to the bigger ship like a terrier on a leash, black plumes of smoke belching out of her stack.

Cripes, even the towline seemed thin for the job. The winch looked underpowered, too, and the *Salvation* herself was dirty, in need of a fresh coat of paint. She was doubtless a good ship—hell, she'd survived since World War II—but she wasn't a salvage tug, and with the weather set to turn, McKenna wasn't about to stand around waiting for Christer Magnusson to prove it.

She picked up the radio. "Coast Guard cutter *Munro*, this is the *Gale Force*."

A pause. Then: "*Gale Force, Munro*. We were just about to hail you, sir—er, ma'am. Can you tell me your intentions in these waters?"

"Sure," McKenna said. "I'm here to salvage the *Lion*."

A longer pause. "Ma'am, it's our understanding that Commodore Towing is handling salvage duties at this time. Have you been in touch with the *Salvation*?"

"I have," McKenna said. "I told them they're wasting your time. That little boat over there is pouring its heart out and it can't move the *Lion*. What's going to happen when this gale hits?"

"As far as we're aware, Commodore's operations are proceeding as planned," the radio operator replied. "If you wish to assist, I'd suggest you try to negotiate something with the *Salvation* herself. We're not in a position to be settling disputes of this nature."

"You will be," McKenna said. "When the operation fails and the *Lion* wrecks on a rock somewhere, you'll have a mess on your hands, I assure you."

She slammed the radio handset back into its cradle. Stared out at the *Lion*, now visibly rocking as the waves crashed against her hull.

"Well, we can't just sit around and wait," Court Harrington said. "I need to get aboard before this weather turns nasty."

At the *Lion*'s stern, the *Salvation* bobbed, no sign of life from the afterdeck or the wheelhouse. McKenna studied the smaller vessel, felt Harrington's eyes on her, knew he was growing impatient, probably doubting her ability to bump Christer Magnusson out of the way.

If your dad was here—

Shut up. McKenna reached for the radio. "Hell, no, we're not waiting," she told Court. "Hello, *Munro*," she said into the handset. "This is the *Gale Force*. I'd like to talk to your commanding officer, please."

THE MUNRO'S CAPTAIN WAS A MAN named Tom Geoffries. He listened as McKenna laid out her argument. But McKenna couldn't convince him.

"The *Salvation* assures me they have the situation under control," Geoffries told her. "Frankly, Captain, this sounds like a load of sour grapes from an outfit who gambled and lost."

McKenna gritted her teeth. "I appreciate how it might sound that way, Captain Geoffries," she replied. "From my angle, I have a high-horsepower, deep-sea tug stocked with the best salvage experts, divers, and naval architects in the business, and none of us can do our jobs because a group of pretenders are standing in our way."

Geoffries came back harsh. "I think you're out of line, Captain Rhodes."

"Sir, you know as well as I do that this weather is only going to get worse," McKenna said. "That ship's rate of drift is going to increase, and assuming she doesn't sink, she's going to hit land sooner or later. And I'm telling you, in this gale we've got coming, that little navy tender over there isn't going to be anything more than a speed bump."

Geoffries didn't respond. McKenna waited. If the Coast Guard captain cut her out, the *Gale Force* would have no choice but to stand down, watch the *Lion* drift toward land, and pray there was still time to act when the call finally came.

The radio crackled. "I'm sorry, Captain Rhodes," Geoffries said at last. "Until they prove they're not up to it, this is Commodore's wreck. I just can't break their contract without cause."

34

This was a nightmare zone.

Okura dangled in darkness, lowering himself slowly down a line of rope, his feet pressed tight to the deck as he walked himself backward, searching the long line of Nissans for the briefcase. The cars hung around him, rocking with the ship's motion. They reminded Okura of an uncut sheet of dollar bills, one single unit moving in unison, rising and falling and rising again.

The weather outside must have worsened considerably. The creaks and moans had become more pronounced, the sway of the ship heavier. A couple times, Okura was thrust up and away from the deck with the force of the swell, tossed into the air and then down again, his grip on the rope slipping, his feet nearly giving out.

Somewhere below him was water. Okura could hear it sloshing in the darkness, something dripping. The decks were slick with oil. It leaked from the cars' engines and drained steadily down the listing deck. Okura imagined the dark frothy mixture at the bottom of the cargo hold, imagined falling into the cold water, drowning in it, coughing up oil and freezing salt water in pitch-black surroundings.

Somewhere below, too, was Tomio Ishimaru. Okura had wrestled the stowaway's body off of its little platform, sent it plunging down to the darkness, heard it collide with something, a car probably, then another. Then he'd heard the splash, and the stowaway was gone.

Fifty million dollars. Now it's all mine.

THERE WAS STILL NO SIGN of the briefcase when he'd reached the end of his rope. Okura wrapped it around his glove, found another bulkhead wall to rest against, then stretched and drank water from the canteen he'd stuffed in his pack. Surveyed the situation.

There were cars everywhere. The darkness seemed to close in around them, bringing with them a lingering, primal fear. This was a madhouse.

Three or four rows down, Okura could see the portside hull of the *Lion*. There was a pool of oily water immersing the first row of cars completely, and part of the second row. Headlights emerged from the murky depths like shipwrecks. There was still no sign of the briefcase.

It must have fallen all the way to the bottom, was probably lying somewhere in that oily water. Okura hoped the briefcase was water-tight, imagined coming all this way to find a case of sodden, pulpy stock certificates, unreadable and utterly useless, the perfect punch line to this entire sick joke.

The rope was too short to continue any farther. Okura suddenly felt exhausted, beaten, and he wondered how many hours he'd spent down here, whether it was still daylight outside.

Magnusson will salvage this ship, he thought, staring down the row of cars toward the icy water at the bottom. *He'll pump out all the*

*water and bring the ship upright, and I'll intercept the briefcase when
the ship has been saved. To hell with staying down here any longer.*

He stood and straightened, already feeling the fresh air on his
face, tasting the hot food in the *Salvation*'s galley. But as he turned
toward the hatchway and prepared to make the climb, he spied
something, a blur as his headlamp passed over it, and then he looked
closer and saw it was the briefcase.

It was lying on the windshield of a sports sedan, five or six rows
away. Only God could tell how Ishimaru had managed to kick the
damn thing so far, but there it lay, dry and unmolested.

Now all that remained was to retrieve it.

35

By morning, the gale was a foregone conclusion.

The waves had grown to ten-foot swells overnight, gloomy gray
rollers that rocked the *Gale Force* fore and aft, coating her decks with
salt spray, spilling coffee and ruining sleep. McKenna and Al Parent
traded off all night, jogging the tug in the swell, keeping her bow
pointed to the waves. McKenna watched the *Lion*, searching for any
sign that she was flooding. Waiting for the moment the big ship finally sank.

Morning was a gray horizon to match the sea, the *Lion* drifting
north at a knot and a half an hour, the *Salvation*'s efforts to arrest the
drift not amounting to much. The wind was gusting to twenty-five,
the gale warning all over the forecast. It would arrive in earnest by

afternoon, and its heavy winds would push the vast, exposed bulk of the *Lion* northeast toward the Aleutians at an increasing speed, until there was nothing anyone could do but pray she sank before she made landfall. If she stayed afloat, McKenna knew, she'd be on the beach within a couple of days.

McKenna called the crew to the wheelhouse. They crowded in, Matt and Stacey and Court Harrington around the chart table, Nelson Ridley beside McKenna at the wheel, Al and Jason Parent by the doorway, and Spike on the dash. They looked out at the *Pacific Lion*, the *Salvation* at her stern, her flimsy towline drawing taut, then slackening as the waves battered both vessels, the *Salvation*'s black exhaust nearly obscuring the *Lion*'s stern.

"He's got to get her moving," Ridley muttered. "What in hell is Magnusson doing, farting around over there?"

"There's no way he can move that ship," McKenna replied, "and he's a fool for even trying. So let's get our pumps and generators ready to go. Climbing equipment, too. Matt and Stacey, I need you inside the *Lion* as soon as we get our line on."

The Jonases nodded. "You know us, boss," Matt said. "We'll be ready."

"Al and Jason, you get the towline ready," McKenna continued. "We're going to rig a bridle at the stern, stabilize her, see if we can't put some distance between us and the Aleutians before this storm takes over. We're going to need every inch of open water, from the looks of it."

"Aye-aye," Al agreed.

"Good. Nelson and I will join Matt and Stacey on the ship. It's all hands for this job." She turned to Harrington. "You have that computer of yours fired up?"

"Just waiting on the numbers," Harrington said.

"Perfect." McKenna turned back to the window. It was eight in the morning, and today, she knew, would determine the *Lion*'s fate—and the *Gale Force*'s. "This is our wreck," she told the crew. "So let's be ready to claim her."

36

The wind howled.

Christer Magnusson stood at the *Salvation*'s wheel. Bill Carew and his deckhand joined him in the wheelhouse. Foss and Ogilvy were in their bunks, resting. They'd drawn the night watch, and it had been a long night.

The other guy, Okura, was still on the ship somewhere. Refused to leave, the maniac. Magnusson studied the *Lion*'s stern, figured the guy would probably wind up dead, decided he was glad he'd asked for that twenty-five thousand up front.

Behind the *Salvation*, the *Lion* dragged at the towline, the wind catching the freighter's hull and shoving it off course, threatening to pull the smaller boat with it. Bill Carew had the *Salvation*'s engines revving high, almost at their limits, but the force of the wind was nearly overpowering the ship, and that, Magnusson knew, was a very bad sign.

Bill Carew met his eyes. "You want to have your men slacken off that winch and we'll release the tow?"

Magnusson didn't answer. The correct thing to do in this

circumstance—the seas getting bigger, the wind moaning through the rigging, foam and salt spray everywhere, an underpowered boat, and a heavy, wallowing tow—was as Carew suggested: slacken off the towline, untether the *Salvation* from the wreck, and turn around, with tail between legs, head back to home base.

But Magnusson hadn't built his career on giving up early. If that woman on the *Gale Force* wanted to take the *Lion* from him, she was damn well going to earn it.

"Slacken the winch?" Magnusson said. "What the hell for?"

Carew opened his mouth to answer. Magnusson cut him off. "Give me more power," he told the captain. "Damned if we're giving up without a fight."

THE BRIEFCASE, at last.

Okura's muscles screamed as he balanced on the windshield of the sports car, clutching the briefcase like a trophy. The ship swayed and rolled. The cars groaned against their fastenings.

Okura didn't care. He was fifty million dollars richer.

He timed his movements carefully. Clambered off the Nissan and onto its neighbor, aiming his headlamp in the direction he'd come. Four cars away, his rope dangled in space. All that remained was to reach that rope and to climb it to safety.

Fifty million dollars. Okura crawled across the front end of the next Nissan. *Thank you, Tomio.*

ABOARD THE MUNRO, Captain Geoffries watched the *Pacific Lion* swing on the end of the *Salvation*'s towline, waves crashing against her exposed hull. He checked the GPS screen in front of him: forty-five nautical miles to landfall, the south shore of Umnak Island. Despite the *Salvation*'s efforts, the freighter continued to drift north.

"Raise the *Salvation*," Geoffries told his radio operator. "Ask them what the hell they're doing over there."

THE SALVATION'S RADIO CRACKLED to life. The *Munro*. "Requesting an update on the status of your operation," the radio operator told Magnusson. "It looks like you're into some difficulty over there."

Magnusson studied the *Munro*. It jogged in the swell, steady and silent and ever-present. Behind the cutter, a half mile away, the *Gale Force* waited her turn.

Magnusson picked up the radio. "No difficulty," he told the *Munro*. He motioned to Carew, who pushed the *Salvation*'s throttles, the twin Caterpillars roaring with the strain. "Everything is proceeding as planned."

37

McKenna stared out at the *Salvation* through her binoculars. "My god," she said as another thick plume of smoke erupted from the little boat's stack. "They still think they can tow that thing."

Beside McKenna, Nelson Ridley shook his head. "They're nuts, skipper. They'll blow their bloody engines."

Through McKenna's binoculars, the *Salvation* struggled forward, white water roiling from beneath her stern.

"The old girl has heart, anyway," she said. "Even if her master's a maniac."

The wind gusted harder. The *Lion* began to yaw sideways on her towline again, fighting the *Salvation*'s efforts to keep her true. The *Salvation* bucked on the end of the line, straining and pulling for all she was worth. McKenna could almost hear the engines howling, knew the noise must have been tremendous, the exertion, as the plucky little boat put fifty-five thousand tons of ship on her back.

At first, she thought her eyes were playing tricks on her. But Ridley noticed the same. "Geez," the engineer exhaled. "Who's towing who, skipper?"

Ridley was right. Little by little, the *Lion* was dragging the *Salvation* around as the big freighter herself turned abeam to the sea, her whole flank now exposed, increasing the wind's hold on her, blowing her back.

The *Salvation* fought valiantly. It was losing. Slowly, inexorably, the wind and the sea took control of the *Lion*.

"Thundering Jonas," Ridley said. "They're going to lose that ship if they're not careful."

McKenna put down the glasses. "Forget the ship," she said. "If they don't change something fast, they're going down with it."

MAGNUSSON LOOKED OUT the aft window of the *Salvation*'s wheelhouse. The towline was stretched taut, the propellers churning up a mighty white wash. Carew had the throttle pegged at the max, the engines howling. But behind them, the *Lion* continued to pull, dragging them into the trough, the waves hitting hard, broadside.

Magnusson swore. Threw open the aft door and hollered down to Robbie, who worked the winch from the afterdeck, paying out line to gain distance from the *Lion*.

"*Don't you dare drop that line*," Magnusson shouted down. "*You don't do a damn thing unless I say so.*"

Magnusson ducked back inside the wheelhouse, his adrenaline running now. The *Salvation*'s engines seemed to take hold, the propeller biting into green water, arresting the *Lion*'s momentum—for the moment.

We're not giving this ship up, Magnusson thought. *I'll be goddamned if that woman takes this job from me.*

It sounded good in his head. But then he looked out the portside window and saw the wave coming, bigger than any other, looming large and closing fast, headed for the *Salvation* and her prize.

RIDLEY STIFFENED. "Oh," he said. "Oh, Lord, no."

McKenna glanced over at him. Looked back at the *Salvation*, binoculars down, and saw what her engineer was seeing.

A wave, the biggest of the day, a freak, maybe thirty feet high— kid's stuff for the *Gale Force*, and even the *Salvation*, but not with this tow behind her. Not like this.

The wave scudded toward the *Salvation*, toward the *Lion* and the towline stretched between them. McKenna watched it come, knew she should feel vindicated. There was no way the *Salvation* could survive with her tow intact. As soon as this wave hit, the *Lion* would be hers.

Instead, she felt emptiness, fear, as if she were watching the wave that had stolen her father all over again. The *Salvation* dropped into the trough. The wave loomed. McKenna braced herself, though she was a half mile away.

38

The wave snapped the towline like the crack of a rifle. Magnusson lunged for the door, called out for the deckhand, watched the line snap back like a whip, heard—*felt*—the loose end hit the wheelhouse like a freight train.

Then the boat was surging forward, down into the trough, the engines at full bore, the load suddenly eased, the propellers churning and driving the *Salvation* into the sea. Carew had fallen over backward, was stumbling to his feet, nobody at the controls. Magnusson hurried over, throttled down the engines, three-quarters power. Turned her bow into the waves.

"Hey," he called down to the galley, where Foss and Ogilvy had damn well better be awake. *"Get your asses up here, right now!"*

OKURA WAS HALFWAY UP the climbing line, the briefcase tucked under his arm, when the wave hit. He felt the *Lion* drop into the swell, knew instinctively what was coming, knew it was a bigger wave than any he'd felt so far. The cars lurched on their mounts, steel screaming in protest. Okura braced himself. Then the wave hit.

It seemed to hit twice. Broadsided the *Lion* with a hard, thudding crash, and then another jolt, not as forceful, but somehow more sudden. And Okura felt the briefcase slip from beneath his arm, felt it falling away.

He loosened his grip on the rope for an instant, reaching down for the briefcase, and then he was slipping. The rope seemed to slide through his fingers, and then it was gone, and he was falling backward, down through the darkness, his headlamp giving brief, photo-flash glimpses of the ceiling, the deck, the cars on their mounts.

No, he thought, time seeming to slow. *Damn it, no. I was so close.*

Then he hit something hard, unyielding and painful, and the impact knocked out his headlamp, and everything was dark and suddenly very quiet.

MCKENNA WATCHED THE WAVE HIT. Watched the towline snap like an overstretched elastic, watched the *Salvation* lunge forward, an explosion of white water breaking over her bow, the towline whipping back, wild, on the tug's afterdeck.

"Bleeding hell," Ridley muttered. "I hope nobody's back there."

McKenna lifted her field glasses. Couldn't see a soul on deck, though at this point she wouldn't be able to see much; the towline had snapped with enough force to cut a man in half.

Christer Magnusson seemed to get the *Salvation* back under control. He throttled down the engine and turned the salvage boat into the waves. She jogged there, for a minute or two, and McKenna relaxed. Maybe disaster had been averted. Maybe everyone on that little ship was fine, and the *Gale Force* could set to work saving the *Lion*.

The radio came to life above her head. *"Man overboard, man overboard. Salvation has a man in the water."*

39

"Man overboard!"

Suddenly, she was back there. Out *there*. That night, her dad, the *Argyle Shore*. It was happening again. And another man would die if she didn't act quickly.

McKenna throttled up the *Gale Force* and got on the hailer. "*Salvation* lost a man overboard," she told them. "Everyone on deck. Pike poles and life preservers, whatever you can find. I need eyes on this guy immediately."

Ridley joined her at the wheel as the tug plowed through the water toward the stern of the *Lion*. "You see him, lass?"

"Not yet." Ahead of the *Gale Force*, the *Salvation* was making a slow turn. McKenna aimed the tug just past the *Lion*, figuring she'd meet Magnusson in the middle. Assuming Magnusson's guy could stay afloat that long, could stay conscious. That water was *cold*.

"Watch that towline," Ridley said. "Don't want to foul a prop."

The *Salvation*'s severed towline hung off the stern of the *Lion*. If it caught up in the *Gale Force*'s propellers, it could cripple the tug.

McKenna picked her way around the towline as Stacey Jonas

appeared at the bow, scanning the water for the *Salvation*'s lost man. McKenna watched her, watched the waves, watched the *Salvation* in the distance.

There's enough wind and wave to make this guy invisible, McKenna thought. *If Christer doesn't have eyes on him, he's lost.*

She picked up the radio. "*Salvation, Salvation,* do you see your man, Christer?"

Silence. Then: "Negative. I lost him when we went into a trough. He was a couple hundred yards back when I last saw."

Shit. McKenna put down the radio and motored onward. Felt her heart pounding, fought the negative thoughts. *Too late. We're not going to get him.*

He's gone.

Then Stacey stiffened on the bow. Jumped and pointed forward, a couple degrees to starboard.

"I think she got him," Ridley said. He hurried to the starboard window, slid it open, and hollered something to Stacey, who called back, never taking her eyes from the water.

"Three boat lengths," Ridley reported. "You see where she's pointing, skipper?"

McKenna stared out at the gray water. Rubbed her eyes, kept the tug moving forward. Didn't see. Then she did. The guy was floating there, his head up, splashing a little to keep his face above water. He looked dulled by the cold already, looked ready to give up.

"We see him," she told the *Salvation* over the radio. Then she turned to Ridley. "I'll bring him up on our starboard side. Make sure the crew's ready."

She idled toward the man in the water until he was about a quarter boat length away, keeping the portside to the wind and the sailor in her lee. Stacey gestured back, *Cut the engines,* and McKenna cut them out of gear and drifted, hoping the poor guy had strength enough to grab a rescue line, or a life preserver, at least.

She went to the starboard window, peered out and back, watched Matt heave a line toward the sailor, Jason hanging down over the rail with a pole.

The first throw missed. Not by much, a few feet, but the sailor was in no shape to swim for it. Quickly, Matt hauled in the line, coiled and threw it again. This time, his throw was true. The line landed on top of the sailor, who took hold with both hands, his movements clumsy and slow.

Hold, McKenna thought as Matt and Jason began to pull the rope back to the tug. *Hold on to that line, man. You're almost there.*

The men hauled the sailor toward the *Gale Force*'s hull, and McKenna returned to the controls, watching her crew on the closed-circuit monitor and keeping an eye on the oncoming waves, ready to engage the propellers or bow thruster if the seas threatened to push her boat down on top of the man in the water.

On deck, Matt and Jason struggled with the pike pole now, their faces tight with exertion as they worked to pull the man to safety. McKenna muttered a silent prayer as Al joined alongside, leaning over the gunwale and reaching toward the waterline.

Careful, she thought. *Don't you guys fall in, too.*

Slowly, Matt and Jason lifted the pike pole. Al strained lower, reached with both hands, came back with two fists full of soggy clothing and the man it belonged to. Matt and Jason helped him haul the man aboard, lay him on deck.

Thank god.

McKenna put the boat in gear, turned her nose to the wind.

"Bring him inside," she ordered over the hailer. "Get him warmed up fast."

MATT AND STACEY had the *Salvation*'s crewman wrapped in a sleeping bag when McKenna came down. The man was shivering, a coffee mug pressed to his lips.

"You guys saved my bacon," he said. "I thought I was done."

McKenna nodded, saw the man's wet clothes lying in a heap on the galley floor. "You got pretty damn lucky you weren't split in two by that towline."

"I jumped," the man replied. "Last second, you know? I saw that cable stretching, and then I heard it snap, and it was all I could do to get out of the way."

"You know you didn't have enough power to pull that ship," McKenna said. "Why risk your life—and waste everyone's time?"

The man looked down at the table. "I mean, I work for the boat, right? This is Commodore's job."

"*Was* Commodore's job. We're taking over."

"Fine by me. Look, I spent most of my time on the wreck with the other guy, Japanese buddy."

McKenna swapped glances with Matt Jonas. "Who?"

"Guy from the *Lion*, Hiroki or something. He paid us twenty-five grand to get him back out to the wreck without telling anybody." He sipped his coffee, his teeth chattering. "The guy's still on the ship, to tell you the truth. Last I saw, he was down in the cargo hold."

McKenna frowned. *What the hell was the guy doing in there?*

She was about to ask the man to elaborate when Al called down from the wheelhouse. "*Salvation*'s coming up alongside us now, skipper," he said. "Better tell the boy to get ready."

McKENNA JOINED THE REST of the crew on deck as the *Salvation* pulled up beside the *Gale Force*. Spied Christer Magnusson on the smaller tug's afterdeck. He met McKenna's gaze, raised a hand in greeting, looked away.

So be it, McKenna thought. *You gambled and lost, now get out of our way.*

Al idled the *Gale Force* close, and Jason Parent stood ready with a long coil of rope as Matt and Stacey Jonas readied the *Gale Force*'s life raft. The *Salvation*'s deckhand started to the rail as Matt and Stacey lowered the raft to the water. Then he stopped and turned around, came back to McKenna.

"Robbie Peters," he said, his hand outstretched. "You guys saved my life."

McKenna shook the man's hand. He had a firm grip, though his hand was frigid. "Glad we got to you in time," she said. "I assume this means you guys are giving up on that freighter."

The deckhand glanced back at the wounded *Lion*. "Hell," he said, "I'll be happy if I never see that ship again in my life."

The two boats inched closer, and Jason Parent heaved the line across the narrow chasm to Christer Magnusson, who made it fast on his end. Then Robbie Peters was climbing over the gunwale and into the life raft, and, gripping the rope with one hand and steadying the raft with the other, he pulled himself across the rough seas to the *Salvation*.

McKenna watched the kid make it home to the *Salvation*'s scuffed hull. Watched Magnusson pull him to his feet, help him into the house. Tried not to think of her dad in the water, lost and alone.

Christer Magnusson didn't stop to help you then, she thought. *He raced right past and claimed the* Argyle Shore *as his own. Sent that damn pile of flowers to the old man's memorial.*

Would he have done what you just did, if it was Jason Parent in the water?

She shook the thought from her mind. Watched the *Salvation* until Magnusson and Robbie Peters were long gone from the deck and Jason Parent had the raft reeled in and the line coiled.

"Okay, enough of this amateur hour," she said, starting back to the wheelhouse. "Let's get our line on that ship."

40

McKenna called the Coast Guard on channel 16, the maritime distress frequency. "We're taking over. The *Salvation* has agreed to relinquish the tow."

The *Munro* responded quickly. "Copy, *Gale Force*. Please advise if there's any way we can assist."

"Actually, there is," McKenna told the radio operator. "The *Salvation* left a man aboard the wreck, one of the Japanese sailors. He's somewhere in the cargo hold, looking for lost property, but the last thing we need is some treasure hunter in our way right now."

A pause. Then the *Munro* returned. "Roger, *Gale Force*. Funny thing, the customs agents in Dutch Harbor reported a missing Japanese sailor. We'll pick him up and make sure he gets home."

McKenna thanked the radio operator and hung up the handset. Then she picked up the satellite phone and placed a call to Japan.

IT TOOK McKENNA THIRTY minutes of holding and transferring before she reached who she was looking for, a vice president of the Japanese Overseas Lines, a man named Matsuda.

"We already have signed an agreement," Matsuda told her. "Commodore Towing is handling our ship."

"Commodore tried and failed," McKenna replied. "Technical difficulties. Gale Force Marine is taking over."

Matsuda didn't answer for a minute. "I assume you are calling to negotiate," he said at last. "In which case, I can offer you an Open Form agreement. Five percent of the *Pacific Lion*'s value, as established by an independent arbitrator."

McKenna laughed. "Commodore brought five guys and a seventy-year-old hulk, and I know you gave them a better offer. I have a crew of salvage experts and a deep-sea tug. You're going to have to do better."

"Double, then," Matsuda said. "Ten percent."

McKenna pursed her lips. Ten percent of the *Lion*'s value would net the *Gale Force* approximately fifteen million dollars. Even after paying off the crew, it would make for a substantial windfall. But McKenna didn't bite.

"Ten percent is the industry floor," she told the executive. "And this is an extraordinary job. We'll sign the Open Form for thirty percent of your ship's value."

Matsuda gave a sharp bark of disbelief. "This is a one-hundred-and-fifty-million-dollar ship, Ms. Rhodes. You're asking me for forty-five million dollars?"

"Those pretenders on the *Salvation* jerked our chain for days," McKenna told him. "Now I'm fighting a gale and a sinking ship. My crew's going to earn every penny of that award. Thirty percent, or I'll let the arbitrator figure it out."

Matsuda went silent again. McKenna pictured the man in his office, hoped he was gripping the phone tight. "Twenty percent," he said finally. "Thirty million dollars. We sign the agreement now, and save the legal costs."

McKenna looked out at the *Pacific Lion* through the wheelhouse windows. The ship wallowed in the swell, waves breaking over her red keel.

Matsuda coughed. "Ms. Rhodes?"

She blinked back to focus. Idled the *Gale Force* toward the *Pacific Lion*'s stern. "Twenty percent," she agreed. "Fax me the paperwork. And Mr. Matsuda?"

A pause. "Yes?"

"It's *Captain* Rhodes," McKenna said. Then she ended the call.

41

Okura woke up in darkness. In cold and damp, with the ship still moving, still shuddering as the waves outside battered the hull. He was lying on something hard, something painful, and for a moment, he couldn't move his arms or his legs, and he panicked, afraid the fall had paralyzed him.

Gradually, though, he regained feeling in his limbs. Brought his hand up to his face, felt blood, warm and sticky. His face hurt, his nose. The side of his head. He reached for his headlamp, but it wasn't there. The cargo hold was pitch-black. Water sloshed beneath him, but Okura had no way of telling how far below.

The briefcase.

He'd landed on a car. He could feel the windshield beneath him, cold steel at his back, the wipers digging through the fabric of his pants. The car rocked with the movement of the freighter, and the tie-up straps groaned.

Where is the briefcase?

Slowly, cautiously, Okura steadied his body with his hands and sat up. Felt the car shift beneath him, unsteady, dangling from the deck. He groped in the darkness, but couldn't find the case. Down here, he was blind.

There was a new noise, unfamiliar, from high above. An irregular banging against steel. Then, there were voices, and light. Okura could see them through the windshields, and the windows of the cars that hung above him, thin beams cutting through the dark. He couldn't make out what the voices were saying.

"Robbie?" Okura struggled to sit up. "*Help me.* I'm down here."

The lights swung around in the darkness, blocked by rows of cars. Okura remained obscured in darkness.

"Anyone down there?" someone called. "This is the Coast Guard. It's time to go home."

Okura watched the men's beams, saw the light play off of their

Coast Guard flight suits. Rescue jumpers, he realized. Survival technicians.

He said nothing.

The men ventured out onto Ishimaru's platform. Peered over, and now their headlamps found Okura's rope. Okura shifted farther into the shadows, felt the Nissan rock unsteadily beneath him. Tried not to breathe.

He'd been waiting for Robbie to return, help him retrieve the briefcase, and rescue him from the ship. But the Coast Guard's arrival meant something had happened up there on the surface. And whatever it was, it was bad news for Okura.

As Okura watched, the techs rigged a harness and looped it over a pipe on the ceiling. One of the technicians climbed inside while the other stayed on the platform, gripping the rope and belaying his partner, slowly, through the rows of cars.

"Hello?" the first technician called. "Anyone down here?"

His light swept over the cars above Okura's head. Shone through the windshield above Okura, paused for a split-second on something alien to this space, something shiny, and Okura felt his breath hitch.

The briefcase.

It lay wedged against a car tire, just above Okura, well within reach. He could retrieve it easily from his position. But the technician was still dropping closer to Okura, closer still. Okura didn't move. Held his breath and stayed motionless until his muscles screamed from the effort. Finally, the technician was passing him, two or three cars away, and as he dropped farther, Okura let himself breathe, let himself shift, just a little.

Then, from above, the other technician's voice, and another beam of light. "Hey, Tommy, over *there*. I think I see something."

42

McKenna stared up at the *Lion* as two Coast Guard ASTs winched something large and black from the listing deck of the freighter to the HH-65 Dolphin helicopter hovering above the wreck.

"What do you make of it, skipper?" Ridley asked beside her.

McKenna frowned. "It doesn't look good," she said. "They were supposed to get that sailor off. I hope nobody got hurt."

Through her binoculars, she studied the helicopter and the cargo on the end of the winch line. The object was long and shapeless, and the ASTs handled it awkwardly. McKenna watched it rise toward the open door of the helicopter, felt a sudden lurch of recognition.

The object was a body bag. Someone onboard the *Lion* was dead.

IN THE CARGO HOLD, Hiroki Okura gripped the briefcase to his chest and thanked the fates for his incredible luck.

He'd nearly given himself up when the technician had called out from above, thought he'd been spotted, that the game was over. But the technician's light hadn't found him; it had swung past, swung deeper into the hold, and Okura listened as the second tech descended to investigate.

"Anything?" the first tech called down. "Thought I saw something that looked human."

A beat. Then: "Oh, it's human all right. But I'd say we're a little late for a rescue."

For a moment, Okura was confused. Then he understood. *Ishimaru. They've found Tomio's body.*

In an instant, Okura realized he'd just won the lottery. The Coast Guard would assume Ishimaru was the missing Japanese second officer. The only men who could correct them were already back in Japan.

This was a gift. Divine intervention. This was a fifty-million-dollar stroke of good luck.

Okura had lain in the dark. Listened to the techs discuss how to retrieve the stowaway's body. Lay still and waited for the men to retreat and leave him alone with the briefcase.

43

McKenna maneuvered the *Gale Force* to the stern of the *Pacific Lion.* Dropped Al and Jason Parent on the big freighter's slanted afterdeck to wrestle the *Salvation's* towing gear off of the bollards. The line still dangled in the water, and McKenna was leery of fouling the *Gale Force's* twin propellers. She idled away from the *Lion* as the Parents struggled with the gear.

As McKenna watched, Al climbed up the listing deck to the *Salvation's* towing bridle and, using an acetylene torch, cut through the heavy chain and shoved it free of the bollard. The gear hit the water with a splash and disappeared instantly, sinking toward the sea floor some three thousand fathoms below.

Then Al Parent's voice came over the radio. "Clear, skipper. We're good to go."

With Al and Jason on the radios, and Nelson Ridley at the winch, McKenna backed the *Gale Force* to the stern of the *Lion* again, guiding her tug with the rear-mounted controls at the back of her wheelhouse. Spike hopped up on the mantle beside her to assess the tug's progress, the self-fashioned master and commander of the ship.

"Keep an eye on things, cat," McKenna told him. "It's all hands now."

She petted the cat absently, and for once Spike tolerated the intrusion. McKenna reversed the tug to within a boat length of the *Lion*, watched as Ridley fired a messenger line across to Al and Jason. The two men were practically standing on the bollards to keep upright, the deck like a high, slippery wall, and they fought to maintain their balance as they hauled in the messenger line.

For an instant, McKenna thought of Al Parent singing songs to his grandson on the satellite phone, Jason Parent kissing Angel and little Ben good-bye on the dock. She watched her crew work, and thought of the body bag the Coast Guard had just pulled from the wreck. Then she pushed the thoughts from her mind. They would do her no good here, not now.

McKenna backed the tug as close as she could to the freighter, conscious of the tug's proximity to the massive, multibladed propeller jutting out of the water just yards away. Al and Jason wrestled the messenger line around the bollards, and Jason heaved the line back to Nelson Ridley, who used the *Gale Force*'s own winch to haul the towing gear from the tug's stern and across to the *Lion*.

It was a slow, painstaking job. Al and Jason kept the line as secure as they could as the heavy towing bridle fell off the stern of the *Gale Force* and was pulled across to the *Lion*. The bridle itself was heavy chain, designed to prevent the towing wire from chafing against the bollards during an open-ocean operation, and Jason and Al labored to maneuver it around the bollards and shackle it back to the line between the ship and the tug.

The seas continued to batter the *Lion*. The men fought the towing gear, and fought to remain upright, and even McKenna, in the wheelhouse, was exhausted by the time the bridle was secured and the towline in place.

This ain't your everyday barge tow, girl.

She crossed back to the front of the wheelhouse, checked her GPS. Waited on Al and Jason to return to the tug, and began to swing both the *Gale Force* and the *Lion* into the wind again, to steady things out a little bit. According to her GPS, the *Lion* was now less than forty nautical miles from the Fox Islands in the Aleutian chain, drifting steadily. Job one was complete; the *Gale Force* had the *Lion*. Job two involved getting the ship upright again, and that came with a ticking clock.

Behind McKenna, Spike leaped down from the mantle. Padded across to the stairs, and paused to look back at the skipper. The cat yowled once, his pessimism obvious, before disappearing down the stairway and out of sight.

Show a little team spirit, cat, McKenna thought, watching him go. *We could use it.*

FORTY-FIVE MINUTES LATER, McKenna stood on the afterdeck of the *Gale Force* as the Coast Guard's HH-65 Dolphin hovered above, lowering down a steel basket to the waiting crew. Nelson Ridley captured the basket and held it steady as Stacey Jonas, outfitted in full climbing gear, stepped aboard, grinning like a kid at the front gates of Disney World. This was what she'd been waiting for, the adrenaline bit, the whole appeal of the job. McKenna figured even the payoff was just a bonus to her diver.

The Dolphin winched Stacey up, then Matt, then Nelson Ridley. McKenna stepped forward, only to be beaten to the basket by Court Harrington, laptop in tow.

McKenna grabbed him by the shoulder. "No way," she told him. "You're too valuable to risk on that ship."

"Bull," Harrington replied. "You need me on board. You're not going to get radio reception inside the hull of that ship. I need to be with you when you take the fluid measurements."

"And what if you get hurt?"

"What if *you* get hurt? Or Matt or Stacey?"

"Difference is, I can find another diver," McKenna replied. "Or Al can run the boat. Nobody can work that computer like you."

Harrington grinned. "Then listen to me," he said. "I need to be on board to do my job, McKenna. Are you going to let me do it, or what?"

She looked up at the helicopter. "Damn it, Court. *Fine.*"

He smiled wider. "Knew you'd see it my way," he said, and climbed in.

As the basket inched skyward, Harrington kept his computer open in his lap, checking numbers, seemingly unconcerned by the heavy gusts of wind that buffeted him, thirty feet above the tug. McKenna watched, wondered why she'd capitulated—*if* she'd capitulated. Wondered if Court even knew she was captain.

She shook the thought away. *Focus on the job.*

"Keep an eye on things while we're gone," she told Al Parent as the basket descended again. "We could be gone for a while."

"Fair enough." Parent grinned. "I won't have the boy cook you dinner, then."

"Better wait for my word on that. But I might call you up for a lullaby." McKenna climbed into the basket and flashed the thumbs-up to the flight mechanic, who started the winch and began to lift the basket from the deck.

McKenna gripped the side of the basket as it rose. She'd never been very good with heights, and dangling in a flimsy shopping cart in a gale wasn't exactly going to help with that. The tug grew smaller and smaller beneath her. Al Parent returned to the wheelhouse, and McKenna almost envied the relief skipper, who would spend the next day or two in the captain's chair, feet up, the ship's cat in his lap and a paperback novel in his hands, his only worry being to keep the tug's bow to the sea and the *Lion*'s drift arrested.

You wanted to chase the big scores. It's going to get much harder yet.

SAFELY ABOARD THE DOLPHIN, Harrington nudged McKenna as the helicopter climbed. Pointed out the window at the *Pacific Lion*, the freighter's portside weather deck only a few feet above the water. Every time the swell hit, the ship dipped and rolled, and the portside railings dropped toward the sea.

Harrington pointed at a series of vents just below the railing. *"I've been looking over the design of the ship,"* he told McKenna, hollering over the roar of the helicopter. *"Those vents are for the cargo hold, to keep car exhaust from building while they're loading. They go all the way down to deck four, the first cargo hold."*

McKenna followed his eyes. Got the point quickly. The way the seas rocked the freighter, those vents were dipping into the water, allowing more leakage into the holds. If the seas got any bigger, those waves could flood the vents, starting a chain reaction that could sink the *Lion* within hours. And the seas were forecast to get bigger, much bigger.

"Not good," McKenna told Harrington. *"How do we fix that?"*

Court studied his laptop. *"Depends on how much water's already on board. I might be able to lessen the list a little bit just by pumping out some of the cargo hold. But we're going to have to hurry."*

"Yeah," McKenna hollered back. *"No shit."*

44

The helicopter dropped McKenna and her crew on the *Lion*'s starboard weather deck, high above the water—or more accurately, onto the wall of the accommodations house on the starboard side of the ship. From there, the *Gale Force* team descended to the cargo holds through an access hatch amidships and a long, dark, tilting stairwell. Ridley remained topside.

The rest of the crew had tied off lines and dropped them into the abyss, then tied loops in the lines to create hand- and footholds to aid the descent. They all wore climbing harnesses and bright headlamps, and they clipped their harnesses into the loops in the ropes as they descended.

Safety first.

It was quieter inside the ship, out of the wind, though the swell swayed the ropes every time a wave hit. McKenna made sure she stayed clipped in at all times. It was a long way to fall if she made a mistake.

There were nine cargo decks on the *Lion*, decks four through twelve. McKenna and the team headed straight to the bottom. It was a long climb down, damp and cold, with the crew's rhythmic breathing as they dropped, the rush of the wind past the postage-stamp patch of daylight above, the crash of the ocean, and the maddening tilt of the stairs, a nine-story drop in the dark.

Finally, McKenna reached bottom, a dark, geometric mishmash of shapes and angles, a watertight bulkhead door mounted on a wall that was now a floor. Beyond it lay the first cargo hold.

There was another watertight door, too, in what had been the floor. It led deeper into the ship, to the decks and passageways beneath the cargo holds. The crew would need to access those areas to check fluid levels in the fuel and water tanks, but for now McKenna had her eyes on a deckload of Nissans.

Matt and Stacey Jonas touched down shortly after McKenna, then Court Harrington behind them. The Jonases were breathing heavily, flushed with exertion. Court nudged Stacey. "Long way from Baja, huh?"

Stacey smiled, unbowed. "Yeah, but the company's better."

"This deck isn't going to be underwater when we open the door, right?" McKenna asked Harrington. "I don't really want to drown today."

Harrington checked his laptop. "There is water in there, but I don't think this deck is fully flooded. Not based on my calculations, anyway."

"How much do you trust your calculations?" Matt asked.

"Completely."

"I guess we'll find out," McKenna said, turning a wheel on the bulkhead to unlock the door. She held her breath as the door unlatched, ready for water to burst through—but nothing happened. McKenna opened the door slowly, peered through. Didn't see water.

What she did see, though, were cars. Row after row of cars, hanging precariously from their mounts on the oily deck. They descended in straight lines, fore and aft, strapped in by heavy-duty tie-down lines, every one of which seemed to protest every time a wave hit the ship. There were hundreds of cars—five thousand of them—dark and ghostly and ominous, descending from the high starboard side of the hold down toward the portside, outlasting the beam of McKenna's headlamp and disappearing into the darkness.

And somewhere down there, McKenna could hear water.

"We have fluid in this hold, as expected," she told the crew. "Court's right. Let's strap in and find it."

Matt Jonas tied off another line at the bottom of the stairs, dropped it through the bulkhead door, then a second line. There wasn't enough room between the cars for a third, so McKenna would follow Harrington down on his line, one at a time, using the deck for handholds when they reached the portside of the ship and the water.

Stacey dropped in first. The diver climbed down steadily, no sign of hesitation, no fear. McKenna knew she wasn't susceptible to claustrophobia or anxiety or panic attacks. She was calm, and she would keep her head, even if things went awry.

And they could very easily go awry. The *Lion* had three massive seven-story cargo ramps for offloading and unloading cargo. The main door sat at the stern, starboard side, well above the waterline. The second one lay amidships, also on the starboard side, so it wouldn't be a problem, either. The third, though, was on the port-side amidships, and because of the way the *Lion* lay in the water, much of that third door was also submerged. It was supposed to be watertight, but there was already water in the hold. Odds were the door was probably leaking, in addition to the vents above, and if it blew out, seawater would flood the hold within minutes.

But there was no sense worrying about that right now. The door hadn't blown yet.

Court Harrington dropped through the hole next. McKenna gave him a minute. Beside her, Matt Jonas watched, stone-faced and silent. If he was worried about his wife down there, he wasn't showing it.

McKenna met his eye and he smiled back at her. "Go get 'em, skipper."

Here goes. She clipped onto the rope and backed through the bulkhead door.

The deck was slick, covered in leaking oil from the fleet of hanging Nissans, and McKenna struggled for traction as she walked herself backward. The cars surrounded her. The ship swayed, and the cars shifted and creaked on their bindings, their deadly potential impossible to ignore.

Then Stacey called up. "Found it. Geez, McKenna, there's a lot of water down here."

Stacey and Harrington were about ten feet below McKenna, waiting at the edge of a lake of green oily water. McKenna could see at least two full rows of cars trapped beneath the surface, maybe more. It was murky down there. The submerged cars looked eerie, shipwrecks in the shadows. But the water wasn't visibly rising, and that was good news.

Stacey reached into a pack around her waist, and pulled out a distance finder, a little laser box similar to an electronic tape measure from the hardware store. She lowered herself as close as she could to the surface of the water, aimed the finder across to where the water met the top of the hold, and reported the distance to Harrington. Then she aimed the finder into the water, between a row of cars, and called out the distance to the portside hull.

Harrington copied the distances into his notebook. "Basic trigonometry," he told McKenna. "If we can get an idea how much water's leaked into this hold, we'll know how the ship will respond when we turn the pumps on her."

"Perfect." McKenna peered over the architect's shoulder at his chicken-scratch handwriting. "So how much water are we dealing with?"

"Let's see." Harrington tapped his pencil on the notebook as Stacey called out another measurement. "Factoring the length of the ship, the cars in the water, the water on the decks below . . ." He paused, wrote down a couple figures. "I estimate we're dealing with approximately fifteen hundred tons of leakage. And there's more coming in with every wave this ship takes."

McKenna studied the architect's notebook again. Couldn't make high or low of anything on the page. "That's a lot of water," she said. "Do you maybe want to run topside, check your work on a calculator?"

Harrington shook his head, because of course he was never wrong. "Not necessary. This is pretty basic math, McKenna. Now all we need to do is get measurements for the other fluids on board the ship—oil and ballast and drinking water and whatnot—and we're good to go."

Another wave hit the ship, rocking the cars on their moorings. McKenna pictured the vents up top, a few feet from the surface, pictured more seawater spilling down inside them every few seconds. There were thirty-three tanks on the *Pacific Lion*, all of them needing measurements. The gale was building outside. There was no time to waste.

"We need to do this in stages," she told Harrington. "This ship won't survive the storm unless we can prevent those vents from flooding."

"We could block them off," Stacey suggested from the waterline. "Weld steel plates over the holes. We have the equipment."

McKenna mulled it over. Didn't really like the idea of parking the *Gale Force* under the *Lion* for any length of time, not in this weather. "What else do we have?"

Harrington wrote something in his notebook. "If we can pump all this floodwater out of the hold, we correct . . ." He tapped his pencil again. "Eight degrees of the list, right away. That would move us from the current sixty-three to a more manageable fifty-five."

"That should give us clearance," McKenna said. "Move those vents higher above the waterline before the storm gets much worse."

"That's a lot of pumping, McKenna," Stacey said. "It'll take all night to get that water out."

McKenna thought about her bunk on the *Gale Force*, Jason Parent's cooking. *Not tonight, girl.*

"That sounds about right," she replied. "So we'd better get started."

45

McKenna climbed ten decks skyward, up to the starboard deck of the *Lion*. Ridley waited for her there, staring out at the low gray clouds. It was a quarter after nine in the evening, but there was plenty of light; the sun wouldn't officially set until midnight at this edge of the world. And while there was still light, there was still time to work.

McKenna raised the *Munro* on her handheld radio. Outlined the situation. The vents, the water in the hold.

"My architect calculates that we can reverse the list about eight degrees if we pump out the floodwater," she told the *Munro*. "Do you mind if we borrow your helicopter?"

The radio operator came back with a laugh in his voice. "No problem at all, Captain. We're billing the shipping company for every minute we spend out here. I'll have that Dolphin on scene in a half hour or so."

McKenna thanked him. Ended the conversation and hailed Al Parent on the *Gale Force*, told him to ready the pumps for pickup.

"Roger," Parent replied. "You planning to spend the night on the wreck?"

"Going to take nine or ten hours to get the hold pumped dry," McKenna told him. "I might send a couple crew back, but I'll stick around and keep an eye on things. We're going to need hoses, too, Al. Miles of them."

"I'll send you every hose I can find. Anything else?"

McKenna surveyed the empty deck. Felt her stomach growl, and tried to remember the last time she'd eaten anything. "Send us some food, would you?" she said. "I'm starving over here."

AL AND JASON PARENT had a care package ready within an hour. Nelson Ridley and Court Harrington helped McKenna wrangle the Dolphin's steel basket into the stairway through an access hatch through the hull on deck seven. They unloaded a lunch bag filled with thick sandwiches and thermoses of coffee, a couple spare sleeping bags, and a flashlight apiece. They stashed the goodies in the corner of the stairs, unloaded a couple long coils of hose, and then set to work maneuvering the heavy pump out of the basket.

The pump was the size of a suitcase, the kind that just barely fits into the overhead bin. McKenna lashed it to a railing inside the stairs, holding the machinery secure as Harrington radioed the all-clear to the Coast Guard aircrew. The helicopter moved down the ship, a couple hundred feet astern, where Matt and Stacey Jonas had set up shop inside their own access hatch. Meanwhile, McKenna, Ridley, and Harrington began to wrestle their pump down three more decks to the water.

It was a long, arduous process. Ridley and Harrington steadied themselves by the access hatch and belayed the pump down the dark stairwell while McKenna descended beside it, guiding the pump through the angled stairs to keep it from bashing against the walls. The men lowered the pump slowly, took their time, the sea doing everything it could to knock them off balance. Finally, McKenna guided the machine to a resting position at the bulkhead on deck four, and let the rope go slack.

"Touchdown, fellas," she called up. "Now send me some hose."

The men lowered the hose down to McKenna. Then they grabbed the sleeping bags and the food and dropped down to deck four themselves, to maneuver the pump into the cargo hold and through the maze of hanging cars, to the water. They tied the pump to four eyebolts in the deck a few feet above the waterline, then rigged up the hoses, one end in the oily green water, the other all the way up at the access hatch on deck seven, pointing out over the hull and down to the ocean.

It was almost full dark when McKenna pushed the hose out of the access hatch. Nearly midnight, the gray clouds above gone black, the wind full of salt spray even this far from the waterline.

McKenna secured the hose. Then she hollered down the stairway to Ridley and Harrington. *"Okay, boys. Fire her up!"*

A pause. Then a rumble as the pump came to life. For a minute, nothing happened. Then the hose coughed and spasmed, and suddenly a gush of oily water spewed out and down the hull.

Two hundred feet away, Matt and Stacey had their own pump working. McKenna waved at Matt from her access hatch. Then she dropped into the ship again, and climbed down toward deck four to find Ridley and Harrington and settle in for the night.

46

He couldn't stay here.

Okura lay across the rear windshield of the Nissan on cargo deck twelve, the Coast Guard long gone, the darkness absolute. He was hungry. His whole body hurt. The storm threw the ship violently, hurled it high atop monster waves and slammed it down into the troughs, bashing the tethered cars into the steel deck, again and again. Okura gripped the briefcase, knew he had to go, escape the cargo hold, find food and water. Wait for the gale to blow over and then attempt his escape.

Fifty million dollars. Yes, but he would die like Ishimaru if he didn't get out of here.

First problem: light. Okura inched to the edge of the Nissan. Leaned down the side of the car, reached as far as he could, fumbled in the dark for the door handle. Found it with his fingertips, stretched as far as he could, and pulled. The door swung open, swung down. Inside the car, the dome light illuminated.

The sudden bright nearly blinded him. He shielded his eyes, waited until they'd adjusted. The cargo hold looked chaotic. The dome light played spooky shadows on the cars nearby. All the same, the light was a comfort. The whole situation seemed surmountable at once.

Okura looked up the slanted deck toward the bulkhead where he'd found Ishimaru. Thirty or forty feet above him. He would have to climb, and climb carefully.

The Nissan was chained in four points to the deck; it was tethered to the cars ahead and behind, on both the driver's and passenger's side. The cars rose and slammed down with every fresh wave, sending spasms of shock through the tethers. Okura knew the storm would try its damndest to shake him loose as he climbed. Knew it was his only chance at escape.

If only I had something to eat.

There was canned food in the galley, lots of it, though the rest had gone bad. Medical supplies in the infirmary, fresh clothes in the staterooms. Even bedding to make a nest for sleeping. Everything he needed was waiting above him. All that remained was to get there.

Okura maneuvered to the rear of the Nissan. Swung his feet over the side and stepped gingerly onto the oil-slick deck. Waited, timing the waves, felt the *Lion* drop into a trough and braced himself for the impact. The swell slammed the hull and moved on, and then Okura made his move.

He dropped down to the deck, grabbing hold of the tethers with one hand, the briefcase with the other. Used his legs to push off from his Nissan's rear bumper, reached high above his head for the next car in the line. Hurled the briefcase ahead and pulled himself higher, his feet struggling for traction against the slippery deck. He felt the *Lion* drop into another trough. Knew if he didn't hold tight he'd be cut loose and falling. Grabbed the briefcase with one hand and a tether in the other, pulled himself to a tire and wrapped it in a bear hug. Felt the momentary weightlessness as the wave hit, and then the crash as the car hit the deck again.

Okura held on. Climbed up onto the hood of the Nissan, scrambled across the roof to its trunk before the next wave rocked the *Lion*. One car. He'd made it one car, and he felt exhausted to his core. Felt like he'd just climbed a mountain. He looked up the long row of cars, the bulkhead just barely visible, and wondered how he would ever make it to the top.

He'd made it one car, though. He could make it one more.

47

McKenna and Harrington bunked at the base of the stairs, by the bulkhead door leading to cargo deck four, while Nelson Ridley climbed back to the weather deck to maintain radio contact with the *Gale Force*. McKenna and Harrington unraveled their sleeping bags and dug into their provisions, and listened to the pump rumble away in the hold.

"We'll go two hours on, two off," McKenna told the architect. "Check the pump every hour or so, make sure the hose is still sucking water. Adjust as you see fit. Sound good?"

Harrington chewed his sandwich, swallowed. "Makes sense to me."

"Remember to clip in. Every time you go up or down that line. Safety first."

"Right, McKenna." Harrington grinned. "This isn't my first rodeo."

It's practically mine, McKenna thought. *And I don't want to lose anyone.* She rummaged in the dinner bag. Jason Parent had made sandwiches, thick ones, roast beef and big hunks of bread, and he'd somehow rustled up fresh lettuce and tomatoes, to boot. McKenna took a bite and savored it. Drank her coffee.

High above them, the wind howled through the access hatch and up the stairway to the deck. Pitch-dark up there now, the only light the cold blue from the LEDs in their headlamps. They were alone here, might well have been the only people left alive on the planet, and McKenna couldn't shake the sense of awkwardness. She hadn't been this alone with Harrington, with so little to say, since she'd told him she thought she was falling in love.

And that hadn't exactly gone over well.

"So we got this thing licked, or what?" McKenna asked after a beat. "You think you can save this wreck?"

Harrington nodded. "I'm reasonably confident."

"'Reasonably?'" McKenna arched an eyebrow. "Okay, but once we get all the fluid levels, you're going to be sure, right?"

Harrington laughed a little, the kind of laugh that made McKenna feel like she'd just asked something dumb. Like she was reading the situation all wrong yet again.

"It's not just the numbers," he said. "We'll get everything we can use, but there's no guarantees."

McKenna stared at him. "You said if we input all the fluid levels into your models, the models would show us what to do. Are you saying that's not true?"

"It's not as simple as that, McKenna. This isn't some video game. There's thirty-three tanks on this ship, and a million other variables. I won't give you a clean, precise solution to a really messy problem."

"But that's what you do," McKenna said. "That's *your job*, Court, to clean up these messes."

Harrington sighed. "I can give you odds," he said. "The *models* give us odds. We decide whether the odds are worth the risk. That's how this works." He paused. "Your dad understood that."

"Yeah, so why can't I; is that what you mean?" McKenna said quickly. "I'm sorry, Court. I thought I had the best scientist in the world for this job, and you're telling me it's a freaking game of poker?"

Harrington started to reply. McKenna beat him to it.

"I need a solution, Court," she said. "I don't need odds, or excuses. I need a plan to save this ship, and I need it fast."

"You'll get your plan, McKenna," Harrington said. "Just let me do my job, and you worry about yours."

I'm the freaking captain, McKenna thought. *My job is to worry about you and your job.* But she kept her mouth shut. Screwed the top on her thermos and peered down the bulkhead to where the pump rumbled away.

Harrington was watching her. Those green eyes, she could feel them. "What happened to us, McKenna?" he asked when it became apparent that she wasn't going to meet his gaze. "How did we get here?"

You know how we got here, she thought. *You know damn well.*

She kept that to herself, though, didn't say it to Court. "It doesn't matter, Court," she said instead. "What matters is how we get home."

"I really liked what we had together. I hate that it ended how it did."

"You mean with my dad dying?" she said.

Harrington made a face. "That's not what I meant," he said. "Before that, when you said all that stuff." He paused. "I was young, and you were young, and I thought we were just having fun. And then, with your dad, and everything fell apart—I guess I just never got a chance to say sorry."

This was a mistake. McKenna wished she were topside. Heck, wished she were underwater. Anything to dodge this conversation.

"Yeah, well, no apology necessary, Court," she said. Then she stood. "I'm going to check on that pump. Get some sleep. I'll wake you up when it's your turn."

She dropped through the bulkhead and climbed down to the pump. It wasn't quite a walk of shame, but it kind of felt just as crummy.

48

By sunrise, McKenna could almost feel the ship righting itself. The water level in the hold had dropped noticeably, and the pumps were still working hard. Up the stairway, the skipper could see the little patch of gray sky, hear the wind roaring. The ship rocked even harder now, the swell more pronounced, and between checks of the pumps, McKenna climbed to the access hatch at deck seven to survey the weather.

It was a grim sight. The wind had intensified overnight, and it was tearing the tops of the waves to foamy shreds. It blasted into McKenna's face, rocked the ship hard, and, far below, she could hear the waves crashing against the ship's keel. The ocean itself was a mess of white water and confused seas, the waves gunmetal gray and haphazard. They built seemingly at random, crashed and died and disappeared again, reappearing as big rumbling masses that steam-rolled across the water to collide with the *Lion*. The gale was in full force, the *Lion* in its direct path, the waves reaching for the vents every time the wreck plunged into the swell. McKenna stared across the water and cursed Christer Magnusson. Knew he'd wasted good time, and she and her crew would pay for it.

Harrington awoke shortly after dawn. He wiped his eyes, sat up, groggy. "Is it my watch yet?"

McKenna didn't answer right away. She'd stayed awake all night, watching the pump, watching Harrington sleep, dreading the moment she'd have to wake him up and rehash the night's conversation.

So she'd let him sleep, avoided the issue.

"I figured you're the brains of the operation, you could use the rest," McKenna told him. "Anyway, it's still early. You can spell me for a while."

Harrington looked at her. Looked ready to ask a question, but didn't. "It feels like it's getting rougher out there," he said instead.

"Supposed to blow forty knots," McKenna said.

"Are you tired?"

"No more than usual."

"I was thinking, I could start surveying the ship. Check the levels in the ballast tanks, start plugging in numbers. If you don't mind watching the pump a little longer."

McKenna considered it. The way the storm was building, the earlier they could get started, the better. And it would be nice to get some distance from Harrington for a while. But she shook her head. "I can't let you wander around this wreck by yourself, it's too risky. Give it an hour or so, then we'll go together."

Harrington hesitated. Then he nodded. "Sure, McKenna," he said. "Okay."

THE COAST GUARD SENT a helicopter over just after seven in the morning. McKenna and Ridley met topside and guided the basket down—supplies from the *Gale Force*. Fresh sandwiches, hot coffee, fuel for the pumps. Then McKenna left Ridley with the amidships pump and took Harrington to the Jonases, who'd built their own nest to babysit their pump.

"How's she looking?" McKenna asked the divers.

"Still sucking water," Stacey told her. "And the noise almost drowns out Matt's snoring."

"Just thought you might be homesick for those big *Gale Force* diesels," Matt replied, laughing. "You love me, don't lie."

He moved in for a kiss that Stacey pretended to deny, and then she gave in, and it was gooey and romantic and awkward as all hell, given the conversation McKenna and Harrington had endured the night before. From the expression on Court's face, he must have felt the same.

Stacey caught them looking. Caught on immediately. "Oh, geez," she said, blushing. "I'm sorry, guys. We get carried away."

Harrington made to answer. McKenna did, too. They talked over each other, and accomplished nothing but prolonging the agony.

"Forget about it," McKenna said finally. "I'm going to take Court on a tour of the ballast tanks. See if we can fill in the blanks on that computer of his. You guys babysit this pump until we get back, or that hold empties, whichever comes first. By then, hopefully, Court will have a plan for us."

Matt looked at Court. "I could go with Court," he said quickly. "If you, you know, need a rest or something."

Good god. This is why you never hook up with your coworkers.

"I'm going," McKenna said firmly. "You guys stay here."

"O-ka-ay." Matt looked dubious. "You two be careful down there. It's bound to be a death trap."

"We'll take it easy," Court said. He'd lost that cocky smile of his, and McKenna wondered if the whiz kid was actually nervous, or just dreading the thought of spending more time with her.

He had a right to be nervous, if that's what it was. The *Pacific Lion*'s ballast and fuel tanks were located at the very bottom of the ship, close to the keel, to keep the center of gravity as low as possible. That meant venturing under the cargo decks, all the way down to deck one, which, on the portside, rested more than seventy feet under water. It would be pitch-dark and cramped and disorienting, and if anything went wrong, there wouldn't be much hope of survival.

At this point, I'll take my chances, McKenna thought. *Anything's better than staying up here and pretending not to talk about me and Court.*

Matt and Stacey's stairwell ended at deck four, but there was a watertight hatch at the base of the stairs, and beyond it another narrow passageway down to the bowels of the ship. McKenna and Court struggled to unlock and lift the hatch open, then tied off a single line and dropped it into the gloom.

McKenna met Stacey's eyes as she lowered herself through the hatchway. "Be careful, you guys," Stacey said. "I mean it."

"Didn't you hear what Court said?" McKenna replied. "We'll be fine."

She clipped her harness to the first loop in the line, and dropped herself through, searching with her feet for the slant of the wall. Slowly, she walked herself deeper.

The *Lion*'s list was easing, she could tell. That meant the portside vents were higher above the water, but it also would complicate maneuvers inside the ship. As the angle of the list moved from sixty-three degrees to fifty-five, the walls would become just upright enough to be difficult to walk on, while the decks remained impossible to traverse. The closer the list got to forty-five degrees, the more difficulty McKenna and her crew would have traversing the interior of the ship.

Moreover, as the team righted the *Lion*, they would expose still more of the ship's hull to the wind, making it difficult for Al and Jason Parent to exert any control over the wreck from on board the *Gale Force*, and with only forty or so nautical miles of open water between the *Lion* and the Aleutian Islands, no one had much room for error.

We need to get this ship upright so we can tow her somewhere safe, McKenna thought as the force of a heavy wave launched her toward the roof of the stairwell. She gripped the rope tight, hung on for her life. Clipped in with shaky hands, and kept her breathing steady.

Try not to fall, girl, she told herself. *Do us all a favor.*

McKENNA QUICKLY DISCOVERED the easiest way to traverse the long subterranean corridors under the cargo decks was by crawling. The steel was ice-cold on her hands, and the deck and the walls met at a frustrating angle beneath them, but it was quicker than trying to balance upright against the list and the ever-present swell.

Harrington led them through a maze of unmarked corridors,

around blind corners to more of the same, relying on his memory of the ship's design to lead them to the fuel and ballast tanks. He seemed to know where he was going.

"You really did your homework," McKenna said, crawling after him.

Harrington glanced back over his shoulder. "Yeah, well," he said. "I told you there was luck involved. That doesn't mean it doesn't take skill."

The starboard ballast tanks were empty. Bone-dry. Harrington made a note in his notebook. "I guess that explains the whole tipping-over thing. Somehow, I don't think they planned it that way."

"Ballast swap," McKenna said. "Except they screwed up and forgot to replace the Japanese water with the American stuff."

"That should make it easy to reverse the procedure, then," Harrington said. "Pump water from the portside tanks to the starboard and hope she levels out."

Hope.

"When you say you'll give me odds on our success," McKenna said, "what exactly does that mean?"

"It means—" Harrington exhaled. "Listen, I've been experimenting with the models on my computer, trying to optimize my strategy, but like I told you last night, there's luck involved, too. Every four or five simulations I've run, the ship tilts upright and keeps going over, until she's all the way down on her starboard side." He paused. "And then she sinks."

"Once out of five?"

"Pocket aces." Harrington twisted back again, grinned at her. "Best starting hand in poker, pocket aces. Gives you an eighty percent chance of winning against any random hand. That's what we're dealing with here, McKenna. Pocket aces."

Pocket aces. "Remind me again how you busted out of that poker tournament?" McKenna said.

Harrington's smile disappeared. "I don't want to talk about it," he said. "Let's keep going."

THEY WORKED ACROSS the starboard side of the ship, checking ballast tanks, fuel, and bilge water. The *Lion* had a waste-treatment tank and freshwater reserves, too, and Harrington checked every one, leading McKenna steadily toward the bow of the ship, writing down numbers in his little book every step of the way.

They reached the forward ballast tank, and it was time to descend again, rappelling down another long narrow hallway to the portside of the ship. The ship was dead quiet down here. Wet, too. Water dripped from the ceilings and puddled on the deck— floodwater from the cargo decks above. The *Lion*'s watertight doors were holding, and Ridley and the Jonases should have nearly been done pumping out the hold, but that was all cold comfort to McKenna. There was water above her, water beside her, and water below.

Harrington shivered. "I guess this is what life on a submarine feels like."

The portside ballast tanks were all full, which made Harrington even more optimistic. "We can just even them out," he told McKenna. "This could be way worse. I mean, at least the hull isn't breached, right?"

"Right," McKenna agreed. She watched Harrington write something in his little book. "How did you get into this stuff, anyway?"

Harrington looked up. "Pumping ballast?"

"Ships," McKenna said. "My dad always said you had a one-in-a-million mind. You could be, like, building rockets or something. Why naval architecture?"

"Why not?" Harrington said. "I don't know, I've always had a thing for ships. My dad used to take me walking down by the water when I was a kid, used to tell me all about the cargo ships we saw anchored out in the harbor. I think he secretly wanted to run away on one, you know?" He shrugged. "Anyway, I grew up thinking I would design ships for a living, but it turns out there isn't much work for shipbuilders in the United States anymore. And anyway, this is more fun." He laughed. "And more lucrative, if you do it right."

"That's a big *if*."

"Still better than an office job." Harrington turned around again. They'd reached another watertight door. "The engine room," he told McKenna. "Just a couple more ballast tanks, and a few random fluid levels, and we're set to pump."

McKenna was ready to breathe fresh air again. "Perfect."

Harrington tried the door. Jiggled it. The door wouldn't move. "Only one problem," he said. "We're locked out."

49

"There's another door on the starboard side," Harrington said. "We'll just climb back up and go that way."

They ventured back through the ship, retracing their steps down the same dark, damp corridors. Passed the stairway where they'd climbed down from deck four, and continued to the engine room doorway. This door was unlocked. But it was blocked from within, and by something heavy.

"I don't think we can move this," McKenna said after they'd shoved and heaved against the door for a while. "Must have tipped over when the wreck happened."

"Yeah, well, we need to get in there," Harrington replied. "We have to get those fluid levels before we even think about beginning the operation."

"There has to be another way in."

"Of course. There are access doors through the accommodations deck, and farther astern. We just have to go all the way back topside."

McKenna checked her watch. Almost noon. The trek through the bottom of the *Pacific Lion* had taken more than five hours, and the weather was only getting worse out there. It would take another hour to reach the engine room, she figured, and a couple of hours to check the rest of the fluid levels. Then Harrington would have to devise his plan of attack, and the crew would have to move the pumps into position, and then the pumping itself—

It was a long day ahead. And that assumed nothing went wrong.

"To the stern, then," she said, starting back toward the access stairway. "But let's hustle, okay?"

THE BATTERING EFFECT of the waves had been muted, seventy feet below the ocean surface, but in the starboard access hatchway, McKenna could feel the full force of the swell again. The rope swung, wild and unpredictable, launching McKenna against the wall of the stairway, and then into the steps themselves. She hit hard, bounced off, hit again, came back clutching her ribs with her free hand.

"Cripes," Harrington called up from below. "You okay up there?"

"Just got the wind knocked out of me," McKenna replied, catching her breath. "I'll be fine."

"We can't do this job without you, either, so be careful."

"Roger." McKenna continued to climb. Three decks, nearly thirty feet in this claustrophobic madhouse. The waves hammered the ship. The rope swayed. McKenna clipped herself in, climbed a couple of loops, unclipped herself and clipped in again. Above her, the watertight hatchway was a swatch in the darkness, only slightly better lit than the access stairs themselves. McKenna focused on the climb. Steadied her breathing. Step by step, she reached the top.

Matt Jonas was waiting when McKenna poked her head through the hatchway. "Stacey's just checking on the pump," he reported, "but I think we've pretty much got it beat. You guys have any luck down there?"

"A little bit." McKenna pulled herself through the hatch, steadied herself as another wave hit. "Just have to check on a few figures in the engine room. Then we're ready for action."

"Right on." Matt gave her a sheepish smile. "Starting to get a little seasick down here."

"It's nautical out there, that's for sure." McKenna peered down the access hatch. "You alive down there, Court?"

The architect pushed out a deep breath. Unclipped himself, clipped back in. "I'm okay," he said. "This swell is kicking my ass, though."

"Couple more loops, then you got it made."

"Yeah." Court laughed. "Then we just have to climb up nine more decks and back down again."

He climbed to the next loop. Unclipped himself. Pulled the carabiner up and fumbled with it, couldn't clip in. Dropped it. It dangled from his harness. "Crap."

McKenna reached through the hatch. "Forget it. I'll pull you up."

But Harrington was still fumbling with the carabiner. He picked it up, snapped it open. Then the wave hit.

It must have been another monster. It jarred the *Lion* sideways, so hard that McKenna thought for an instant that the ship must have been sinking. The steel shuddered and groaned. The cars shifted on their mounts in the cargo hold. McKenna steadied herself, caught her balance, just in time to see Harrington lose his grip on the rope.

The architect's eyes went wide. He opened his mouth but didn't scream, locking his gaze on McKenna as he fell, dropping fifteen feet and then pinwheeling off a wall or a staircase or something, hurtling down out of sight, his headlamp like a strobe against the steel walls. A moment later, McKenna heard the thud as the architect hit bottom.

"Court!" McKenna was on the rope in an instant. Hollered up at Matt to call the Coast Guard as she dropped through the hatch and down toward Harrington, moving too fast to bother clipping herself in. She hollered Court's name as she dropped, was vaguely aware of Matt scrambling up the other rope to the surface, nearly lost her grip as another wave hit—not as hard but hard enough—held on tight and kept going, down, down, into the darkness.

Harrington lay on his back at the base of the stairs, his body bent at an impossible angle. McKenna dropped off the rope next to him, her heart pounding. *"Court,"* she said, kneeling beside the architect. "Come on, Court. Talk to me."

Harrington stared up at the ceiling, his eyes unfocused.

"Court. Where are you, buddy?"

Harrington blinked slowly. "Randall?" he said. "Shit . . . that hurt."

Then he was out, unconscious. McKenna felt for a pulse. It was there, but it was weak, and Harrington sure wasn't talking.

"Get me some help," she called up through the ship. *"Damn it, I need some help down here, now!"*

50

The Coast Guard's Dolphin arrived on scene after twenty long minutes. The AST took another twenty minutes to make his way down the access stairway to where McKenna waited with Harrington.

The architect hadn't opened his eyes. McKenna checked his

pulse again; it was weak, but it was there. The way Court's vision swam as he'd looked at her, though, McKenna figured it was decent odds he had a head injury. Broken bones, definitely. Figured it was a coin flip whether he ever walked again.

The AST touched down beside McKenna. "Guess you guys got the same wave we did. Had to be thirty feet, easy."

McKenna said nothing. The AST looked Harrington over. "Yeah, okay," he said. "Sit tight. I'm going to get the medevac board down here."

It was another twenty minutes before the board arrived. One hour since the fall now. McKenna could feel the minutes slipping away, just as fast as they'd passed with her dad in the water.

Come on, come on, come on.

Matt Jonas lowered the board from the top of the access stairs. It was long and unwieldy, and it banged and crashed against the walls of the stairway as it dropped. McKenna wondered how the hell they would get Court out without hurting him any further.

The AST laid out the board. With McKenna's help, he got Harrington situated. The architect still hadn't regained consciousness. He was breathing, but barely.

"Here's what we're going to do," the AST told McKenna. "You're going to climb back up to that hatch, and you and your partners are going to haul this guy up. I'm going to climb up alongside him, steady the board, make sure he doesn't crash into these walls too hard. Then we'll do it again up the second set of stairs."

"Roger that," McKenna said, reaching for the rope. She looked back at Harrington. "Just be careful, okay?"

The AST didn't look up from the medevac board. "I'll look out for him," he said. "You get going."

. . .

McKENNA CLIMBED AS FAST as she could. Tried to cover the ground without clipping herself in, but then another wave hit and knocked her sideways, nearly knocked her clean off the line. She closed her eyes, saw Harrington falling, heard the thud as the architect hit the deck. Opened her eyes and reached for her carabiner and clipped herself in all the way to the top.

Stacey was with Matt at the top of the stairs. She stood back as Matt and McKenna began to pull Harrington skyward. The whiz kid wasn't so heavy, not with two people hauling him, and somehow this struck McKenna where it hurt.

The most important member of the team, and you couldn't lay off him. God help you if he's dead because of you.

Slowly, Matt and McKenna hoisted the medevac board to the access hatch while the AST climbed beside. Harrington's eyes were still closed when he came through the hatchway. Stacey stifled a gasp, her hand to her throat.

The AST paused at the bulkhead. "One more time," he told McKenna and Matt. "You got enough left in the tank?"

"If they don't, I do," Stacey told him. But her husband was already following McKenna up the line.

The wind howled outside as McKenna reached the surface. The helicopter hovered overhead, buffeted by the gale. The sky was the same dull gray, the clouds hanging low, the wind whipping more froth off the water.

Ridley helped McKenna to her feet. Took the rope and helped her and Matt pull Harrington to the surface.

The job seemed to take hours. The wind attacked in force.

McKenna heaved on the line and tried to fight the feeling that the whole job had just gone to hell.

Finally, Harrington was on deck. The AST climbed after him, signaled to the crew of the Dolphin to lower the hauling wire. It took the flight mechanic a couple of tries with the wind. The wire flew everywhere, landing thirty feet away. McKenna and Matt ran to it, dragged it back to the AST and Harrington, helped the AST clip the medevac board to the guy wire, and watched as the mechanic winched Harrington skyward.

The AST was next to go. McKenna gripped his arm. "How bad is it?"

"We'll give him the best we've got, ma'am," the AST replied, avoiding her eyes. "If our guys can fix him, they will."

51

Hiroki Okura peered out through a porthole at the salvage crew clustered on the starboard wall of the accommodations house. Listened to the drone of the Coast Guard helicopter as it climbed high in the air and flew away, out of sight. They'd taken someone with them, an injured man. Something had gone wrong.

It was serious, judging by the expressions on the faces of the crew members left behind. They stared up at the gray sky after the helicopter, faces flushed red from the bitter wind, eyes as dark as the water below. For a long time, nobody moved. They seemed to be waiting for someone to tell them what to do.

They were an interesting assortment, the salvage crew. Two women, and that alone was a rarity, this far out at sea. Stranger still, the younger of the women appeared to be in charge. She was in her thirties, Okura decided. He wondered how she'd managed to find herself aboard this wreck.

It didn't matter. The salvage crew hadn't noticed Okura, and that was perfectly fine with him.

He'd survived the perilous climb up the long string of Nissans, little by little, inch by inch, wave by thundering wave. He'd rested at the bulkhead where he'd killed Ishimaru, exhausted and weak from hunger. It hadn't just been the money that had spurred him to keep moving, but also the knowledge that if he died here, he would die no better than Ishimaru—a failure, alone, in this cold, hellish pit.

So he'd climbed. Found the rope he'd left behind and lifted himself up the stairwell, clutching the briefcase and walking up walls, taking breaths where he could find flat ground, somewhere to set his feet. His muscles burned from exertion. Still, he pulled himself skyward, fought gravity and the storm and his own failing strength.

He didn't know how long he'd climbed, but it could have been hours. Finally, when he'd nearly had enough, the darkness changed, almost imperceptible, yawned open in front of him, and he could suddenly see forms again, walls, the silhouette of his hands, the briefcase. The air became marginally fresher, cooler. The sound of the storm became louder. And he'd felt the knot where the rope tied off to a handrail, and then he knew he'd won.

Okura had collapsed in the hallway, the central spine of the *Lion*. Dragged himself and the briefcase behind to the galley, the food stores, and laid waste. Much of the ship's food had gone bad; the galley reeked of overripe fruit and meat gone to rot, but Okura was too hungry to care. In the dim light from two salt-encrusted portholes, he'd eaten everything he could find, most of it stale: the cookies left out for the overnight watch, a whole box of rice crackers, chocolate. He'd found a can opener and drank chicken soup, cold, ate a whole tin of peaches, then a tin of pears.

With his strength mostly restored, he'd climbed his way back out of the galley and into the nearest stateroom, pulled the bedding and pillows from the bed and made a nest in a crook of the listing wall. He lay down and wrapped himself in the soft, letting the storm lull him into a well-deserved sleep.

NOW HE WAS AWAKE.

He'd heard the helicopter approach, listened as it settled into a hover above the ship. He'd pushed the blankets away and climbed up the stateroom to a porthole facing down the weather deck aft. Looked out just in time to watch the Coast Guard technician disappear down a hatchway, fifty feet away.

A man stood balanced on the wall nearby, a big man, older, a considerable mustache. He'd waited, his brow furrowed, occasionally walking to the hatchway and peering down into the abyss. Once or twice, he'd glanced back at where the stateroom jutted out from the accommodations superstructure, and for one brief, terrifying instant, Okura thought he'd been seen. But the man didn't investigate, just looked up at the helicopter and then back down the hole, waiting on the Coast Guard technician's return.

The man hadn't been aboard the *Salvation*. None of this crew had been; they weren't Christer Magnusson's people. The Commodore team had carried themselves with a swagger, a certain confidence. They'd dressed alike, looked alike, didn't speak much.

This crew was different. They didn't have Magnusson's cocksure demeanor, for one thing, but there was something else, too: these people were familiar, the way they interacted. The way their eyes met, how they seemed to communicate without needing words.

This wasn't the *Salvation*'s people, no. This crew looked more like a family. But they were a family who had lost one of their own, and now they stood, impossibly small against the scale of the ship, with the vast, colorless sky above, looking up at where the helicopter had disappeared and waiting on their leader to make the first move.

Okura peered up at them through the porthole. Hoped that whoever the injured man was, his injury wouldn't jeopardize this crew's ability to bring the *Lion* to harbor. The second officer had fifty million American dollars riding on their success. His survival depended on it.

52

McKenna surveyed the *Lion*'s unsteady deck. The wind roared. The waves battered the ship. The gale surrounded her. It was hellish, and Court Harrington was gone.

Stacey Jonas reached the top of the stairway. Matt hurried over to help her out of the hole. Nelson Ridley stayed put. Watched McKenna.

The ship shuddered constantly, threatening to knock McKenna and her crew off their feet. Just descending into the engine room would be a hell of a job, and even if McKenna could gather the fluid levels for the rest of the tanks, she'd be damned if she could figure out Harrington's computer.

Sometimes the ship just keeps going, the whiz kid had said. *The ship tips all the way over onto her starboard side. And then she sinks.*

McKenna shivered. There was no way she would try to right the *Lion* without Harrington. And right now Harrington was clinging to life in the back of a Coast Guard helicopter.

"We can't just wait around for him, skipper," Ridley said, reading her mind. "They're talking forty-five-knot winds in the next couple of days. We stick around here, we might lose the tow. We gotta make something happen, and fast."

McKenna knew he was right. Knew they were already testing their luck, knew it couldn't hold forever.

And it hasn't. Down one crew member. How many more to go?

"We can put another line on this wreck," Ridley said. "Tow her out away from land, as far as we can get her. Buck into the storm and hope she doesn't sink on us."

"We won't make much progress," McKenna replied. "Not in this wind. Not with this tow. If the weather gets as bad as they're saying, it could drive this ship onto the rocks, no matter what we try to do. We just don't have the power to hold her steady forever."

McKenna leaned against the starboard deck. Stared up at the sky, the clouds racing by overhead. Tried to picture her charts in her head, the Aleutian Islands to the north.

"There's a pass," she told Ridley. "Between the Aleutians. I saw it on the map. We put that second line on the ship, ride the flood tide right through to the Bering Sea. Take shelter in the lee of the islands."

"Be a hell of a job to drag this wreck through. Just turning her in the right direction will be a chore. And then getting her there in a following sea—"

"It's our only play, Nelson. It will be calmer on the other side. We can anchor up and wait for Court to recover. Buy us some time."

Ridley's brow furrowed. He didn't say anything.

"Thirty million dollars," McKenna said. "If our boat sinks, our money sinks, too."

"Fine." Ridley's eyes darkened. "But what if the kid doesn't make it?"

McKenna looked at him.

"You saw the kid. It was bad, skipper," Ridley said. "What if he doesn't come back?"

McKenna saw Harrington's face, the look in his eye as he fell. Saw his broken body at the bottom of the stairway. The grim look in the AST's eyes as he maneuvered Harrington skyward.

You did this. You lost another one.

Ridley cleared his throat. "Skipper?"

McKenna shook her head clear. "We cross that bridge when we come to it. First, let's get this ship through the pass."

ABOUT AN HOUR LATER, McKenna dropped from the *Munro*'s backup Agusta helicopter onto the afterdeck of the *Gale Force*. The Dolphin was gone, airlifting Court Harrington back to Dutch Harbor.

The architect's prognosis was not great. "He's surviving, Captain," the *Munro*'s radio operator had informed McKenna. "He's still unconscious, last we heard, and it looks like he's bleeding internally. The doc managed to get him stabilized, but that's about the best I can tell you."

"How bad could it get?" McKenna asked. "Worst-case scenario. Do you know?"

A pause. "I'm sorry, Captain. I can't say."

"You can't say? Or you don't know?"

"I don't know, Captain. I'm sorry."

McKenna stared out at the gale through her tug's wheelhouse windows. "We're taking the ship through the Samalga Pass," she told the radio operator. "It's too miserable to work out here. We're going to tow her across to the Bering Sea side."

Another long pause, this one stretching for miles. "Uh, stand by, *Gale Force*."

McKenna stood by. Waited for twenty minutes, and when the radio came to life again, it was Tom Geoffries, commander of the *Munro*.

"Captain Rhodes, I've talked to my superiors in Kodiak, and there's no way I can let you through that pass. Not in this weather. Not a single tug."

"The weather's only getting worse," McKenna told him. "Short of opening the seacocks and scuttling the ship, there's not much my crew can do in these conditions. If you want the ship saved, this is our only option."

Geoffries was silent. "Let me make a call, Captain," he said at last.

McKenna stood by again. In the back of her mind, a little voice whispered something, reminded her of the *Gale Force*'s troublesome starboard turbo, that hair-raising encounter with the oil tanker in the Columbia River.

She pushed the thought from her mind as Geoffries hailed back over the radio. "We have Kodiak on board," he told McKenna. "You can have the pass, Captain Rhodes, but if you screw up—" A beat. "If you screw up, Captain, it's both of our asses. Understand?"

"Roger that, sir," McKenna replied. "We'll make it work."

Ridley fixed that engine, she thought as she replaced the radio. *She's bulletproof. No way she conks out again.*

She looked around—the pounding, incessant swell, the wind howling through the *Gale Force's* stay wires.

She'd better *not conk out,* she thought, *or we'll have a heck of a lot more to worry about than a lost paycheck.*

53

YOKOHAMA

The man standing on the opposite side of Katsuo Nakadate's desk was, by every account, highly regarded in his industry, and extremely well accomplished. He was a man accustomed to receiving respect, a man not used to deferring to others. But as Nakadate studied the master of the *Pacific Lion*, he didn't see an alpha male in command of his situation. Rather, he saw a frightened little boy.

"You know who I am," Nakadate said, and the captain swallowed and nodded. "Good. Then we can dispense with the formalities. Did you have a pleasant flight home?"

The captain nodded again. Stole a glance around Nakadate's

office, at the two young men standing wordless by the only exit. "Y-yes," he said, stammering a little, his voice dry. "It was fine."

"I'm sorry to bring you here so unexpectedly," Nakadate told him, "but there's an urgent matter that I believe you can assist me with." He gestured to a chair. "Please, sit."

The captain sat. He had reason to be frightened, of course. Confused, at the very least. The two young men standing behind the captain had intercepted him on his regular early-morning jog, spirited him away in a waiting Mercedes-Benz, and driven him here, to a skyscraper in downtown Yokohama, a lavish corner office amid the clouds—and an audience with Katsuo Nakadate himself. The captain had been angry when he'd been brought into the office. That anger had changed to fear when he'd seen Nakadate, recognizing him from the newspapers, placing his face.

"What do you want from me?" the captain asked. "I've done nothing wrong. I'm a good man. I'm not a—not a gangster."

Nakadate smiled inwardly. He didn't consider himself cruel by nature, but there was always some humor in observing the contortions people put themselves through to avoid causing him offense— as if the head of the Inagawa-kai syndicate would be so petty as to kill a man over an ill-chosen word. Regardless . . .

He opened a folder on the desk in front of him. Flipped through until he'd found the photograph he was looking for. Removed it, and slid it across the desk.

"Your family, Captain Ise," he said. "Your beautiful wife, and two little boys."

The captain went pale as he studied the picture. It was recent: taken the previous morning, in front of the boys' school. A crude gesture, yes, but a point to be made.

The captain pushed the picture away. "This isn't necessary," he said. "Whatever you want to know, I'll tell you as much as I can. Please—tell me what this is about?"

"Very well." Nakadate found another photograph, a single man this time, removed it. "Have you seen this man before?"

The captain looked. Squinted. "No, I haven't. Who—"

"That man is named Tomio Ishimaru. Until recently, he was a valued member of my staff of accountants. Until shortly before your ship sailed, in fact."

Ise started to respond. Nakadate cut him off with the wave of his hand.

"The day of your departure, Captain Ise, Tomio Ishimaru murdered three of his colleagues and escaped with something very valuable to me."

One more picture from the file folder. Nakadate held it out to the captain. The captain glanced at it, then looked away quickly.

"We've managed to trace Ishimaru to the docks," Nakadate continued. "The man in the picture you're holding is—*was*—a customs agent. After some encouragement, he admitted to us that he'd accepted a bribe from Ishimaru in exchange for access to a ship. *Your* ship, Captain Ise."

Ise glanced at the photograph again. Looked like he might be physically ill. "I don't know— I don't have anything to do with this," he said. "Please—you—this has nothing to do with me."

"Someone allowed Tomio Ishimaru on board your ship, Captain. We've obtained security footage of a sailor meeting him at the gangway. Unfortunately, it's too dark to make out the sailor's face. But we know Ishimaru had help. And I need you to tell me who it was."

Ise said nothing.

"Captain?"

"I told you," Ise said, "I have no idea. I couldn't be on the docks at the time you suggest. I was on the bridge with the harbor pilot. He can verify this."

Nakadate leaned back in his chair. Turned slightly to gaze out the tall windows at the city and the harbor beyond. "Someone helped the smuggler," he said. "One of your men, Captain."

Ise still didn't respond. Stared down at the picture, the customs agent's ruined face. Nakadate gave him a moment, a long one. Then he looked past the captain to the young men by the door. Nodded to the older of the two, a man named Daishin Sato, who stepped forward, cracking his knuckles.

Ise caught the gesture, the meaning. Sat straight in his chair. "Okura," he said, realization dawning on his face. "Hiroki Okura, my second officer. He was on the bridge when the ship capsized. He refused to leave the wreck with the rest of us. The Coast Guard was forced to send a helicopter back to find him."

Nakadate made a note. "And did they find him?"

"They found him, and they brought him back to Dutch Harbor with the rest of us. But . . ."

"Yes?"

"He escaped," Ise said. "He disappeared from the community center in Dutch Harbor. Nobody could find him. He didn't come home with the rest of the crew."

Nakadate sat forward, tented his fingers. "Where could he have gone, Captain?"

"Nobody knows. The town was very small. But Okura simply disappeared."

"Did he carry a briefcase, the last time you saw him?"

Ise didn't have to think long. "No. None of us carried anything. I would have remembered."

Nakadate studied Ise some more. The captain waited, emboldened enough now to return his gaze briefly before looking away.

"We are most appreciative of your help, Captain Ise," Nakadate said finally. "My secretary will be happy to call you a taxi. Please, have a pleasant afternoon. and if you think of anything else I should know . . ."

"I will contact you," Ise said quickly. "I swear it."

Nakadate gathered the photographs, returned them to the file folder. Stood, and motioned to Sato to open the door.

"See that you do," he said. "Good day, Captain."

54

McKenna sat in the skipper's chair in the wheelhouse of the *Gale Force*, monitoring the tug's progress toward the Aleutian Islands. Night had finally fallen, the crew in their bunks or watching a movie in the galley.

It was good to be back on the tug. The wheelhouse was warm and quiet, the coffee fresh, the deck and the walls resting at the proper angles—the storm-tossed seas notwithstanding. Even Spike seemed marginally friendlier. The cat slept on the bench beside the skipper's chair, closer to McKenna than his usual spot on the dash. Probably had more to do with the wave action than McKenna, but the skipper figured she'd take any victory she could get.

The *Pacific Lion* was under tow. The tug was making good time, running with the seas behind her, and her engines had held up thus far. She and the crew had deployed a sea anchor from the *Lion*'s bow—a massive, radio-deployed, high-tech parachute that Randall Rhodes had ordered custom-built for situations like this. The anchor would stabilize the *Lion* in a following sea, keep her parallel to the waves instead of turning broadside, prevent her from surfing down on the *Gale Force* as the waves passed beneath her.

With luck, the *Gale Force* would make Samalga Pass for tomorrow morning's slack tide, bring the wreck through without incident. By evening, McKenna hoped to have found a nice, quiet spot behind one of the Aleutian Islands to shelter from the storm.

And then what?

The Coast Guard had updated McKenna on Court Harrington's status. The architect had been airlifted to Dutch Harbor, and there were discussions about flying him on to Anchorage. Nobody on the other end of the radio had sounded anything better than cautiously optimistic, but Harrington was going to survive, anyway. He might or might not come back to the job, but in the short term, the crew of the *Gale Force* was going to have to work on saving the *Lion* without him.

McKenna mulled her options. Nelson Ridley was holding on to Harrington's laptop, and Stacey Jonas had salvaged his notebook after the fall. McKenna and her crew had access to all of the fluid levels on the *Lion*, as well as the model Harrington was planning to use to right the ship. How hard could it be to plug in the numbers?

Very hard, as it turned out.

"Clearly, there's a technique to this we just aren't getting," Ridley told McKenna after they'd sunk the virtual *Pacific Lion* nine or ten times. "No wonder the other outfits all wanted Court on their team. This is like building a spaceship."

"We still have the stern tanks to measure," McKenna said. "Maybe once we get the fluid levels locked in, we'll be able to make sense of this thing."

"You want to take a gamble on that? You and me, with thirty million dollars riding on it?"

The answer was no. McKenna imagined towing the *Lion* to a sheltered harbor somewhere, imagined the days of pumping and clambering around the ship. Imagined watching the damn thing roll over and capsize because she'd messed up the pumping algorithm, watching the whole operation sink to the bottom of the Bering Sea, taking the *Gale Force*'s big payday—and a few more of her crew—down with her.

"We can't do this ourselves, McKenna," Ridley said. "We need to assume Court isn't coming back and prepare accordingly."

McKenna didn't answer. Reached out, petted Spike. The cat purred, arched into her touch, spent about a minute in total bliss. Then he opened his eyes, saw McKenna, stiffened, stood, and leaped from the mantel.

McKenna watched him pad out of the wheelhouse. Looked back through the rear windows at the twin towlines stretching back off the stern, toward the lights of the *Lion*. With any luck, the *Lion*'s watertight doors were holding, keeping her afloat. God willing, they would make it through the pass.

And then?

McKenna straightened. "I know, Nelson," she said. "I'm working on it."

. . .

AT A QUARTER AFTER TEN the next morning, McKenna found herself staring out from the wheelhouse as the *Gale Force* approached the mouth of the Samalga Pass, waiting on the tide to turn.

The pass was a desolate, primeval place: to the east lay Umnak Island, seventy miles long and mountainous, shrouded in fog. To the west were the volcanic Islands of Four Mountains, an uninhabited cluster of barren, forbidding rock. The nearest island, Chuginadak, climbed a mile into the fog. Its volcano lay quiet today, but according to Tom Geoffries on the *Munro*, it was named after an Aleut fire goddess and known to be restless.

It wasn't the volcano that had McKenna preoccupied this morning, but the pass at its base. Fifteen miles wide, Samalga cut through the Aleutian Islands from the North Pacific to the Bering Sea, and the tides could be wicked. The ocean floor climbed from six hundred fathoms at the mouth of the pass to eighty in the middle, and there were shallow patches and seamounts where it reached as high as thirteen fathoms, less than eighty feet below the surface. As the tug and her tow arrived, with a gale force wind and the tide running opposite, the mouth of the pass was a turbulent mess, a standing swell with steep, twenty-foot waves; a chaotic, boat-swallowing pit.

The *Munro* joined the *Gale Force* outside the pass. McKenna could see that Captain Geoffries was taking care to steer well clear of the shallow water, keeping alongside the *Gale Force* and the *Lion* in seven hundred fathoms of water, more than three-quarters of a mile. The gale continued to blow, and the seas were agitated, but the deep water was peace compared to the hell at the mouth of the pass.

McKenna surveyed the roiling water through her field glasses. Then she picked up the intraship telephone and called Ridley down in the engine room. The engineer answered. "Coney Island Pizza."

"How's it looking down there?" McKenna asked him. "We going to have enough oomph to make it through this thing?"

"We're gravy, skipper," Ridley replied. "I've been watching the engines all night. No problems whatsoever."

"How's that turbocharger on the starboard main? Not going to crap out again, right?"

"Compression is fine. These engines are rock solid. Nothing to worry about."

"If you could see what I'm seeing," McKenna said, "you'd be worried, too."

"Nah. We're going to drag this thing through, easy-peasy. You find us a new whiz kid, yet?"

"Not yet. I'll keep trying once we're through that pass." She ended the call. Put down the phone and looked out through the windows at the volcano in the distance, the churning water, the long, dark mass of Umnak Island to the east. Had no idea how she was going to scare up a replacement for Court Harrington, but this wasn't the time or the place to be trying, anyway.

Once the *Gale Force* entered the pass, McKenna would have to maintain enough speed to keep water past her rudders or she would lose her ability to steer the tug, and the *Lion* behind her. The tide would take hold and propel them forward like an amusement park ride, and the *Gale Force* would need every ounce of power she could muster. If the turbos crapped out, or the engines gave way, the tug and the massive freighter behind her would be driven straight onto the rocks.

The radio came to life. "*Gale Force,* this is Captain Geoffries. This tide is about to turn. How are things looking on your end?"

McKenna glanced back through the aft windows to the stern, and close behind, the listing hulk of the *Lion.* Al and Jason Parent had shortened the towline in preparation for the pass, closing the gap behind tug and tow. It would increase McKenna's ability to control the freighter, but would also give her less time to react in case something went wrong. Still, it was the only way to maneuver the *Lion* in such close quarters.

"We're ready to rock and roll here," McKenna told Geoffries.

"Excellent. We'll let you lead and tuck in behind your tow, keep an eye on things from the rear. That work for you?"

"Sounds perfect to me, Captain."

"Just make sure you give a wide berth to that fire goddess on your portside. There are shoals south of the island where the tide rips something fierce. It'll drag that ship away from you if you don't watch it."

"I saw that on the charts," McKenna said, "and I can sure see it now out my wheelhouse windows. We'll stick to the middle of the channel."

She signed off and hung up the handset. The tide was slackening outside, and the standing waves at the entrance to the pass were diminishing. Soon after the slack, the tide would reverse, and the North Pacific would rush north between the islands into the Bering Sea, carrying the *Gale Force* and her tow along like a piece of driftwood in the current.

A piece of driftwood with nearly ten thousand horses under the hood, McKenna thought. *Assuming those engines hold.*

McKenna surveyed the pass one more time. The grim, unforgiving shores on either side of the water. The *Lion* would wreck if the tug's engines failed. She would wreck if the towlines parted. But she would also wreck if she stayed out here; it was only a matter of time. The only way to save that ship was through the pass, so, damn it, it was time to get moving.

55

Hiroki Okura ventured forward to the bridge of the *Pacific Lion* and found himself in Armageddon.

The ocean around the freighter was a savage. It leaped at the ship, clawed at the hull, dropped away and reared back to leap again. A following sea, monster rollers lurking behind the *Lion*, catching up, overtaking, lifting the freighter high and then plunging her down again, daylight all but gone in the bottom of the troughs, the view panoramic from the wave tops. And everything tilted, twisted sideways, dark and cold.

The view was unsettling. Now and then a wave broke, sending white water over the portside railing and toward the bridge windows. A rogue wave could do worse, Okura knew; smash open the windows and knock him from his chart-table perch, even flood the vents that led down to the cargo hold. There was nothing to do but hope that didn't happen. No way to react until the sea threw the first punch.

The salvage crew was moving the ship. Okura had pieced

together the rest of their plan as soon as he'd seen the islands off to starboard. Those would be the Aleutian Islands, the only landmasses for hundreds, even thousands, of miles. And with the wind and the waves coming from astern, there'd be no reason to drag the ship closer to landfall, unless . . .

The salvage crew intended to drag the stricken freighter *through* the island chain and out to the other side, use the land as a wind block to continue their work. Okura couldn't see anything dead ahead of the *Lion*, with the towlines being rigged to the stern, but he hoped the pass was large and the tug was stout. This was no weather, no place, to be fooling around.

Since he'd spied on the salvage crew, he'd been hiding out in the crew quarters, sleeping in his makeshift bunk, venturing down into the galley to raid more of the stores when he could stomach the nauseating smell, and fiddling with the lock on the briefcase, trying to crack the combination.

But he had made this excursion to the bridge as the salvage crew tugged the *Lion* north. He'd determined to rest up on the ship, regain his strength, wait for the salvage crew to reduce the ship's list and bring her closer to land before he attempted to make his escape. The salvage crew had no idea he was on board. They didn't know about the briefcase, the stolen bonds. Okura was confident he could elude them and make his retreat from the *Lion* in secret.

But it never hurt to have a little insurance.

So Okura had braved the maddening, bucking-wave action and the narrow skewed hallways, and he'd ventured forward to the bridge, where he stood, transfixed by the storm, until he remembered why he'd come.

He turned his back on the storm. Found the locker at the rear of the bridge, the small safe inside. A couple of feet in length, the same in width and depth, a combination dial on the door.

Okura hadn't been given the combination. Captain Ise guarded that information jealously. But Ise was getting old, and his memory was fading. Okura had found the combination stored in the captain's stateroom, a Post-it note stuck to the desk.

Now Okura held himself steady with one hand as he worked the dial with the other, the crash of the sea and the ship's maddening list making even this simple task difficult. It took time, maybe ten minutes, but finally Okura dialed to the last number, tried the handle, heard the lock disengage. He swung the safe open and peered inside.

The *Pacific Lion* carried cash, thirty thousand dollars in American currency—petty cash for port fees and pilotage, the occasional bribe to a corrupt harbormaster. The cash was the captain's to dispense, and the captain's alone. But Captain Ise was gone now, back to Japan. Okura filled his pockets with three neat stacks of banded hundreds.

It wasn't the money, though, that had prompted this visit. Behind the cash lay a pistol, a Beretta M9, and a handful of magazines. Captain Ise's last-ditch protection against piracy or mutiny.

Okura took the pistol and the spare magazines. Left the safe open and climbed back to the chart table, where he studied the gun. It was sleek, matte-black, deadly, and it sent a jolt of satisfaction through Okura just to look at it.

He'd never shot anyone before. He didn't plan to shoot anyone now. But as another wave caught the *Lion* and lifted her high, Okura gazed out from the bridge and saw the cutter *Munro* in the distance, an ever-present white knight, and decided he liked his chances just a little bit better, now that he'd picked up some firepower.

56

The tide ripped through the pass like a raging river, pulling the *Gale Force* and the *Pacific Lion* along with it.

McKenna stood in the wheelhouse, knees and body braced against the swell, her eyes moving constantly as she guided the tug forward.

She watched the *Gale Force*'s progress through the wheelhouse windows and on the GPS screens, keeping the tug in the middle of the pass, away from the dark islands on either shore. She watched the instrument panel, her eye on the engine temperature gauges, the RPMs, the tug's speed through the water. She looked back through the aft windows at the towlines stretched tight across the tug's stern, at the big wallowing freighter listing behind the tug, watching to make sure the tide wasn't running the freighter too close to the *Gale Force*. She kept her eyes everywhere, forward and back, her whole body a coiled spring. Knew she wouldn't relax until she'd brought the *Lion* through to the other side.

Ridley was in the engine room, watching the big diesel engines for any sign of trouble. Al and Jason Parent monitored the towlines. Matt and Stacey Jonas stood by, a couple of extra pairs of eyes on the instrument gauges, the charts, the tow. Even Spike was on duty, perched on the bench beside the skipper's chair, the master of the ship, his yellow eyes alert as they darted around the wheelhouse.

McKenna had called the crew to the house just before slack tide, laid out their assignments, and set them to work. Then she'd guided the *Gale Force* into position, pointed her northeast, up the middle of the pass, toward a nameless point of land on the eastern side of Chuginadak Island. The tug had responded beautifully. The *Lion* followed like an obedient dog. The seas were calmer at slack, not nearly as chaotic as when wind and tide ran opposed to each other. Heck, the ride had almost started to seem pleasant.

Then the tide changed, barely noticeable at first, and then faster and faster. It was ripping north and pulling the *Gale Force* along with it as McKenna turned the tug and tow north-northeast, dodging Samalga Island at the apex of the crescent pass. She pushed the throttles higher, kept the towlines stretched taut, the mighty tug pulling, her twin propellers gripping and churning the water, her rudders responding to McKenna's every touch of the wheel.

The *Munro* on the radio: "Looking good from the stern, *Gale Force*. Your tow looks stable and the sea anchor is holding. How are you feeling up front?"

"Yeah, *Munro*, we're doing fine," McKenna told the cutter. "This tide is something else, though."

She put down the handset. Looked back at Matt and Stacey Jonas. "So?" she said, exhaling a long breath. "Are we having fun yet, or what?"

Matt grinned at her. Started to answer. And then an alarm sounded, drowning out his reply.

57

The alarm sounded, *loud*, shrill and incessant above McKenna's head. She recognized it immediately: the bilge pumps. *Shit.*

At the very bottom of the *Gale Force*, well below the waterline, was a compartment called the bilge, where water that hadn't drained from the tug was collected. Every ship had a bilge compartment, and the *Gale Force*, like all ships, possessed pumps to remove the excess water that amassed there. These pumps worked automatically when the water level reached a certain height. The alarm McKenna was hearing meant the pumps weren't doing their job.

Now's not the time, McKenna thought, fighting the tug's wheel and throttles as she struggled to keep ahead of the tide. She glanced back at Matt and Stacey. "One of you want to take the wheel?"

Matt stood and hurried across, replaced McKenna at the controls.

"Keep her in the middle of the channel," McKenna told him, already reaching for the intraship phone.

She dialed Ridley in the engine room. "You hear that?" she asked the engineer when he answered. "The bilge pumps are failing."

"Pumps are working fine, skipper," Ridley replied, not even a hint of panic in his voice. "But they're overwhelmed. We're taking on water somewhere."

Shit.

This was the beginning of the worst-case scenario. If McKenna couldn't find the source of the water rushing into the bilge, she stood to lose the tug, the tow, and possibly her life. The water would continue to rise, spilling out of the bilge and into the engine room, where it would drown the tug's engines, rendering her powerless. From there, it was only a matter of time before the tug sank, capsized in the swell, or was driven onto the rocks on either side of the pass. Or it was crushed underfoot by the *Lion*.

McKenna picked up the hailer. "All hands," she said. "We're taking water. I need this whole tug inspected for leaks right away."

Stacey was already headed down the wheelhouse stairs, and McKenna knew Al and Jason Parent were no doubt already springing to action as well. She hesitated, debated calling the *Munro*, filling them in. Before she could make up her mind, another alarm began to blare.

"**ENGINE TEMPERATURE**," Ridley reported over the intraship phone. *"Portside engine's burning up."*

"On my way." McKenna set down the phone. Picked up the hailer. "Al Parent, meet me in the engine room," she ordered. Then she hurried to the stairs herself.

McKenna had a suspicion what was happening now, and it was both good and bad news. In order to cool the *Gale Force*'s twin diesel engines, the tug took in cold water from outside the tug, circulated it through the engine and expelled it back out to the sea. If the engines were overheating while the bilges were flooding, it probably meant a failure in that cooling system somewhere. Water was coming in, but it wasn't making it to the engines. The trouble was locating the leak.

We can't deal with this right now, McKenna thought as she raced down through the tug to the engine room. *Not here, with this tide. Not in this pass.* But she didn't have a choice.

She met Al and Stacey in the engine room with Ridley. The engineer was covered with grease and sweat, bleeding from a cut on his forehead. He shook his head when he saw McKenna.

"We can't keep the port engine online much longer, skipper," he said, yelling to be heard over the noise of the diesels and through the industrial-strength ear protection they were all wearing. *"We'll lose her for good unless we shut her down."*

One engine against this tide. The starboard engine, to boot, with its faulty turbocharger. *Shit, shit, shit.*

"Wait as long as you can," she told Ridley. "Then cut it. We have to fix that leak."

A GOOD SKIPPER KNOWS *her tug inside and out, McKenna.* Randall Rhodes had insisted his daughter learn the engine room, every inch of it, even as she'd protested that that was what Ridley was for.

And if Ridley's unconscious? You have fumes in the engine room and he's incapacitated, what are you going to do then?

She hadn't had an answer.

The skipper leads from the front, McKenna. You learn every inch of this boat, every job. And you make sure you can solve every problem.

She'd hated her dad for it, the long extra hours, the harbor days in the engine room instead of in town or on some paradise beach with the rest of the crew. Resented the work, the lack of free time, but hell was she grateful to the old man right now.

She'd never dealt with this problem before, not exactly, but she knew her engine room, all right. And she led Al and Stacey down the diamond-plate decking between the two engines, searching for the portside raw-water-intake pipe, where seawater entered the ship.

The alarms kept sounding. The engines roared. The engine room was a sauna. The tug swayed and bounced. McKenna pictured Matt at the wheel, hoped the diver had it under control. Knew the tug would get sluggish the more water she took on, knew as soon as Ridley cut that port engine, they'd risk handing control of the tug over to the racing tides.

Damn it.

McKenna knelt at the hull of the *Gale Force*, behind the portside engine. Lifted a piece of diamond plating and found the intake pipe, traced it away from the hull and toward the engine, until she found the problem.

A burst pipe, below the deck plating, spewing seawater everywhere at a dizzying volume. McKenna hurried back to the hull, found the seacock valve that closed and opened the pipe, turned it closed.

"Tell Ridley to cut the engine," she told Al. *"And bring me another length of pipe."*

While Al disappeared forward, McKenna led Stacey aft to Ridley's workshop. As with the rest of the engine room, the engineer kept his shop tidy and organized, and McKenna muttered a silent prayer of gratitude as she searched through Ridley's tools for the equipment she needed.

By the time she'd found her supplies, Al was back at the burst pipe, a length of replacement in his hands, the portside engine offline behind him. The engine room was marginally quieter, the motion of the tug in the current more pronounced. Now it was a race against time, against the tide, a desperate hope that Matt could keep the *Gale Force* in control of the *Lion* until McKenna could get both engines back online.

And if that damn starboard turbocharger goes, we're all screwed.

She took the fresh pipe from Al's hands. Knelt down and pulled up more of the diamond plate beneath them, slipped on a pair of safety glasses, and reached back to Stacey for Nelson Ridley's reciprocating saw.

As her crew looked on, McKenna cut out the damaged piece of pipe. Measured the gap, and cut the replacement pipe to fit. Then she swapped in the replacement pipe, fastened it at both ends, and screwed the fasteners tight—she'd have preferred to weld it, but that would have to wait—and motioned to Al to open the seacock again, and to Ridley to fire up the intake pump.

Then all four of them held their breath and waited as the pump spooled up and sent cold water back through the replacement length of pipe, watching for any sign of a leak, a poor fastening, anything. But the replacement held, and McKenna stood, swapped a quick grin with Stacey, and then hurried back to the stairs with Nelson Ridley behind her.

"Best to leave that engine to cool for a while, skipper," Ridley told her. "If we can afford it."

"Stand by on that," McKenna replied. Then she turned and hurried upstairs through the tug toward the wheelhouse, her heart pounding, her adrenaline through the roof.

Holy cow, she thought. *I sure owe you for that one, Dad.*

58

The alarms had stopped sounding by the time McKenna made it up to the wheelhouse. As she hurried to where Matt stood at the controls, she scanned through the forward windows, looking for any indication of trouble.

"We still winning this thing?" she asked.

Matt didn't look back at her, kept one hand on the wheel and the other on the throttle. He'd kept the *Gale Force* mostly on course, McKenna saw from the GPS, and behind the tug, the *Lion* still followed.

"We're winning," he told her, his jaw set, "but barely. That starboard engine is busting its ass for us right now."

He still had control. Still had enough water moving over the tug's rudders to keep her responsive to his commands. But there was still plenty of ocean to cover before they cleared the pass, and McKenna could only pray that Ridley's fix on that faulty turbo would hold.

If the turbo blew up again, the starboard engine was shot, and they'd have to fire up that portside diesel and hope it could limp them somewhere quiet, somewhere safe, somewhere to anchor up.

There was nothing to do but hope, though. Fight the tide, and keep moving, and trust the tug would see them through.

The radio crackled. "*Munro* here. *Gale Force*, we notice you've wandered offline a little bit. Everything all right over there?"

McKenna picked up the handset. "Just fine, *Munro*. We had a little issue with our engine coolant system, but we have it licked now."

A pause. McKenna figured Tom Geoffries was probably having a panic attack in his captain's chair at the moment, picturing the *Gale Force* broken down, the *Pacific Lion* on the rocks.

You and me both, Tom.

"Okay, *Gale Force*," the *Munro* replied, the radio operator sounding dubious. "Keep us advised as to the situation over there, please."

McKenna agreed. Hung up the handset, and relieved Matt Jonas at the controls. Tried to calm her racing heart and focus on getting the tug through the pass.

SHE GUIDED THE GALE FORCE onward. North, past the top of big Chuginadak Island, its volcanic peak glowering down through the fog, then up along the smaller islands, Kagami and Ulaga to the portside, and, to starboard, tiny, rocky Adugak Island, so small it looked like a pimple jutting out from beneath the waves, a few miles offshore from Umnak.

The tide carried them forward as the pass widened, doubled in width, as the currents dissipated and the Bering Sea opened up before them. The starboard engine didn't fail. The turbocharger didn't blow. The towlines stayed strong, and the *Lion* didn't capsize behind them. The ocean floor dropped down to six hundred fathoms, and the wind died a little in the lee of the islands. The *Lion* didn't wallow so much behind the tug anymore. The waves didn't crash and batter near as violently.

They'd made it.

The *Munro* on the radio again. Captain Geoffries. "Congratulations, Captain Rhodes. Now, do you have any idea where you want to park this thing?"

McKenna turned to her GPS screen, searched the charts for somewhere to hide the *Lion*. Found what she was looking for almost instantly.

"Inanudak Bay," she told Geoffries. It was an uninhabited inlet on the north side of the island, ten miles wide, like someone took a bite out of the rock between Umnak's three volcanoes. It looked sheltered enough to give the crew of the *Gale Force* a calm place to work, while wide enough for maneuverability if something went wrong.

"Good thinking," Geoffries replied. "Should be flat as a mill pond in there."

McKenna plotted a course. "It's four thirty now," she said. "We'll run up there tonight and make sure it's a good spot. Drop the anchors and see if we can't all get a good night's sleep, for a change."

"Roger that. Let us know if you need a hand, Captain. Our resources are yours for the asking."

McKenna thanked the captain. Wished him a good afternoon and signed off. Stood at the wheel, looked out at the calmer seas, the easing wind. Heck, even Spike was back asleep.

Through the pass on one engine, she thought. She crossed to the depth sounder, the picture of her dad in that old pewter frame. Studied it, the smile on his face, in his eyes, *felt* his presence around her, even though the wheelhouse was empty.

Couldn't have done it without you, she thought, and as she went to set the picture down, the light caught the glass on the frame and showed McKenna her own reflection. It shocked her a little, caught her off guard.

She was filthy, she realized. A grease stain on her forehead and a smudge under her eye. Blood smeared across her cheek, though coming from where, she couldn't be sure. Her knuckles, maybe; she'd scraped them raw. She looked tired, beaten-up, ragged—but she was smiling, the same smile as Randall Rhodes in the picture, worn-out but content.

Through the pass on one engine, she thought again, setting the picture down. *Girl, you're a bona fide towboater now.*

59

Court Harrington awoke suddenly, confused and disoriented. Heard the *beep* of machines beside him, someone calling on a PA system, and for a minute he figured he was on the *Gale Force,* in his bunk, waiting on Randall Rhodes to call him back to work.

But his bed wasn't rocking with the motion of any waves. And the room was more spacious than his berth on the tug. And—*geez*—he wasn't wearing any clothes, just a thin cotton gown beneath the bedsheets.

Also, his head hurt like a mother. It hurt to breathe, too. Heck, every part of him hurt. And his body was stiff and unresponsive when he tried to move. There were wires leading out to those beeping machines from underneath his gown, an IV in his arm.

He was in a hospital, he realized. He'd been here a while, he knew. But just why, he couldn't remember.

Harrington tried to think. *It can't be that serious if you can't remember,* he thought. *That's how it works, right?*

He'd been on the *Gale Force*—on the wreck, the *Pacific*

Lion—he remembered that much. He'd been exploring the ship with McKenna Rhodes—because Randall was dead, long dead—and McKenna was giving him grief about the models he was running to right the ship.

He remembered that. He remembered that McKenna didn't like him very much; she'd been pissed off with him ever since he boarded the tug in . . . Where?

Ketchikan.

Right. So he remembered that much. He remembered being belowdecks on the *Lion* with McKenna, and then the engine room had been locked and they'd had to retreat, and then . . . ?

And then nothing. And then now this hospital room, wherever *this* was.

Harrington wiggled his fingers. His toes. Felt them move, hands and feet, so that was a plus. Next step, walking. Harrington pushed himself up in his bed, felt dizzy and blinked and closed his eyes until the dizziness went away. He pushed the blankets off his body, pulled the gown down to cover as much as it could, and swung his legs over the side of the bed, feeling the diodes on his chest pull as he moved.

The machines continued to beep. His head continued to hurt. But Harrington figured he needed a damage report.

He set his feet on the cold floor. Pushed his ass off the bed and stood, gripping the side of the bed to stay upright. Put weight on his legs. Slowly, cautiously, he loosened his grip.

Then he collapsed to the floor.

Instantly, there was a nurse beside him.

"What on *earth* do you think you're doing?" she asked Harrington, scooping him back up and helping him into bed. "How long have you been awake?"

"Damage report," Harrington replied, his mouth dry. "I needed to— What the hell happened to me, anyway?"

"You had a fall," the nurse said. "You broke a couple of ribs, and you have a serious concussion, and with it, a fair bit of memory loss. But frankly, Mr. Harrington, it's a miracle you aren't paralyzed."

Harrington lay back on the bed. "I fell on the *Lion*?"

"Is that a ship? Because you fell on a ship."

"Yeah, the *Pacific Lion*. What happened after I fell? Where am I now?"

"You're in Dutch Harbor," the nurse said. "You were airlifted here by the Coast Guard. They're going to send you on to Anchorage now that you're awake."

"Yeah, but the ship," Harrington said. "What happened to the ship?"

The nurse shook her head. "No idea. I just take care of *you*, Mr. Harrington."

Harrington stared up at the ceiling. Couldn't remember his fall, couldn't remember anything after he and McKenna had found the engine room locked.

"I need a telephone," he told the nurse. "I need to make a phone call, right away."

THE PHONE in the wheelhouse was ringing.

McKenna sat at the chart table with Court Harrington's laptop, trying to decipher the whiz kid's models—or, barring that, find a list of genius friends Harrington may have had, classmates, anyone who could help her crack the code. They'd have the *Lion* anchored down in Inanudak Bay within a few hours, and McKenna wanted to have a salvage plan set by dawn.

Matt Jonas answered the phone, and McKenna only half listened, focusing her attention on Harrington's screen. But then Matt was holding the phone out, telling her that the call was for her.

"Who is it?" McKenna asked. "I'm a little busy, Matt."

But Matt was unswayed. "You want to take this, skipper," he said. "I promise."

McKenna looked at him. Matt shrugged. Held out the handset, and, after one more look at Harrington's models, McKenna sighed and took the phone. "Captain Rhodes," she said. "This had better be good."

"Define 'good.'"

A man's voice. A Carolina drawl. McKenna recognized it, felt the breath sucked from her lungs. "Court?"

"You gotta get me out of here, skipper," Harrington said. "They took all my clothes."

McKenna didn't answer. Couldn't.

"McKenna?"

McKenna blinked. Felt tears, and for once in her life, didn't mind. "Yeah, I'm here," she said. "It's good to hear your voice, Court."

"Yeah, I know it is. But you gotta fly me back."

McKenna stared out the dark wheelhouse and over the *Gale Force*'s bow. Could see nothing but night, and the odd whitecap on the water ahead. She pictured Harrington in a hospital bed, banged-up and bruised but awake. *Alive.*

"Fly you where?" she replied. *"Here?"*

"I know you can't save that ship without me," Harrington said. "And you know there's no one else who can do it. The way I see it, you have no choice."

"You're hurt, Court," McKenna said. "They said you might never walk again."

"Yeah, well. They were wrong about that. I broke some ribs and busted an ankle pretty good, got some new brain damage, that's all. I'm fine, McKenna. I can walk, and if you tell them to wrap up these ribs real tight, I can sure as hell help you rescue that ship."

McKenna shook her head. "I appreciate the enthusiasm, Court, but—"

"Who else are you going to get? Don't tell me you're going to try to work through my models yourself." Harrington paused. "Look, I'm telling you, I'm fine. I want to help. Let's get this ship right, and then I swear I'll check back into the hospital, first thing. Just let me do this, *please.*"

McKenna closed her eyes. Tried to imagine what her dad would have done. Figured if her dad were Harrington, he'd have fought off the nurse and bought his own ticket back.

"You swear you're okay?" she asked the architect.

"I'm fine, McKenna. It hurts to breathe a little, and I'm going to limp for a while. But I'm still the best architect that you know."

Crap.

Somewhere behind the *Gale Force*, the *Lion* wallowed on the end of its tow, waiting for someone to plot a way to save her. McKenna figured she didn't really have a choice.

"Damn it, *fine*," she told Harrington. "But as soon as we're done here, I'm taking you back to the hospital myself."

60

There was a Coast Guard petty officer waiting for Court Harrington when the nurse wheeled him out through the lobby of the Iliuliuk Family and Health Services clinic in Dutch Harbor. She was a young woman with a short, clipped haircut, who looked him over, skeptical, as he struggled up from the wheelchair.

"Good morning, Mr. Harrington," she said, handing him a cup of coffee. "Are you sure you're up for this?"

"Pretty sure," Harrington replied. That might have been a stretch. He ached all over, his head swam, and every breath felt like a stab wound. Walking, too, wasn't the most fun in the world. But this petty officer probably jumped out of helicopters for a living, Harrington figured. She wasn't going to sympathize with a couple bumps and scrapes.

He shook his head. Winced. "I mean, definitely. Once we get going, I'll be fine."

The petty officer didn't look convinced. Behind Harrington, the nurse grumbled her protest, handed Harrington a couple of forms to sign. He did, and then he was free, and the petty officer was leading him out through the parking lot to a waiting van. She helped him into the passenger seat and closed the door for him, waited until he was settled before driving away from the building.

It was a ten-minute drive to the airport. Harrington focused on trying to breathe without hurting, on trying to remember the fall.

Wondered, briefly, if he was making a mistake, but he knew that the crew of the *Gale Force* couldn't do this without him.

The petty officer pulled into the airport, parked the van at the far end of the runway. Directly ahead was a Coast Guard helicopter, low slung and military-looking, like some kind of robot bug.

"Jayhawk," the petty officer said. "You're riding in style this morning."

THE HELICOPTER didn't do much to help Harrington's pain threshold. The engines roared and rattled, and the whole machine shook as it sped westward, jarring Harrington's brain inside his skull, the seat belt digging tight into his bandaged midsection, the broken ribs wrapped tight under his brand-new UNALASKA! tourist T-shirt. Outside, the view was nothing but gray clouds; the pilot must have been navigating by computer alone.

Two technicians joined Harrington in the back of the helicopter, both young, friendly looking guys in orange jumpsuits and helmets. They'd given Harrington a helmet to wear, too, with ear protection but no radio, so he couldn't hear what the crew members were saying. He sat and looked out the window, found a grab bar to steady himself, hoped he wouldn't be sick or pass out in front of these tough guys.

The Jayhawk flew west for an hour or so. Then the pilot said something to the copilot, and one of the flight technicians smiled at Harrington and yelled something he couldn't make out over the roar of the engine.

He could feel the helicopter slowing down, though, and beginning its descent, and then clouds were gone and the helicopter was dropping, down toward a cold-looking black sea surrounded by rocky cliffs and featureless, verdant green mountains, and in the middle of the water was the *Pacific Lion*, lying on her side just as Harrington remembered, the Coast Guard cutter on one side, and the *Gale Force*, looking impossibly small, on the other.

The pilot aimed for the tug, and as he descended, Harrington could see the cluster of crew waiting on the deck aft of the wheelhouse, watching the Jayhawk as it dropped to a hover forty feet above.

The flight technician slid open the side door while his partner readied the basket, and Harrington inched across to the open door and climbed into the basket, felt the sudden blast of wind, the chill air, the basket swaying with every movement, and every movement sending spasms of pain through his chest. Suddenly, the hospital didn't seem so bad anymore.

The technicians worked the hoist, winching him down, and as the basket descended, Harrington could pick out the crew, Matt and Stacey, and Al and Jason, and Ridley, who caught the basket and helped Harrington to the deck, led him back to where McKenna stood, watching, looking him over.

"Welcome back, Court," she said. "You look like shit."

61

McKenna's first thought, on seeing Court Harrington struggle out of the basket dangling from the Coast Guard helicopter, was to curse the whiz kid six ways from Sunday, and then start looking for a seventh.

Just fine, my ass, Court, she thought, watching him limp across toward her, nearly slipping on the seawater-slick deck. *You don't look much better than the last time I saw you.*

Harrington still had that smile, though, that cocky grin, as if he knew a secret that no one else did, and McKenna figured it was a good sign, that his spirit hadn't been broken, even if his body sure looked like it had been.

"I can't believe you came back," she told him, leading him into the tug and up to the wheelhouse. "I can't believe I *let* you come back."

"You know I wouldn't miss this," Harrington replied. "You guys keep my laptop handy?"

McKenna found Harrington's laptop. "Kept all your data intact," she said. "Just have the engine room and the stern ballast tanks to check."

"We're going to have to do a full check all over again," Harrington replied. "It's been a few days, right? Who knows what kind of leaks could have sprung?"

"Fine. Matt and Stacey can take the forward compartments. I'll have Jason help me work the engine room."

Harrington reached to take the laptop from her. "What about me?"

"You stay topside," McKenna said. She held on to the computer. "Better yet, stay here. We'll take the readings and feed the numbers back to you."

Harrington shook his head. "I need to be on board."

"Not an option. We can't risk it. What if you have another accident?"

"So I won't have another accident." He made a grab for the laptop, an edge to his voice now. "You think your old man never worked hurt?"

McKenna hesitated. Wondered if she'd made a mistake even flying him out here. If she was setting Harrington up to kill himself trying to save the *Lion*. Finally, she handed over the computer. Watched Harrington set it down on the chart table, watched his face as the machine booted up.

He'd looked happy and relaxed a moment ago. Now his jaw was set, and any trace of that smile was gone.

Fifteen minutes from friendly to fuck off, McKenna thought, watching him. *That has to be a record, even for me.*

THEY FLEW BACK to the *Lion* that afternoon. Dropped down onto the starboard deck, where, despite Harrington's protests, McKenna left the architect topside with Nelson Ridley and took Jason Parent into the engine room.

The engine room sat in the middle of the ship, width-wise, surrounded by cars on cargo decks on the port and starboard sides. McKenna led Jason down an aft access stairway into darkness, that same maddening repetitive descent: clip onto a loop, step down, unclip and reclip and step down again. No light but from their headlamps, no sound but their breathing.

They reached the bottom, deck one on the starboard side, and stopped to rest by a watertight door. McKenna pointed her headlamp in Jason's direction. "You having fun?"

Jason was panting. "I went rock climbing once," he said. "On a first date. It was nothing like this."

"How'd you do?"

"Put it this way." Jason smiled, a little. "There wasn't a second date."

McKenna laughed. "Well, you don't have to worry about that today," she said. She turned to the watertight door. "If I have this right, the engine room is right here."

She unlatched the door and pushed it open. Beyond was more darkness, but the sensation, impossibly, was of open air and vast space. McKenna peered inside, scanned the room with her headlamp. She'd been correct; they'd reached the base of the ship's massive power plant, a four-story behemoth surrounded on all sides by catwalks and piping, instrument gauges and ductwork, and the massive propeller crankshaft. Water dripped from somewhere out of sight. The air was colder here. Nothing moved.

"I guess I was right," McKenna said. "Let's get to work."

THE WORK WAS SLOW-GOING.

Jason Parent was a game partner, but this wasn't his job on the *Gale Force*, and it showed. He lagged back, cautious, hesitant, eating up time, and McKenna had to remind herself they had no hurry, not now.

You lose Court, it's a sad story, she thought. *Jason's a new dad. Let's make sure his little boy grows up with a father.*

They started on the starboard side of the engine room and worked their way down. The room was huge, six stories tall, at least, and the catwalks and stairways that accessed the power plant's nooks and crannies hung angled and unsteady, every one of them a death trap.

McKenna worked quickly, dangling in space to read off from the lubricating-oil tanks, the diesel fuel reserves. Parent went slower, copying the numbers into Harrington's notebook, trying to keep up.

"Give me one second," he called down to McKenna. "You're throwing up a lot of numbers here, boss."

"Take it easy," she called back, hanging in space near a seawater-intake gauge. "We have nothing but time."

They worked their way down the ship, from starboard side to port, high to low. Finally, they'd cleared the room. Just the ballast tanks to go.

The *Lion* had two ballast tanks at her stern, one on the portside and one on the starboard. There were also the bilges, the very bottom of the ship, where any wastewater or other leaked fluid would have accumulated. McKenna and Jason crawled and clambered their way to each of the final tanks, and McKenna waited while the deckhand copied the numbers by the light of his headlamp.

Finally, high on the starboard side again, atop the last ballast tank, Jason straightened. "Got it," he said, peering down at the notebook. "What next?"

McKenna double-checked her own plans, Harrington's map of the ship. "That's everything," she said. "Back to the surface."

Jason exhaled. "Thank god."

62

The wait was maddening.

Court Harrington rested on the starboard wall of the *Pacific Lion*'s accommodations house and cursed the bad luck that kept him topside on the wreck while McKenna and the rest of the crew had all the fun down below. Nothing against Nelson Ridley, who leaned against the starboard deck, eating a sandwich, but Harrington wasn't used to letting other people do the work for him.

Heck, the way the ship rested, he couldn't even *pace* properly. All he could do was stand there and freeze and stare up at the sky, the clouds scudding past overhead, pushed by the gale that still raged on the other side of the island. Stare at the sky, and wait.

Ridley beckoned to him with a half-eaten sandwich. "So, is it true that you can't remember what happened, lad?" he asked. "The fall, and all that?"

"That's right," Court replied. "I got nothing from when I was down bottom with McKenna to when I woke up in the hospital. But everyone seems to think it was bad."

"It *was* bad," Ridley said. "They were saying you might not ever walk again. Hell, they thought you might die."

"Well, I didn't die." Court maneuvered his way over to the engineer. "And here I am walking, but damned if I don't still feel useless."

"Useless?" Ridley laughed. "Lad, you're the most important part of this job—after the skipper, of course. You just have to learn patience."

He dug out another sandwich. Held it out to Court. "Here, eat up and get comfortable," he said. "You'll be back at it soon enough."

OKURA STARED OUT THROUGH A PORTHOLE, envious, as the two salvage men ate their meal on the *Lion*'s weather deck. Sandwiches, simple, but to Okura's hungry eyes, a feast: thick pieces of bread, healthy cuts of meat. Tomatoes and lettuce and plenty of cheese, all of it fresh—or fresher, anyway, than the slim choices that remained in the *Lion*'s stinking, noxious galley.

Okura had been eating canned food for days, cold tins of beans, soup stock, preserved fruit. He'd polished off the ship's store of chocolate and candy, a case of Coca-Cola for good measure. He wouldn't starve on this vessel, no matter how long the salvage crew took to do their work. But that didn't mean he couldn't long for a nice steak, some fresh fish, a glass of cold beer or a bottle of wine—or even a decent sandwich, for god's sake.

The crew moved with less urgency, now that they'd brought the ship into the lee. They weren't quite relaxed, but the worry that had defined them wasn't etched so firmly on their faces. Okura supposed he should be happy; the crew seemed to believe they could save the *Lion*. He wished they would hurry up and get started.

Someone was looking at him. Okura scanned the deck, and locked eyes for an instant with one of the men—the younger one, the one who'd been injured—no more than twenty feet away. Okura flinched, and drew back, down into the stateroom, his hair on end, his heart racing. Dropped as stealthily as he could down the skewed stateroom floor, slipped out into the bowels of the ship.

ON THE WEATHER DECK, Court Harrington frowned. "Hey, you see that?"

Ridley followed his eyes to the porthole. It belonged to a stateroom that stuck out a few feet onto the weather deck, the window looking aft, down the deck toward them.

"I didn't see anything," Ridley replied. "Did *you* see something?"

Court pushed himself to his feet, limped his way down the deck to the porthole, and peered inside. The glass was filthy, stained, almost useless, and the stateroom beyond was dark. Nothing moved inside.

"Thought I saw something in there," he told Ridley without lifting his eyes from the porthole. "Some*one*."

"Could be Matt or Stacey coming back. The skipper, maybe." Ridley paused. "Mind you, they did pull a body out of the cargo hold earlier. And I won't say there haven't been times on this ship I've felt like I'm being watched."

Harrington pressed his face to the porthole. Tried to replay the image in his mind. Whatever he'd seen, it hadn't been for long; just a shift of the light, a suggestion of movement, and then stillness again.

Still—for the briefest of moments, he could have sworn he'd seen a face.

"I'll be right back," he told Ridley, pushing off from the wall. "I'm probably crazy, but I won't sleep tonight if I don't check this out."

Ridley looked at him. "You're going in?"

"Sure. McKenna isn't back yet. We have nothing to do but wait." He grinned. "Why not go hunt us a ghost?"

63

Okura hunched behind a bulkhead and listened to the voices reverberate down the hallway. Men's voices, at least two of them, inside the ship.

They *had* seen him. Not good. Not good at all.

He'd left the briefcase in the stateroom where he spent his nights. It was hidden, tucked under the tilt of a now useless bed, but its absence still made Okura's mind race.

The salvage men could find it. They would take the money. *His* money. He couldn't let it happen.

Okura slipped the pistol from his waistband. Listened to the men's voices, the sounds of their feet on the deck, on the walls, as they descended farther into the *Lion*.

COURT STRUGGLED AHEAD of Ridley down the narrow hallway and wondered why he suddenly felt so ill at ease.

The freighter's accommodations deck, after all, wasn't nearly as foreboding as the very bowels of the ship, the dark corridors beneath the cargo decks, the vast inky abyss of the holds. This hallway was relatively well lit; the air was fresher, and the ocean where it was supposed to be—belowdecks.

But this was a ghost ship. A man had died here. And Harrington was sure he'd just seen a face.

What the hell are you doing here, man?

The men reached the midpoint of the ship, the long central corridor interrupted by watertight bulkhead doors. This corridor was darker, the air still, the sounds from above muted in the stillness.

Court gestured left, toward the stern of the ship. "First stateroom on the left," he said, whispering now. "That's where I saw him."

He let go of his rope and stepped into the central corridor, felt his broken ribs protest, the pain inescapable no matter how tight they had bound his chest. Behind him, Ridley followed, neither man speaking, hardly daring to breathe. Court could feel his heart thudding behind those busted ribs, wondered what he would do if there actually *was* someone else aboard the freighter.

Wet your pants, probably. And scream like a girl.

Then Court thought about McKenna, decided that wasn't a very good analogy. The skipper of the *Gale Force* would probably handle a stowaway—or even a ghost—with a little more aplomb.

The men reached the stateroom door. It opened inward on the wall above their heads, a beam of dusty light falling onto the forward wall. Court reached up, took hold of the doorframe, and tried to pull himself up, couldn't do it. Not without crying, anyway.

He eased back, wincing, forced a smile at Ridley. "Maybe you'd better."

Ridley nodded. Pulled himself through the doorframe with a grunt. Court watched the engineer's feet dangle as he surveyed the room. Waited, tensed, for some confrontation.

But nothing happened. "Nothing in here," Ridley called down, and then he dropped back onto the corridor's portside wall, kept his balance. "Just another empty stateroom."

"Huh," Court said. "Guess I was wrong."

He looked farther down the corridor, unwilling to believe that his eyes had deceived him. About ten feet down, on the portside of the ship, another door hung open. Harrington maneuvered down the corridor, leaning on the skewed deck and walls to support himself. Stopped above the open doorway and bent over, best as he could, to peer inside.

"Ridley," he said, his heart racing even faster. "Come have a look at this."

The stateroom looked lived in. As in, *after* the wreck. There was a pile of bedding in the corner, a stack of empty Coke cans, some candy bar wrappers.

"This is a nest," Court told Ridley. "Someone's been in here."

"Could have been that dead guy," Ridley replied. "Or Christer Magnusson's crew."

Court considered this. His whole body was tired, his mind, too. His chest ached, his head was kind of swimming, and all he really wanted was to crawl into his bunk.

But still.

"Maybe," he said. "But then, who'd I see staring out at me just now?" He struggled to stand. "Come on. McKenna's not back yet. We can keep looking."

. . .

THEY WERE COMING CLOSER.

The men had discovered his sleeping space. Now their curiosity was inflamed. They would know they'd seen a man in that stateroom, and they would want to find him.

They would send him back to Japan. The yakuza would likely kill him. And the salvage crew would find the stolen bonds, earn a nice bonus on top of the salvage award.

Fifty million dollars. Your money.

Okura backed down the corridor, his mind working supersonic. If he were forced to shoot the men, the noise would alert their friends. The Coast Guard would be called. They would bring guns of their own.

Damn it.

But he didn't have a choice. If the men found him, he would have to shoot them, and hope the noise of the shots died in the still air within the ship. Then he would retrieve the briefcase, and . . .

And what?

Okura couldn't afford to waste time on that question, not now. The men were still approaching. He thumbed off the pistol's safety. Retreated from the bulkhead, searching the darkness for any sign of the men.

64

The galley stank.

Something was rotting. Scratch that: *everything* was rotting. The *Pacific Lion* had been adrift for weeks now, and just about everything in the kitchen had spoiled. Court pulled his shirt over his nose and mouth, tried not to breathe as he limped into the mess, their headlamps cutting swaths through the dim.

"If there's somebody on board this ship, lad," the engineer said, coughing, "I really doubt he's hanging around here."

Court glanced back at him. "I mean, the guy's gotta eat, right?" he said. "Unless he really *is* a ghost."

They'd peered into every stateroom off the main corridor, looking for more signs of a stowaway. Found nothing. But Court remained unconvinced.

"Come on," he told Ridley. "Better than freezing our asses off on that deck up there, anyway."

Ridley looked like he'd beg to differ, if he hadn't been focused on trying not to throw up. The wreck of the *Lion* had wreaked havoc on the galley; there was food spilled everywhere, pots and pans on the floor, unidentifiable liquids pooled at the confluence of deck and wall. The scene was of chaos at an impossible angle. The smell only compounded the disorientation.

Court poked through a pile of empty cans, a half-eaten chocolate cake that had smeared on the floor and congealed into something else entirely. Made his way to the dry-goods locker and peered inside.

"Not much in here at all," he called back to Ridley. "I guess they were due for a shopping trip when they reached America."

There was something wrong here. Court was sure he was missing something, but he couldn't figure out what it was.

"Guess he's not here, whoever he is," Ridley said.

Court started to agree. Then he noticed the freezer, a walk-in, sliding door open a couple of inches. "Unless . . ."

"Oh no," Ridley groaned. "Lad, nobody in their right mind would be hiding in there."

"Only take a second to check," Court replied, climbing across the galley toward the freezer. "Set our minds at ease, right? Why not?"

HIROKI OKURA waited in the back of the freezer, wedged between a wall of spoiled ice cream and a couple of slabs of beef gone very, very ripe. The smell was appalling, unbearable, and Okura felt he might die if he didn't breathe fresh air soon.

But he had more pressing concerns than air quality. He could hear the men outside in the galley, hear the clatter as they pushed through the debris toward the freezer door. They were coming.

They would find him.

He wedged himself against the ice cream. Raised the pistol and aimed it at the freezer door. Wondered how it would feel to shoot someone, wondered how he'd allowed himself to get to this place.

He waited.

. . .

COURT HAD JUST REACHED the freezer door when something moved in the corridor outside. Both men stiffened, spun to the doorway, expecting to see the stowaway or, barring that, the ghost.

Instead, they saw Stacey Jonas, braced against the portside wall and looking in at them, quizzical.

"What the heck are you guys doing?" she asked. "The Coast Guard chopper's topside. Everyone's waiting on you two."

Ridley shrugged, turned to Court, who'd paused, his hand on the freezer door.

"We thought we saw something in one of the staterooms," Court told her. "Thought we should investigate."

Stacey raised an eyebrow. "And?"

"And, I guess," Court said, "I guess we found a nest?"

"What, like a bird?"

"A *person*," Ridley said. "A bundle of bedding wedged against the wall. Someone was sleeping there, *after* the wreck."

"Probably that sailor who came back with Magnusson," Stacey said, shrugging. "He was on here for a few days, remember?"

"Right," Court said. "But then he died."

Stacey waited for the punch line.

"I swear, I saw a face in that stateroom," Court continued. "Just now, while we were waiting. And then we find that nest? Can't be a coincidence."

Stacey shifted her weight. "It's probably your mind playing tricks on you, Court," she said. "You had a concussion, for Pete's sake."

"Stacey—"

"Anyway, the Coast Guard's burning fuel waiting on you two," Stacey said. "And the skipper is already pissed."

"Roger," Court said, turning back to the freezer. "Just let me check—"

"*Court.*" Stacey's voice was sharp, and it stopped Court cold. "Did you hear me? I said McKenna is pissed. It's time to go."

Court paused, torn. Hand on the door.

"If there's anything in that locker, it's long dead by now," Stacey said. "Just like your ass will be, if you don't bring it topside."

Court sighed. "Damn it," he said, sighing. "I know what I saw."

But he let go of the freezer door. Turned away. And struggled to follow Stacey and Ridley back down through the galley toward the door.

65

Okura waited until he could no longer hear the voices of the men outside. Then he waited longer, until he couldn't breathe the rank air in the locker for one minute longer. He crawled to the door, listened a moment, and slid the door open to the galley beyond.

Relief. Even the stale galley air was fresh, compared to what he'd been breathing. And nothing moved amid the mess of spilled food and kitchen equipment. The galley was dark. The men were gone.

Okura loosened his grip on his pistol. His fingers ached, he'd been holding the weapon so tight.

He navigated the hazards that littered the galley. Made the bulk-head door and pulled himself up to the long central corridor. Crept down to the stateroom where he'd made his nest. Dropped in, and felt under the bed for the briefcase.

It was there. The men hadn't taken his money.

The crew was gone. They hadn't discovered him, and they'd left the briefcase. But Okura knew he would have to be careful while he waited for the salvage team to finish their job. They would be wary now.

66

"You disobeyed a direct order," McKenna said, pacing the wheel-house. "You did *exactly* what I told you not to do, Court, and you put yourself, and this job, back in jeopardy."

Six hours since the Coast Guard's Dolphin helicopter had re-turned her and the crew of the *Gale Force* to the tug, and McKenna was still steaming mad. Could hardly look at Harrington, who sat at the chart table, his laptop in front of him and the ship's cat on his lap.

The rest of the crew was downstairs, in the galley. Jason Parent had cooked up a delicious salmon steak dinner with roast potatoes and a passable, if slightly limp salad, and McKenna had eaten with the rest of the crew, though she'd barely tasted a bite.

"I know what I saw, McKenna," Harrington said. He wouldn't look at her. "Someone made a nest on that ship."

"I don't give a damn if you saw my dad himself in that stateroom,

Court," McKenna replied. "I told you to stay topside and keep out of trouble. And you went exploring instead."

Court said nothing. Stared down at Spike like he was hoping the cat would bail him out of this jam. But the cat only purred, apparently unbothered by the fight.

Traitor, McKenna thought.

"You're confined to the tug," she told the architect. "I can't trust you on that ship anymore. You can radio your instructions from here, but you're not setting foot on that wreck again. Are we clear?"

Harrington didn't answer right away. He looked up slowly, looked straight at McKenna. And then he *laughed.*

The bastard *laughed* at her.

"You can't be serious," he said. "McKenna—"

"*Captain Rhodes,*" she replied.

"*Captain Rhodes,*" Harrington said. "Whatever. You need me on that ship if you want me to save it. You can't just confine me somewhere."

"I can and I will," McKenna replied. "In case you forgot, this is my goddamn tug." She glared at him. "And you're going to respect that, or I'll ship your ass back to Dutch Harbor."

"And do what? Sink that ship over there just to prove a point?"

She wanted to strangle him. "If I have to, I will," she said slowly. "I'm not going to fight you, Court. This is my boat. You work for me. You're going to remember that, or you're not going to last."

Harrington said nothing. He looked at her, and he wasn't smiling anymore, and for a long moment, neither of them said anything.

Then Harrington shifted. "This is about your dad, isn't it?" he said. "This is you trying to make up for what you think you did." He blew out a breath. "That's what it is, isn't it? You—"

McKenna shook her head, cut him off. "This conversation is over," she said, starting for the wheelhouse stairs. "You have your numbers. Make me a model. I want to start pumping tomorrow."

She hurried out of the wheelhouse before he could reply. Fairly *ran* to her stateroom, closed the door tight, leaned against it, and felt her eyes brim with tears, and freaking hated herself for it.

That cocky bastard, she thought. *I never should have hired him on for this job.*

But she couldn't raise the *Lion* without him, she knew, and Harrington knew it, too. And that was the part that pissed her off the most.

67

UNALASKA AIRPORT, DUTCH HARBOR

The four Japanese men stepped from the little plane and onto the tarmac. They paused briefly to breathe in the cool air, to survey the town and the mountains and the water. Then they walked into the terminal and out to the parking lot, where a couple of taxis stood idling beside a handful of private cars. A young woman stood waiting beside an American SUV. She held a sign that read GRAND ALEUTIAN HOTEL, and she straightened as the four men approached.

"Need a room?"

Three of the four men looked at the fourth, the young, slim man named Sato. "Yes," Sato said. "We will need two rooms, if possible."

The woman looked back at the terminal, the rest of the flight walking out with family members, friends, heading to well-worn pickup trucks. "Looks like I'll have plenty of space," she said. "Jump in."

The men stowed their gear in the trunk, and climbed into the SUV as the young woman fired up the engine. Three men sat in the back of the truck. Sato sat in the front.

"What are you in town for?" the woman asked him as she pulled out of the lot. "Business, or pleasure?"

"Business," Sato replied.

"Something to do with that ship that wrecked?"

Sato shook his head. "Fishing," he said. "We represent a major investor."

"Aha," the woman said. "Well, you're in the right place for that."

THE DRIVE TO THE GRAND ALEUTIAN took all of five minutes. The woman—her name was Hannah, she'd told Sato—parked the SUV and opened the trunk.

"The shipwreck you mentioned," Sato said as he followed Hannah into the lobby. "Did they save the crew?"

"The crew? Sure, no casualties." Hannah paused. "Wait, I lied. One of those guys went AWOL, ditched the rest of his guys and went back to the ship on Bill Carew's boat. What I heard, he was looking for something, but he shouldn't have bothered. They brought him back to Dutch in a body bag."

"How very sad."

"You said it. Just goes to show." Hannah shrugged. "There's nothing in this world so important it's worth dying over, right?"

She led Sato to the check-in desk, took his credit card. "How long are you staying with us?"

"We're not sure," Sato replied. "It depends how quickly we meet our objective."

Hannah nodded. "Well, we're nowhere near capacity," she said. "I'm sure it won't be a problem if you need to stick around for a while."

68

Harrington worked on the models through the night. He made coffee in the galley as the light disappeared outside the tug. Brought it up to the wheelhouse and sat with Spike at the chart table and stared at the computer and tried to conjure a way to guarantee the *Pacific Lion's* survival.

Tried to chase the fight with McKenna—*Captain Rhodes*—from his mind.

The night passed quickly. It was only six hours long at this latitude, anyway. At dawn, Nelson Ridley came up into the wheelhouse. "We didn't give your bunk away, lad," he said. "You're allowed to take a nap."

Harrington rubbed his eyes. "No rest for the wicked. I'm kind of stuck here at the moment."

Ridley walked to the wheel. Checked the instrument panel, the GPS screen. "You must be beat," he said. "No sense working all night."

"This stuff has to get done, one way or the other. The captain led me to believe she wanted to get the pumps going right away."

"Sure," Ridley said, shrugging, "but you're still allowed a couple hours' shut-eye. Hell, take all day, if you need it. After what you've been through, you've got to take care of yourself."

Harrington laughed. "*You* want to tell her that?" he said. "We're kind of on the outs at the moment."

"Who, McKenna?"

"I think she prefers *Captain Rhodes*."

Ridley frowned. "Oh," he said, and he studied Harrington, his brow furrowed. "It was my fault, what happened yesterday, lad," he said. "I shouldn't have let you into the ship."

"No, that's on me," Harrington replied. "I dragged you into it, but it was my call. Anyway, I think it goes deeper than that. She doesn't think I respect her, or something."

"Do you?"

Harrington looked up, surprised at the engineer's bluntness. "I mean, yeah, of course. Of course I respect her. Why wouldn't I?"

Ridley rubbed his chin. "But is she the captain of this vessel, lad? Or is she still your old flame?"

"Can't she be both?" Harrington replied.

Ridley looked at him. Clucked sympathetically. He disappeared down the stairs, and reappeared a moment later, carrying a fresh mug of coffee.

"You think on it," he said, setting the coffee down for Harrington. "And don't kill yourself with this computer work. It's only a job, after all."

"Yeah," Harrington said. "But what a job it is."

HE WOKE UP GROGGY a few hours later. Lifted his head from the chart table, wiped the drool from his cheek. Downstairs, in the galley, someone else was awake, bashing pots and pans, making breakfast. His computer was dark, fast asleep; the cat, too. Harrington thought of his bunk longingly. Then he shook his head clear.

He sat up, rubbed his eyes, switched the computer back to life. His 3-D model of the *Pacific Lion* glared out at him, every fluid level rendered in exact detail. Harrington studied the screen for a moment. Then he stood, stretched, and limped down the stairway to rouse Captain Rhodes.

"I THINK THE SIMPLEST way is the best way," Harrington told McKenna. "The portside ballast tanks are full, and the starboard tanks are empty. If we can ballast the tanks, the ship should regain equilibrium."

They'd returned to the wheelhouse. The captain sat beside Harrington at the chart table, Harrington's laptop open in front of them. They hadn't talked about last night yet, but Harrington knew they would have to.

He needed to be on board that ship.

McKenna looked at the model. "What about the rest of the fluids? Fuel and fresh water, et cetera. Don't they factor into your thinking?"

"They do," Harrington said, "but every tank but the ballast is already balanced for ocean sailing. The more we mess around with ancillary fluids, the greater the risk we destabilize the ship even further."

"And those models?" McKenna said. "Still no way you can really predict what the ship is going to do?"

"Not one hundred percent. But eighty percent, definitely."

McKenna looked at the computer again. Looked at Harrington, at Spike. "Pocket aces, huh?"

"Best we can do." Harrington paused. "There's one more thing," he said. "I know you're mad about yesterday, and I'm sorry. But I really need to be on board the *Lion* if we're going to make this work."

McKenna shook her head. "I can't trust someone who doesn't respect the chain of command, Court."

"Look." Harrington sighed. "It's not about respect."

"No?" Her eyes flashed. "You would have disobeyed my dad just the same?"

"I don't know. Probably not. But your dad was your dad, and you're—"

"One of your old hookups."

"My *friend*." He looked at her. "I thought we were friends, McKenna— *Captain Rhodes*, sorry. This whole *chain of command* thing is hard to get used to, okay?"

McKenna didn't answer. She stood, and walked to the front of the wheelhouse, looked out through the windows toward the hulk of the *Lion*. Harrington waited.

"This is a thirty-million-dollar job," the captain said finally. She hadn't turned away from the windows. "This isn't about friends, or old hookups, or anything else. You almost died on that ship, Court. The last time this tug ran an operation this big, my dad drowned. If we don't have rules—if we don't have trust, and respect—then we're putting our lives at risk just being here."

"I'm sorry," Harrington said. "You're right."

She turned from the window. Met his eyes. "You do what you

need to do to get that ship raised. If that means you're on board, then so be it. But don't spit in my face and call me your friend, Court. I give an order, you damn well follow it."

He nodded.

"I beg your pardon?"

"Yeah," he said. Cleared his throat. "I mean, aye-aye, Captain Rhodes."

69

They left Al Parent on the *Gale Force* to tend to the tug—and, via sat phone, to his insomniac grandson. The rest of the crew flew to the *Lion* in the *Munro*'s Dolphin, the last of their portable pneumatic pumps hanging from the helicopter's hoist.

McKenna watched the *Gale Force* shrink beneath the helicopter, and tried to work through her strategy. More accurately, she tried to figure out how to implement Court Harrington's strategy while risking the least number of her crew.

"We'll work in teams," she told the others. "Matt and Stacey, you guys take Ridley to the bow. Get one pump in position, then move your old pump from the cargo deck down to deck one as well. I'll take Jason aft. Court, you're topside."

Everyone nodded. "Sounds good," Matt said.

"Those pumps are heavy. A hundred pounds apiece. We're going to need all of them, so take your time. Don't try to be a hero, just get the job done."

"Speak for yourself, skipper," Ridley said, grinning. "You know you're the only hero we've got."

McKenna shook her head. "No heroes today. Strictly professional. Let's get it done."

HARRINGTON'S PLAN INVOLVED pumping seawater from the *Lion*'s portside tanks to the starboard tanks, until the ship was properly balanced, then taking stock of the list and adjusting as necessary. It meant McKenna and her team would have to lug four one-hundred-pound pneumatic pumps to the lowest reaches of the ship—the labyrinth on deck one—and run pumps and hoses across the width of the bottom deck.

The portside tanks were full, and fully pressurized, and any mistake could send that ballast water flooding into deck one, drowning whoever was down there within minutes. There were four pumps. Four opportunities for failure.

McKenna and Jason Parent wrestled the first pump through the after stairway and down the narrow access hatch to the first deck. Hustled back up to help Harrington lower the heavy hoses down behind.

The pump was heavy, a beast to maneuver in the ship's narrow confines. McKenna and Jason sweated and swore, muscling the pump through the access hatch and easing it, slowly, down to the lowest deck.

"Cripes," Jason said, wiping sweat from his brow. "You're kind of a badass, skipper."

"You and me both," McKenna replied. "This is teamwork."

They wrestled the first pump into position, just ahead of the engine room on deck one. Then they climbed again, up to the fourth deck, where McKenna descended among the Nissans to where the second pump waited, left over from the crew's initial efforts to pump out the hold. The skipper untied the pump and fastened a line to it, guided the machine up between the long row of vehicles as Jason hefted it back up to the stairs.

Then they maneuvered the pump through the access hatch to the first deck again, hauled it through the maze to the stern ballast tanks. They tied down the pump and ran hoses in both directions, up to the starboard tank, and down to the portside. McKenna connected the hose to the starboard tank's emergency valve.

"I'm going to wait until the rest of the pumps are hooked up to do the portside," she told Jason. "Don't want to get this party started too early."

Jason looked at her, then past her, down the long corridor to the portside tank. He shivered. "Yeah," he said. "I'd say that's a good idea."

THE CLIMB TOPSIDE was as long and arduous as ever. The rest of the crew was waiting there. "What took you so long, skipper?" Ridley asked. "You take the lad on a tour?"

McKenna wiped the sweat from her face. "Just lazy, I guess. You guys been here a while?"

"He's just messing with you," Stacey said. "We just got here. All the pumps in position."

"Perfect," McKenna said. "Okay, we need four people down below to watch the pumps. I'll take one. Ridley, Matt and Jason, you guys take the others."

Stacey and Court swapped glances. "What about us?"

"Stay up here. Get ready to relay information down to us, if necessary." She looked at Stacey. "I don't want you and Matt down there at the same time. If something goes wrong—"

"If something goes wrong, I don't want to be left alone on this earth without my husband," Stacey finished. "I appreciate the sentiment, skipper, but this is your operation. We could use you and Court topside to coordinate."

McKenna thought about it. "Damn it, fine. But be careful, all of you. Find somewhere safe to camp out, somewhere you can get out quick if something goes wrong, understand?"

"Got it," Stacey said.

"Aye-aye," said Matt.

McKenna looked at Jason Parent. The kid looked nervous, a little, but he wasn't about to admit it.

A married couple and a new dad, McKenna thought. *You could be sending them to their deaths.*

She shook the thought away. "You good?" she asked Jason.

Jason stood straighter. "I'm good."

"Okay. Synchronize your watches. I'll give you an hour to get down to your stations and in position. Sixty minutes from now, we start pumping. Good luck."

She watched her crew disperse, Matt and Stacey toward the after two access points, Jason and Ridley toward the bow. Court Harrington stood beside her. He was watching, too.

"This going to work?" McKenna asked him.

Harrington set his jaw. "Yeah," he said. "Yes, damn it, it will."

70

Matt Jonas found the pump ahead of the engine room on deck one. He checked that the hose was connected to the starboard tank's emergency valve, then rappelled down the corridor to the portside valve.

He checked his watch. Ten minutes to zero hour. Matt picked up the loose end of the hose, fastened it to the portside tank's emergency valve.

A noise, behind him. Footsteps, labored, someone navigating the tricky path through the corridor. Matt turned, saw a headlamp at the top of the hall, the starboard side, peering down at him.

"It's McKenna." The skipper's voice echoed through the empty ship, an eerie, ghostly sound. "Just making sure you're all set."

"Doing fine," Matt told her. "Just about to open the portside valve, start pumping this thing up."

The skipper hesitated. "Right," she said finally. "Okay, cool."

"This thing going to work?" Matt called up to her.

"I hope so," she replied. "I think so." Then, quickly, "I mean, the whiz kid says it's pocket aces, best shot we have."

"Pocket aces, you said?"

"That's right."

Matt looked around the corridor. "Those are good odds. Eighty percent, right? Best starting hand in poker."

"Yeah," the skipper replied, "but did he tell you how he busted out of the World Series?"

Matt shone his light up toward her. He could see the skipper in the distance, a hundred feet up, peering down at him.

"None of us would be here if we didn't like to gamble, right?" Matt said. "Aces get cracked now and then, but hell, that's just variance. You sure as heck wouldn't fold them."

"Dad was always a gambler," McKenna said. "Guess I'm going to find out if I've got that itch, too."

Matt smiled. "You wouldn't be here if you didn't." He checked his watch and looked up at her. "I'm about due to open this valve up, skipper."

"Roger that. I'd better check on the others." A pause. "Be careful."

"Always." Matt listened to the skipper's footsteps until they were nothing but echoes. Then he checked his watch again. Time to gamble. He hesitated a moment, thought about Stacey and the rest of the crew.

Variance, he thought. Then he opened the valve, tensed as the hose filled, muttered a silent prayer, and waited.

71

McKenna made her way forward through the bowels of the ship. Checked in on Ridley, could barely hear the engineer's answer over the roar of the pumps.

"She's looking fine, skipper," he reported. *"No leaks, no mess. We're in business."*

"Keep it that way," McKenna told him. Then she crawled along the starboard side of deck one to the bow, where Jason Parent was babysitting his own pump, the bright orange hose filled with water and pumping steadily into the starboard tank.

"You okay?" McKenna shouted down to him.

Jason flashed her a thumbs-up. *"All good down here."*

McKenna returned the thumb. *"Keep it going."* Then she found the kid's access hatch, climbed up and through to deck four, and up the stairway to the outside world again.

She couldn't feel a thing as she stood on the *Lion*'s accommodations house. The list remained constant, about fifty-five degrees. It hadn't begun to ease yet, but the ship wasn't sinking, either.

That was probably a good sign.

She radioed back to the *Munro*, reported her crew's status. Then, as an afterthought, "You guys still have that helicopter handy?"

"That's affirmative, Captain," the radio operator replied. "The Dolphin is standing by."

"It might be nice," McKenna told him, "if they could stand by a little closer while we're pumping. Can you get them in the air above us?"

"I'll dispatch them now. Get you some eyes in the sky, huh?"

And some quick response if this all goes sideways, McKenna thought. *No pun intended.* She thanked the operator and signed off. Gazed down the deck and found where Court Harrington had set up shop by an access hatch, a couple of hundred feet astern.

She picked up the radio again. "I noticed we haven't sunk yet, Court."

A pause. McKenna watched Harrington pick up the radio. "Say again?"

"I said we aren't sinking," McKenna said, feeling dumb. "Just a joke. But it's a good sign, right?"

"Oh." Harrington laughed a little. "Yeah. Not yet."

"Small victories, right?"

"Yes, ma'am."

"We keep an eye on things, take it slow, we might just make it out of here. You doing okay over there?"

Harrington laughed again, more this time. "Just hoping our aces hold out."

"You and me both," McKenna said. She straightened. "Okay, back to work. I'm going to go check on those pumps."

"Roger that," Harrington replied. "I'll be here."

HARRINGTON COULD FEEL THE DIFFERENCE, within a couple of hours. It was getting harder and harder to sit on the *Lion*'s accommodations house.

Fifty degrees, maybe less, he thought, trying to find a place to set down his laptop. The closer the ship came to a forty-five-degree angle, the tougher it would be for the crew to maneuver. Harrington grabbed a handhold, a ladder up to the ship's massive exhaust funnel. Hoped that the pumps would hold out and push the ship into a more comfortable position quickly.

McKenna Rhodes appeared, down the deck. She climbed out of an access hatch, stepped out onto the wall of the accommodations house, and slipped and nearly fell. Settled for sitting down awkwardly. Harrington picked up the radio.

"At least we're making progress," he said. "Even if it does suddenly feel like we're drunk."

The captain picked up her own radio. "I was hoping you weren't watching," she said, laughing. "I feel like Bambi on ice over here."

"It shouldn't last. And we're moving in the right direction. A few hours, we'll have enough water in the bow and stern tanks. We can kill those pumps and put all of our focus amidships."

"We can't just keep them all running?" McKenna replied. "Fill the tanks up faster, and keep this thing moving?"

"We'd get more control if we're only filling two tanks. Plus, you can use the extra crew to relay messages from up here."

McKenna picked up her radio again, but didn't reply. Harrington could tell she was thinking it through.

"Yeah," she said finally. "Okay."

"You're running this operation, though. We'll probably be fine with four pumps. It's your call."

"No," the captain said. "I don't know a damn thing about how to right this ship. This is *your* call, Court. You tell me how you want to play it."

Harrington studied her down the long deck. Couldn't quite see the captain's eyes, but could tell they were fixed on him. He picked up his radio again.

"Two pumps," he said. "Just to be safe."

McKenna pushed herself to her feet. "I'll tell Ridley."

72

The young doctor gave Daishin Sato a pained expression. "I hate to tell you this, sir, but you took the wrong flight. They flew your brother's body to Anchorage already."

Sato let his eyes drop, tried to play the role he'd chosen: grieving brother, come to retrieve his sibling's remains. He'd found the doctor at work in the town of Dutch Harbor's small medical center, tending to a Aleut girl with a broken arm. Assumed a pitiful countenance and asked for information.

Both the smuggler Tomio Ishimaru and the sailor Hiroki Okura were still missing. One of the men was dead. Sato wanted to know which.

"Anchorage," he repeated. "Tell me, why did they move him? Are you not equipped to deal with the deceased at this hospital?"

"Most of the time, sure," the doctor said. "But if the death is suspicious—"

"Suspicious? I was told he died alone on his ship."

The doctor winced again. "I'm sorry. Someone should have really gone over this with you. There were some questions that arose when I looked at the body. The cause of death wasn't maybe as clear as we thought. So I sent the body to the state medical examiner in Anchorage, standard procedure. They'd be able to give you more information."

He began to turn away. "I'm really sorry. This is— I don't know why someone didn't tell you this stuff already."

"Wait." Sato took hold of the doctor's arm. With his free hand, he retrieved a photograph from his pocket, Hiroki Okura. "My brother— Tell me, this was him, yes?"

The doctor glanced back at the injured young girl, her mother behind her glaring at Sato. He sighed. "I'm sorry," he said again. "I really—" Then he looked down at the picture. "Wait a minute."

"Yes?"

The doctor took the picture. Studied it close, squinting. *"This* is your brother?"

"Hiroki Okura. My brother. This is the dead man, correct?"

"I don't . . ." The doctor stared at the picture. "This isn't the body I saw," he said. "What the heck?"

"You're sure?"

"Pretty sure." The doctor still hadn't taken his eyes from the photo. He scratched his head. "The body— His eyes were set closer. And his mouth, it was different. It was—" He shook his head. "This wasn't the guy."

Sato took the picture back. "Thank you," he said. "That is excellent news."

He turned away from the doctor, walked out of the hospital. Heard the doctor call something after him, but didn't look back.

73

The *Lion*'s progress slowed with only two pumps online, but Harrington's plan was working. By nightfall, the big freighter's list was reduced to forty-five degrees.

McKenna radioed back to Al Parent on the *Gale Force*, asked him to make up a care package of sandwiches, fresh coffee, and sleeping bags to send over via the Coast Guard's Dolphin. Asked him how little Ben was doing, got a laugh in response.

"He likes 'Twinkle Twinkle Little Star,'" Al said. "Knocks him right out. 'Ramblin' Man,' not so much."

"Maybe stick to the classics?" McKenna replied.

"'Ramblin' Man' *is* a classic, boss. Soon as we get home, I'm playing that baby Waylon's entire back catalog."

The helicopter arrived as the last light of day faded away. Its bright spotlight lit up the *Lion*'s deck, found McKenna and Court Harrington in the center of it, and the flight mechanic lowered his shopping basket with Al Parent's provisions inside.

Harrington helped McKenna unload the cargo. Then the architect bent down, wincing, to gather up a couple of the sleeping bags, and began to parcel out the sandwiches and coffee. "I'll take these back to Matt and Stacey," he told McKenna. "Get them settled in."

McKenna shook her head. "I'll do it."

"You have Ridley and Jason to take care of," Harrington replied. "I'm not going to go AWOL on you, I promise. Just trying to help."

"You're still recovering," McKenna said. "I'm not sending you down thirteen decks. I'll do both." She gestured to the flight basket, which she was still holding steady. "Get in."

"What?"

"Go on back to the tug. We can handle things overnight. Get some sleep, have a hot meal. We'll see you back here in the morning."

Harrington frowned. "Are you serious?"

"This isn't me trying to power-trip," McKenna said. "But you've been working nonstop for a good couple of days. If anything goes wrong, we'll call you."

The helicopter's engine roared overhead.

"If I wasn't so tired, I'd fight you harder on this," Harrington muttered, climbing into the basket.

McKenna smiled. "And I'd still be the captain. Get out of here."

She waved up to the helicopter, watched as the flight mechanic began to winch Harrington skyward. Watched the architect climb aboard, watched the lights of the helicopter as it disappeared behind the *Lion*, stood there until she couldn't see anything anymore.

Then she picked up the sleeping bags and the food and headed aft to Matt and Stacey, to get them tucked in for the night.

FROM HIS HIDING SPACE in the infirmary, Okura could tell the list was easing. It had happened slowly, imperceptible, but now, as the hours passed and the *Lion*'s walls became walls again, Okura found he could stand on the deck nearly without support. The salvage crew was winning. They were righting the ship.

And that meant they would soon be towing it back to civilization. As long as he kept hidden until then, he could find his way off—steal a lifeboat, maybe, or wait until the ship was tied to a dock—and use his passport and the stolen bonds and the thirty thousand in cash from the ship's safe to disappear into America and start a new life.

He'd moved to the infirmary, near the rear of the crew accommodations deck. Brought the briefcase, too; stashed it in a medicine locker. He had food—stale, but edible—and enough bottled water to survive another week, at least. And he had the pistol.

Okura checked the weapon. Hoped, again, that he wouldn't have to use it, but he knew he'd have no choice if the salvage team found him.

So be it.

McKENNA DIDN'T SLEEP MUCH.

She carried supplies down to Matt and Stacey at the stern of the ship. They'd set up a nest on deck one, at the base of the closest access hatchway to their pump. McKenna handed out the sleeping bags, the sandwiches and the coffee, a paperback adventure novel to help them pass the time.

Stacey looked at the book's cover, all gunfights and swarthy heroes and scantily clad women. She made a face. "I mean, really? You expect me to read this?"

McKenna grinned. "Al sent it over. Could be from his private collection."

"Great." Stacey tossed it in the corner with the sleeping bags. "Desperate times, huh?"

"Stay safe," McKenna said, heading back for the climbing rope and the surface. "I'll be topside if you need me."

She climbed back to the weather deck and carried the rest of the provisions down to Nelson Ridley and Jason Parent at the forward pump.

Ridley looked through the sandwich bag. "Couldn't find us a cigar?"

"We pump out this ship, I'll fly you to Cuba," McKenna told him. "In the meantime, you'll have to make do with roast beef."

Ridley spread out the sleeping bag. Unpacked a sandwich. "Get some shut-eye, lad," he told Jason. "I'll take the first watch."

McKenna and Ridley waited until Jason had made himself as comfortable as possible in the damp, dark corridor. They ate sandwiches by the light of their headlamps, drank coffee.

"Seems like it's working," Ridley said, gesturing at their confines. "We're getting there, boss. Little by little."

He was right, McKenna knew. The ship had passed the forty-five-degree point by now; the pumps were moving her in the right direction.

"I just hope we can stop the list when we need to," she said. "From what Harrington says, there's still a chance this thing could kill us all."

"Nah. The kid's got it licked, skipper. You wait and see."

"Mmm," McKenna said, unconvinced.

Ridley didn't say anything for a while. Then he shuffled a bit closer to her, lowered his voice. "You know, he's not such a bad guy, McKenna. He's a cocky bastard, to be sure, but he doesn't mean any harm."

"Whether he means it or not is irrelevant," she said, meeting his eyes. "He doesn't respect me, Nelson. And if he doesn't respect me, I can't trust him."

"I get it," Ridley said. "I do. It's just . . ." He paused. "There's a history between you two; there's no point pretending otherwise. You're never going to be merely captain and crew."

She set her jaw. "So, what? I should just let him walk all over me? I'm supposed to forgive insubordination because we hooked up a couple times?"

"No, skipper," Ridley said. "No, you're right about that. I'm just saying that this is hard for him, too. He's trying to find his place on that tug, same as you."

He finished his coffee and didn't say anything more, and Mc-Kenna couldn't read the expression on his face, his eyes dark and inscrutable.

"I'm going topside," she said, standing. "Make sure you get some rest."

74

By morning, the *Lion*'s list had dropped to thirty-eight degrees. McKenna climbed the ropes down to Ridley and Jason Parent, found the engineer asleep and Jason awake, flipping through some kind of cheesy romance novel.

"My dad packed it in," the deckhand said, shrugging. "I wish he'd chucked in a *Car and Driver* or something."

"Matt and Stacey got an adventure story," McKenna told him. "You give it here, I can see if they'll trade."

Jason looked at McKenna's outstretched hand, then back at the book. The kid was blushing a little. "It's just, I'm kind of invested by now. The characters, you know?"

McKenna laughed. "Suit yourself. Everything okay otherwise?"

"Perfect. Except Ridley snores like a diesel engine."

"Good to hear," McKenna said. "It'll keep you awake."

She made her way along deck one to Matt and Stacey's nest, made sure the Jonases and their pump were in working order.

"Everything's fine, but we're almost out of fuel," Stacey reported. "How's the rest of the crew?"

"Jason's feeling romantic, and Ridley's fast asleep," McKenna replied. "And Al's singing Waylon Jennings to Jason's little boy."

Matt laughed. "Don't let your babies grow up to be cowboys?"

"Surprisingly, no. But I bet if you requested it, he'd be glad to oblige."

"How are *you*, McKenna?" Stacey asked. "Did you get any sleep?"

"I'm fine," she said, set to brush off the question. Then she met Stacey's eyes. "Sent Court back to the tug for some bunk time last night, so that kind of eased the tension a little bit."

Matt and Stacey both nodded like they knew exactly what she was talking about. "He's still Court," Stacey said. "That's for sure."

"Still a genius," Matt agreed. "And still a little boy."

"And still my ex-boyfriend, or not even," McKenna said. "Ridley thinks I'm being extra hard on Court because I still hold a grudge."

The Jonases swapped looks. "I mean," Matt said. "I wasn't going to say anything, but—"

"You guys have some stuff to work through, is all," Stacey finished. Then she smiled brightly. "But who doesn't, right?"

"Sure," McKenna said. "I guess I was just hoping I wouldn't have to work through all this stuff with a hundred-million-dollar ship on the line." She shrugged. "Anyway, I'll get that fuel for you. Give me an hour or so."

She left Matt and Stacey to tend the pump. Climbed back up topside, where the sky was still gray but getting lighter, and the clouds still whipped around the bases of the volcanoes on Umnak Island, obscuring their peaks. It still looked like a hell of a gale on the south side of the island, and from what McKenna had picked up from the weather forecast, the storm wasn't set to die yet. Another couple of days of a real solid blow, at the very least. She looked up at the racing clouds and shivered, thankful they weren't still out in open water.

Around eight in the morning, the Coast Guard helicopter returned, bringing fuel for the pumps, and more food, and Court Harrington.

"Brought you a case of Red Bull, too," Harrington told her. "Figured you probably didn't get much sleep last night."

McKenna helped him unload the rescue basket. Thought about last night's conversation with Ridley, forced herself to meet the architect's eyes. "You'd be right about that," she said.

"We still okay, though? I mean, the ship's looking better."

"Everything's good," McKenna said. "No problems. Still pumping away. You okay?"

"Slept like a baby," Harrington said, grinning. "First time in my life that old bunk felt comfortable."

They got the basket unloaded, marshaled the supplies on the deck. "You know, you could head back to the tug for a little bit," Harrington said. "Get a little rest yourself. It's going to take another day or so for the ship to level out."

McKenna finally looked at him. A good night's sleep had done

Harrington well, put some color on his face; he looked refreshed and energized and ready to work. *And you look like you spent another sleepless night on a smelly old shipwreck.*

"I have these supplies to distribute," she told Harrington. "Pumps to refuel, food to pass out. Those guys down below could probably use some fresh air."

"They can help me haul down the food," Harrington said. "I feel good today. I can spell them down there. No need for you to do everything, skipper."

"We have a job to do," McKenna said, picking up a fuel canister. "I'll sleep when it's done."

Harrington cocked his head. "I swear, I'm not trying to give you back talk this time," he said. "But how can you keep working? Aren't you, like, exhausted?"

"I know you're not, and I am exhausted," McKenna said. She nodded to the case of energy drinks. "But that's what those are for."

75

McKenna took a walk as the ship leveled out beneath her. It was late afternoon, and the pumping operation continued to proceed as planned. Still, she wanted to inspect the ship, now that the deck was flat enough to walk: about twenty degrees of list remained, and steadily decreasing. The ship was upright enough now that she'd been able to hook up a generator to the emergency power. The *Lion* was still largely dark, but the crew had managed to get a few of the lights back on.

Anyway, there was something bothering her, though she was loathe to admit it. Both Harrington and Ridley had reported a nest in the accommodations house; stranger still, they'd both claimed they'd seen some kind of ghost.

McKenna didn't believe in ghosts. But a man *had* died on this ship, a man who'd apparently bailed on his crewmates to return here. She wanted to set her mind at ease, prove to herself that her architect and her engineer were mistaken.

Harrington was somewhere aft, working through some calculations on his laptop. McKenna checked in with Ridley and Jason, told the deckhand to be ready to head back to the *Gale Force* tonight.

"Spell your dad," she said. "Sleep in your own bunk. Call your son and sing him something more soothing than Al's outlaw country."

Jason nodded, his nose in that romance novel. "I just want to see if she gets the guy in the end."

"Kid's a born-again romantic," Ridley said. "Heart of gold."

He and McKenna laughed at the blush that spread over the deckhand's face. Then McKenna climbed back up to the deck—using the ladder and the stairs this time, instead of walking on the walls—and set out to survey the ship.

She walked up and down the starboard deck first, gazed out over the railing at the vast bay that spread out in front of her. The terrain up here was like some kind of painting: no trees on the shore, just rock and low lichen, electric-green. The bay itself was deep blue, almost black, rippled with wind and whitecaps. It was a lonely place, even with the Coast Guard cutter anchored nearby. The land was windswept and barren, the air bracing. The place was a moonscape, a frontier.

People aren't supposed to be here, she thought. *Not places like this. But here we are, anyway.*

The thought made her feel uneasy, and the uneasiness made her feel stupid, but there you had it. This was a strange, hostile place, and that was before you factored in Harrington's "ghost."

McKenna walked down the starboard deck to the exhaust funnel at the stern, then back up to the bridge. Opened the bridge door and peered inside, at the papers and charts strewn everywhere, the spilled coffee creamers. The electronics were dark, and the room was quiet, filled everywhere with the reminders of the men who'd fled the *Lion* not so long ago.

McKenna found the passageway down the middle of the ship. Switched on her headlamp and followed the passageway aft, past the captain's suite, the officers' staterooms. Found the stateroom where Ridley and Harrington had claimed they'd seen someone, the starboard side, scanned the room and saw nothing amiss.

A few doors down, on the portside of the ship, was where they'd claimed to have found the nest. McKenna tried to muffle her steps as she approached the door. Could feel her heart rate start to increase. When she'd reached the threshold, she counted to three and looked in the doorway. A pile of bedding on the floor, and in the corner, just as the men had reported, a pile of trash beside it.

But the ghost, whoever he was, wasn't here.

McKenna continued aft. Checked the rest of the staterooms, came to the galley. Held her breath to avoid inhaling the rancid air, and scanned the dark room with her headlamp. Another pile of empty cans, ten, fifteen easy. Thrown away in the corner. McKenna felt ice up her spine, and it might have just been because she was spooked out, a little, but her spidey sense was tingling just a little, too.

They pulled a body from this wreck.

McKenna took a breath, had to, immediately regretted it, the air was so foul. The galley was devoid of life, anyway; no sense hanging around here. She backed away from the door and continued down the passageway aft, checking the crew quarters and finding nothing amiss.

Just past the galley, a stairway down to the cargo holds. And here, more mystery: a pair of climbing ropes, lying discarded on the stairs. McKenna followed the stairs down.

The lines stopped at the first cargo deck. There was a watertight bulkhead door at the landing, and it lay open. On the other side, McKenna could see more signs of human life: energy bar wrappers, a couple of batteries. The crew of the *Salvation* had stopped here, clearly.

McKenna paused again, to listen. Heard nothing but her heart in her chest. She was getting kind of freaked, she realized.

There's nobody here. What would they even be doing on this ship? Why wouldn't they have shown themselves, like, a week ago?

She followed the climbing lines back to the accommodations deck. Continued down the passageway aft, past more crew quarters, the officers' lounge. An exercise room. All empty. That left only the infirmary. Fine. She was ready to get back out to fresh air.

The door to the infirmary was closed. McKenna turned the handle and pushed, felt resistance. *Strange.* The door was unlocked, but there was something blocking it from within. She pushed harder, and the door gave a little. She tried again.

Why are you even doing this? she thought. *So something shifted during the wreck. What are you trying to prove?*

She was trying to prove that there wasn't a ghost, she decided. She was trying to prove to Court Harrington that he was wrong.

She pushed again. This time, something crashed to the deck behind the door, and the door fell open. And McKenna stumbled into the infirmary, and found herself face-to-face with the barrel of a gun.

76

Okura held the pistol level at the young woman's forehead, trying to keep his hand from shaking.

"Get back," he said, his voice ragged from days of silence, trembling from the fear and the sudden adrenaline rush. "No sudden movements."

He'd been asleep in the sick bay, nothing better to do, when he'd heard footsteps approaching. Held his breath and waited, hoped the cabinet he'd lodged against the door would deter any visitors. Prayed whoever was out there would leave him alone.

But she hadn't. As soon as Okura heard the door turn, he knew in his heart he was made. He'd muttered a silent curse, and reached for the pistol.

And of course, the woman—the salvage master—had felt the cabinet blocking the door and must have known what it signified. Okura had waited as she'd labored to move the cabinet, fighting his racing pulse and the nervous thrill that came with the knowledge that, yes, now he would have to shoot someone.

The cabinet fell. The door swung open, and the woman was there. And Okura was ready for her, ready, at last, for action.

EXCEPT HE'D MADE A MISTAKE, another one. As the young woman backed away from the pistol, Okura looked into her eyes and knew he should have pulled the trigger sooner, shot her as soon as he'd seen her, and finished the deed quickly, instead of letting the woman live long enough to show her face.

She was indeed young. Her face was pale, her eyes wide. She was scared, but there was something else, too, something like resignation—or disgust.

Okura motioned with the pistol, back, out of the infirmary and into the hall, buying himself time. Nearly tripped on the fallen cabinet and lost his balance, almost squeezed the trigger prematurely. The woman's eyes got wider, like she'd seen it coming. Like she'd expected to be dead already.

Killing Tomio Ishimaru had been easy. The man was yakuza, a criminal, a killer himself—and he'd been half dead, anyway. Killing him had been no harder than killing an ant. A mosquito.

"Please," the woman said. She held up her hands, backed away from him slowly. "Whatever you're planning to do, think it over. I'm sure there's a way we can get ourselves out of this."

"Silence." Okura followed her into the corridor. Motioned forward, toward the cargo stairs. He would have to kill her in the hold; the sound of the gun would be too noticeable here. Okura prodded the woman, pushed her toward the stairs.

He would have to kill this woman. Then he would need to escape. With luck, her mates wouldn't discover her for hours.

"You don't have to do this," the woman said. "Whatever you're doing here, it's not worth killing me for, I promise. This isn't the only way out."

Fifty million dollars, Okura thought.

He held the gun steady. "I'm sorry," he told the woman. "This is the only way."

77

McKenna felt the barrel of the stowaway's gun in the small of her back, her fear fighting with the realization that this ridiculous, improbable set of circumstances was how she was going to die.

Shot to death in the cargo hold of a shipwreck. In the middle of Nowhere, Alaska. Why? Who knows.

She might have laughed, if she hadn't been so scared.

The stowaway prodded her down the stairs to the cargo holds. He was silent behind her, his breathing heavy. He didn't want to shoot her, McKenna could tell, but she figured he'd made up his mind.

The worst part was not knowing why.

"Listen, what is it you want?" she asked him, trying to keep her voice light, conversational. "Why are you here? Whatever you need, I can help you."

The stowaway didn't answer.

"This is my ship now," she said. "It's worth a heck of a lot of money. Is that what you want?" She laughed. "Let's make a deal."

The stowaway laughed, too, but there was no humor in it. "You don't have enough money to negotiate, I'm afraid."

"Are you serious? My cut on this ship is thirty million dollars. That isn't enough for you?"

"No," the stowaway said. She felt his hand on her arm, firm. "Stop here."

They'd reached deck eight. The stowaway nudged her toward the bulkhead door, and she caught his meaning and turned the wheel to unlock it. Opened the door, and stepped through. Walked a couple of paces into the first row of cars, the hold lit by a few feeble emergency lights and the beam of her headlamp.

She turned around. Slowly, so she didn't freak the guy out, though she supposed it didn't matter. If this guy was going to shoot her, she was going to see it coming.

No Rhodes ever died on her knees.

The stowaway winced as he looked at her. "I'm sorry," he said, and McKenna knew this was it. And then, just as the stowaway steeled himself to finally pull the trigger, just as McKenna closed her eyes and prayed it would be quick—

Court *freaking* Harrington poked his head out from the stairwell behind them. "Captain Rhodes? You down here?"

And the stowaway spun at the sound of Harrington's voice, and then he really *did* pull the trigger.

78

"Court, get down!"

McKenna leaped at the stowaway as the gun roared, the explosion near deafening in the low cargo hold. Had just enough time to see Harrington go down, and then she was tackling the stowaway, football-style, wrapping both arms around the man's waist and knocking him to the ground, McKenna close behind.

The pistol came out of the stowaway's hands, jolted free from the impact. It immediately began to slide down the listing deck. The stowaway grabbed for it, missed, bucking McKenna off his back, but both of them were scrambling down, too, toward the distant portside, bilge water and darkness.

It was not a smooth ride. The deck was grooved steel, studded with anchor points. McKenna reached for a handhold, something to arrest her fall, her hands slick with engine oil and grasping at nothing, her body picking up speed as she tumbled down.

The fall took forever. Kicked the shit out of McKenna every inch of the way, tore up her knees, her legs, scraped open her palms and slashed at her arms. And then—*SLAM*—she collided with the hull on the portside of the ship, a foot and a half of oily water, her headlamp hanging off her head at a crazy angle, leaving her near blind and disoriented, the whole world a graveyard of ruined Nissans and steel.

McKenna struggled to her feet, feeling every fresh bruise. Fixed her headlamp and searched the gloom for the stowaway, found him three cars from the hull, bashed up against a front tire and reaching for the pistol.

The gun had become tangled in a web of tying straps just above the stowaway's head, and somehow he'd had the presence of mind to stop his fall nearby. Now, as McKenna watched in horror, the man pulled himself to his feet, wiped his hands on his pants, and leaned down and picked up the pistol.

Shit.

McKenna ducked behind the closest Nissan as the stowaway fired again. Heard the bullet strike steel behind her, ricochet; she saw sparks. Another shot, and another, the stowaway coming closer, keeping her pinned as he closed the distance.

Gotta move.

Stealthily as she could, McKenna crept away from her makeshift cover, pulled off her headlamp and held it in her hand, tried to keep her head low and out of sight in the dim light.

Before she'd gone twenty feet, she knew she was made.

"Stop," the stowaway said, his voice unreasonably calm. "Give me your flashlight, or I'll shoot you right there."

McKenna didn't turn around. Exhaled a long breath. "Hell, you're going to kill me anyway," she said. Then she reached back and chucked the headlamp away, threw a strike down the length of the hull, and ducked away quickly, bracing for the shot.

But the shot didn't come.

Instead, McKenna heard a wheeze, the air punched out of the stowaway's lungs. Heard the clatter as the pistol fell to the deck, the splash as it slid into the bilge water. Then another splash, bigger, as the stowaway fell himself.

Slowly, McKenna stood. Stayed low, searched the darkness,

caught the vague shape of a figure in the glow of the hold's emergency lights. Court Harrington. He'd lost his own headlamp, she saw, but he'd brought his laptop with him. And he'd used it, she surmised, to neutralize the stowaway pretty damn hard.

"Captain Rhodes?" Harrington called out. "You okay?"

McKenna checked herself. No bullet holes. "You saved my life, Harrington," she said. "I think at this point, you can call me McKenna again."

79

"I found him in the infirmary," the skipper told Harrington as he helped her haul the unconscious stowaway up the cargo deck to the bulkhead. "Guess he moved out of that first nest once you found him, barricaded himself away where he thought we'd never look."

Harrington grunted, feeling the exertion. The stowaway wasn't big, but it was no easy task dragging him up to the listing deck, not with his ribs still taped up like he was a mummy. "Sure," he said. "So who is this guy?"

"No idea. Guess we'll find out soon enough."

With his free hand, Harrington gripped a Nissan's mirror and pulled himself forward. Whoever the guy was, Harrington was pretty damn grateful he wasn't much of a shot. The sneaky bastard had spun and fired wild, missed him by ten feet, but he'd thrown himself to the deck anyway, nearly cracked his laptop. It was a damned painful maneuver, besides, and when he'd stood up again, both the skipper and the shooter were way down at the portside hull, continuing their grudge match.

"Why was he so hell-bent on killing you, anyway?" Harrington asked. "You say something to piss him off?"

The skipper looked at him sideways, smiled just a little. Kept climbing. "That's what I can't figure out," she said. "I guess he was just mad that I found him."

Harrington glanced over at her. They'd almost reached the bulkhead door, almost time to call the Coast Guard, and hand this joker off.

There was more to this story, he figured. Nobody just stowed away on a shipwreck for weeks without a damn good reason.

And Harrington was a curious guy.

So he helped the skipper lug the unconscious stowaway to the bulkhead door, stood guard over the guy as McKenna ventured topside to call in the Coast Guard. Waited as the Coast Guard took the man into custody, two big, burly rescue swimmer types. They braced the stowaway on each side, and carried him upstairs to the helicopter.

Harrington followed. Joined the crew on the weather deck and regaled them with his story, told them all how he'd had a question for the captain about the pumps, how he'd followed her inside the ship, heard her voice in the cargo stairway, and followed her down. Played himself off as dumb and clueless when it came to the attack, held up his laptop, the screen cracked, and told them they were all lucky the guy's skull wasn't thicker.

And then, when the Coast Guard flew away, and the crew dispersed back to their pumps, Harrington ventured inside the ship again, and down the central corridor to the infirmary. He found the cabinet with which the stowaway had blocked the door, the sick bed where he'd slept, the piles of garbage he'd accumulated. And then, hidden in a medicine cabinet beside the stowaway's sick bed, he found the briefcase.

It was slim, stainless-steel, a few nicks and scratches on its sides. It looked like something from a spy movie, something totally out of place in the infirmary, hell, on this ship. It was undoubtedly what the stowaway had been guarding.

Harrington knew he should tell the skipper about what he'd found. She was the captain, after all, and whatever was inside the briefcase—it was locked, he discovered—was important enough to kill over.

This was the kind of thing the captain would want to know about.

But Harrington knew McKenna pretty well, and he knew she liked to play by the rules. He knew that if he gave her the briefcase, she would feel obliged to hand it over to the authorities. And he *was* curious. What would possess a man to hide out on a shipwreck for days—weeks—without telling anyone? What kind of secret could make someone so desperate? This was a mystery, and he wanted to solve it himself.

The *Lion* was a shipwreck, Harrington reasoned. By maritime law, everything aboard was the property of the *Gale Force*. It wouldn't hurt to investigate the briefcase a little more.

So Harrington took the briefcase from the medicine locker, carried it out of the infirmary and back through the accommodations and out to the deck of the *Lion*. Stashed the briefcase with his sleeping bag and a couple of empty fuel canisters, and set off to find Captain Rhodes again.

This was probably a bad idea, but damn it, life was a gamble. And Harrington figured gambling was precisely why he was here.

80

By the middle of the next morning, the *Pacific Lion* had leveled out.

On Harrington's instruction, the crew had killed the forward pump when the list hit fifteen percent, just before darkness fell. The skipper had sent Ridley back to the tug, kept Matt and Stacey on the first deck to babysit the last pump. She'd tried to send Harrington back, too.

"I'd rather stay, if it's okay with you," he said. "This is crunch time. I need to be here."

The captain made to argue, then seemed to think better of it. "I guess you're right. If anything's going haywire, it's happening tonight."

"It's not going haywire," Harrington told her. She didn't look convinced.

They'd found a platform in the access stairway on cargo deck seven, midway from the surface to the Jonases on deck one, close enough to the open air that the radios still picked up a little reception, and they could holler down to Matt and Stacey for status reports. They'd brought down their sleeping bags, some food, and the last of the Red Bull. Harrington had bundled his sleeping bag so the skipper wouldn't notice the briefcase inside.

He needn't have worried. The captain was spent. She'd wrapped herself up in her sleeping bag, made a cursory attempt at conversation, lay her head back on the wall of the stairwell, and passed out cold, finally asleep.

Harrington had watched her for a moment, studied her face as she slept. He'd missed her, he realized. More than he'd expected to. He'd pushed her away when she'd fallen for him, sure; he was young then. She'd surprised him. He wasn't planning for commitment.

He wasn't so young anymore. He wasn't so scared to get serious. And he'd never known anyone quite like McKenna Rhodes, no matter where he looked. He just didn't have a clue how to tell her this stuff without messing up the, ahem, *chain of command*.

McKenna slept soundly. Harrington leaned over and switched off her headlamp. He pulled a sleeping bag over his shoulders, and settled in to wait.

The night passed, uneventful. Morning came. The last pump kept working, and the list continued to ease. By midmorning, the *Lion* was nearly at zero degrees.

Harrington had supervised the last hour of pumping. Monitored the water level on the fifth starboard-side ballast tank, one eye on the gauge, the other on his battered laptop. Then the skipper had woken up, sheepish, hadn't said much. Headed topside to call the Coast Guard.

IT WAS TEN FORTY-THREE in the morning when McKenna heard the final pump shut off. She was standing on the starboard deck—on the deck now, not the wall—waiting for the Coast Guard to send Captain Geoffries over with a party to survey the *Lion* and pronounce her saved.

McKenna would wait for the Coast Guard and the shipping company to give her the final verdict, but from where she was standing, the job looked done. The *Lion*'s list was erased. She sat level now, steady in the water, a ship again. Her owners would get her engine repaired, offload her cargo of Nissans, and put her back to work, whereas last week they'd been ready to write her off as gone.

McKenna looked up and down the deck, from the bridge to the exhaust funnel. Saw the access hatch where she and Matt and Stacey and Ridley and Jason Parent and Court Harrington had entered the ship, where they'd muscled down their pumps and walked on the walls, where they'd curled up with sleeping bags and sandwiches and those paperback novels, where they'd cheated death to save the ship.

And now the ship was saved. The prize was theirs. The job was finished, save a few minor details. Court Harrington's plan had worked, the crew had played their parts perfectly, and the big freighter was nearly as good as new. Soon, Gale Force Marine would be thirty million dollars richer.

And none of it would bring her father back to life.

McKenna knew she should be happy. Knew her crew would tell her she'd done the old man proud. Knew, by rights, she should be jumping for joy and grinning ear to ear and pricing out Corvettes on the Internet. But she couldn't enjoy the moment, not completely.

She just really wished her dad had been here to see this.

81

The *Gale Force* set out from Inanudak Bay that evening, the *Pacific Lion* on a short leash behind it. It had taken Captain Geoffries and his crew most of the day to survey the *Lion* and verify she was ready to move. Taken the crew of the *Gale Force* a few hours more to move their hundred-pound salvage pumps up from the bowels of the ship. But now the pumps had been transferred back to the tug, the Coast Guard had signed off, and the *Gale Force* was moving.

McKenna settled into the skipper's chair as the towline went taut behind the stern of her tug, and the big freighter followed behind, docile as a sleepy cow. It was about a hundred-mile run from Umnak to Dutch Harbor, all in the lee of the Aleutian Islands, and McKenna figured it would take a day or two, give or take, to get the *Lion* delivered.

She'd phoned Japan already, raised the Japanese Overseas Shipping Company, and told them when and where to expect their ship. According to Geoffries on the *Munro*, weather in Dutch was too foul for commercial flights, so the Japanese had chartered their own jet. They were due sometime within the next couple days.

The islands protected the *Gale Force* from the heavy winds on the North Pacific side, and the Bering Sea swell was behaving itself as well. Spike was curled up on the bench beside the captain's chair, had even let McKenna pet him a couple of times. He hadn't purred, mind, or even looked particularly pleased, but he didn't claw at McKenna, or run away, and that was a start.

She watched the wheel for an hour or two, followed the *Munro* out of Inanudak Bay and up alongside the northwest side of Umnak Island. The crew—aside from Nelson Ridley and Matt Jonas, who were camping out on the *Lion*—was downstairs, doing the dishes, watching another movie, grabbing some well-deserved rest in their bunks, and McKenna knew she should feel exhausted herself, but she didn't, not now that the job was almost done.

She checked the autopilot, plotted a course on the GPS. Turned on the satellite radio, some old Springsteen, her dad's stuff. Crossed to the depth sounder and the pewter picture frame beside it, picked up the frame and brought her dad's face into the low light from the GPS screen.

Her dad smiled back at her, that old flannel shirt and the stained baseball cap, kind eyes and beard going to gray, and even though McKenna knew it was stupid, she found herself waiting for him to come alive in that picture, say something, smile wider. Share in her success and everything she'd accomplished.

You did this, Daddy, she thought. *Your crew and your boat, and everything that you taught me. You raised that ship from the dead.*

It wasn't enough, though. It was never enough. No crew, and no tug, would ever bring Riptide Rhodes back.

She stared at her dad's picture until the tears blurred her vision, and she was crying for her dad, and for the *Lion,* and for everything else, and she kept staring at the photograph, waiting for a sign, for some indication that her dad was there with her, that he'd been there all along.

But there was nothing. A dark, empty wheelhouse, and a sleeping cat, and an old pewter frame, the picture inside going yellow with age.

And then there were footsteps on the wheelhouse stairs, heavy and uneven. McKenna turned quickly, wiping her eyes with the back of her hand. Found Court Harrington climbing into the house, a steaming cup of coffee in his hands.

"Stacey said you were going to be up all night. Figured you'd need coffee, so—" Then he must have seen the tears, because his eyes widened and he stepped back. "Whoa, sorry. Everything okay?"

McKenna wiped her face again. Felt herself go red. Turned away, furious with herself, put the picture away.

"Everything's fine," she told him. "Perfectly fine. You can just leave the coffee on the table, thanks."

But Harrington didn't move. "Are you crying, though?"

Bastard.

McKenna steadied her breathing. Still didn't trust herself to look at Harrington, so she stared out into the night instead. "It's nothing," she said.

Harrington came closer. Picked up the picture and held it close to his eyes, squinted at it. "Your dad?"

She nodded.

"It's like he's here, isn't it?" Harrington said. "Don't you feel like he's right here along with us?"

McKenna couldn't answer that without risking more tears, so she shook her head.

"I do," Harrington said. "I sure as heck do. I see him in every stroke of good luck we've had on this job, everything that's gone right. And you'd better believe he was looking out for me when I had that fall. I could have been a goner."

"He would still *be* here," McKenna said, "if I'd made that turn quicker."

Harrington didn't say anything for a while. "You saved my life. You know that, right? If you didn't have your shit together, I would have died on that shipwreck."

McKenna said nothing.

"But you know what? Even if I had died, it wouldn't be your fault," Harrington continued. "This is a dangerous job. People have accidents; people get hurt. Your dad knew that as well as anyone. You do what you can to mitigate the risk, but in the end your luck's going to hold or it's going to give out, and there's nothing you can do about it."

McKenna studied the instrument panel, the engine gauges, the radar, and the dim GPS screen. Anything to keep from looking at Harrington. "I just miss him," she said finally. "I miss him so much. This is all I ever wanted, but it's so damn *hard* without him."

"But he *is* here," Harrington said. "Don't you see? Everything you've done has his stamp on it. Every time I look at you, I see the daughter Riptide raised. And I see a damn fine salvage captain, to boot."

McKenna laughed. Couldn't help it. Turned to see Harrington looking at her with such an earnest expression that it only made her laugh harder.

"What?" Harrington held the straight face for another beat. Then he gave it up. "I guess that was pretty cheesy, huh?"

"I just feel like I should be paying you extra, making you play therapist to some raging bitch with daddy issues."

Harrington's smile grew. "You're not such a bitch."

"You weren't saying that a couple days ago."

"You got better," he said, unfazed, and they smiled at each other until the moment stretched just a little too long, and then he straightened and nodded at the coffee in her hand.

"Anyway, there's lots more where that came from," he said. "Coffee, I mean. Plenty of Red Bull, too, if you need it."

"I should be all right," she said. "Thanks."

He turned to go. "Well then, good night, Captain Rhodes."

McKenna, she thought, but she didn't want to confuse the guy, and maybe she was getting a little confused herself.

"Good night, Harrington," she said, and then he was gone, and she stood up by the wheel, replaying the conversation, seeing those green eyes in her mind, and wishing like hell she knew some way to chase them.

82

There was a new buzz in the town of Dutch Harbor. Daishin Sato could sense it, feel the electricity in the air and in snippets of conversation. At the same time, he'd noticed an increase in traffic on the town's little roads. Something was happening, and it related to the *Pacific Lion.*

Even Hannah seemed to feel the change. The Grand Aleutian's desk clerk had been preoccupied all day, typing on her computer and talking on the phone, issuing instructions to the cleaning staff, and primping the brochure rack in the lobby.

Sato was interested. The search for Hiroki Okura had stalled. The *Lion*'s second officer was alive, Daishin was fairly certain of it. And he'd stolen away to the *Lion* aboard a local salvage boat, Hannah said. But the body the Coast Guard had removed from the *Lion* belonged to Tomio Ishimaru. That meant Okura was still out there, somewhere.

"What's all the excitement?" Sato asked Hannah. "The whole town has changed."

Hannah's smile seemed to brighten her whole face. "It's the shipwreck. That salvage team saved it. They're towing it to Dutch as we speak."

"Ah," Sato said. "That's big news."

"You said it. There's like seven executives from the shipping company coming in from Japan on a private plane. Booked up the whole top floor of the hotel." She grinned. "I'm hoping they have to stay for a while. This could make our whole season!"

"With luck," Sato said. Then he frowned. "But is this all that has the whole town so nervous? Everyone is talking about the *Pacific Lion*, at every store and restaurant. Are visits from the Japanese so rare?"

Hannah looked at him blankly. Then she laughed. "Oh," she said. "Ha! I see what you did there. That's funny."

Sato smiled back. Tried to be patient, though a part of him would have liked to have strangled this happy, cheerful woman.

Polite. Conversational. Friendly.

His patience paid off. Hannah leaned in conspiratorially. "There is something else."

"Yes?"

"I heard there was a gunfight on that ship," she said. "Some stowaway was on board for some reason, and when the salvage crew found him, he tried to shoot one of them."

Sato feigned surprise. "Goodness. I hope nobody was hurt."

"I don't think so. Not seriously, anyway." Hannah shrugged.

"They got the guy under control and off the ship, from what I heard."

"And what will they do with him?"

"No idea," she said. "But they brought him here, to the cop shop. He's under arrest. As far as I know, they're still debating who has jurisdiction."

Sato nodded. "How exciting."

"You're telling me," Hannah replied. "Gunfights and everything. This is like from a movie!"

83

Hiroki Okura sat in the little cell in the back of the Dutch Harbor Department of Public Safety's police station, staring at the wall and wishing he'd never encountered Tomio Ishimaru in that smoky mah-jongg parlor.

His head hurt from where the salvage man had beaned him. He remembered trying to work up the nerve to shoot the young woman, remembered a glimpse of her partner before he'd knocked Okura to the deck. Then he'd woken up on the Coast Guard cutter, and nobody would talk to him or look him in the eye.

They'd bandaged his head, refused him any painkillers, kept him under observation, took his belt and his shoelaces.

"Suicide watch," someone said. "Have to make sure you don't do anything crazy."

At that point, Okura would have welcomed death. Certainly, he had no future to live for, not now. The Coast Guard crew had put him on a helicopter, flown him to Dutch Harbor, where a couple of members of the town's small police force were waiting to take him to jail.

They'd fingerprinted him. Booked him. Refused him a shower, though he smelled absolutely foul after weeks on that ship. They'd locked him up in this cramped little cell, three walls of bars and a fourth of cinder block, a stainless-steel toilet in the middle.

"Debating whether to prosecute you here, or just send you home," one of the policemen told Okura. "Seems you've caused something of an international incident."

Excellent, Okura thought. *So much for anonymity.* At the best case, he would spend years of his life in prison. In the worst-case scenario?

Okura didn't want to think about it. There would be plenty of time for that later. But just as he'd succeeded in chasing the thoughts from his mind, the door in the corridor was unlocked and swung open. And in walked a police officer, trailing that worst-case scenario in the flesh.

"Guess I have some good news," the police officer told Okura. "Looks like your brother's here to see you. Moral support, or whatever."

He unlocked Okura's cell door. Stepped aside so the man who called himself Okura's brother could walk in, then locked the door behind.

"Ten minutes," he said, and retreated to the outer door again, leaving Okura alone with the man.

. . .

THE MAN WAS YOUNG, in his mid-twenties, and thin. His eyes were dark, almost as black as his hair. He wore a black suit, a white shirt, a skinny black tie, and his hair was artfully mussed.

He was not Hiroki Okura's brother. Okura didn't have a brother, and if he did, this man would not have been him.

The man didn't bother to introduce himself. He walked to the center of the cell. Sniffed, made a face. Then he fixed his eyes on Okura and smiled, wide. His teeth were white; Okura could have sworn they were jagged, like a shark's.

"Katsuo Nakadate sends his regards," the man told Okura. He reached into his suit pocket, removed a folded piece of paper. Unfolded it, and held it out to Okura.

Okura hesitated. The man gestured, *Take it*.

Okura took the paper, though he wanted nothing to do with it. He forced himself to look down. Swallowed.

His sister. Her daughter. A photograph from a distance, outside of their house.

"We aren't barbarians," the man continued. "Maybe you didn't know what you were doing when you helped Ishimaru. You were old friends, yes? We can understand that. We're not cruel."

Okura said nothing. Felt his legs begin to shake, tried to focus on standing upright, maintaining control of his bladder.

"Mr. Nakadate simply wishes to be returned what has been taken from him. I assume you know what I'm speaking of?"

Okura nodded yes.

"Do you know where it is?"

Okura nodded again.

"Tell me, Okura-san. I give you Katsuo Nakadate's word that your niece and her mother will not be harmed."

Okura closed his eyes. Hoped desperately that what he said next would absolve him, wash his hands of this mess, keep his sister safe.

"On the ship," he said, soft enough that the man had to lean in to hear him. "In the infirmary, in a medicine cabinet. If it's not there, it was taken by one of the salvage crew."

The young man grinned again. Shark teeth. "Thank you, Okura-san. I hope, for your family's sake, that we recover the property without delay."

He turned and called for the guard, who appeared quickly. Walked out of the cell and down the corridor, stopping before the outer door to turn back and wink, once, at Okura. And then he was gone.

Okura sank to the hard concrete bench. The man had left him the picture, his sister and his niece. Okura stared down at it for a long time. There was nothing else he could do.

84

A small collection of Japanese men waited at the fuel dock when the *Gale Force* tied up in Dutch Harbor.

It was morning, a day and a half after the *Gale Force* departed Inanudak Bay. The *Pacific Lion* was secure, tied to a couple of mooring buoys in Unalaska Bay, about a mile out from the town. The tow was complete, and the crew of the tug was ready to hand the freighter back to her owners.

McKenna watched the men on the dock as she nudged the tug against the wooden pilings. There were seven of them, all in black coats bundled tight. They studied the tug, and turned to talk among themselves. One man, slight and middle-aged, his hair thinning, stood with them but said nothing. He didn't look away from the tug.

This man was Matsuda, McKenna would find out, when the tug was tied fast and she'd climbed down to the dock. The shipping company's vice president stepped forward from his group, bowed slightly. "Captain Rhodes," he said. "It's a pleasure to meet you at last."

McKenna cocked her head. "Is it?"

Matsuda hesitated. Then he looked McKenna in the eye. "I'm sorry," he said. "I want to apologize for the stance my company—for the stance *I* took with you and your team. Truthfully, I didn't think your organization had the capability to handle a job so demanding."

McKenna cast her eyes across the water to where the *Lion* rested on her moorings. "I guess you were wrong."

"Indeed, and my company is grateful for it. You and your crew have accomplished an incredible feat."

Yeah, McKenna thought. *Now let's see how long it takes you to pay us.*

Matsuda frowned, as if he could read her mind. "I'm truly sorry to have underestimated you, Captain Rhodes. Be assured, it won't happen again."

McKenna met Matsuda's eyes. The executive looked tired from his journey. He seemed genuinely humbled. McKenna forced herself to be gracious. "Don't mention it," she told him. "Let's have a look at your ship."

. . .

MCKENNA FERRIED THE Japanese Overseas contingent across the water on the *Gale Force*. Maneuvered her tug to the stern of the *Pacific
Lion*, and waited as Al and Jason Parent made her fast. Then she
helped Matsuda and his colleagues up and onto the afterdeck, the
same perilous spot where Al Parent and Nelson Ridley had secured
the towline just days before.

The deck was safe now, the list erased, the ship more like a ship
again than a sadist's climbing wall. McKenna and Ridley led the
inspection party through the ship, from engine room to cargo holds
to bridge, the shipowners talking among themselves in Japanese,
making notes, taking photographs.

Matsuda was quiet. He didn't talk to McKenna, and he didn't
talk to his colleagues. He walked ahead of them without pause, as
though he knew its layout intimately. He studied the Nissans in the
cargo hold and the spilled papers and coffee creamers on the bridge
with the same careful, conscientious eye.

"They will not be able to sell these cars, you know," he told Mc-
Kenna as they climbed a staircase between decks. "Already, there is
outrage in the American market. A newspaper suggested the manu-
facturer could refurbish the vehicles and sell them as new on their
lots. Do you believe this, Captain?"

McKenna glanced back, through the bulkhead door and onto
the cargo deck, the Nissans still strapped in and secure, the steel
deck still slippery with oil and transmission fluid. "No," she said. "I
don't believe it."

"I'm told that most of the cars remained dry, at least," Matsuda said. "Maybe they are salvageable, maybe not." He shrugged. "Whatever the case, they won't be sold in America. Your country's love of litigation will ensure it."

McKenna said nothing. *Five thousand Nissans. Brand-new, all of them, and all of them headed for scrap.*

"The ship, though," she said. "You're going to keep using the ship, right?"

"Oh yes, the ship can be fixed." Matsuda laughed. "Maybe you'll even pass her in the harbor someday on your tugboat. You can look at her and see a monument to your determination."

It was a happy sentiment, sure, but you couldn't pay a fuel bill with sentiment. The payout remained foremost in McKenna's mind as she followed Matsuda through the ship, casting glances back at the executive's colleagues with their iPads and digital cameras and notebooks. The survey took hours, and the shipping executives seemed to make note of every chip, dent, and scratch they came across.

Finally, though, Matsuda and McKenna led Ridley and the executives onto the starboard weather deck, the survey complete. Matsuda conferred with his colleagues. Ridley joined McKenna at the rail.

"I bet they try to screw us," Ridley said. He sounded nonchalant, but McKenna knew there was real fear in his words. "I bet we fight this thing out in court for *years.*"

The engineer had a right to be afraid, McKenna figured. For thirty million dollars, Matsuda and his colleagues might very well be tempted to haggle on the price, judging that Gale Force Marine lacked the resources to fight a long legal battle.

And they'd be right, McKenna thought. *I have barely enough cash on hand to pay for fuel and transit back to the Lower 48, much less retain a team of maritime lawyers.*

She stared out over the railing at the town of Dutch Harbor in the distance. "I really hope it doesn't come to that."

Matsuda coughed quietly behind them. Ridley nudged McKenna. "Here it comes."

McKenna turned. Found Matsuda standing alone, a few feet away, his colleagues watching silently from behind. "Captain Rhodes," Matsuda said. "Can we discuss?"

McKenna glanced at Ridley, who grinned, sardonic, like, *Wait for it.* Then she followed Matsuda to the forward lifeboat.

"I wanted to express my apologies again," Matsuda told her. "I was wrong to underestimate you, Captain Rhodes. You've done remarkable work."

"Thank you," McKenna said. *Now stick the knife in me.*

"We have no interest in making enemies of you, Captain, or any of your crew," Matsuda continued. "And I, personally, have no interest in making this partnership any more adversarial than it already has been."

"Good," McKenna said. "Me, neither."

Matsuda paused. Broke eye contact, and McKenna thought, *Here it comes.* Then the executive looked at her again. "Our insurance assessment of the value of the ship and its cargo will take some time," he said. "However, we estimate the total will amount to something more than the hundred and fifty million dollars you and I discussed previously."

McKenna frowned. "Okay?"

"I'd like to therefore make a proposal," Matsuda said. "The Japanese Overseas Shipping Company will make Gale Force Marine a good faith payment of twenty million dollars, effective immediately. We can settle the remaining balance when we have processed the assessment, which you of course will be allowed to review."

He met McKenna's stare. "You are welcome to propose another arrangement, but I think this is a fair offer."

McKenna didn't answer for a beat. Felt her heart pounding. Realized, for all the work, she hadn't quite been prepared for this moment. "Yes," she said, and her voice came out strangled. "That's more than fair."

"You'll need to provide the company's banking information. My colleagues will process the transaction."

"Of course," McKenna said.

Matsuda studied her face, the ghost of a smile on his lips. "Will you shake my hand, Captain Rhodes?" he asked. "And accept my friendship, once and for all?"

McKenna blinked her head clear. Looked at the shipping executive, who waited, his hand outstretched. "Damn right, I'll shake your hand," she replied, and she did just that. "It's a pleasure doing business with you."

85

Through the window of his rented pickup truck, Daishin Sato stared across the pier at the salvage tug, trying to conjure a strategy.

Beyond the *Gale Force*, the freighter *Pacific Lion* sat peaceful and upright in the middle of Unalaska Bay, almost close enough to touch. And somewhere onboard, or somewhere nearby, fifty million dollars' worth of Inagawa-kai bearer bonds waited to be claimed.

The sailor, Okura, claimed the bonds were in a briefcase in the infirmary. If they weren't there, they were in the hands of the salvage crew already. Dutch Harbor was a small place. There were only so many ways to leave it. Sato was confident he and his colleagues could recover the briefcase. The more pressing concern was that of stealth: How to retrieve the bonds and escape this barren rock without being noticed?

Sato did not want to have to resort to violence. Violence would attract undue attention, but these situations invariably required a strong hand, and Sato was not averse. His job was to recover his employer's stolen property. There would be no credit given for mercy.

The *Lion* sat alone in the middle of the bay, visible to all in the tiny town. For all Sato knew, there may still have been men aboard her, Coast Guard men, or salvage men, or shipping company men. But even if the ship were unoccupied, it would be foolish to attempt to gain access during daylight. No matter how stealthy, no one could cross a mile of open water in daytime without being seen.

But it would be dark soon enough. And there was work to be done. From his pocket, Sato produced a satellite phone, and used it to place a call to his colleagues at the Grand Aleutian Hotel.

"We move tonight," he told the man who answered. "Send one man to the pier to keep watch over the salvage crew. Tell him to report immediately if he sees the stainless-steel briefcase."

"I'll send Masao," his colleague replied. "And what of the rest of us?"

Sato started his engine. "You'll meet me outside the hotel," he said, shifting into reverse. "Five minutes. We'll need to locate some adequate firepower."

86

McKenna and Ridley delivered Matsuda and the rest of the shipping company executives from the *Pacific Lion* back to shore. One of Matsuda's companions, an accountant named Hayata, copied Gale Force Marine's banking information on the short ride across the harbor. He entered it into a laptop equipped with a satellite transmitter, pressed a few buttons, and then nodded to Matsuda.

"You can call your banker," Matsuda told McKenna. "You should receive payment within thirty minutes."

McKenna thanked him, shook his hand again. Shook Hayata's hand, too, and the rest of the executives'. Ferried them to the pier and helped them off of the tug, wished them all a happy goodbye and a safe return to Japan. Then she called the crew into the wheelhouse.

They gathered, Matt and Stacey, Ridley and the Parents, and Court Harrington.

"The Japanese Overseas men have surveyed the ship," she told them. "And they've accepted delivery. Our job is officially finished."

The crew cheered. Hugged. High-fived. McKenna shook hands with Al and Jason Parent, hugged Matt and Stacey and Ridley. Hugged Court Harrington, too.

"Ain't finished until we get paid, though," Ridley said. "I told Carly we'd redo the kitchen, soon as I finished up here. She wants granite countertops, skipper. Help me out."

McKenna grinned at him. "You can tell Carly to go ahead and start working," she said. "Though she might want to look into marble counters, instead. The really expensive stuff."

She addressed the crew again. "The shipping company figures the *Lion*'s value at somewhere north of a hundred and fifty million dollars. Based on the contract we signed, which gives us twenty percent of that figure, Mr. Matsuda and his team have offered to make a good faith payment to the *Gale Force* up front, with the outstanding balance to be worked out once we've all had a chance to run the numbers."

"Okay," Harrington said. "So what's the payout?"

"Twenty," McKenna replied.

A pause. "Twenty what?" Stacey said.

"Twenty million. The money's in transit as we speak."

The crew stared at her. Said nothing. McKenna knew they were running the math, calculating their own payouts. Ridley was the first to break the silence.

"Well, thundering Jonas," he said. "Forget the kitchen. I'll buy Carly a new house."

Stacey nudged Matt. "What do you think, honey?" she asked. "Want to take me to Antarctica? Hang out with some penguins?"

"Might need a different plane," Matt said, kissing her. "But I'm game if you are."

All eyes turned to Al and Jason Parent. Al shrugged. "Think I'll finish up that old Mustang in my garage. Finally get her up and running again."

"What about you, Jay?" McKenna asked.

Jason blushed a little bit, looked down. "Probably put most of my share into Ben's college fund. Make sure he's set up really well for the future."

He paused. The rest of the crew waited. Finally, Jason looked up, and there was a shy smile on his face, too. "And maybe I'll get a new truck," he said.

"Sure you will." Nelson slapped him on the back. "A really big truck, my friend. This calls for a celebration!"

"Heck yeah, it does," McKenna said. "Find us a decent restaurant, and the best-looking bar on the island. Dinner's on me tonight, gang."

LAUGHING AND JOSTLING, the crew disappeared belowdecks to their staterooms to dig out their fancy Sunday-go-meeting clothes and prepare for dinner. Work was over. Time to relax, to eat a steak and drink a beer, to shower and sleep and feel like a human being again.

Court Harrington hung back. He'd been quiet all day, kind of withdrawn, and McKenna felt the first tendrils of worry as she watched him. She'd come pretty damn close to opening up to him the other night, showed him more of herself than she liked, and she caught herself wondering what he was thinking about, if he'd seen what she'd showed him and was judging her for it.

Don't be so self-absorbed. The job's over, and the guy's probably still in pain from that fall. He's wondering how soon is too soon to book a flight out of here.

"I'll get you on the next plane," McKenna said, figuring to cut him off at the pass. "Find you a specialist wherever you want to go, everything on me."

Harrington blinked. "A specialist?" he said. "No, I—"

"If it's about the money, we still do it like my dad did," McKenna told him. "Divvy it up, like on a fishing boat. The tugboat, the *Gale Force*, Gale Force Marine, whatever you want to call it, the company takes half. As the skipper, I take a double share of the rest. Crew gets a full share."

"I don't care about the money," Harrington said. "Whatever you think is fair."

"Eight shares total, including my two. Means your share—every share—is worth—"

"One point two five million dollars," Harrington finished.

"That's right. It's not World Series of Poker money, but I hope it's a decent consolation."

"One million–plus is top nine, easy. And in case you forgot, I busted out of that tournament."

"That's the game," McKenna said. "Here, just like Vegas. You bust out, you get nothing—and we bust out plenty. You win, you take your cut of the spoils."

Harrington didn't say anything.

"You'll have to give me your bank information," McKenna said, for nothing else than to keep the conversation going. "I'll get the money to you as quick as I can, obviously."

Harrington still said nothing. "You okay?" McKenna asked him.

"Yeah," he said slowly. "Just trying to wrap my head around it, is all. I mean, I knew it was a big score, but . . ."

"It's crazy," McKenna agreed. "Like I said, this is the biggest job I ever pulled. Probably top ten for my dad, maybe even top five."

"I wasn't even thinking about the money," he said. "I was going to—" He looked at her. "It just all happened so fast, right? Like, two weeks ago I was at a poker table, never thought I'd see you again. Now it's like, what, we just go our separate ways?"

"There will be other jobs. You're going to need some recovery time, I bet, but I have your number."

He made a face. "That's it? 'I have your number'?"

McKenna shrugged again. Didn't know what he wanted, didn't know how to give it to him. Couldn't meet his eyes, either.

Then she had an idea, figured she might as well just run with it. "Wait here," she said. She ducked downstairs and into her stateroom, dug out a bottle she'd been saving for a while, two glasses. Brought it all back to the wheelhouse.

"We don't usually drink on my boat," she told him as she handed him a glass, "but I bet they pour lots of champagne if you win the World Series of Poker."

She popped the cork clumsily and filled his glass, then hers. Hesitated a moment, searching for words.

"To a job well done," she said finally, holding her glass aloft, and he laughed at her, shaking his head, and she knew she'd picked the wrong words.

"That's what you want to toast to?"

McKenna looked at him. Then her glass. "What do you suggest?"

"I don't know," Harrington said. "The way things were going, I was kind of hoping you were headed somewhere a little less professional."

"Damn it." She frowned. Fumbled. "Okay," she said at last. "To renewed friendships. Is that better?"

Harrington smirked. "I guess it'll have to do."

He was close to her now. They touched glasses and drank, and he was still looking at her, and she realized with some alarm that he was about to try to kiss her. She straightened, backed away a little bit.

"Oh, shit," she said. "I'm sorry. Don't—you don't want to do that."

"Why not?"

His smile didn't waver, and McKenna realized she didn't really know *why* she was backing away from Harrington, realized there was a part of her that actually kind of wanted him to kiss her, even as the rest of her was screaming, *Abort! Abort! Abort!*

As it was, she was saved from a decision. Before she could answer Harrington, one way or another, there was a noise outside the wheelhouse, and McKenna looked past him to see Matsuda climbing the stairs from the afterdeck to the wheelhouse. The shipping executive peered in the window, saw McKenna, knocked lightly.

Harrington laughed. "Damn it," he said. "That guy *really* needs to work on his timing."

McKenna laughed, too. *Thank god,* she was thinking. *Saved by the bell.*

87

"Captain Rhodes." Matsuda gave McKenna a smile as he let himself into the wheelhouse. Then he noticed Harrington. "Please, forgive my intrusion."

McKenna glanced back at the champagne bottle, the empty glasses, felt herself start to blush. *Busted,* she thought. *No way to hide it.*

She cleared her throat. "No problem at all. What can I do for you?"

"I had another proposal I thought you might be interested in," Matsuda told her. "No obligation, of course."

"Of course."

"We need to transport the *Pacific Lion* to Seattle," Matsuda said. "We will unload the cargo there, and have the vessel inspected by a proper shipyard. Her engine is, of course, out of operation, and in any case, your Coast Guard would not permit us to sail the ship to Seattle ourselves."

McKenna got it. "You need a tow."

"We do. You're the closest boat, and we're confident in your capabilities. Gale Force Marine is my company's first choice."

McKenna thought about it. It was probably a ten-day tow to Seattle, she figured. McKenna had been hoping to get home fast, had imagined she was done with the *Lion.*

"We would pay a fair rate," Matsuda continued. "You, your boat, and your crew, plus all expenses. Essentially, Captain Rhodes, you can write your own contract."

The *Gale Force* did have to get home somehow. It would be a nice little bonus if the ride home wound up paying. *Hell,* McKenna thought. *When did Dad ever turn down a job?*

"I'll have to check with my crew," she told the executive. "But this sounds good to me."

Beside her, Harrington raised his glass. "Consider one crew

member on board already," he said, and those green eyes sparkled at her again. "When do we leave?"

McKENNA THOUGHT ABOUT IT. Kept it in her mind all through dinner, as she pitched the job to her crew, and all through the night and the next day, as the *Gale Force* worked with the Coast Guard and Matsuda and his colleagues to ready the *Pacific Lion* for the tow.

It was a nice thought. A week or so on a boat with Harrington, nothing really to do but sleep and eat and relax, catch up with the architect a little more, see if there really could be a spark there again.

And McKenna knew if she turned down Harrington's offer, she would spend the next ten days wondering—and probably more— because she *was* still attracted to him, kind of, even as cocky and smartass as he might have been. It had been a solid couple years since her last decent relationship, a long time to live without human companionship. Part of her wanted to say, *To hell with it*, and just dive in to ten days with Harrington, a pleasure cruise on the way home to reality.

She avoided Harrington as the Coast Guard surveyed the *Lion* again, searching for flooding and finding none. Thought about the architect as she and Nelson Ridley lashed the freighter's massive rudder into a fixed position. As they worked to repair the ship's emergency generator and restore power. As she worked with Ridley in the tug's engine room to make a proper fix to that portside intake pipe. She was tempted, really tempted. She almost told Harrington yes.

But she didn't. She didn't because she had enough in her life to worry about without getting moony over the crew, Harrington in particular. She was happy with her career, and her life on the tug, and she'd been down this road with Harrington before. The architect was way too smart to wind up with some awkward moody bitch of a tugboat captain anyway.

Why tease each other? Why start something they knew could never end well?

So, at the end of the second day, with the *Lion* cleared for departure and the crew of the *Gale Force* prepping to cast off in the morning, McKenna sat down with Harrington in the wheelhouse and told him she was sending him home.

"I told you I'd get you to a hospital," she said. "You shouldn't even be here right now, not after that fall."

Harrington laughed. "I'm fine," he said. "We're talking ten days of rest and relaxation, not another salvage job. I think a cruise would do me good."

"And if you reaggravate an injury?" she asked. "You could mess yourself up for life, if you don't treat this right." It all sounded so weak when she tried to explain it.

"So you're kicking me off," Harrington said. "That's what you're doing?"

McKenna shrugged. "Come on, Court," she said. "There's no point, for either of us. You get back to dry land, back south again, you'll wonder what the hell you were doing wanting aboard a smelly tug for another ten days."

Harrington didn't say anything. Pursed his lips and looked off through the window, and let the moment stretch out, the gulf widen between them.

Captain up.

McKenna stood. "I'll book you a flight home," she said, crossing the wheelhouse to the phone. "No sense dragging this out any longer."

McKenna met his eyes, and his eyes were stone hard, but she could see behind them that she'd hurt him. He was hurt.

But he looked away. "Aye-aye, captain," he said. "Whatever you say."

88

Ridley drove them to the pier in the *Gale Force*'s Zodiac, and then he drove them to the airport in the fuel-dock owner's truck. McKenna and Harrington didn't say much to each other on the drive.

It's better this way, McKenna thought. *No chance anybody gets hurt this time around, anyway. No more hurt than we are already.*

She wasn't sure she believed it, though, and she knew Harrington didn't.

Ridley drove across the runway and parked the car outside the terminal building. Waited behind the wheel as McKenna and Harrington climbed out. It was a decent day outside, not too cool, overcast, the fog just starting to drift in over the mountains. Harrington's plane wouldn't have any trouble getting out of town, not today.

She waited as Harrington retrieved his carry-on from the back of the truck, then led him into the terminal building. Through the window, McKenna could see the architect's plane waiting, a twin turboprop PenAir Saab 340.

"Kind of a puddle jumper," she said to make conversation. "Might be bumpy, but you'll be okay."

"I made it to the tug on a Coast Guard rescue helicopter," Harrington replied. "I think I can handle it."

"You're booked through to Anchorage, then down to Seattle. You can pick up your tickets from Alaska Airlines when you get to Anchorage."

"Okay." He wasn't looking at her, and she wasn't really looking at him, either. They were both kind of marking time, and McKenna wondered what more she was supposed to say here.

"Anyway, thanks for coming out," she said finally. "You should have the money in a day or two, tops."

He wouldn't meet her eyes. "Thanks," he said. He hoisted his carry-on bag. Exhaled. "See you around."

McKenna watched him walk away, out through the security checkpoint and into the waiting room. Watched him join the line of other passengers, present his ticket to the agent, walk out the other side of the terminal and across to the plane. He climbed the stairs to the cabin, found McKenna through the glass, and waved, once. Then he ducked inside the plane, and only then, when she couldn't see him any longer, did McKenna walk away.

HARRINGTON WATCHED THROUGH THE WINDOW as the little plane rocketed down the runway and lifted off above Dutch Harbor. He could see the airport below, could see Nelson Ridley's borrowed truck waiting outside the terminal, could almost convince himself he saw McKenna walking out as the plane banked and climbed. In the distance, he could see the *Pacific Lion* in the harbor, the *Gale*

Force tethered to her bow. He could see it all, briefly, and then the plane was climbing into the clouds, and he could see nothing but gray. He sat back in his seat and tried to forget about McKenna Rhodes, steeled himself for the long flight south.

UNNOTICED BY McKENNA, and Court Harrington, too, was the well-dressed young Japanese man who'd arrived at the terminal in a taxi shortly after the three *Gale Force* salvors, hurried to the PenAir desk with barely a glance at where Harrington and McKenna carried out their awkward goodbyes, purchased a last-minute ticket to Anchorage and, while Harrington hoisted his carry-on bag and turned away from the salvage captain, slipped past and through security to the waiting area.

When Harrington boarded, the young man was already on the plane, tucked into a window seat near the rear, his nose in his phone, steadfastly ignoring the other passengers.

Harrington might have seen him, might not have, but he didn't notice, in any case. The man was just another passenger on a half-full flight, another refugee from the edge of the world.

89

From his hiding place at the water's edge, Daishin Sato felt his phone vibrate. He removed it from his pocket. A new text message.

The American has flown to Anchorage. I am following him.

Sato waited.

As he'd expected, the phone buzzed again.

He was not carrying a briefcase.

Sato replaced his phone. "We proceed as planned," he told his colleagues, who waited in the shadows. "The American does not have the briefcase."

For all Sato knew, the young American man had transferred the stolen bonds into his luggage. He might have discarded the briefcase, and taken the contents back with him to the mainland. If that were the case, Masao would find out soon enough. In the meantime, Sato and the other two men would operate under the assumption that the bonds were still aboard the freighter.

He and his colleagues had spent the last night and day waiting for the Coast Guard to release the ship, once again, to the salvage crew's custody. Waiting for the salvage crew to pronounce the ship ready to tow. Ready for the darkness, for their own opportunity.

Waiting, and preparing.

They had liberated a small rowboat from the government docks near the town. Such was the size of Dutch Harbor that the boat was simply tied to a piling, no locks or alarms. It had simply been a matter of untying the rope, climbing aboard, and rowing the little dinghy around the point and out of sight. There, they had stocked it with food and provisions for the next stage of the task.

The Dutch Harbor citizens' relaxed attitude toward security extended, Sato had discovered, to their firearms. This was a frontier town, full of hunters and fishers and men and women of the wild, and nearly all of them owned guns. Sato and his colleagues had drifted from house to house, trying back doors and finding them largely unlocked.

They'd searched the empty houses, found what they needed quickly. Amassed two pistols and three rifles, sufficient ammunition. Sato would take no chances with this stage of the operation. There was a good probability that success would demand violence.

Sato tucked the phone into his trousers. He and his men had dressed in black: pants, sweaters, watch caps. They would blend in with the dark water after night fell. Nobody would see them as they crossed the bay.

"As soon as there's darkness," he told his colleagues, "we row for the *Lion*."

90

Early the next morning, McKenna Rhodes stood at her tug's wheel, plotting a course through the Aleutian Islands as the *Gale Force*'s mighty engines pulled the *Pacific Lion* away from her moorings in Unalaska Bay.

Dutch Harbor lay behind the big freighter, fading into the fog. The airport was closed again. Even if McKenna had wanted Harrington back, she couldn't have him. She still wasn't sure she'd made the right decision sending him away.

Working at sea was a lonely business. For the most part, McKenna could handle the loneliness when she was working, when there was a job and a rhythm and a simplicity to life: the tug, and the tow, and the ocean beyond. It was harder on dry land, when the grocery stores and streets and sidewalks were filled with happy couples, romantic movies, love songs. It was easier to take refuge out on the water, easiest to just shut yourself off from romance completely.

She'd had a long, sleepless night to think about the architect, to remember the strength in his arms as he'd held her, the wry humor behind those eyes. Now, in the morning, she was tired of feeling heartsick. Tired of longing for a man who'd already kicked her aside once, for a life she damn well knew was impossible. She had a job to do, a ten-day tow worth another half a million dollars, easy—and it *would* be easy, compared to the challenge of saving the *Lion* in the first place.

Behind the *Lion*, the Coast Guard cutter *Munro* idled away from her dock. The cutter would tail the *Gale Force* up and out of Unalaska Bay, and back down through busy Unimak Pass, between Unimak and Akun Islands, just east of Unalaska. The pass saw more than three thousand freighters a year traversing the Great Circle Route between Asia and the Pacific Coast of North America. Things weren't liable to get near as hairy as in Samalga Pass, but Captain Geoffries on the *Munro* wanted to see the *Pacific Lion* safely across to the North Pacific before he let McKenna on her way.

McKenna didn't mind. If she were honest, she appreciated the support. The waters around the Aleutian Islands were tricky and treacherous, and given the *Lion*'s history, it couldn't hurt to have someone around who knew the local currents.

The crew was mostly down below. Jason Parent cooked breakfast. Al Parent was asleep, resting for his wheel watch. Ridley was in the engine room, and Matt and Stacey Jonas had returned to the *Lion*, camping out on board the freighter to keep an eye out for flooding or any other mishap. Everyone was where they should have been. The *Gale Force* was operational, solvent, triumphant. And McKenna still felt the same gnawing loneliness she'd felt since she'd watched Court Harrington board his plane. She figured she would be happy if the feeling was gone by the time she reached Seattle.

Beside her, Spike jumped onto the bench beside the skipper's chair. From there, he leaped onto the dash and picked his way around the instrument panels, surveying the wheelhouse. He looked at McKenna with his big yellow eyes, and meowed, mournful.

"I know, buddy," McKenna told the cat. She settled into her skipper's chair, tried to get comfortable for the long journey home. "I kind of miss him, too."

SATO COULD FEEL THE SHIP MOVING, feel the steady, rhythmic motion as the *Lion* and her escort sailed out of the bay and into the open ocean.

So the ship was going somewhere. Doubtless, the owners saw little merit in keeping the vessel in the tiny town of Dutch Harbor any longer. And given that the crew of the tug was American, Sato surmised that they were headed for civilization, mainland Alaska at the very least, the Lower 48 in the best case.

This was good news. This would alleviate the need for Sato and his men to conjure a way out of Dutch Harbor with the bonds. They'd brought provisions aboard with them; they could survive for two weeks, if absolutely necessary. And when the ship docked in America, they would find their way off of it, disappear into the crowd. Find sympathetic friends to facilitate their passage back to Japan.

The ship's movement was a blessing. Far more troubling to Sato was the issue of the stolen bonds themselves. They were not where the sailor had claimed. Sato and his colleagues had searched the infirmary top to bottom and found nothing but discarded bedding and empty food containers—evidence of Hiroki Okura—but no sign of the briefcase.

Compounding the matter was the issue of the two Americans who'd made camp on the accommodations deck. To Sato's amusement, they hadn't claimed any of the many staterooms aboard the ship; rather, they'd spread sleeping bags in the officers' lounge and claimed it as their bedroom. He'd had one of his colleagues, Fuchida, spy on them at night while they were sleeping.

A man and a woman, middle-aged, Fuchida had reported. They looked romantically involved, perhaps married. They did not look armed.

They would wish that they were. If Sato and his colleagues couldn't find the bonds on this vessel, they would have to resort to more aggressive tactics.

And that was bad news for the man and woman who'd camped up above.

91

Two days out of Dutch Harbor, the satellite phone in the *Gale Force*'s wheelhouse startled McKenna out of the blissful rhythm of another morning at sea. She'd been tending to the autopilot, satellite radio blasting some classic Stones, looking out through the forward windows at a flat calm sea and enjoying every minute of the slow, monotonous journey south.

She'd all but pushed Court Harrington from her mind, forgotten about the cocky North Carolinian who'd almost—*almost*—bewitched her into losing her sense again, back there in Dutch Harbor.

And then the satellite phone rang, and it was Harrington on the other end. And he sounded, well, sheepish.

"Hey, uh, skipper," he began tentatively. "How's it going?"

"Going fine, Harrington," she replied. "Seas are flat calm and we're plowing along. You'd have been bored out of your mind by the first night out."

Harrington laughed, but it was something more nervous than funny. "Yeah, I bet."

"Where are you? You make it down to a hospital, or what?"

"I'm in Seattle," he replied. "Found a good physiotherapist, and she's working me hard. Sounds like I'm going to be here for a little bit." He paused. "But listen, skipper . . ."

McKenna frowned. "Uh-huh?"

"This is awkward," he said. "There's no easy way to say this, but, uh—" *Sigh.* "I left something on the tug. In my stateroom."

"Oh," McKenna said. "That's no problem. Give me a forwarding address, and I'll have it sent your way as soon as we hit the docks. Unless it's dirty underwear or your personal stash of porn, in which case you're SOL."

"It's not porn. It's not underwear, either. It's not—" Another nervous laugh. "Actually, it's not even mine."

He let that one hang there, long enough that McKenna should

have asked him to elaborate, but she didn't bother. Figured if he was going to spill something rotten on her, she wasn't going to beg for it.

And then he did. Told her a whole sordid story, the ghost on the *Lion* and how it led to the ambush, Harrington saving McKenna's life in the nick of time.

McKenna knew all this. This was old news. But Harrington had more to tell.

"I started wondering why this guy stuck around so long," Harrington said. "Turns out he was after this briefcase. Stainless-steel, like in a James Bond movie or something. It was hidden in a cabinet in the infirmary."

A briefcase. McKenna felt the first stirrings of nausea. "You never mentioned anything about a briefcase before, Court."

"I wasn't—" Pause. "I knew we'd have to give it up if I made a big deal out of it. You know, with the guy trying to kill you and all."

"So you kept it."

"We're a salvage operation. Everything on that boat belongs to us, rightfully, by law, right?"

"Court." McKenna rubbed her eyes. "We made thirty million dollars–plus on that job. If someone wants to kill me for a briefcase, heck, they can have it."

"I was just curious, is all. Wouldn't you be?"

"So you left the briefcase in your stateroom, is that it?" McKenna replied, dodging the question. "And what do you want me to do with it? What was inside, after all that?"

"I don't know," Harrington said. "I was waiting until things calmed down, and I was going to show it to you and we could open it, but then . . . you know."

You tried to kiss me and I got cold feet and put you on the next plane out of my sight. I know.

"McKenna— Captain Rhodes?"

"I'm here, Court," McKenna said. "I'm just trying to process this."

"I just thought you should know. I'm sorry I didn't tell you."

"Yeah, well." She corrected the autopilot. Shook her mind clear. "Nothing to do about it now. Let me have a look at the briefcase and I'll get back to you."

"Okay," he said. "Thanks." Then after a beat: "Tell the gang I say hi, okay?"

"Yeah," she said. "Okay. Will do." And she ended the call.

HARRINGTON TOOK THE PHONE from his ear. Stood for a minute outside the front doors of the hospital, looking up at the sky. It was a pleasant, sunny day, warm and summery, the sky a cloudless blue, but Harrington barely noticed.

She's going to kill me, he thought, tucking the phone into his pocket and starting toward the hospital entrance. *That woman is going to straight-up kill me.*

He disappeared inside the front doors, intent on finding his therapist for another day's labor. The doctor was pretty cute, kind of a hardass, and she seemed to find Harrington's salvage stories exciting. It wasn't the worst situation in the world, but Harrington wasn't focused on the doctor right now.

He found the elevator, pressed the call button, and waited, tapping his foot and mentally kicking his ass—completely unaware of the nondescript Chrysler rental idling out in the parking lot, or the driver inside, who'd been watching him close ever since he'd left Dutch Harbor.

92

Daishin Sato found an access hatch in the hull of the *Pacific Lion*, midway between the accommodations deck and the waterline. He unlocked the bulkhead door and swung the hatch open, revealing an endless expanse of azure sea and blue sky, a gentle rolling swell, the *hush* of the water as the *Lion* plowed through it.

Sato took a moment, admired the view. Breathed the fresh air. He and his colleagues had been imprisoned belowdecks for three days, confined mostly to darkness and the stale air of the holds. He'd ventured up to the weather deck once, when the cargo hold started to seem suffocating, but it had been nighttime, the ship's minders asleep in the lounge, the air outside cold.

It was a beautiful day. It had been an uneventful voyage, so far, for better or for worse. Sato wasn't seasick; that was a positive. Perhaps the only positive, at this point.

He produced his satellite phone. Entered the number he knew by heart, and waited to be connected.

The connection took time, longer than a cellular phone, and Sato held the phone to his ear, and watched the waves roll by. Then a click, and the connection was made. *"Hai."*

"The product is not here," Sato told the man on the other end of the line. "We've looked exhaustively."

There was a pause. The connection clicked and coughed. Sato waited.

"Very well," the man said at last. "We will have to escalate the matter."

"I'll wait for instruction," Sato replied.

The other man didn't bother to answer. He killed the call, leaving Sato alone again with the vast, open ocean, and the sky equally limitless. Sato indulged the view for another minute or two.

Then he closed the hatch and locked it, and set out to return to his colleagues.

THREE THOUSAND MILES away from the *Pacific Lion*, Katsuo Nakadate replaced the handset on his phone.

He turned in his chair, away from his desk and his computer, to stare out through vast picture windows at the city of Yokohama and the ocean beyond. He thought, with a long moment, about what he was going to do.

The syndicate's interests remained in jeopardy. The bonds remained unrecovered. Nakadate would use any means to recover them, but still, he had hoped to confine any violence to the accountant Ishimaru, and perhaps to his accomplice on the freighter.

He didn't relish the prospect of initiating conflict with civilians. He had hoped that Sato and his colleagues would have located the bonds on the freighter, that his most pressing concern would be bringing his men home.

But the bonds had disappeared. And that meant someone—an American—knew of their whereabouts.

Nakadate swiveled in his chair again, back to his phone. Picked up his handset and instructed his secretary to make another call.

He waited briefly. Then the call was placed, and Masao Tanaka answered on the first ring.

"Your colleagues have had no luck," Nakadate told him. "It's your turn to act."

93

Four days into the tow.

McKenna made fresh coffee in the galley, and then climbed the stairs back to the wheelhouse. Nelson Ridley had the controls this morning. The engineer heard her coming, glanced back to greet her, and let his eyes fall meaningfully on the chart table by the stairs, the stainless-steel briefcase that sat upon it.

"You ever going to look inside that thing, skipper?" he asked McKenna. "It's kind of giving me the heebie-jeebies here."

McKenna handed Ridley a cup of coffee, took a sip of her own. Surveyed the wheelhouse, looked out through the windows. It was a nice enough day on the water: not much sun to speak of, but no wind, either, and nothing more than a low, westerly swell, as far as the seas were concerned. The *Pacific Lion* followed the *Gale Force* as she had for days now, and McKenna found it almost hard to believe that the well-behaved freighter dawdling behind the tug was the same beast of a ship that had nearly killed Court Harrington.

Of course, there was a reason that saving the *Lion* was worth thirty million dollars, and towing her to port only paid a fraction.

Ridley took the coffee, but he wasn't about to let the subject drop. "I mean, be honest. Aren't you at all curious?"

McKenna looked back at the briefcase, felt her body tense involuntary, constricting around her lungs just enough to be uncomfortable. She'd found the briefcase just where Harrington had described it, stashed under his bunk with a whole family of dust bunnies, had brought it up to the wheelhouse and looked at it for a while, long enough to make her feel uneasy. Then she'd set the thing down on the table, tried to forget about it. Tried to focus on the tow.

"Of course I'm curious," she told Ridley. "But it's locked, Nelson."

Ridley raised an eyebrow. "We're the roughest, toughest salvage tug on the North Pacific," he said. "We raise ships from the dead. You don't think we can open a briefcase?"

"I'm quite sure we can," McKenna said. "It's just—"

She trailed off, unsure how to tell Ridley how that damn case gave her the creeps, too, how she could close her eyes and hear the gunshots that had almost killed her and Harrington, see the look in the gunman's eyes as he'd prepared to pull the trigger.

"I know," Ridley said. "It's weird, all right. But the kid's got a valid argument. It's lawfully our property." He gave her a devilish grin. "What if there's a million bucks in there, skipper? Wouldn't you want to know?"

"I've already made my millions for this trip." She forced a smile, gestured to the controls. "Let me take over here, would you? Grab a sandwich or something."

Ridley paused, like he was debating pressing the issue. Finally, he shrugged. "You worried I'm going to crash your big boat?"

"I'm just saying, I've seen you drive that motorcycle of yours. Go on back to the engine room where you can't wreck anything."

"You'd be surprised." Ridley retreated, casting one more meaningful glance at the briefcase before disappearing down the stairs and out of sight.

McKenna listened to her engineer fumbling around in the galley. Checked the autopilot, the GPS, replotted her course, anything to keep from thinking about that case.

The tug was making good time anyway, made it halfway across the Gulf of Alaska already. Another couple days, they'd home in on Cape St. James, the southern tip of the Haida Gwaii archipelago off the British Columbia coast. They'd skirt down the western side of Vancouver Island to the Strait of Juan de Fuca, cut in and down to Puget Sound in Seattle, and home, easy as pie. If the weather held, they might make it in early.

But the briefcase still gnawed at her. *Throw it overboard,* she thought. *Forget about it. Hand it off to the authorities when you get to Seattle. Wash your hands of the whole ordeal.*

Yeah, she thought. *Maybe.*

But even that wouldn't guarantee safety. What if whoever owned the case came looking for it?

What would your dad do, girl?

Riptide Rhodes? McKenna couldn't be sure, but she had a damn solid suspicion her dad wouldn't be turning the case in to any authorities, not until he'd figured out what was inside.

It's lawfully ours. Rules of the sea.

Her dad would have been curious. Hell, McKenna was curious. Just not enough to do anything about it, not yet.

She replotted the *Gale Force*'s route on the GPS screen—again— the vast expanse of ocean, not another soul around for hundreds of miles. Sooner or later, though, the tug would reach landfall, and McKenna wondered what—or who—would be waiting for them when they arrived.

It was a worrying question, and McKenna had days and days to mull it over. She settled into an uneasy discontent, and it hung over her head and didn't go away.

94

Court Harrington had just returned to his suite at Seattle's Fairmont Olympic Hotel—hey, he was a millionaire now—when there came a knock at the door.

Harrington sighed. He was tired, and he was hungry. It had been a long day of physical therapy, feeling weak and helpless as the cute doctor put him through a succession of strengthening exercises. A steak sounded pretty damn good right about now. So did alcohol, for that matter. He'd earned it.

Three knocks, quick and solid. Someone meant business. Harrington crossed the suite to the door and peered through the peephole. Saw a man standing in the hall, young, a black suit.

"Yeah?" he called through the door.

The man seemed to fix his eyes on Harrington's own, even through the tiny looking glass. "Hotel security, Mr. Harrington," he said in an accented voice. "There is a matter we need to discuss with you."

"Security?" Harrington frowned. "What are they saying I did?"

"It's nothing so serious," the man replied. "Please, there are some questions about your account with us. If you'll allow me to verify them with you, I can leave you in peace."

Damn it. Harrington sighed again, felt his stomach rumble in protest as he slid the security chain loose and unlocked the door. Swung it open to reveal the slender security man, smaller than Harrington had first imagined. He gave Harrington a wide smile.

"My name is Tanaka," he said. He gestured into Harrington's suite. "Please, make yourself comfortable."

This was weird. But the guy was small, and Harrington figured if the joker tried anything, he could take him.

"You said you had questions about my account?" he asked, turning to walk into the suite's spacious living area as the door swung closed behind Tanaka. "Listen—maybe you should show me some ID, first."

He turned back, pleased with himself, figured he'd put the guy on the defensive, see how he liked it.

Felt significantly less clever when he caught sight of the gun.

THE GUN had been easy for Masao Tanaka to obtain.

The Inagawa-kai was yakuza, after all, and the yakuza had friends in Seattle. One discreet phone call to one of those friends, one late-night meeting in one empty parking garage, and Tanaka found himself the proud owner of a Beretta 92FS 9mm pistol, with a Gemtech GM-9 suppressor thrown in for good measure. An easy transaction, to be sure, but a worthwhile one, judging by the expression on Court Harrington's face.

Tanaka backed the American farther into his suite. Gestured to a plush chair in the corner. "Please," he said. "Sit."

Harrington sat. He hadn't taken his eyes off the pistol.

"Very good." Tanaka smiled at the American again, still friendly, harmless. "I'm not planning to hurt you," he said. "I don't want to have to alter my plans. Do you know why I'm here?"

Harrington nodded. Tried to speak, wet his lips, tried again. "I guess it's the same reason that other guy drew down on me and my skipper. Y'all really want that briefcase back, huh? What do you have in there, gold bars?"

"It contains important documents that were stolen from my employer. It's imperative that I recover them."

"Huh." Harrington clasped his hands together. Looked down at the floor for a beat. When he looked up again, he was smiling. "Well, I hate to disappoint you, man, but you came a long way for nothing. I don't have your briefcase."

"Where is it?"

Harrington shrugged.

Inwardly, Tanaka rolled his eyes. Could nothing ever be easy? He raised the pistol, took aim at the American's forehead.

"Your name is Court Harrington," he said. "Your parents, David and Ashley Harrington, live in Sylva, North Carolina. Shall I recite their address for you?"

Harrington said nothing.

Tanaka kept the pistol aimed square. "Perhaps you are willing to die to protect a briefcase. Are you willing to kill your parents also?"

The American's smile was gone now. He exhaled a long slow breath and looked down at the floor again.

"I'm afraid I have some more bad news for you, bud," he said at last. "I don't have your briefcase. I left it behind."

"It's not on the *Pacific Lion*. We know this for a fact. Try again."

"Did I say it was on the *Lion*?" Harrington shook his head. "It's on the tug, smart guy. Way out there in the middle of the Pacific Ocean."

Tanaka nodded. "Good." Kept the pistol trained, and with his free hand, produced a cellular telephone. Pressed the call button, and waited.

"Hai," came the response.

"On the tugboat," Tanaka said in Japanese. "I believe the American is telling me the truth."

He ended the call.

"Who was that?" Harrington asked. "Who did you call?"

"My employer," Tanaka replied. "I was pleased to inform him that you had offered us a good lead."

"Oh." Harrington relaxed a little bit. "So, great, what happens now? I guess you can go, huh? Let me grab a little dinner?"

Soon as this guy gets out of my hair, he thought, *I'll call McKenna and tell her to watch her six.*

But Tanaka smirked. "Not yet," he said, and he dragged a chair from a desk along the wall and sat, facing the American. "First, we wait to know if you've been truthful with us."

95

Katsuo Nakadate replaced his handset and studied his computer screen with satisfaction. Masao Tanaka's information had come at a fortunate time.

Nakadate had discovered, purely by accident, that he could follow the path of the *Gale Force* across the North Pacific simply by typing the name of the tugboat into an Internet search browser. The tug transmitted a GPS signal that was monitored and rebroadcast by a number of marine traffic websites, all of them dedicated to tracking the progress of ships across the sea.

If the *Pacific Lion* had been making a routine voyage, Nakadate surmised that he could have followed her path just as easily. The Internet site featured maps that were filled with hundreds of cursors, like an air traffic controller's screen, each cursor representing a cargo ship, a tug, or a large fishing vessel.

Right now, Nakadate could see that the *Gale Force* had crossed the Gulf of Alaska to the Haida Gwaii archipelago, and turned in a southwesterly direction to follow the coast of the Canadian Vancouver Island toward Seattle.

The western length of Vancouver Island, Nakadate had learned, was remote and rugged, and mostly uninhabited. But there were settlements, mostly toward the southern end, fishing villages and tourist towns. They would have to do.

Nakadate picked up the phone. Called Daishin Sato on his satellite phone. Sato answered, apologized for the poor reception, and

Nakadate could hear the man's breathing as he ventured, presumably, somewhere better.

Then Nakadate could hear the wind, and perhaps the ocean. Whatever it was, Sato's voice came through much clearer. "We are ready."

"The briefcase is aboard the tug," Nakadate told him. "You will retrieve it under cover of darkness. Take whatever steps necessary to maintain secrecy. Then you will retreat to Vancouver Island, a town named Tofino. I will arrange for your retrieval there."

"As you wish," Sato replied. Nakadate ended the call. Checked on the progress of the *Gale Force* again. Then he brought up the tugboat company's website. It was a minor site, plain and amateurish. A picture of the tug, and a picture of the captain—a woman named McKenna Rhodes. Nakadate studied the pictures. The tug was handsome and well-kept, her owner surprisingly young for such a position. Her eyes were clear, though, and her gaze direct. She didn't look like someone who would brook Sato's ambush without a fight.

So be it, Nakadate thought. *If she is lucky, she won't even notice Sato's presence aboard her tug. But I will have my property returned, one way or the other.*

He clicked off of the Gale Force Marine website. Brought up the GPS map again. The *Gale Force* inched across the ocean, little by little, beating her steady path down the Canadian coast.

96

The weather began to turn again as the *Gale Force* reached the top of Vancouver Island. The wind picked up to about fifteen knots, and the swell built to six feet. The tug led the *Pacific Lion* down the west side of the island, dodging the treacherous Brooks Peninsula, which jutted out ten miles from shore like a hitchhiker's thumb, a nest of hairy weather and unpredictable seas.

By the time the tug and tow reached Estevan Point, just north of the little surfing town of Tofino, the radio was broadcasting a wind warning and a small-craft advisory, and McKenna was checking the barometer and hardly daring to sleep. The *Gale Force* could handle a little rough weather out in the open ocean, but tomorrow would see the tug enter the Strait of Juan de Fuca, that narrow, busy channel to Vancouver and Seattle, and she hoped the weather would cooperate for that tricky stretch.

Right now, there was nothing to do but wait and watch and worry, though at least it took her mind off of the briefcase. McKenna caught a few hours of sleep around Estevan Point, woke up and relieved Al Parent at the wheel as night fell, and the tug and tow approached Tofino. Their course kept them offshore by about twenty miles, the rocky Vancouver Island invisible off the portside, but McKenna looked out at the heavy rolling swell scudding in toward land, and imagined the surfers on Tofino's Long Beach would have a field day in the morning.

Nelson Ridley was in the wheelhouse with McKenna when the

radio squawked. Just brief, mostly static, probably a stray pickup from somewhere long-range.

But then it happened again. And this time, both McKenna and Ridley could hear Stacey Jonas's voice, clear, and clearly panicked.

"There's someone on the freighter, McKenna. We're under attack! They—"

Stacey's words were drowned out by something in the background that sounded a heck of a lot like gunshots. Then there was static, and then silence.

IF CIRCUMSTANCES HAD BROKEN just a little differently, Stacey Jonas wouldn't have survived long enough to make that panicked call.

It had happened so fast. She'd set out for a walk, a little fresh air before bed, knew the weather was turning and it might be her last chance, the rest of the trip probably booked solid keeping watch on the bilge water and ballast tanks, looking for flooding. Matt was in the officers' lounge, lazing about, reading another one of Al Parent's paperback romances. He'd yawned, waved her off, said it looked cold out, and she'd called him a baby and bundled up tight.

The wind *was* blowing hard, and the swell had picked up, but the air was refreshing anyway, and Stacey turned up her iPod and jogged in place a bit, got the blood pumping, was thinking about sprinting down to the exhaust funnel and back—and then she saw them.

Men, three of them, by the aft portside lifeboat. They were dressed in black and fiddling with the davits, almost blending into the shadows around them. Stacey watched, frozen in place a hundred feet away, couldn't quite believe what she was seeing.

Where did they come from?

What are they doing here?

And, scariest of all: *Have they been here the whole time?*

And then it didn't matter, none of it did, because one of the men had looked up and seen her, said something to his friends. And then one of those friends pulled out a gun.

NELSON RIDLEY WAS FIRST to spot the blip on the radar screen. McKenna was at the radio, trying to raise Stacey again, heart pounding, when Ridley called her over.

"C'mere, skipper," the engineer said. "I think you want to have a look at this."

McKenna joined him at the dash. Studied the radar screen. Then looked back through the aft windows at the lights of the *Pacific Lion*, fifty yards behind.

"Okay," she said. "What the heck are we seeing?"

The *Gale Force*'s radar had a minor blind spot directly aft. It wasn't configured to pick up small, fast-moving objects, particularly in heavy seas. If McKenna hadn't known what to look for, she never would have seen it.

But it was there, an intermittent blip on the screen. It was tiny, moving distinctly from the *Lion* on the freighter's portside. Moving faster, too, closing the distance between the freighter and the *Gale Force*.

"Whatever it is, it's coming in hot," Ridley said. "I'm going to try Stacey again."

McKenna took her field glasses to the aft windows. Searched the gloom behind the tug's stern as Ridley tried Stacey, got only static. McKenna kept looking. Couldn't see a thing but the *Lion* and the black, empty ocean.

"Nelson, raise the Coast Guard," she said. "I think we're going to need some help out here, fast."

97

Sato expected the salvage crew would know he was coming. He hoped that it wouldn't matter.

Fuchida had seen the woman first. She'd picked an inopportune time for a walk, and it had nearly cost her her life. Would have, if Tsunoda was a better shot with his pistol.

The first shot had missed badly, and the woman didn't make the mistake of waiting around for another. She'd turned and ran, sprinted for the first door and hurled herself inside the freighter.

"Find her," Sato told the others. "*Now*. Her partner, too."

But the woman was fast. She'd disappeared down the hall before Fuchida and Tsunoda could catch up, and though they'd followed her heavy breathing resonating down the steel corridor, they hadn't been quick enough.

She'd gathered her companion. Locked themselves in a stateroom, a heavy bulkhead door. Fuchida had opened fire, nearly killed himself, and Sato and Tsunoda as well. Did no harm to the door whatsoever. And inside, through the steel, Sato could hear the woman's muffled voice as she called her own colleagues for help.

So be it. We are armed. We will retrieve the briefcase.

"Leave them," Sato told the others. "They aren't of any consequence now."

RIDLEY HAD THE Canadian Coast Guard on the radio. "Coast Guard, this is the tug *Gale Force*. We are currently transiting Canadian waters with tow, seventeen nautical miles off Long Beach. We, ah, have reason to believe that we are under attack."

Ridley caught her eye, shot her a grim look. McKenna read it immediately. Unlike their American counterparts, the Canadian Coast Guard wasn't considered a part of the military. The organization focused on search and rescue and environmental enforcement, not coastal defense, and its cutters weren't equipped with deck guns or any other heavy weaponry.

The radio crackled back. "*Gale Force*, this is Tofino Traffic," the operator said. "We have the lifeboat *Cape Ann* in your vicinity. Can you confirm the details of your situation?"

"I said we're under attack, Tofino," Ridley said. "You got any guns on that lifeboat?"

The operator paused. "*Gale Force*, I can't broadcast that information on this channel. Do you have reason to believe the attackers are armed?"

"We heard gunshots," Ridley said. "Look, we're fearing for our lives here, Tofino. Do you have any way to protect us?"

Footsteps on the stairs. McKenna looked back, saw Al and Jason come up, brows furrowed, questions on their faces. On the radar, the blip continued to close distance. It looked small enough to be hampered somewhat by the heavy swell, but not nearly enough. They were coming, McKenna knew. That swell wouldn't stall them for long.

The Coast Guard operator came back. "*Gale Force*, I've passed your information on to the Royal Canadian Navy. They have the coastal defense vessel HMCS *Nanaimo* outbound in the Juan de Fuca Strait. Estimate arrival on scene in approximately six hours."

McKenna crossed the wheelhouse, took the radio from Ridley. "Tofino, *Gale Force*. Six hours doesn't do us a lick of good out here."

"I have an RCAF Sea King helicopter ready to fly from the 443 Maritime Helicopter Squadron in Victoria as well, Captain," the operator said. "Again, they estimate two hours to get to your location."

"Two hours. And what do you suggest we do until then?"

Another pause. "*Gale Force*, we recommend you, ah, initiate anti-piracy measures and do what you can to keep them off of your ship. However you can protect your crew, Captain, we suggest you do it."

McKenna looked at Ridley again. Ridley rolled his eyes. For the short term, anyway, the *Gale Force* was alone in the water.

"Antipiracy measures," Al Parent said. "Do we have any of those?"

"We have firefighting equipment," McKenna replied. "Water cannons, fore and aft. I want Jason on the forward cannon, Al on the aft. Try and blast them as best you can if they try to board us."

"That's it?" Jason said. "We're going to spray them with water?"

"They're here for the briefcase," McKenna said. "If we give it back to them, they'll leave us alone."

"And if they don't?"

McKenna looked at him. At the rest of her crew. "If that doesn't stop them?" She crossed the wheelhouse to a locker on the starboard side, secured with a combination lock. Spun the dial, opened the locker. Pulled out a Remington pump-action shotgun.

"If that doesn't stop them," she said, "we use this. But let's pray it doesn't come to that."

She looked around at her crew. The crew stared back, their eyes wide. Ridley met her gaze, frowning, and McKenna knew what he was thinking.

One shotgun and two water cannons. It was hardly an arsenal.

98

Sato stood in the cockpit of the lifeboat, listening to the little engine whine as it closed the distance between his men and the target.

The master of the tug had turned on her spotlights, and they crisscrossed the water, searching the dark. The tug was quite large up close, its red-and-white superstructure rising tall and proud over its rugged black hull. The tug was still plowing through the water as though nothing at all was the matter, as though they hadn't noticed the lifeboat's approach.

But Sato knew that wasn't true. He'd heard the woman on the freighter calling for help, had monitored the captain of the *Gale Force* talking to the Coast Guard on the lifeboat's radio. He knew the Coast Guard had informed the military, and that the quickest response was still two hours away.

In two hours, Sato thought, *we'll have made landfall. And we will have that briefcase with us.*

All the same, they would have to work quickly. There would be no time for creativity, just simple brute force. The captain would produce the briefcase. Sato would ensure it. It was only a matter of time.

The heavy ocean was slowing the lifeboat's progress. The engine punched and struggled, and the little boat climbed up and crashed down on the large waves. The tugboat ground on ahead. Sato could see action in the wheelhouse, two figures silhouetted in the windows. A third man appeared on the afterdeck, fiddling with something that looked like a deck gun. Sato stared at the man. For a moment, he even felt concerned. Then the deck gun began to spout water.

A firefighting tool. A giant water gun. The crew of the tug intended to use it for defense.

The tug's spotlights crossed the water. Landed on the lifeboat, momentarily blinding Sato. He ducked away, called ahead to Fuchida, who stood at the lifeboat's bow door with a rifle. "Send them our regards."

Fuchida shouldered his rifle, took aim. Fired three shots across the water, sending the man at the water gun down to the deck.

There, Sato thought. *What do you think about that?*

"DOWN!"

McKenna and Ridley hit the floor as the attackers opened fire. Bullets struck the wheelhouse walls, a hail of sparks along the tug's superstructure.

At the after water cannon, Al Parent fell. McKenna staggered to her feet, half crawled to the starboard door, away from the attackers in their little lifeboat. Opened the door and looked out onto the deck, expecting to see her first mate cut to pieces. *"Al!"*

But Al wasn't dead. He'd ducked behind his cannon, hiding for his life. *"Get the hell off that deck,"* McKenna told him. *"Get in here, now."*

Al pushed himself to his feet and made a dash for the doorway just as the attackers fired again. More sparks, everywhere. The tug plunged and rolled in the swell, and Al slipped, lost his balance. Picked himself up as the bullets whizzed past.

McKenna leaned out the doorway, grabbed the first mate, and pulled with all of her strength until the man was safe inside. Then she hurried to the forward starboard window and called down to Jason Parent on the bow.

"Get your ass inside," she hollered. *"Never mind the cannon!"*

Jason peered around the portside of the tug. Ducked back again quickly as more shots sounded out. He hurried around the starboard side of the tug and into the house.

"Take Al and Jason and lock yourselves in the engine room," McKenna told Ridley. "Stay there and don't move until I come and get you, okay?"

Ridley's brow furrowed. "What are you going to do?"

McKenna checked the autopilot. Checked back at the attackers, now about fifteen yards out, and closing. A lifeboat. They'd taken a damn lifeboat. *But where the hell had they come from in the first place?*

"I'm going to give them what they came for," McKenna said, reaching for the radio. "Now take the others and lock this tug down."

. . .

SATO WATCHED AS THE TUG'S crew scrambled to hide from Fuchida and Tsunoda's barrage of fire. The lifeboat pushed through the waves, approached the tug's stern. Five minutes, maybe less, and Sato and his colleagues would be able to board.

The people in the tug's wheelhouse disappeared. Sato could only see one of them left. He wondered what the rest of the crew was doing. Hiding, probably.

Then the radio came to life.

"We have what you came for." A woman's voice, the captain. "If you'd stop shooting at us, I could hand it over."

Fuchida and Tsunoda looked back at Sato. He lifted a hand. *Cease fire.* Then he picked up the radio. "Show me."

A pause. Then: "Yeah, okay. Just give me a second."

99

McKenna edged out onto the *Gale Force*'s afterdeck, keeping the tug's big winch between her body and the attackers' guns, holding the briefcase aloft so they could see it.

"This is what you want, right?" she yelled, though she knew they couldn't hear her over the roar of the engines, hers and their own.

She peered around the winch. Saw the lifeboat lit bright as day in the *Gale Force*'s spotlight, ten yards off the port quarter. The little boat wallowed in the swell, one man on the bow, and one perched above the stern, both armed with rifles. They'd stopped shooting, anyway. That was a plus.

I should have done this earlier, McKenna thought. *As soon as I saw them, I should have hailed them on the radio and told them come get what they wanted. Hell, I should have passed this thing on to the Coast Guard as soon as Court called. Whatever it is, it's not worth dying over.*

The lifeboat approached the tug. McKenna looked out from around the winch, waved the briefcase over her head.

"Just take it," she called out. *"Take this damn briefcase and leave us alone!"*

The men on the lifeboat lowered their rifles. Whoever was inside driving the thing motored the boat past the *Gale Force*'s stern and up the portside of the tug. It rolled in the swell, but the men on board kept their weapons gripped tight as they watched McKenna.

That's some serious firepower, she thought. *We wouldn't stand a chance if they boarded us.*

She edged out from the winch. Picked her way across the deck to the port gunwale, careful to stay as hidden as possible, holding the briefcase in front of her like a shield. It wouldn't stop the bullets, she knew, but it might give the shooters pause if they were planning to kill her.

The lifeboat idled, fifteen feet off the *Gale Force*'s starboard side. The men watched McKenna approach. McKenna held out the briefcase.

"Take it," she called out again. *"It's all yours."*

She began to step out to the gunwale, ready to beckon the driver of the lifeboat closer so she could heave the thing over. The gunman on the stern leaned into the lifeboat's cabin, said something to the driver, and the little boat turned and motored down the top of a wave toward McKenna.

Okay, she thought. *Nice and easy. Throw them the briefcase, and then duck for your life.*

She knew as soon as she threw the briefcase, she was fair game for the men. She thought about dying. Thought about her father.

Might see you sooner than either of us planned, Daddy.

Then something exploded from somewhere above McKenna's head. Instantly, there was a hole in the lifeboat's bow. The shooters ducked for cover, disappeared inside the orange canopy. McKenna heard a noise from above, a familiar *chu-chunk* from the wheelhouse door. Looked up and saw Ridley with the pump-action Remington, swinging the barrel around to the lifeboat's stern.

Ridley fired again. One of the lifeboat's plastic windows disappeared, along with the back of its canopy. The lifeboat shuddered and wallowed. The shooters stayed down. Ridley pumped another shell, fired at the bow again. Made another hole.

McKenna could only watch. *What the hell are you thinking, Nelson? That shotgun only holds five rounds. What are you planning for when the ammo runs out?*

Ridley fired his fourth shell at the lifeboat, amidships. Shot spattered the hull, pitting it with holes. One more shell.

The shooters were regrouping now. McKenna could see the barrels of their rifles poking out from the lifeboat's mangled canopy. Ridley pumped the shotgun one more time.

"*The brake,*" he called down to McKenna. "*Release the brake, skipper.*"

McKenna blinked. Didn't get it right away. Ridley caught her eye through the stairway's metal grating.

"The winch brake," he shouted. *"Let her go."*

The shooters let off a rapid barrage of shots from the lifeboat. Ridley ducked down as sparks exploded around him. Stood up again and fired his last shell at the smaller boat. This one put another hole in the bow.

Ridley ducked into the wheelhouse and slammed the door. Bullets spattered the superstructure around him. The lifeboat's engine whined loud, working hard. The attackers would close the distance in no time, climb aboard the tug and kill them all.

McKenna hurried to the winch. Looked up to the wheelhouse and saw Ridley at the aft controls, yelling something through the window. She reached the winch, heard bullets all around her. *Felt* them fly past. Found the manual brake on the winch, pulled it out of its chock. Instantly, she heard the tug's engine roar.

The *Gale Force* bolted like a spooked horse. The winch paid out towline, no longer restrained. The thick wire spooled out, fast as a train, as the tug's twin propellers churned white water at her stern.

The lifeboat kept pace. The bullets kept coming. From behind the winch, McKenna saw the driver aim his ailing vessel at the tug's stern. But the lifeboat was hurt. It was underpowered already, and Ridley had blasted a couple big holes in her bow. Every time a wave hit, the boat took on more water, sagged lower.

Ridley had the tug's engines revved to the limit. Now the lifeboat dropped back. The driver sold out for the *Gale Force*'s stern, one last-ditch Hail Mary. One of his shooters climbed to the bow. Readied himself, crouched, leaped at the tug. Seemed to hang in the air a long moment, then fell into white water. The lifeboat wallowed in the *Gale Force*'s wake. The shooting stopped.

McKenna watched the little boat settle in the water. It was listing to starboard now, thanks to Ridley's new holes, and it was sinking fast. The shooters had clambered atop the lifeboat's ruined canopy, the highest, driest point, the tug and the briefcase forgotten.

Inside the wheelhouse, Ridley powered down the engines a little. Took them off redline. It didn't matter now, McKenna knew. The lifeboat was a goner. The *Gale Force* was safe.

McKenna heard a noise above her head. Looked up to see Ridley step out of the wheelhouse door, survey the damage on the wheelhouse wall, pockmarks and bullet holes. Nothing a little spackle and some paint wouldn't fix.

"You want to tell me what that was all about, Nelson?" McKenna asked, her heart still racing.

Ridley didn't answer. Tracked the spotlight back to follow the lifeboat, its bow submerged by now.

"I had this thing resolved," McKenna continued. "They put their guns down. I could have thrown them the briefcase and resolved this thing peacefully."

Ridley studied the lifeboat some more. McKenna watched him. He came down the stairs without ever taking his eyes off the attackers.

"You do what you want with that briefcase," Ridley said. "You can turn it in to the police, throw it overboard, hell, turn this tug around and drop it in the water next to those assholes. I don't care."

He looked at McKenna, and his eyes were hard. "I told your dad I'd keep watch over you, lass, if he ever couldn't do it himself. And as long as I'm your engineer, no one, but *no one* is going to bully this boat around."

McKenna studied his face. Realized she appreciated Ridley's resolve, though she would never admit it.

"I guess we should go back and rescue those guys," she said.

Ridley followed her gaze. Narrowed his eyes. "Nah," he said. "Coast Guard's on its way. That little dinghy they're riding won't fully sink for a little while yet. We'll keep the spotlight on them, let them stew in their bad decisions for a bit."

McKenna looked at the lifeboat. The bow was underwater, most of the passenger compartment flooded. The three shooters clung to the stern, to the ruined canopy, as the wreck bobbed in the swell. Far behind, the *Lion* followed the *Gale Force*, but it would slow before it reached the shooters, McKenna could see, drift away from them.

In the distance, she spied lights on the horizon. The Canadian Coast Guard lifeboat, closing fast. The shooters wouldn't drown in the water, but their bad night wasn't over just yet.

"Fine," she said, straightening. "Let the Coast Guard haul them in. Get the Parents out of the engine room. Let's clean up this tow and get a move on."

100

Nakadate stared at his computer in disbelief.

A Google News alert: MORE DRAMA ON THE *PACIFIC LION*. Three Japanese nationals rescued from a sinking lifeboat. Firearms recovered in the wreck. Reports of an audacious attack on the *Pacific Lion* and her tugboat escort, the *Gale Force*, the same tug that had rescued the ship after her near-capsize in the North Pacific three weeks ago.

The three attackers were safe, Nakadate read, but were in Canadian custody. The *Pacific Lion*, meanwhile, would continue her voyage to Seattle—though from now on, with a military escort.

Nakadate read the article over again. Sato and his colleagues had failed. The *Lion* continued. There was nothing about a briefcase. No mention of his stolen property.

Perhaps there was no need. The scope of Sato's failure was so vast that Nakadate could be sure the briefcase remained in the salvage crew's possession. That was a problem, but it was not yet a disaster.

He picked up the phone. Placed a call to Masao Tanaka. The crew of the *Gale Force* retained the stolen bonds. Nakadate wondered how eager they would be to trade.

"THERE IS ONE THING I've been wondering," Stacey Jonas told McKenna over the radio. She and her husband had emerged from their hiding place, called over to the *Gale Force* to check in on the crew. She and Matt were scared half to death, but otherwise they were fine.

"What's that?" McKenna asked, watching the lights of the *Lion* inch closer to the stern of her tug, the winch drawing the big freighter back close again. Beyond the *Lion*'s stern, the Canadian Coast Guard lifeboat had rescued the three shooters; above, a big Royal Canadian Air Force helicopter stood guard.

"It was like they knew something," Stacey said. "Like, why would they even move on the *Gale Force* at all?"

"Maybe they talked to the sailor," McKenna said. "The Coast Guard brought him to Dutch Harbor. Best I can tell, that's where these three got on."

"Yeah, maybe," Stacey said. "That would put them on the ship, for sure. But there's no way they could have checked out the whole freighter since we left Dutch, is there? I mean, they didn't even bother to ask me and Matt if we knew anything."

McKenna said nothing. Thought back to Dutch Harbor. Thought she might remember, vaguely, a man on the dock, a pickup truck. A man at the airport, Court's flight.

Probably nothing. Just paranoia.

"Those guys were on a mission, McKenna," Stacey continued. "They knew where to look. How do you figure they got that information?"

Damn it. McKenna stared out the window, the near-black night, the ocean.

"I'll get back to you," she told Stacey. "I'd better make a call."

101

Court Harrington still hadn't eaten his steak.

Oh, the nice Japanese man with the silencer on his pistol had allowed Harrington to order room service, sure; the men had to eat while they waited, after all. And they'd been waiting a long time already.

But there was something just *wrong* about eating a steak at gunpoint. How could a guy fully enjoy the meal, knowing some lunatic was one ill-timed sneeze from blowing your head off?

So he'd ordered hamburgers, chicken fingers. A turkey club sandwich. Soda, instead of beer, because damn it, he wanted to save that first ice-cold Budweiser for the celebration. And this, whatever it was, was far from a celebration.

They'd sat here all day and night and through the day again, Tanaka and Harrington. Tanaka didn't sleep, best as Harrington could tell. He went to the john, sure, but he kept the door open—and he made sure that Harrington remembered that he knew his parents' address every time he had to go.

Harrington was bored. He was worried. He wondered how much longer this would take, how it would end.

He hoped McKenna Rhodes was all right.

If she's hurt, it's on you, you asshole, he thought. *One hundred percent, you screwed up.* The thought kept Harrington awake through the night.

But he'd turned the TV on a few hours ago. Kept the volume low, just background noise, something to distract him while he waited. Didn't even care what program, what channel, just wanted something to take his focus away.

Now, the news was playing. And Harrington heard something that made him reach for the remote.

"Another twist in the saga of the *Pacific Lion,*" the anchor was saying. "The freighter that nearly sank three weeks ago in Alaska was involved in another high-drama, high-seas event, this time a foiled act of piracy."

Foiled. Does that mean they're okay?

Now Tanaka's phone was ringing. The man stirred in his chair, removed the phone from his jacket with his free hand, brought it to his ear. Waved at the TV, at Harrington, *Turn the volume down.*

Harrington didn't. Tanaka stopped waving. Pointed the gun at his forehead. Harrington reached for the remote. And then the room phone began to ring, too.

Tanaka turned away a split second, distracted. Accepted the call on *his* phone, brought his gun hand to his ear to block out the noise. And Harrington decided he'd had enough waiting around, figured he was about ready to eat that steak.

He leaped at Tanaka and knocked the man to the floor.

102

The hit man went down easy. Crashed to the carpet, Harrington on top of him. Had a moment while falling to choose what to hold, chose the phone. Chose wrong. His pistol flew sideways, landed under the couch.

A struggle ensued. Harrington pushed off of Tanaka. Dove for the couch, didn't quite get there, felt the smaller man clawing at him. Prayed the guy didn't have another gun hidden somewhere, kicked like swimming lessons until the guy let him free.

The hotel phone was still ringing. The TV was blaring. Harrington hardly heard it, leaped again for the gun.

This time, he got hold of it. Rolled on his back and aimed it at Tanaka, who'd climbed to his feet and was coming for Harrington. The hit man stopped when he saw the gun. Smiled a little bit.

The bastard was still holding the phone.

"Back," Harrington told him, pushing off of his back and to a standing position. "Back *way* up, buddy."

Tanaka did as instructed. Stood there, waiting. The hotel phone was still ringing, and then it stopped. The TV was still on. Harrington had a pistol, and he had no idea what he was supposed to do next.

He had an idea.

"Give me your phone," he told Tanaka. "Toss it to me. Don't move."

Tanaka obeyed. Tossed the phone softly to Harrington, who managed to catch it, though not at all gracefully. Harrington kept the pistol trained at Tanaka, as he'd seen Tanaka do all night. With his other hand, he brought the phone to his ear.

"I'm going to make a few assumptions," he told whoever was on the other end of the line. "I'm going to assume you're involved in this scheme Mr. Tanaka is running, first off."

Silence.

"Second, I'm going to assume that you're calling because you just saw the same news story we did, and now you know your buddies were, you know, *foiled* in their little act of piracy."

Silence, still.

"And I guess I'm going to assume you were calling to tell Tanaka what to do with me, because you still don't have what you're looking for."

More silence. Harrington was out of assumptions. Fortunately, he didn't need any more.

"Suppose you're correct," came the reply. The man on the other end of the line sounded measured, composed. He wasn't nearly as riled up about this whole escapade as Harrington. "What is it you'd like to tell me?"

"What I'd like to tell you?" Harrington went to scratch his forehead, remembered he was holding a gun. Nixed that idea. "I'm telling you, I'm in charge. I got your buddy's phone, and I got his weapon, too. So that means, whatever you were planning to do with me, you can't. Understand?"

More silence.

"*Understand?*"

The man actually *chuckled*. "Yes, I understand. Go on."

"You come after me again," Harrington said, "I call *my* buddies, and they dump that case of yours over the rail, never to be seen again. Get it? And that goes for my parents, too. Whoever you have watching them, call them off now."

Another pause. Then, before Harrington could prompt him, the man sighed. "We won't harm you," he said. "You, or your family."

"Swear it."

"I give you my word." He said it as though Harrington should know his word meant something. Harrington figured that was as good as he was going to get. He tossed the phone back to Tanaka.

"Talk to your boss," he said.

The hotel phone began to ring again. Harrington nearly shot the thing. Instead, he kept the gun trained on Tanaka. Crossed to the phone, picked it up. "What?"

"Court?"

McKenna. Harrington blew out a breath he didn't know he'd been holding. "McKenna—Captain Rhodes—you guys all okay over there?"

"We're fine, Court," the captain said. "Are *you* okay?"

Tanaka was ending the call with the big boss. Harrington kept the gun where the hit man could see it.

"I'm fine," he told McKenna. "All good. Never better. Just in the middle of something here, you know? I'll call you back in a bit."

The captain started to protest. Harrington hung up on her. Felt bad about it briefly, but he had other things to worry about. "We square?" he asked Tanaka.

Tanaka frowned.

"Are we okay?" Harrington clarified. "Like, you're not going to try to kill me again?"

"I will not," Tanaka said. "Katsuo Nakadate gave you his word."

"Perfect." Harrington kept the gun on Tanaka. "Then I'm leaving. Follow me, and I'll call my friends on the tug and get you in deep shit with your boss, get it?"

Tanaka was smiling again. "Get it," he said. "Okay."

"Okay." Harrington backed to the door. Tanaka hadn't moved, so Harrington lowered the gun, tucked it under his shirt. Felt around for the door handle and let himself out of the room.

103

Katsuo Nakadate stared at his phone and couldn't help but laugh.

Anything that could possibly go wrong, he thought, *will. I will have to do this myself.*

He placed another call, to his secretary this time. "Book me a flight," he told her. "I'm going to America."

104

Harrington walked quickly down the hall away from his suite. Made the elevators and pressed the call button about fifteen times before the car showed up, rode it down to the lobby and walked straight to the concierge.

"There's a strange guy on my floor impersonating security," Harrington told him. "Slim, short guy in a black suit. He's giving me a really bad vibe."

The concierge colored. Reached for the phone. "I'm very sorry, sir," he said. "I'll have our *actual* security investigate."

Harrington thanked the man. Hurried out of the hotel, made a right turn, and started up the hill toward anywhere but where he was. Stopped in an alley a couple blocks away, turned his back to the street, took out the pistol, and fumbled to release the magazine. Figured it out and dropped the pistol in a dumpster. Was walking to the next block, the next dumpster, with the loose magazine, when he stopped.

Whoever the heck Katsuo Nakadate is, he thought, *his word ain't worth spit to me.*

He turned on his heel. Walked back to the dumpster, climbed up the side, and nearly fell in trying to retrieve the pistol. But he got it. Slid the magazine back in, a far more satisfying feeling than the opposite. Then he started up the hill again, away from the hotel. Figured he would call his parents, tell them it was high time they took a vacation.

And then, damn it, he was eating a steak.

105

"Well, we *have* to open it now, don't we?"

Another storm was brewing. McKenna and the crew of the *Gale Force* had lingered off the coast of Tofino long enough to reel in the *Pacific Lion* again and clean up the tow. They waited as more Coast Guard and Canadian military arrived on scene, as the weather picked up, and the ocean swell increased, as the wind began to hum through the *Gale Force*'s rigging.

By morning, the weather service was predicting a gale. McKenna consulted with the Coast Guard, the Canadian Navy, the crew of the Sea King helicopter that circled above them. The Sea King lowered a man to the tug's deck to have a look around. He surveyed the pitted steel on the rear of the wheelhouse, took McKenna's shotgun as evidence, and returned to the afterdeck to winch back up to the helicopter.

"Too rough to do the investigation out here," he told McKenna. "We'll escort you into the Strait, get you to Seattle. Send our guys to take a look at the freighter once you're in calmer waters."

"Sounds good to me," McKenna replied. "I'd like to get some ground covered before this weather kicks up."

"Happy sailing," the Navy airman said, and he gave the thumbs-up to his winch man and ascended back to the Sea King.

. . .

NOW McKENNA AND NELSON RIDLEY stood with Jason and Al Parent in the wheelhouse, studying the briefcase on the chart table in front of them, trying to figure out what to do.

Outside, the Sea King was gone, headed back to Victoria to refuel, replaced by a bright yellow Royal Canadian Air Force Cormorant search-and-rescue helicopter, which had followed the *Gale Force* and her tow down the coast of Vancouver Island and into the Strait of Juan de Fuca, where the Royal Canadian Navy's HMCS *Nanaimo* picked up the escort.

The *Nanaimo* was a short, kind of stubby vessel. Painted a flat naval gray, she lingered off of the *Lion*'s portside quarter, blending in with the dull sky and slate ocean. Apart from a perfunctory introduction by her radio operator, the *Nanaimo* stayed quiet, a constant, silent presence, always visible through the aft windows of the *Gale Force*'s wheelhouse.

McKenna didn't mind. She was still rattled. Thirty-plus years around the water and she'd never been fired on before, didn't think her dad had been, either. The rest of the crew felt it, too, she could tell; they lingered in the wheelhouse, Nelson and Jason and Al, eating snacks and not saying much, everyone jumpy, everyone wired. Jason had called home, Nelson, too, and McKenna listened as both men assured their wives they were okay, nothing serious, that the news reports they'd been watching were way overblown.

"Just Hollywood stuff," Nelson told Carly. "These American news guys always have to make it sensational, you know?"

But he didn't sound quite nearly as unflappable as normal, and he listened more than he talked, reassured Carly he'd be home soon, safe and sound. When he'd ended the call, he'd mopped sweat from his brow.

Even the ship's cat could tell something was up. Spike had climbed into McKenna's lap in the skipper's chair, purred once, turned around twice, then sat and quickly fell asleep. McKenna knew she should have been flattered by the cat's attention, but instead she was worried. If the cat was willing to forgive such a well-established grudge, well, something must really be wrong. And it gnawed at her, as the *Gale Force* beat eastward, between the remote Vancouver Island shore and the high peaks of the Olympic Peninsula. She wondered what would be waiting for her crew when the tug arrived in Seattle.

And then Ridley had shifted his weight as the *Gale Force* plowed a wave, caught McKenna's eye. "Well," he'd said. "We *have* to open it now, don't we?"

And now, here they were, the briefcase before them, Ridley armed with every tool and drill he could carry up from his workshop. Al and Jason weren't saying much, weren't showing their hands, but McKenna could see how they looked at the case. They were intrigued, too.

She wasn't sure, though. She'd been thinking about ditching the thing, chucking it off the boat and being done with it.

"Aren't you curious?" Ridley asked her. "I mean, those assholes were ready to kill us all. Gotta be something important, right? They'll probably send more guys to try and take it from us."

McKenna nodded. "Probably."

"So? You going to let me do this, or what?"

She looked at Al and Jason again. Jason avoided her eyes, kept stealing glances at the briefcase. Al shrugged. "Would be kind of interested to know," he said.

This isn't a democracy, girl. You're the captain here.

But McKenna realized she wanted to know, too. Figured she *deserved* to know; she'd sure been shot at enough.

So she lifted her hands, let them fall. "Go for it," she told Ridley. "You want to take a look, be my guest."

TEN MINUTES AND NEARLY thirty new swear words later, Ridley stepped back, wiped his brow. "But damn it," he said. "That was some kind of lock."

The briefcase had given a good fight. But Ridley, assisted by an assortment of power tools, and a helping of brute force, had finally cracked it. And now the crew crowded around what remained, eager for a look inside.

By rights, Matt and Stacey would be here, too. Seeing how they nearly died for this thing just like the rest of us.

But the Jonases were on the *Pacific Lion*, and McKenna was reluctant to do any more broadcasting over the radio, given the Royal Canadian Navy presence nearby. No sense arousing any suspicion— and you never could be totally sure who was listening in.

Ridley caught her eye. Gestured to the briefcase. "I think the honor is yours, Captain Rhodes."

"Better not be a bomb," McKenna replied. She stepped to the table. Took hold of the briefcase, counted to three in her head. Then she lifted it open. And saw—

Paper.

"What is it?" Jason Parent asked, craning for a look.

McKenna leaned closer. She'd been expecting money, maybe, stacks of hundred-dollar bills. Diamonds, perhaps. Or some kind of cutting-edge technological advancement, the likes of which would make the bearer wealthy beyond her wildest dreams. Instead, paper?

But as she looked closer, she could see that inside the briefcase wasn't just any paper. They looked like certificates.

"Bonds," Ridley breathed out, beside her. *"Thundering Jonas."*

He was right. They were certificates, all right, stock certificates, each carrying a value of five hundred thousand—*what*, she thought, squinting, reading. *Euros?*

Each piece of paper was supposed to be worth half a million euros. And there were stacks of them.

"Ho-lee," Al said, leaning closer. "Are these—these are good as cash, right? As long as we hold them, they're ours?"

McKenna snapped the lid closed. "If you can find someone to buy them," she said. "And judging by the character of those guys who just tried to kill us back there, I'd say these belong to someone we really don't want to mess with."

She looked at Al Parent. "You know what happens if we try to sell these? Some more men with guns track us down, *take* them from us, probably kill us for good measure." She shook her head. "No way, boys. These are bad freaking news."

Ridley had a look on his face like he'd just found the mother lode. "Okay, skipper, you're probably right. but just in case, don't you think we should at least figure out how many of those bonds we're dealing with here?"

No, McKenna thought, but she knew she was outvoted. She sighed, and opened the case. "Soon as we hit Seattle, we're turning these in to the authorities, understand?"

"Sure," Ridley said. "Of course. Let's just count them first."

So they counted. McKenna opened the briefcase, and they each took a stack of bonds, and by the time they were through, they'd piled ninety of the certificates on the wheelhouse table.

"Ninety times five hundred thousand," Jason Parent said. "Shoot, that's like . . ."

"Forty-five million euros," his father finished.

"Right. And how much is a euro worth again?"

Ridley was typing something on his phone. "A euro is equal to approximately a dollar and a nickel. So that puts us—"

"Close to fifty million dollars," McKenna said. "My god."

"That's more than we made for the *Lion*," Jason said. "Holy shit."

Holy shit is right. McKenna was glad suddenly that she knew these men, that her father had hired good crew, that even fifty million dollars piled on her wheelhouse table did nothing to diminish her trust in them.

Still, though, this was a heck of a lot of money.

Ridley was the first to step back from the table. "That's a hell of a score, lads," he said, "but it's the skipper's call." He turned to McKenna. "Whatever you decide, this crew will follow, McKenna. You have my word."

"Thank you." McKenna knew he wasn't lying. Still, she could see the conflict on her men's faces, knew she would hurt a few feelings if she just gave the money away.

Ridley gathered up the bonds. Tucked them back into the briefcase. Rummaged in a locker and came out with a roll of duct tape, taped the briefcase closed. Then he handed it to McKenna.

"All yours," he told her. "Go with your gut."

The briefcase felt heavier now, impossibly so, now that McKenna knew the contents within. The weight seemed almost too much to lift.

"We've still got a long run to Seattle," she told the men. "Let me think on this."

106

Fifty million dollars.

The HMCS *Nanaimo* shadowed the *Gale Force* through the day and into the night. At Port Angeles, across the water from the very bottom of Vancouver Island, McKenna and her crew towed the *Pacific Lion* back into American waters, and the *Nanaimo* ducked away, replaced by a bigger—and heavily armed—Coast Guard cutter.

By morning, the *Gale Force* and her entourage were sailing south down Puget Sound, back into the tugboat's home waters. There was something calming about the familiar scenery, the blue sea and green forest, the white, double-ended Washington State ferries trundling across the Sound. McKenna supervised the crew as they shortened the towline, increasing maneuverability in the Sound's tight confines, and she knew she should feel relaxed now, money in the bank, and the boat almost home.

But there was the briefcase to deal with. Fifty million dollars, or thereabouts. And McKenna knew she should just hand it over to the police, the Coast Guard, the Canadian Navy, whoever. But she was still a Rhodes, wasn't she? Still Riptide's daughter, descended from gamblers and thrill-seekers. The smart thing would be to surrender the briefcase to the authorities, she knew. But nobody in McKenna's family had ever been accused of being smart.

Wait until we tie up in Seattle. Then give it to the cops, and forget about it.

Yeah, she thought. *Maybe*.

BY MIDMORNING, the *Gale Force* and her tow had Seattle in sight. the crew gathered in the wheelhouse to watch the Space Needle appear, the city skyline, busy Elliott Bay with its ferries and fishing boats and massive container ships.

Four harbor tugs waited to dock the *Pacific Lion*, powerful little bulldogs, and McKenna slowed the *Gale Force* and supervised the handover, retrieved Matt and Stacey Jonas from a gangway down the side of the big freighter. Soon, the *Lion* was out of her hands—for good, this time—nudging into a berth in the vast harbor facility south of downtown, across the raised Alaskan Way viaduct from the sports stadiums where the Mariners and the Seahawks played.

McKenna let the tug linger near the *Pacific Lion*, looking from the ship to the city skyline, feeling at home and adrift at the same time. That damned ship had been her responsibility—her *life*—for nearly a month, and now that she'd finished the job, she wasn't quite sure what to do. Life on dry land was infinitely more complex than life on the water, and part of McKenna wished she could stay at sea forever.

She doubted her crew felt the same, though, and she turned the tug north again, toward the West Point light and, beyond, the Ballard Locks. The *Gale Force* felt light, almost weightless now, freed from the burden of the heavy tow.

McKenna called Matsuda as she guided the tug through the locks. Let the shipping executive know that the tow was complete, the *Lion* arrived safe in Seattle. She didn't mention the incident off the Canadian coast, and Matsuda didn't ask. He thanked her, and promised to wire her payment. The conversation was a short one.

Al and Jason Parent took their positions at the bow and stern as the *Gale Force* approached her berth in Lake Union, and McKenna looked up at the city beyond, and felt that same sensation of aimlessness return. Her crew had worked hard. They'd saved the *Lion*. Now what?

Now we deal with the briefcase. She tried to steel herself for the phone call she knew she had to make. The Coast Guard, probably. Maybe the FBI. Someone would know what to do.

Then she heard voices outside the wheelhouse, happy shouts from on deck, and she looked out the window at the approaching pier and saw a figure there, waiting. It was Harrington.

The architect looked stronger than he had the last time she'd seen him, stood straighter, moved easier. He looked tanned and happy, smiling that cocky smile and jawing at Al Parent across the tug's bow. McKenna smiled, despite herself, but as she brought the tug closer, she could see the fatigue behind Harrington's eyes. Judging by his face, he'd aged five years since he'd boarded the flight in Dutch Harbor.

With the bow and stern thrusters going, McKenna guided the *Gale Force* to her berth. Nudged her in gently, and watched Jason and Al Parent scramble to secure the lines, forward and aft, Matt and Stacey assisting on the spring lines amidships. McKenna waited in the wheelhouse until the tug was secure, hurried through her shutdown ritual, and ducked out of the wheelhouse and across the deck to the dock, where Court Harrington was already exchanging hellos with the rest of the crew.

"What, you're not sick of us?" she said as she climbed over the gunwale. "You some kind of glutton for punishment?"

Harrington smiled, sheepish. "Had to make sure you all were okay," he said. "Those guys you were dealing with, they're bad news."

Jason Parent met her eyes. "Court says they followed him to Seattle. Took him *hostage*."

McKenna arched an eyebrow in Harrington's direction, but the architect couldn't quite return her gaze. He shifted his weight, lifted his shirt slightly, and she saw the butt end of a pistol tucked into his waistband.

"What the hell?" she said. "Harrington, what are you doing with that thing?"

Harrington shrugged. "Let's just say your last phone call was pretty fortunate timing. I think the guy holding me prisoner was about to use this on me."

And you didn't tell me? Damn it, Court.

"Anyway," Harrington continued, "you guys figure out what's in that briefcase, or what?"

"*Fifty million dollars.*" That was Jason Parent again. The deckhand went red, covered his hands with his mouth. "I mean, *nothing.*"

"Seriously?" Harrington said. "He's not serious, is he? I figured it was something crazy, but *fifty*—"

McKenna made to answer. Wanted to strangle Jason. But before she could do either, she caught movement in her peripheral vision, the top of the pier. a big Cadillac SUV pulled up and parked. A man climbed from the driver's seat, a young, slender Japanese man. He looked down at the crew as he circled to the rear passenger door, seemed to pick Harrington out of the crowd.

"Oh, dang," Harrington said. "That's him. That's the guy from my hotel room!"

The young man opened the rear door of the Cadillac. An older man stepped to the pavement, slight, but handsome, immaculately dressed. He said something to his driver, who closed the door and hung back, glaring down at Harrington from the top of the pier.

The strange man picked his way down the ramp. Crossed the dock toward McKenna and the tug. He walked with confidence. He was smiling, but his smile carried no warmth.

"Captain Rhodes," the man said, when he'd reached them. "My name is Katsuo Nakadate. I believe you have something of mine."

107

McKenna led Katsuo Nakadate into the wheelhouse of the *Gale Force. So here it is,* she thought. *One way or another, this saga ends now.*

Spike looked up from the dash as McKenna entered the wheelhouse. The cat gave one look at the skipper and her guest, stood straight and jumped down to the carpet, bolted downstairs and out of sight. Nakadate didn't appear to notice.

They sat at the chart table. Nakadate looked relaxed, comfortable here. Somehow, this set McKenna's nerves even more on edge.

"You're here for the contents of that briefcase," she said.

"Yes," Nakadate said.

"You sent your men to attack my boat. To kill me and my crew."

"I sent them to retrieve stolen property," Nakadate said. "I did not send them to kill you."

"Regardless, they fired on my tug. Whatever your instructions, they intended to hurt us."

Nakadate studied her across the table, his face serene, unworried. "The contents of that briefcase are very important to me. My employees know better than to return to me empty-handed."

"They could have explained their position. We could have talked things over."

"And you would have returned what is mine, Captain Rhodes?" Nakadate asked, the hint of a smile on his face. "You would have handed it over, if asked?"

"I intended to, yeah," McKenna told him. "Your *employees* fired on me before I could communicate my intentions. We hadn't even opened that briefcase."

Nakadate winced. "I am sorry to hear that," he said. "Truly."

He said nothing more, for a long beat. McKenna held his gaze, kept her expression neutral, a poker face. Whoever this man was, he must be very powerful. McKenna imagined that if she knew Nakadate's story, she wouldn't be so calm.

Good thing I don't know. Ignorance is bliss.

Nakadate scanned his eyes around the wheelhouse. Then he sighed, and the smile was gone from his face, and he suddenly looked tired.

"The contents of that briefcase are very important to me," he said, again. "I regret that this situation has resulted in violence. I simply want returned what is rightfully mine."

McKenna didn't reply right away. She'd had an idea. Wondered if she had the guts to pull it off.

"What's the deal with that briefcase, anyway?" she asked him. "We opened it, and I know you have bonds worth a heck of a lot of money inside. What I want to know is *why?*"

Nakadate shrugged. "Each of those bonds comprises a share of ownership in a numbered company based in Switzerland," he said. "Essentially, Captain Rhodes, by holding the contents of the briefcase, you are the owner of one of my companies."

"You're talking about money laundering."

"Those are your words. I would merely say that the bonds are ideal for purposes of anonymity."

The man before her was a hundred times scarier than the pirates who'd attempted to kill her crew, McKenna decided. This was a man who would kill at an arm's length, with instructions and innuendo. This was a dangerous, dangerous individual.

Nakadate seemed to read her thoughts. "You can see, perhaps, why it is in both of our interests to resolve this issue. I would like my property returned, and I am confident that you would not enjoy any prolonged connection to me or my business ventures."

"Is that a threat?" McKenna asked.

"No," the man replied. "I only mean that you will find it difficult to offload my property to anyone else, and that even if you do manage to liquidate your holdings, you may find the authorities knocking at your door someday, wondering about your involvement with such unsavory activities."

Nakadate had a point. McKenna didn't know the first thing about selling stolen bearer bonds. Nor did she relish the thought of explaining the bonds to the FBI.

Here goes nothing.

She fixed her eyes on the man. Willed her voice to stay firm. "I'm a salvage master, Mr. Nakadate," she said. "I find lost things, and I return them to their rightful owners. That's what I do for a living."

Nakadate sat back. Tented his fingers. Smiled at her. "Are you suggesting I pay you for my own property, Captain Rhodes?"

"I just rescued a cargo ship worth a hundred and fifty million dollars. The owners paid a reward."

"They were bound by the rules of the ocean. You and your crew had the law on your side, the convention of the sea. Here, you have nothing."

"I have the briefcase."

"You will have to show me the briefcase before I pay you any fees, Captain."

"Fair enough," McKenna said, "but this isn't the open ocean anymore. This is America, and your time is running out. Sooner or later, the police, the Coast Guard, or the navy, is going to want to talk about why three armed pirates attacked my tugboat, and I'm going to have to hand over those bonds. You'll have a far easier time negotiating with me than with them."

Nakadate mulled his over. "The briefcase is on this vessel. Logic demands it."

"Sure. But I'll be damned if I'm letting you search it. and even with your bodyguard, I'd say you're outnumbered."

Nakadate studied her again, for a long time. McKenna willed herself not to flinch. Felt her insides shaking, hoped Nakadate couldn't tell.

Finally, he sat back, and sighed. "Very well, Captain. What finder's fee do you propose?"

McKenna shrugged. "In my business, we usually start at ten percent."

"Ten percent. Am I to assume you've tabulated the value of the bonds?"

"Forty-five million euros," McKenna replied. "A little more, in American dollars. Call it five million dollars, flat."

"And if I don't accept?"

"We continue to negotiate. but I'll tell you, given the work that my team put in to recover your property, the risks we took—not to mention the damage we sustained in the attack on our tug—I think five million is eminently fair."

Nakadate said nothing. *This is it,* McKenna thought. *This is the all-in push on the river card, the big bluff.* She held the gangster's stare, felt her heart pounding. Nakadate didn't say anything for a minute, two minutes.

Then, finally, he nodded. "Five million dollars," he said. "I will need to see the briefcase before I transfer any funds."

108

McKenna retrieved the briefcase from her stateroom. Passed Ridley in the galley. The engineer motioned upstairs. "Everything all right?"

"Perfectly fine," McKenna told him. "Just doing a little business."

She walked back upstairs to the wheelhouse. Paused before she reached the top, half expecting to find Nakadate waiting with a gun in his hand. But the gangster's back was to her, a cell phone in his ear. He spoke very quickly in Japanese.

Nakadate turned as McKenna set the briefcase on the chart table. Crossed to the table and lifted the mangled lid, rifled through the stock certificates inside. Then, satisfied, he closed the briefcase again. Turned it back to McKenna.

"Your bank information," he said.

McKenna dug a notebook out of a drawer at the front of the wheelhouse. Found the information and relayed it to Nakadate, who repeated it over the phone. Then the gangster ended the call.

"Call your banker in ten minutes," he told her. "You will have the money."

McKenna pulled out her cell phone. Found the number for her bank in the notebook and punched it in.

"I will create the necessary documentation," Nakadate told her. "One of my legitimate companies. We will agree that we are paying you the money as a consultation fee relating to the *Pacific Lion* incident. Five million American dollars. That should be sufficient to deal with any tax implications."

"Thank you," McKenna said, realizing that she hadn't quite thought that far ahead.

Nakadate gave her another ghost of a smile. "We are businesspeople, Captain Rhodes. I'm glad we could arrive at a civil arrangement."

McKenna called her bank. Checked the balance of the Gale Force Marine account and the latest transaction. Nakadate was a man of his word. The five million was there.

She ended the call. "We're set," she told Nakadate. She handed him the briefcase, and the gangster took it, bowed slightly. Then he held out his hand.

McKenna hesitated. Then she shook it.

109

McKenna walked Nakadate off of the *Gale Force,* back onto the dock, where Court Harrington waited with the rest of the crew, talking quietly and trying not to let on they were watching.

They went silent as McKenna and Nakadate appeared, watched them walk to the ramp at the foot of the pier, watched McKenna wish the man well, and waited as he climbed the ramp to his waiting Cadillac. They watched McKenna watch the SUV drive away, watched her turn around, finally, and walk back to the tug.

"So?" Harrington asked, as he approached. "That guy was the big boss, right, skipper? Are we, like, cool?"

"That was the big boss, all right," she replied. "It was his briefcase."

"But you gave it back to him." This was Ridley. "What happened to turning it in to the cops?"

McKenna studied her crew. They circled around her, waiting. They were good people. Solid, dependable, competent sailors. They were exactly the team she would want if she were to tackle the *Pacific Lion* again.

"I didn't *give* it, Nelson," she said. "I negotiated a salvage contract. Mr. Nakadate agreed to stop sending men to shoot up our boat if I promised to give him back the contents of that case."

The crew swapped looks. "That's it?" Jason Parent said. "Is that the contract?"

"Well, no. There was the matter of our fee." McKenna tried to keep her poker face. "Mr. Nakadate and I agreed that ten percent was probably fair. He's already wired us the money."

"Ten percent," Stacey Jonas said. "That's nearly five million dollars."

"We called it five, even. And I figure we'll split it like bonus money, between the seven of us. That's a little over seven hundred thousand per person. Sound fair?"

"Hell," Ridley said, "sounds fair to me."

"I'll take it," Stacey said. "Those jerks tried to kill me."

"Fine by us," Al said. Jason nodded in agreement.

Court Harrington hadn't said a thing. McKenna caught his eye. "You're awfully quiet."

Harrington studied the dock. "I could have got you guys killed," he said finally. "You don't have to cut me in. Keep the money."

McKenna shook her head. Made to argue. Ridley beat her to it. "Nah, that's bull," the engineer said. "No one ever claimed salvage was easy. You earned this money, lad, just like the rest of us."

"You're crew," Stacey said. "Like it or lump it. You gambled, we won."

"And," McKenna said, "I don't want you getting a swelled head or anything, but you kind of saved our bacon up there in Alaska. Consider it a performance bonus. Donate it to charity. Chalk it up to brain damage from that fall you took. But you're taking the money, and you're never, *ever*"—she looked at him, hard—"pulling a stunt like this again, understand?"

Harrington met her stare. *Those green eyes.* Held it a moment. Then finally, he grinned. "Aye-aye, Captain," he said. "Thanks."

"Settled." McKenna clapped her hands. "Now, shall we celebrate?"

"Hell, yes," Harrington replied. "I could *really* use a beer."

McKenna climbed back aboard the *Gale Force*. Locked up the wheelhouse, made sure the rest of the tug was secure. The crew had already begun making their way up the ramp by the time she'd returned to the dock. All except Court Harrington.

He was waiting for her, watching her with those eyes, his mouth set and serious. McKenna cocked her head at him. "What?"

"I wanted to apologize," he said. Hitched a thumb up the dock to the rest of the crew. "I mean, I know I already said sorry to them, but I wanted to apologize to you."

"For the briefcase?" McKenna said. "Yeah, well. You don't do it again, we won't have any problems."

"Not just for the briefcase. For what happened in Dutch. For taking things too far when you were just trying to work."

McKenna said nothing. Looked away.

"I know I messed this up," Harrington said. "You won't let me give back the money. What can I do to make this up to you, McKenna?"

She didn't look at him. "This crew needs an architect, Court," she said. "You're the best guy I know. And I like you, I care about you, and—damn it—sometimes, I still miss you. But this crew needs an architect more than I need a man in my life, understand? I can't afford to lose you just because we gambled on an old flame."

He nodded. "Yeah, I get that."

He was looking at her again, earnest, and she could feel something give in her, some kind of grudge. Knew the crew was watching from up on the pier, and figured he knew it, too, figured he just didn't care.

Figured she probably didn't care that much, either.

"Give it some time, Harrington," she said, turning away, turning up the dock toward the rest of the crew. "I'm not saying no yet, I'm just saying *stand by*."

"Stand by," Harrington said, and she could hear the laugh in his voice. "And what should I do while I'm waiting?"

"While you're waiting?" She turned. "You can start by buying this crew dinner, Whiz. Fending off a pirate attack really works up an appetite."

110

A few days later, and nearly five thousand miles away from Mc-Kenna Rhodes and the *Gale Force*, Hiroki Okura was woken by a knock at his door.

His life had been unpleasant, these last weeks, since his return from Dutch Harbor. As he'd expected, he'd been terminated from his position with the Japanese Overseas Lines. He'd been visited by police detectives, investigators. He faced criminal charges for his role in the *Pacific Lion*'s near capsize, for Tomio Ishimaru's presence on the *Lion*, and subsequent death, for his own, unauthorized disappearance from Dutch Harbor and his attack on the American salvage crew aboard the *Lion*.

The charges were coming. The Americans had shipped him back to Japan on the promise that justice be served. It was only a matter of time.

And now, a knock on the door, and Okura, in sweatpants and a stained T-shirt, opened the door and stood blinking in the harsh light of day and saw that it wasn't the police who'd come for him, at last, or his former employer, but a third party, a familiar face.

The man who stood on the other side of Okura's door wore almost exactly the same uniform as the man who'd visited the sailor in the jail in Dutch Harbor: a black suit, a white shirt, a skinny black tie. An air of menace, barely contained. Okura realized he'd been waiting for this.

He'd heard about a high seas shootout off the Canadian coast while the *Pacific Lion* was being towed to Seattle. Apparently, the crew of the salvage tug had foiled the attack. Okura took this to mean the briefcase was still at large. He took the thug's presence at his door to mean that Katsuo Nakadate still required his help.

Okura stared out at the man. Scratched the patchy growth of hair on his unshaved face. "I don't know how I can help you," he said, sighing. "I've told your boss everything that I know. The briefcase was aboard the *Lion*. If you still haven't retrieved it, I don't—"

The thug raised one hand.

"My employer has regained his stolen property," the thug told him. "He requires, now, to know how it was taken from him in the first place."

Okura stared at the thug. "It was Ishimaru, obviously. I was told he murdered his colleagues."

"You knew him, did you not? Ishimaru? You were schoolmates together?"

"I—" Okura swallowed. "We were, yes. And I—I may have helped him by smuggling aboard my vessel. But that's all I did, and I've paid for that, a heavy price. I'm ruined. You—"

"You were observed meeting with Ishimaru," the thug said. "In the days and weeks before the theft. Tell me, what did you talk about?"

Okura didn't answer.

"You had heavy debts, yes? A robbery would have served you just as well as it would have Ishimaru."

The thug didn't wait for Okura to answer. He thrust something into the sailor's hand. a photograph, the same as he'd seen in Dutch Harbor. His sister, his niece.

"My employer would like to meet you," the thug continued. "He hopes very much that you'll accept his invitation."

Okura's mouth went dry. He felt the same sick, hollow sensation in his stomach as when the *Pacific Lion* began its off-kilter slide into the sea, the crushing sensation in his chest that had been present ever since.

He'd known there would be consequences for his actions. He'd prepared himself mentally for jail. He had not, he realized, imagined that Katsuo Nakadate would uncover the depth of his involvement in Ishimaru's robbery.

Okura looked down at the photograph. He studied his niece's face in the picture. His sister.

"He will not hurt them," the thug said. "You have his word. So long as you meet with him now."

He stepped aside from the door, gestured back to a long, black

Mercedes sedan that sat waiting at the curb. He smiled, disingenuous, as though neither man knew exactly where that car was headed.

There was nothing to do but surrender. Okura looked back into his house, one last time, the dirty, unkempt living space of a man who'd gambled and lost everything, a man who'd engineered his own ruin.

The thug gestured again. "Come," he said.

Okura closed his eyes. Then he followed the man to the waiting sedan, and every step he took he felt the pressure in his chest diminish, in his lungs, as though he'd been trying to keep from drowning, and he was finally letting go.

111

SOME MONTHS LATER

They'd worked hard for this. Labored long hours and spent many sleepless nights down in Ridley's engine room, the lot of them, slaving over the *Gale Force*'s twin engines.

It was no easy job, overhauling a pair of twenty-cylinder diesel train engines. Especially not when they were lodged at the bottom of a tugboat. But McKenna and Ridley and Al and Jason Parent had done it, and now they would reap the reward.

McKenna guided the tug from its berth along the shore of Lake Union. Navigated the lake, and the shipping channel to the Ballard Locks, waited as the locks descended the tug to sea level.

Then they were free, steaming out into Shilshole Bay, and to Puget Sound, beyond. It was a beautiful day, sunny and crisp, the last days of a glorious Indian summer. McKenna kept the wheelhouse windows open, the satellite radio playing "Gimme Shelter," called Ridley down in the engine room on the intraship telephone.

"How are they running?" she asked the engineer.

"Aye, they're like new, skipper," Ridley replied. "Just like the day Riptide bought this old beauty."

"Well, then, get your ass up here," McKenna told him. "It's too nice out to spend any more time down there."

Al and Jason were on the afterdeck with Angel and little Ben, and Carly Ridley, Nelson's wife; they'd brought lawn chairs, and Jason was setting up for a barbecue while Al, in full doting Gramps mode, cradled his grandson in the crook of his arm, and pointed out at the ferries and freighters they passed on the water. This was the turnout run for the new engines, sure, but there was no reason they couldn't have fun while they did it.

She ran the tug across to Bainbridge Island, up to the top, where Hedley Spit curved north from the island, and then back again, like a horseshoe, a long, pretty beach and a row of waterfront homes. Then she cut the tug out of gear, let her drift for a while, asked Nelson and Jason to drop the anchor, and ducked down to her stateroom.

She emerged onto the back deck a short while later, dressed in her swimsuit underneath shorts and a tank top, a Gale Force Marine ball cap, and a pair of sunglasses. Pulled up a lawn chair out into the sun, looked over to where Jason had burgers on the grill.

"How's it coming?" she asked him, and he grinned back, flashed five fingers. *Perfect,* she thought, and she sat back, and basked.

Matt and Stacey were gone, headed off to Antarctica, Matt saying something about catching a penguin. They'd made McKenna
swear to call the next time she had a gig, promised they'd be on the
next flight. They'd hugged, said their goodbyes, and McKenna already missed them, though she knew it wouldn't be long before they
crossed paths again.

It wouldn't be *soon*, either, though. The *Lion* had exhausted Mc-
Kenna, body and soul, and she'd set to work on the engines as soon
as they'd hit the dock in Seattle. She'd spent a ton of money, paid off
her dad's loans, worked hard to get the tug and the company into
good standing. And now?

Now she just wanted to relax.

JASON'S BURGERS WERE FABULOUS. Nelson and Carly had brought
a potato salad, and McKenna had a case of cold beer in the cooler.
The sun shone down, the weather was calm. The *Gale Force* bobbed
happily on its anchor, and the day passed.

After she'd eaten, and sunned herself for a while, McKenna
stood, and walked to the chocks at the very stern of the tug, looked
down at the water beyond.

They'd spread her dad's ashes not far from here, in this very water. She'd wanted to take them further out to sea, the open ocean,
couldn't spare the fuel costs, and she'd always wondered if her dad
would be truly happy here, more or less landlocked.

"He'd be proud of you, you know." Nelson Ridley had snuck up
beside her, read her mind like he always did. "Not just for the *Lion*,
but for all of it, lass. For all you've become."

She didn't say anything. Didn't dare look at him, lest the sight of his face burst the dam in her eyes.

"I wish we'd held on to his ashes," she said, at last. "Kept them on the tug, brought them with us. There's been plenty of times I could have used him around."

Ridley chuckled. "What, and keep Riptide Rhodes from the sea?" he said. "Madness."

She looked at him, laughed, too. Wiped her eyes. Ridley clucked, put his arm around her.

"The thing about the ocean, skipper, is it's everywhere," he said. "And your dad's a part of that, now. Everywhere this tug goes, he'll be with us."

He pulled her close, patted her on the shoulder. "You'll be all right, McKenna," he said. "You'll be just fine."

SHE STOOD THERE AT THE STERN for a little while, gazing out at the dark water, the ferries and sailboats beyond, the blue sky above.

No sense lingering on it, she thought, and she straightened, peeled off her shorts and her shirt, draped them in a pile on the gunwale.

"Going to be cold, skipper," Al Parent called across the deck. "Even this time of year."

"Probably," McKenna called back, grinning. "Are you all too chicken to join me?"

Ridley and Carly had excuses, and Al Parent, too. Jason and Angel told her they'd think about it, after the food settled a little. That left McKenna to herself, and she shrugged and turned, climbed up on the gunwale and dove over the side, arched down and sliced through the water, dove deep.

The ocean was cold, as predicted. It felt glorious, bracing, refreshing, and McKenna felt the stress and tension of the last months begin to slip away.

She surfaced, laughing, floated on her back away from the tug, the crew on the afterdeck watching her. They had the sun at their backs, and they were all silhouettes, and looking at them, McKenna could almost convince herself Harrington was here—heck, that her dad was here, too.

But Harrington was gone, and that was for the best. McKenna figured the Whiz Kid was better off having fun, enjoying his millions, that he didn't need to tie himself down just yet. And she hadn't had time to think of anything but the tug, wasn't in any headspace for romance.

Someday, maybe. Then again, maybe not.

And her dad? Her dad was gone, but the crew he'd assembled was still there, still together. The tug he'd shaped in his image was in better shape than ever. And the daughter he'd raised was a captain.

McKenna treaded water, studied her tug. Felt the sun on her face and closed her eyes, lay back and just floated. She could feel her dad with her, now, in the sun, and the sea, and the tugboat in the distance. She could feel him, and she knew he would always be there.

ACKNOWLEDGMENTS

It might be something of a cliché to claim the ocean is in one's blood, but I am descended from generations of mariners, and I've always wanted to write a deep-sea adventure story like *Gale Force*. That this dream has come to life owes a lot to my agent, Stacia Decker, who practically ordered me to write the first draft over cocktails at some raucous convention bar. It owes just as much to my editor, Neil Nyren, whose enthusiasm, encouragement, and keen editorial eye truly gave birth to McKenna Rhodes, and brought the *Gale Force* and her crew to life.

I'm ever grateful, as always, to the all-star cast at Putnam for everything they've done and continue to do behind the scenes to get books like this out into the world. In particular, thanks to Ivan Held, Alexis Sattler, Katie Grinch, and Carolyn Darr; it's a privilege to work with you all, year after year.

Thanks again and again and again to Rob Sternitzky and the rest of the copyediting and proofreading squad. I say this every year, but copy editors are the true unsung heroes of this business, and I've had the good fortune of working with the best. Any foolish errors that remain in the text are my responsibility and mine alone.

A huge thanks to Clive Cussler, C. J. Box, John Sandford, Lee Child, Linda Castillo, Boyd Morrison, Justin Scott, Meg Gardiner, John Lescroart, Steve Berry, Gayle Lynds, Robin Burcell, and Ace

Atkins for reading early proofs of this book and lending their names to its cause.

I'm grateful to the captains and crews of the fishing vessels *Koskelo* and *Nicole & Terri Lee* for taking me aboard and putting me to work, on both the Pacific and Atlantic Oceans: Joey and Suzi Laukkanen; Chad Accettura; Earl Stoesigger; Stevie, Travis, and Logan Gibbs; Louis Peters; and my dad, Ethan Laukkanen.

To my family—Ethan Laukkanen, Ruth Sellers, Andrew and Terrence, Laura Mustard, and little Ethan—my thanks don't ever seem like enough, but I'll give you them anyway, and all the love I have in the world.

But most of all, this book wouldn't exist without my dad, because it's through him that my love for the sea first took hold. *Gale Force* has its roots in our walks along the breakwater in Victoria's Outer Harbor, and in the bedtime stories of shipwrecks and seafaring heroism he'd read to me when I was a child. It was born of ferry rides, and lobster pots, and in the first rudimentary knots he taught me before I set out for my first summer on the water. Dad, this book is for you, with gratitude and love, and with hopes for many fine days and full pots ahead.